Write My Name on the Sky

Write My Name on the Sky

Bonnie Schroeder

Published by Bonnie Schroeder, Boise, Idaho

Copyright © 2017 and 2022 by Bonnie Schroeder

This is a book of fiction. Names, characters, places, and incidents are either the product of the author's imagination or are used fictitiously. Any resemblance to actual persons, living or dead, business establishments, government agencies, events, or locales is entirely coincidental.

International Standard Book Number 979-8-9857529-2-2

Library of Congress Control Number 2022916303

CREDITS:

Cover Photo: Lisa Fotios – Pexels

Cover Design: Paula L. Johnson

Author Photo: McCarthy Photo Studio

FIRST EDITION 2017

SECOND EDITION 2022

Printed in the United States of America

To Marilyn and Pat: sister, brother, cheering section.
With gratitude and love.

Setting the scene...

The Summer of Love began in San Francisco, California, in 1967 and launched a social, cultural and political movement that is unrivaled to this day. Young people wearing bright patterned clothes, often with a joint or a hit of acid in their pockets, called themselves hippies, or flower children. Espousing peace, love and freedom, they gathered at Love-Ins, on grassy park hillsides, to celebrate freedom from convention, listen to the music of Jesse Colin Young or Joan Baez, and give themselves over to the dance, arms outstretched.

Their movement spread south to Los Angeles, a city otherwise known as the City of Angels, although those who really knew the town called it the City of Fallen Angels. It was there, by the summer of 1968, that peace and love experimented in the Los Angeles air...

Chapter One
July 1968

W here the hell was Arlene?

Kate Prescott scanned the crowd of sweaty strangers, searching for her co-worker, who had coaxed Kate into driving to the Griffith Park Love-In on a hot Saturday afternoon. As soon as they arrived, Arlene had moseyed off with a fellow wearing a crown of flowers in his long black hair. Kate feared she'd seen the last of Arlene for the day; it was impossible to pick her out in this ocean of bodies and noise and blinding colors.

People jostled past, and the summer sun singed Kate's skin. Had she ever felt more out of place?

A grubby man approached, dirt-caked hand extended. He grinned, revealing two rows of yellowed teeth. "Here, sister."

Kate backed away, shaking her head as her silver earrings jingled. No way in hell was she going to take the brownie he offered; her stomach clenched, and she was sure there was more to that brownie than eggs, butter and baking chocolate.

"Don't get all uptight, Blondie."

"My name isn't Blondie—it's ... Alice. And you need to back off!"

With his free hand, the man stroked his sparse beard; his disheveled auburn hair looked like it hadn't been washed in a month.

He squinted red-rimmed eyes at her. "Come on, then, Alice. This will help you get where you want to go."

Behind Brownie Man, the hills of Griffith Park had turned summer beige, rising to meet a fair blue sky, oak and Manzanita branches puncturing the shimmering canvas. More revelers oozed past, giving off odors of perfume, incense, and cigarette smoke. Pucci prints swirled against glistening bare skin.

The scruffy guy took a step closer.

"Alice," said a voice behind her, "there you are! We've been looking all over for you."

Kate turned, baffled because she didn't recognize the man who'd spoken, but he seemed to be talking to her. *Who are you?*

In worn jeans and a blue shirt, he still looked cleaner than Brownie Man. Curly brown hair, a little on the long side. And eyes the color of dark chocolate.

He held out his hand. "Come along, Alice. The Wonderland Express is leaving."

He winked at her, and time stopped. She was no longer alone in a sea of frolickers who all knew something she didn't. Drums and voices faded as she took a step toward this man she didn't know but somehow *recognized,* the two of them apart from the crowd.

She took his hand: strong, with spatters of blue and green paint along the back.

He nodded to Brownie Man. "It's cool, we're already trippin'."

"Thanks," she murmured to the man who held her hand.

He pointed toward the shade of a nearby eucalyptus. "My friend over there says he knows you, but he was too stoned to help you out."

When he released her hand, Kate wished he hadn't. She squinted through the sunlight at a long-haired fellow leaning against the eucalyptus. Then she made the connection: Leonard Ryder, from Bright Street. They'd been neighbors until high school graduation. But he looked so *different* that afternoon.

She remembered Leonard as acne-scarred and pudgy, but this guy was slender, and a beard camouflaged his pitted cheekbones.

"Little Katie Prescott," he said, "fancy meeting you here."

Speechless, Kate groped for a greeting. In their senior year,

Leonard had discovered music, playing his guitar and singing folk songs in coffee houses, using only his last name.

"Hello, Ryder," she replied eventually. "Thanks for sending your friend to save me."

Ryder's smirk and his indifferent posture triggered memories of summer afternoons on Bright Street, playing hide and seek with other kids on the block. Ryder always lost; he was too slow and too chubby to find good hiding places, but he always pretended not to care.

"My friend," Ryder said, "*wanted* to save you. But did you need saving?"

"Probably," Kate replied. She turned to Ryder's companion. "I'm Kate Prescott."

"Jack Morrison." He extended that wonderful, paint-spattered hand again. "And what brings you here, Kate Prescott?"

Kate forbid herself to prolong the handshake. "Curiosity."

"Which killed the cat," Jack Morrison pointed out with a slow grin.

"But satisfaction brought it back."

Jack looked at Ryder. "You didn't tell me she was smart."

Kate studied his profile for a moment; he was quite handsome.

"I came with somebody from work," she continued, "but she ditched me."

Ryder sat down, cross-legged, and motioned her to join him. "Work? I thought you were a college girl."

Kate sat, fanning her sundress around her knees. "You haven't been home lately, have you?"

Ryder flinched. "Shit, that's right. Man, what a bummer about your dad. I really liked him."

Kate started to tell him more when a line of dancers snaked past in a wild swirl of bright colors. Tambourines and voices drowned out any chance of conversation, so she leaned back and breathed in the thick, minty fragrance of eucalyptus, mingled with incense and another, sharper smell.

Jack Morrison eased down on the grass next to Kate and raised his voice above the racket. "You stick with us. Pretty girls shouldn't run around here on their own. Too many stray wolves hunting."

Kate shivered. "Thanks for the cheerful thought."

He smiled, and the world turned brighter.

Ryder reached into his shirt pocket and produced a thin cigarette. *Weed*, Kate realized, as Ryder lit it, inhaled and offered it to her. Kate shook her head.

"Come on, Kate—join the party," Ryder said as he exhaled.

Reluctantly, Kate put the joint to her lips and took a careful puff, unable to suppress the urge to look over her shoulder.

Jack's laugh came out low and throaty. "Don't act so nervous. Pretend it's a cigarette. Breathe in. Good."

The smoke tasted strangely sweet. A cough rose in her throat, and she swallowed it away, then handed the joint to Jack.

Their hands touched, and she felt a sizzle along her skin, as if she'd brushed a live electric wire. Did he feel it too? He gave no sign but inhaled deeply and held the smoke in his lungs for an impossibly long time as he passed the joint to Ryder.

Through a stream of exhaled marijuana smoke, Jack asked, "So what were you doing before you got lost?"

"I wasn't lost," she told him.

"We're *all* lost, but some of us don't know it."

"Be careful of him, Katie Girl," said Ryder. "He's a mad artist."

He turned away to gaze at the people flowing past, tapping his thighs in time to the drums. Kate watched the collision of colors, reds and greens and golds and blues, merging and separating. She felt drab in comparison, a wren among flamingoes and peacocks.

The chain of dancers circled back. Bangle bracelets jingled as they beckoned. Ryder pinched out the roach, swallowed it, and rose in one graceful movement, as if defying gravity, brushing leaf fragments from his jeans.

"C'mon, folks, let's groove." He swayed and clapped in time to the tambourines' tempo.

Kate shook her head. "I'm a terrible dancer—don't you remember?"

"Nobody cares. C'mon."

"Let her be," Jack said. "She can keep me company."

Ryder cocked his head and started to say something, but a woman whose breasts were falling out of her orange tank top grabbed his arm and pulled him into the crowd.

Jack took out his Marlboros and offered her one. Kate studied the pack, and he laughed—a soft, teasing sound.

"They're plain old cigarettes," he told her, so she accepted and cupped her hands around his as he struck a match flame and touched it to the tip of her cigarette. Kate's flesh tingled again.

"Thanks," she said, breathing smoke into the pristine summer air.

Jack blew two small, perfect smoke rings and poked his finger through one as it drifted skyward. Kate giggled.

"So, did you like that weed?" he asked.

Kate considered her answer. "I guess. Don't feel it all that much."

"Give it time," Jack said.

She reclined on her elbows and waited.

"You have good skin," he said.

"Me?" Kate tried not to look surprised.

"I've started noticing the models' skin in drawing class," he said, as if that explained the off-the-wall compliment. "You don't go out much in the sun, do you?"

She shook her head. "I burn." She looked down at her bare arms. "I'll be sorry I wore this dress today."

He motioned her closer, into the deeper shade of the eucalyptus, and she scooted toward him.

"You'll be a beautiful old woman when the rest of them are wrinkled crones," he said.

Kate felt the blush on her nineteen-year-old cheeks. "I have a long wait."

Silence descended. *Say something!* Kate admonished herself. Here she was with a good-looking man who paid her *compliments*, and she was totally tongue-tied. She'd never had this kind of trouble talking to men before; had she lost the ability to flirt? Her vocal cords were tight, her muscles as taut as her mother's back-yard clothesline, her brain slow and useless.

Finally, a few feeble words came to her. "How do you know Ryder?"

Jack rubbed the tip of his smoldering Marlboro into the grass to extinguish it. "Roommates," he replied.

"At college?"

His smile held a touch of something she didn't understand. "Yeah. Off campus."

"Which college?"

"You've heard of Chouinard?"

She had. "The art school? Ryder's in *art school*?"

Jack smirked. "Not anymore—but don't tell his folks, okay? They're under the illusion he'll make more money as an artist than as a folk singer. Which I suppose he could, if he got a teaching credential."

"Is that what you're working toward?" Kate asked.

In answer, Jack pulled a folded paper and a pencil from his jeans pocket and began to draw. A few minutes later, he held up a remarkably flattering sketch of Kate herself. She took the drawing and studied it, unable to keep from grinning. He'd made her look prettier than she was, her hair smoother and longer, her nose straighter.

"Very nice; I wish I looked like that."

"You do. Very Alice in Wonderland, except for your green eyes."

He'd noticed her eyes. She'd have to be careful with this guy.

When she offered to return the drawing, he said, "No—keep it. A souvenir."

Kate folded the sketch carefully and tucked it in her pocket. "Thanks." After a pause while she searched for clever words and failed to find them, she asked, "Are drawings your specialty, then?"

He clicked his tongue. "Mostly paintings, but they're harder to carry around. Someday maybe I'll show you, though."

Kate fought more embarrassing shyness. "I'd like that."

"So you know Chouinard."

Kate nodded. "My dad went there."

"Your dad's an artist?"

"To me he was. He was an animator at Disney."

"Was?"

Pain, the non-physical kind, stabbed through her. "He died last year. Drunk driver ran into him."

He put his hand on her bare calf. "I'm sorry."

She should have expected the tears, but they took her by surprise and she swiped at them, mad at herself for acting maudlin. *Time to grow up, get used to it. Get over it.*

He didn't question her tears, and she was grateful for that. Kate couldn't explain why, but she cared what Jack Morrison thought of her.

"And you," he continued. "You've had more education than most, haven't you?"

Kate mimicked his way of putting out a cigarette but found herself empty-handed; she waved toward the mountains surrounding the park. "I almost did."

"Almost?"

"A year at UC Santa Barbara—liberal arts stuff. Nothing you can earn a living with."

"Is that why you quit?"

"Sort of. When my dad died, the money ran out."

"Ouch."

She shrugged. "Life's a bitch sometimes."

He smiled, and again there was that touch of something the exact opposite of mirth. "Right."

Then he lay back on the grass, staring up at the eucalyptus canopy. His eyes drifted shut, and Kate thought he might have fallen asleep, but she didn't mind. Somehow being next to him made her feel safe.

A woman in a vivid emerald gown glided up to them, a matching green scarf around her shiny black hair. Her skin was the color of dark chocolate. She held out her hand, fingers long and tapered. In the middle of her palm was a small white pill.

"One to grow on," the woman said, then threw back her head and laughed. She had immense white teeth.

Kate shook her head and echoed the polite refusal she'd heard Jack use. "Thanks, but we're already trippin'."

The woman laughed again and frolicked off.

Jack sat up. "You learn fast," he said.

Kate watched the woman move away. "What *was* that?"

He pursed his lips. "Acid, probably. LSD. You know LSD?"

"Of course. I didn't just fall off a turnip truck."

What a stupid thing to say. But he seemed to accept it. Kate began to feel like Jack Morrison would accept almost anything she said, or did. He had her father's attitude of competence and comfort in his skin.

"And you know better than to take candy from strangers," Jack said, and Kate felt a glow of pleasure.

That one hit of pot had begun to muddy her thoughts and perceptions, and the voices around her became an incoherent buzz. The air reeked of burning marijuana and incense; her pulse throbbed in sync with the bongos.

Then she heard other sounds: a whistle's shriek and an amplified voice. "THIS IS THE LOS ANGELES POLICE DEPARTMENT!"

Panic seized her. She'd seen news reports of uniformed officers, faces hidden by reflective shields, wading into crowds of unarmed hippies, cracking clubs against skulls and hauling scores of people off to jail—all for the bad luck of being in the wrong place at the wrong time.

The crowd began to disperse like stampeding cattle. Kate scrambled to her feet, and so did Jack.

"We have to get out of here," he shouted above the commotion.

"I know a back way," Kate yelled. "What about Ryder?"

Jack shook his head. "No time. Besides, Ryder always lands on his feet."

She felt a momentary flash of protectiveness for her old neighbor, always the butt of childish jokes, always the one left behind. She wanted to try and find him, and her co-worker Arlene, but the pandemonium made it impossible. She took Jack's hand and pulled him toward a parking lot above the carousel, away from the field where people churned in noisy confusion.

Kate knew the way by heart; she and her dad had hiked every trail in Griffith Park at one time or another. The parking lot ended in a rough strip of asphalt, ringed by a low stone wall topped with a chain link fence. And there, right where she remembered, was the slash in the fence some impatient hiker had cut years ago. Kate squeezed through, Jack followed, and she led him up a bridle path, around the parking lot, above the melee playing out in the park.

Sirens wailed in the distance, and she heard screams and shouts and whistles.

Jack patted her back. "Nice going, Girl Scout. But now what? We can't camp out here all night."

"We don't have to," Kate told him. She pointed to her left. "That takes us down to the road. My car's half a mile from here."

He rubbed his chin. "Well, I'll be damned. Looks like I picked the right person to rescue."

I sure hope so.

"Can you give me a lift home?" Jack added. "I came with Ryder."

Well, well. Maybe the universe is finally giving me a break.

Chapter Two

"That's it on the right," Jack said, pointing to a two-story chunk of brick and concrete, next to a vacant lot. The neighborhood —an industrial section east of downtown Los Angeles—looked dismal and deteriorating, with litter-strewn sidewalks and painted-over storefront windows.

"Pretty ugly, huh?"

Kate shook her head. "It's perfect for an artist."

"If you say so. Park here."

She guided her Chevy into an open space at the curb and turned off the engine. They sat without speaking. *Now what?*

Through the silence came a muffled cackle from the vacant lot, followed by the crack of shattering glass.

Would he shake her hand now, offer thanks for the ride, say goodbye and walk away without looking back?

Jack turned toward her, his face shadowed. "Thanks to you, we escaped the long arm of the law. Feel like Jesse James?"

Kate's grip on the steering wheel relaxed. "Yeah—except for the guns and money."

"So—want to come in and see my paintings?"

Kate laughed to cover her nerves. "That's an offer I don't get very often."

I shouldn't, I don't know him...but he's Ryder's roommate. I've known Ryder forever.

He waited a few seconds. "I'll even feed you dinner. I make great sandwiches."

She hesitated a few more heartbeats.

Jack reached for the door handle. "Come on, you're probably safer with me than with Ryder."

Kate got out of the car and followed him to a door near the car. He unlocked a deadbolt and motioned to a steep flight of stairs, then relocked the door behind them.

"I hope Ryder's okay," she said as they climbed.

"He is. Ryder has big survival mojo."

Jack hit a switch at the top of the stairs, and five fluorescent tubes flickered to life.

Kate stood still, catching her breath from the climb.

The loft opened out from the stairwell into what looked like infinity. Dust motes danced in the light beams, and unfamiliar shapes loomed in shadowy corners of the cavernous building.

"Pardon the mess," Jack said. "The housekeeper hasn't shown up lately."

Kate looked around. "Maybe she got lost in here. This place is *huge*."

He laughed. "It takes a little getting used to. Come on, I'll give you the tour."

The floorboards had been painted utilitarian gray, and part of the space was partitioned off as a kitchen: sink, hot plate, refrigerator, table, and a tall cabinet, door ajar to reveal plain white dishes and a cluster of cereal boxes.

"The bathroom's in there," Jack said, gesturing to a louvered half-door past the sink. "Not fancy, but safe—I promise."

Then he pointed to the front of the loft, dusky with afternoon shadows, where she saw large canvases on a white freestanding wall, another space swathed in plastic sheeting, and a curtained-off area to the right.

"My workshop and sleeping quarters," he said.

Kate pulled her hair back off her face. "You've got all the essentials."

He nodded. "And nobody cares if Ryder makes racket all night— well nobody but *me*, and I can tune it out. I don't get yelled at if I spill paint on the floor, and Ryder doesn't complain about the smell of turpentine." He paused and looked troubled. "It's a little messy—"

"No," Kate said quickly. "It's great. Really. Now show me your paintings."

His expression brightened and then flickered to uncertainty. "They're a little odd, I warn you."

"I like odd," Kate replied.

"What I mean is, they don't exactly follow the current trend."

"Which I wouldn't know if it bit me on the toe," Kate said.

The canvases were larger than she'd first thought, at least five feet wide and almost as tall. A few depicted trees and animals rendered in perfect, realistic detail, but as she moved along the wall, Kate noticed the subjects' edges began to blur, turning impressionistic. Kate liked impressionist art, and Jack's work had a Renoir vibe.

The last group of canvases were bold swathes of blues and greens and golds, blending and separating in dazzling sequences, forming unrecognizable shapes. They hypnotized her and drew her in.

"Wow," she said, annoyed at her inarticulate response.

He didn't say anything, while Kate struggled to come up with a more intelligent remark.

What came out of her mouth was, "They're so *big*."

Jack didn't seem offended.

"So if size were the main criteria, I should be famous?"

"I didn't mean to say that! They take my breath away. Honest. And, evidently, they short-circuit my brain, too."

He didn't react, so she stumbled ahead. "I can't give you some bull-shit opinion of how they echo neo-classic themes merged with tradi-tional impressionism, but—"

"You didn't sleep through art history, then," he said. Now that she was all flustered, he seemed amused. And maybe a little relieved.

Kate pointed to the area inside the plastic sheeting, where an easel held a half-finished canvas. "Work in progress?"

Jack led her past the sheeting. The floor was covered with colorful splatters, and despite an open window the smell of oil paint hung thick in the air. Stretcher bars and a roll of canvas rested against one wall. The painting on the easel was, apparently, going to be one of those enchanting abstracts. A broad line of brilliant turquoise swept across the primed canvas, intersecting a dark brown triangle, edges smudged into the primer.

Kate cleared her throat. "Do they have names?"

He shrugged. "Untitled Number 9281."

"Don't you take them more seriously than that?"

"I take them plenty seriously," he replied, "But I think titles limit them." He pointed at the unfinished work. "What would you call this, if you were bestowing titles?"

She hesitated before answering. *Come on! Think of something brilliant!* "Conjunction," she said, dismayed at hearing the word out loud. Did it sound as stupid to him as it did to her?

His dark brown eyes locked onto hers, and Kate saw something in them, something vast and comprehending.

"Maybe that's what I'll call it then," he said.

Kate could not have turned away from him to save her life, but she was relieved when he broke the gaze and rubbed his hands together.

"Now," he said, "who's hungry?"

* * *

Jack's tiny refrigerator held sliced roast beef and cheese, lettuce and tomatoes.

"My mom sends care packages," he said. "Her crusade to keep me out of fast food joints."

He put the sandwiches on plates, popped open two Pepsis and pointed to the table. "Have a seat—dinner is served."

Halfway through the meal, Jack paused and sat back in his chair, spreading his long legs out under the table. One of his calves touched hers. "So—you know a lot of interesting stuff, like secret ways out of the park, and you have educated opinions about art. What else is in that pretty head of yours?"

Kate tried to ignore the rub of denim on her leg. She sipped cola and hoped she sounded worldly and casual when she answered. "Junk, mostly. I'm kinda boring."

"I doubt that. What were you studying in college? What did you want to be?"

"That's the stupid part," Kate said. "I hadn't decided. I thought I had plenty of time to figure it out."

She didn't mean to go back to the story of her father, but Jack seemed to want to hear it, so she told him how, after a drunk in a pickup truck blew through a red light and broadsided her father's little sedan, killing him on the spot, she and her mother discovered Dad had under-insured both his car and his life. The pickup driver had no insurance at all, and no assets except his ruined truck. All of which led to Kate dropping out of college to move home, get a job and help support her mother and her kid sister, who was in her junior year of high school.

"Man," said Jack when she finished. "You must be really pissed off about all that." He shifted in his chair, and she felt a twinge of regret when his leg moved away from hers.

Kate filled her mouth with cola, stalling as she sought a way to describe her feelings. She didn't know which emotion came through strongest, grief or rage; they seemed to be holding a contest inside her.

Jack reached out and stroked her arm. At another time, the gesture would have seemed incredibly sensual.

She hated self-pity and fought it away. *Lighten up.*

"Can't change what happened," she replied.

"No," Jack said softly, "that never works."

He sounded like he *did* understand.

"So I racked up a year of totally useless stuff at the university, sampling what's out there, to see if anything clicked. I wanted—want —to do something important with my life. Something that *matters*."

"Be an artist like your dad?"

Kate traced a circle in the condensation on her Pepsi can. "No talent for that—but I enjoy *looking* at art. My dad loved taking me to galleries and museums and explaining the paintings. He could've been a great artist if he hadn't had a family to support."

She was going on like Daddy's Girl. *Stop it!*

"Anyway," she continued, "I put off declaring a major; I was gonna do it in my sophomore year. And…"

"And then it was too late," he finished for her.

"And then it was too late," Kate echoed. "Only it isn't—not *theoretically.* There's night school."

"Oh, *that'd* be fun. Work all day and study all night."

"You do what you have to."

He studied her face for a minute. "For a kid, you're pretty smart."

Kid? He couldn't have more than two years on her.

* * *

After they ate, Jack lit a Marlboro and passed it to her, then fired up a second one for himself. They smoked in silence, and it was the easiest thing in the world to be sitting there, not having to make conversation.

After Jack ground out his cigarette in an abalone shell ashtray full of butts, he asked, "Want to get stoned again?"

Kate had only smoked pot a couple of times; she didn't like feeling out of control.

She extinguished her Marlboro. "You bet."

He led her toward the front of the building, past a curtain and into a space where a double bed, covered with a paisley quilt, rested against one brick wall. Windows opened out to the street below, and Kate heard the hiss of tires. Darkness was settling in, she noticed with a jolt of surprise. The curtain fell back into place with a whisper.

Kate's adventurous spirit wavered. Where was this headed? A cool breeze drifted in through the open window. Until that moment she hadn't noticed the summer heat in the room.

Jack pointed to a wing chair, upholstered in worn pink velour. He snatched up a tangle of rumpled clothes and swept the chair seat with his hand.

Kate sat, trying to camouflage her nervousness. Jack tossed the clothes onto a pine chest, opened its top drawer, and pulled out a joint. He held it up and looked at her, eyebrows raised.

"I don't share the good shit with just anybody," he said.

Kate's muscles unclenched. "I'm flattered."

He lit the doobie, sucked in a massive breath, then passed it to Kate. This smoke tasted different, more astringent, and stronger. Her mind went soft, and as she exhaled, Kate felt like she was releasing her troubles.

Jack sat across from her, on the bed, and she gave the joint back to him. He took another hit, held it in and let it go. The air grew thick with marijuana smoke.

"So," she said, "what's *your* story? Have you always wanted to be an artist?"

He handed her the doobie. "Pretty much. Although I was on my way to reform school by seventh grade—dumb stuff like shoplifting cigarettes."

"In seventh grade?"

Kate took a deep, long hit. She felt like a pretty accomplished pot smoker at this point. Her thoughts came together and scattered like dandelion fluff, which amused more than bothered her.

"I got an early start," Jack replied. "My dad was a career Marine before he retired, so we traveled a lot. You know the drill—the new kid in school always has to prove something."

He took back the joint and inhaled.

"Stealing cigarettes to fit in?"

A stream of smoke came from his mouth as he answered. "Yep. Then I started drawing. Cartoons of people at school—stuff like the science teacher mooning the class. It made the other kids laugh, and I liked that."

"And you got caught."

"Damn straight. Nearly got expelled."

"But your drawings were so good they forgave you, right?" Kate asked.

Jack lifted his eyebrows. "Sort of. The principal suggested art lessons." He paused and raised his hand dramatically. "And the rest is history."

Kate took another toke, then started to cough. Jack stood and patted her back. "Let's get you some water. I forgot you're a rookie at smoking dope."

"Not a rookie," Kate protested between coughs. "But this shit is *strong*."

He cupped her elbow in his hand and helped her stand. He kept his arm around her and guided her to the kitchen and into a chair.

As Kate watched him fill a glass with water, his shape undulated. She rubbed her face, then stared at her hand: *was it transparent?* She blinked as a cool sensation ran through her fingers; Jack was putting the water glass in her hand.

It took all her concentration to hang on to the glass. She sipped until the raw tickle in her throat eased up, and then she gulped. The plain Los Angeles tap water tasted exquisite.

"Easy," Jack said, and he seemed to be fighting back laughter. "Don't drown."

Kate drained the glass. Her vision steadied, her flesh no longer flickered.

"More?" he asked.

Yes, she did want more: more water, more dope, more Jack. She wanted more of everything.

Chapter Three

Kate heard a door slam, then heavy footsteps on the stairs.

"Ryder," Jack murmured.

Kate swallowed. She'd forgotten that her old neighbor from Bright Street shared Jack's loft. Jack refilled her water glass while Kate tried to tame a flutter in her chest.

Ryder came into the kitchen area, pulled a beer from the fridge, gulped it, and belched.

"Hey, man," Jack said. "Glad you got away. I thought maybe I'd have to bail you out." He handed Kate the water and sat next to her.

Ryder chugged more beer and wiped his mouth. "I went into the wind, man. How'd *you* get away?"

Jack tilted his head toward Kate. "I tried to play hero, but she had better tactics."

Ryder looked at Kate as if he didn't recognize her. She felt disconnected, like watching a movie scene, as she sipped the water and licked her lips.

"Hey, Ryder," she said, "how's it goin'? You still singing?"

He kept staring at her. Did he not remember who she was? Who *was* she, anyway? How did she get here?

Jack's foot hooked a chair and pulled it away from the table. "Sit down, dude. Tell Kate what you've been doing. Besides smoking dope, getting drunk, and getting laid."

Ryder sat and took another swig of beer. "Singing. Yeah, I've been doing that. Singing my ass off."

"At the *Quartermoon*," Jack said.

"The Quartermoon?" Kate was impressed. She'd heard of the hip club on Melrose. Arlene from work had raved about it. "They still have folk music there?"

Ryder peered into his beer can. "Folk is dead, haven't you heard? Even Dylan went electric. Rock 'n' roll is where it's at."

"And your old pal is right in the center," Jack said. "Driving the little girls mad."

"Nah, that's *your* scene, man. I do my music and if they come and listen, fine."

Kate chewed on her lower lip. "What do you sing now? Still play guitar?"

"I keep the ol' Gibson around, but its days are numbered." He beat his palms on the tabletop. "The times they are a-changin'," he sang, and then added, "Hell, they done changed."

Ryder turned to Jack. "Where's that killer weed of yours?"

Jack shrugged, all innocence. "I think you smoked the last of it."

"Don't give me that shit. You two are stoned out of your gourds."

Suddenly self-conscious, Kate became aware of her dry, dry mouth; her tongue felt like cotton. She lifted the water glass, which seemed heavier than it should, and took a drink, swallowing carefully so as not to dribble, then set the glass down with fierce concentration. She tried to prop her elbow on the table and missed.

"It's in my stash drawer," Jack told him. "Help yourself."

Ryder clomped into Jack's bedroom and brought back a joint. He fired it up and held it toward Kate.

She shook her head. "I'm already six feet off the ground."

Ryder gave her a "lightweight" look and handed the joint to Jack, who inhaled appreciatively before returning it to Ryder.

Kate tried again. "You get paid to sing now? Great."

Ryder exhaled smoke. "Not so great—and not so much. Doesn't nearly pay the bills. Morrison covers me when I come up short. Or his mom does, only she don't know." He smirked. "Wonder what she'd say if she knew how much of your allowance you spend on weed?"

Jack glared at Ryder. "She doesn't care where it goes."

Ryder wiggled his eyebrows. "You show Kate your etchings, man?"

Kate straightened her back. "Paintings, Ryder. You should know the difference. And yes, he did—they're wonderful. He paints like you sing."

Jack tapped the back of her hand with his index finger. "Be careful. You haven't heard him sing lately." He reached for the joint, took a hit and returned it to Ryder.

"I remember how great you sounded at the talent show," Kate said to Ryder, and although she sensed him retract a little, she continued, to Jack. "High school—senior year. He comes out on the stage and starts singing 'Long Black Veil' and... and it was *so* beautiful."

Her thoughts were tangling, and Ryder didn't react to the compliment. Did he not like her anymore? Why not? "I knew he had a good voice," she added, "but that day—that day he sang like an angel."

Ryder snorted. "Some angel. Everyone acted so fuckin' surprised."

"Everyone *was* surprised. It was phenomenal."

"Phenomenal," Jack repeated, softly. "I imagine it was."

This was going all wrong. Jack would think she was hung up on Ryder—the last thing in the world. She had to turn the conversation around.

"Anyway," she said, fumbling in her purse for a cigarette, "I think you should both be famous; it's not fair that so much junk is out there when the really good stuff gets ignored."

Jack lit her cigarette and smiled, but there was sadness in his smile. "That's the way the world works."

Ryder drained his beer and got another, then sat back down and scooted his chair closer to Kate's. "See, Katie Girl, that's the thing you never got, about life." He exhaled another pungent smoke stream. "It's fucking unfair from the get-go."

Kate tried not to lean away from him, but she couldn't help herself; his red eyes and messy hair made him look faintly menacing.

"Ryder," Jack said, "let's not get into the heavy stuff, man. Chill."

"I'm talking to *her*, man." He put his booted foot on his knee and rubbed his calf. "Think about it. Morrison here gets an allowance from his folks—money Pops made fighting wars. You have to give up college and bust your butt to earn a living because your dad got mowed down by a drunk. See?"

She noticed Jack's worried expression; he seemed to be fighting to keep his mouth shut.

"And what about your life, Ryder?" Kate asked. "Where's the unfairness there?"

Ryder fastened the roach to a clip and took another toke, then passed it to Jack. "Besides the detour I had to take when my folks insisted I become a cartoonist like your dad?"

"Animator," Kate protested. Jack offered her the roach, and she accepted. The tip singed her nose when she inhaled, but she suddenly needed that hit. She held the smoke in her lungs as long as she could, proud when she didn't cough.

Ryder reached for the roach, casually pinched it out, and rubbed the remains into the end of a cigarette. "Aren't you the little word fanatic. Animator then, whatever. Hell, even your sister called him a cartoonist."

"That sounds like Debbie, the little snot." Then it hit her. "You talk to my sister?"

Ryder lit the loaded cigarette and didn't offer to share. "Didn't know this was an interrogation. Christ—she lives two houses away from my folks, she hangs around sometimes, comes to hear me sing. What's it to you?"

Kate started to touch his arm, but this new Ryder was too bristly. She sent Jack a "save me" look.

He got it. "Your sister's a groupie? Does she know how perverted this one is?"

Ryder rolled his eyes.

Jack grinned. "Oh, excuse me. Was I talking to you?"

Ryder stood and stretched. "I'm beat. Later." He shambled off to the back of the loft.

"Was he always this moody?" Jack asked.

Kate lowered her voice. "He got that way in high school. Until then he was kinda sweet. But people change, I guess."

"And they're never exactly who you think they are." Jack winked at her. "That keeps the game interesting."

"You like things to be interesting, don't you?"

"I do," he replied. "And I find you, Miss Kate, very interesting."

Pleasure rippled through her. She'd never worked at being *interesting*, but if Jack Morrison thought she was, then she had to be.

Chapter Four

Ryder left silence in his wake.

"I should get going," Kate said, but she didn't want to leave.

"No way," Jack said. "You're too stoned. Your eyes are red as Rudolph's nose. But I know a better place to talk while you come down."

He stood. "We need provisions." He grabbed two Pepsis from the fridge, then reached into the cupboard and pulled out a bag of M&Ms. "Follow me."

For a second Kate thought he'd lead her back to his bedroom and was more curious than disappointed when he led her around the kitchen partition to a wooden ladder rising into darkness.

"I'll go first," Jack said. "It jiggles a little, but it's safe."

The ladder did more than jiggle; it wobbled and groaned. A dizzying fear stopped her. What the hell was she doing?

But with Jack ahead of her, she couldn't turn back. Kate clutched the ladder's splintery edges and pushed herself up into the shadows.

"You okay?" Jack called out.

"Sure," Kate replied. Her mouth had gone dry again.

"Almost there, hang on."

She heard hinges creaking. A rectangle of sky, lighter than the shadows around her, opened up above.

Jack climbed out and reached for her hand, pulling her up onto the roof.

Kate's legs were trembling, but an instant later the neon splendor around her erased anxiety. Office buildings glittered against the night sky. Company logos in blue and orange, green and gold glowed atop the towers. Lighted windows revealed empty chairs at empty desks. The sight felt magical and secret.

"A real Wonderland," she said.

Jack laughed. "Thought you'd like it."

Kate pointed out the squat shape of Permian Oil's headquarters, barely visible to the west except for a mammoth yellow "P" inside a white circle shining from the façade. "That's where I work."

"Isn't that convenient," Jack murmured.

A breeze brushed her face, bringing city scents: cooling pavement, exhaust fumes, grilling meat. And something floral and sweet, faint as the touch of a fairy's wing. She squinted at the shimmering lights, blurring them into multicolored starbursts. A horn blared in the distance, and tires squealed on asphalt.

Jack popped open the colas and handed one to Kate. The cold sugary fizz tickled her nose.

She tilted her head back and studied the sky. A few stars hovered in the darkness, muted by the city's glare.

"The stars are hard to find, but they're there," Jack said, his mouth so close that she felt his breath on her cheek. He pointed to a faintly glowing cluster in the southern sky. "Centaurus. Don't look *at* it. Look *beside* it and you can see it better."

She leaned her head against his shoulder to look where he was pointing. "How cool." *Great vocabulary, Kate.* She took a step back. "Where'd you learn that?"

He took a drink, keeping his eyes on the distant constellation. "My dad. Soldiers learn survival stuff, like how to navigate by the stars. If we ever get lost in the desert, I can get us out. In theory."

No brilliant reply came to her, so Kate said, "I bet he taught you some good stuff."

Jack pulled out his Marlboros and offered her one. She took it and savored the contact while she shielded the match flame. Did he feel that electric current when their hands touched?

"Not so much." Jack blew a cloud of smoke into the darkness. "He was gone a lot, and when he came home it'd be weird at first. And when I'd get used to it, he'd leave again. Or we'd move to some new base with him."

"So you lived in a lot of different places. It must've been hard—starting over, making new friends."

He leaned against the waist-high wall surrounding the roof. "Sometimes, yeah."

Kate stretched her back. "I've lived in Burbank all my life—except for that time in Santa Barbara."

Silence cloaked them for a few heartbeats.

"Once I got into art," Jack said, "that helped me make sense of everything, in some weird way. I didn't feel so alone—I felt like it all meant something."

He seemed to be talking more to himself than to her.

"You're lucky to have figured that out," she said.

He faced her, all focus. "Maybe. But it takes you over. It—God, this sounds so damn pretentious, but… ah shit, it's hard to explain."

"It defines who you are?" Kate offered.

His white teeth flashed in the darkness. "Yeah. You understand."

"I think so. I'm still trying to find something that means as much to me as painting does to you."

"You'll get there. Don't ever quit looking."

"You sound like my dad." Kate deepened her voice, *"Don't ever settle. Find your passion and follow it."*

How many times had Dad told her that? And had he truly found *his* passion?

"Your dad was right. You should never settle for the easy answer. You look and look, go down blind alleys, bang your head against the wall trying to get it right. You rub your fingers raw reaching for it. And then all of a sudden one day—bam! There it is."

He seemed to be talking from experience, and Kate envied him.

"Is that how it is with you? The search?"

"Lots of times, yeah. But that feeling when you nail it down? Like you said before—doing something that matters. That's the best high there is. It's like you're writing your name on the sky."

"That's what I want," Kate told him. "That's it exactly. But I don't know how to get there."

"You'll do it," he whispered. "I'll show you how."

Kate couldn't interpret anything in Jack's dark brown eyes. He held out his hand, and she took it.

"Stick with me," he said, "and I'll help write *your* name on the sky."

She'd never confided her yearning to anyone except her dad, that craving to be important, to do something big. Yet by some wild coincidence, she'd met someone who understood how she felt.

"Maybe we can help each other," she murmured.

"Maybe so." Jack ground out his cigarette on the roof's dark asphalt, and Kate did the same. Then he cupped his hand under her chin and lifted her face toward his. He kissed her first on the cheek, then on her lips, tiny butterfly kisses that warmed her skin and drowned out everything except a wild exhilaration.

He tasted of cola and cigarettes; his tongue flicked against her lips, and she let him in, and the feel of his mouth on hers, his tongue, his hands, his body leaning into her—it set fire to her senses. She didn't want the moment to end, didn't want him to let go of her. Not then. Not ever.

Jack stepped back, smiled, and brushed a strand of hair off her face. "You're so pretty."

She turned away before he could read the longing on her face.

"Bet I know what you want," he whispered. She felt a hot rush of shame as cellophane rustled behind her.

"Hold out your hand," he told her, and she did.

At first she didn't understand what he'd given her. Then recognition struck: the M&Ms he'd picked up earlier. Kate smiled and popped the candies into her mouth.

"Oh my God," she said, "this is the best thing I've ever tasted."

He didn't reply but turned her toward the lavishly lit buildings of downtown. His fingers went to work on the tight places in her shoulders, gently kneading away tension, and she pushed against him. His breath warmed the back of her neck.

"When I went to the Love-In," Kate told him, "I sure didn't expect the day to turn out like this."

"What *did* you expect?"

"A little fun, a break from the grind."

"Sometimes life sends you what you need, even if it's not what you think you want."

"I never thought of it that way."

Jack laughed. "We're all at the mercy of the universe, kid."

"I worry about that," Kate replied.

"You worry a lot, don't you?" Jack said. "I saw it in your eyes when I met you. You take life seriously."

"I don't know how *not* to."

"Share the worry," Jack said.

Kate leaned against him and surrendered to the comfort of being held, without needing to speak or explain anything to Jack Morrison.

A few minutes later, the eastern sky lightened, a gentle pink tinge that deepened to rose and then turned fiery gold as the sun breached the horizon, sharpening silhouettes, dimming lights to pale flickers, then extinguishing all but the brightest.

Kate sighed. She wanted to stay there forever in the protection of Jack's arms, but she had to pick up the threads of her life. She could tell that Jack didn't go for the clingy type anyway. He wanted *interesting*.

He kissed her again, outside by the car, and promised to call her. Kate pretty much believed that he would.

Chapter Five

"Where the hell have you *been*?" Helen Prescott demanded from a shadowy corner of the living room as Kate came in.

"Mom, you scared me to death! What are you doing?"

Helen stood and followed Kate to the kitchen. "What do you think? Waiting for you to come home, or the police to call."

Ah, shit, here we go. Kate tossed her car keys on the counter; they skittered across the tile and fell to the floor.

She bent to retrieve them. "I'm sorry, Mom."

A door opened down the hallway, and her younger sister Debbie poked her head out. "What's going on?"

Helen ignored the question, snatched a pack of Old Golds off the kitchen table and lit one with a flick of her chrome lighter. Kate almost didn't recognize her mother's face, taut with rage; she'd gotten used to sad, dazed Helen.

"Why didn't you call? Did you see the news? The police came!" Helen said. "They broke up that *thing* in the park, and for all I knew, you'd been arrested. Or worse."

"I went home with a friend," Kate said. "I'm sorry. I should have called."

"You're damn right you should have! Don't you ever think of anyone but yourself?"

Kate's mouth opened, a sharp reply on her tongue, but Debbie eased herself into the kitchen and spoke first.

"Yeah, Kate. Don't you?"

"Come on, Mom. It's over. I'm home, and I'm sorry. Didn't mean to get anyone all uptight." Kate frowned at her sister. "Make yourself useful for once. Help me fix breakfast."

"Oh, sure, pretend nothing happened, pretend it's another ordinary Sunday." Helen blew out a thick stream of smoke and shook her head. "I try to look out for my girls, I try to make this a nice home." She turned on Kate again. "You think it's easy, taking care of the two of you on my own?"

The thing was, Kate understood the fear behind her mother's anger. Her father had set out on an innocent errand and had never come back. And from the moment Kate found out about his death, the world never again seemed safe. That shared fear should've drawn her closer to her mother, but it didn't. Somehow Helen had twisted things around. Whenever she got upset, she blamed Kate, regardless of the real cause, and that act was getting old.

Hostility surged up, and Kate couldn't stop it. "Okay, Mom. I get it. But it's not my fault Dad died."

Sharp and shrill, her voice filled the tired old kitchen with its scuffed maple cabinets and the dripping faucet they couldn't afford to get fixed.

Helen's face turned white, and for a moment Kate thought her mother might slap her. Debbie covered her mouth with both hands and looked ready to cry.

Fine, Mom, let 'er rip. Get it out. Quit whining.

Instead, Helen lit another cigarette from the one still burning at the tip of her fingers. She ground out the other in short, harsh jabs, shoving around the chipped green glass ashtray that overflowed onto the scarred Formica table top. "All I ask is a little consideration. If you want to run wild and stay out all night, fine. But have the courtesy to call, so I'll know where you are."

Kate's energy evaporated as if her mother had sucked the life force right out of her. Her arms and legs felt like they had ten-pound weights attached, and it was hard to even form words. She wanted to crawl into bed, pull a pillow over her head, and sleep.

"I will. Now can we please drop it?"

"Did you ever think what Debbie and I would do if anything happened to you?" Helen put her hands on her hips, the cigarette dangerously close to the sleeve of her fluffy pink bathrobe. "We count on you."

"Nothing's going to happen to me, Mom."

"And if it did, wouldn't I just be the last person to find out!"

From the doorway, Debbie watched with an eager expression on her face, but for once she had the good sense to keep quiet. She was wearing one of Kate's oversized t-shirts, without permission of course.

Kate scowled at her mother. "That's ridiculous!" Despite her exhaustion, Kate heard herself shouting. "And I'm sorry if for one afternoon I actually thought about something besides what you and Debbie need. It won't happen again. What more do you want?"

I have to move out of here, Kate thought. *I have to get my own place.*

Helen leaned against the counter, taking deep puffs on her cigarette and glaring at her older daughter. Kate looked away first. There was no winning this one. She walked out of the kitchen and down the narrow hallway with its grimy yellow paint. Somehow, she kept herself from slamming her bedroom door behind her.

Debbie came in without knocking, face flushed, hazel eyes wide with wonder. "Wow, is she mad at you or what?"

"Yeah, and thanks for egging her on."

Sarcasm was wasted on Debbie, who flopped on the bed and watched Kate peel off her sundress and get into her nightgown. "So how was the Love-In?"

"It was fun. Your friend Ryder was there."

"I thought he would be. He's so cool."

"Does Mom know you hang out with him? He's a little old for you."

"I don't hang out with him. I just like to talk to him when he comes to see his folks. He's so cool! He's practically famous, and they asked him to sing at the—"

"At the Quartermoon, yeah, I heard. I still don't think he's the kind of person you—"

Debbie's expression slid from cheery interest to resentment. "What do *you* know?"

As Kate shook out her sundress to put in the laundry basket, paper rustled in the dress pocket. Jack's sketch. She retrieved and unfolded it.

"What's that?" Debbie asked.

"None of your business," Kate murmured, gently touching the drawing.

Debbie rose from the bed and came over, all curiosity now. Damn it, she always snooped in Kate's room, and she'd find it anyway.

Kate held out the sketch. "A guy I met at the Love-In did it."

Debbie's eyebrows rose, and she seized the sketch. "The one you were with all night?"

"Never mind. Give it back."

Debbie held the drawing behind her back, and Kate fought down an urge to grab Debbie's curly brown hair and pull on it until she screamed.

Instead, she held out her hand and repeated, "Give it back. And quit taking things that aren't yours."

Debbie gave her the sketch. "How come it's okay for you to spend the night with some guy you just met, but I'm not supposed to be friends with Ryder?"

"Because I'm older than you."

"Like you're so smart, Kate." Debbie tugged at the sleeve of the t-shirt. "Why are you so mean? Dad didn't die just for *you*. Stop using it as an excuse to be a big bitch."

She stomped out of the room, and she *did* slam the door.

Great. The only family I have left is pissed off at me.

Kate put Jack's sketch away in her top dresser drawer and tried to regain the mellow feelings she'd had with him. Then she combed the tangles from her hair and wondered if sleep was out of the question.

Chapter Six

"So this is the famous Quartermoon," Kate said, as she passed under a neon crescent. Posters lined the walls of the entrance, and Ryder's face stared out from one of them with an impudent smirk, defiant eyes, and a messy halo of dark blond hair.

"Are you impressed?" asked Jack.

She was. But not by the Quartermoon itself, or even seeing her friend's photo on display. What affected her most was the reality of Jack Morrison, his arm encircling her waist as he guided her to a table near the stage. *This isn't a dream. I really am here.* Their first date, one week to the day after they met.

"I can't believe *Ryder's* singing here," Kate said as Jack pulled out a chair for her.

Jack handed her a drink menu. "Sometimes I can't, either."

Kate thought she could probably get away with ordering a real drink but decided to stick with Pepsi. No stranger to alcohol after her year at the university, she was still amateur enough to be careful. The last thing she wanted was to get plastered and end up passing out on Jack's shoulder—or puking on his shoes. Jack, who she learned was already twenty-one, went with scotch and soda. Kate made a mental note of his choice.

When the drinks came, they clinked glasses. "To Ryder," they said at the exact same time.

The noise level nearly deafened her as the room filled, and the air thickened with cigarette smoke—and another kind of smoke, from the acrid whiff she caught now and then. She tried not to gawk at the audience, a wild assortment of people who would've drawn open-mouthed stares on the tidy street where she lived: men with hair to their shoulders, strutting in their bell-bottom jeans; women in bright peasant blouses, cut low to display acres of bare skin, feather boas draped around their necks. Perfumes mingled and clashed: patchouli and roses, sandalwood and cinnamon.

Jack's hand covered hers. "You look nice."

Kate felt a warm flush on her cheeks. "Thanks."

She'd agonized over her appearance, first sweeping her hair into a chignon, then letting it fall soft and natural to her shoulders. She tried on half a dozen outfits before settling on a short navy skirt with dark tights and a pale blue silk blouse, but now she wished she'd gone for something more radical.

"Blue is a good color on you," Jack said.

"Thanks," she said again, wincing at her lack of originality and tucking a stray lock of hair behind her ear. "You look pretty groovy yourself."

He did. Jack had a tall, lean body that held clothes gracefully, and his jeans and gray shirt fit in seamlessly with the Quartermoon crowd. He leaned back in his chair, looking supremely comfortable in this strange world, drumming his fingers on the tabletop.

She'd brought a soft pack of cigarettes that took up most of the space in her tiny purse. As she pulled out the Marlboros, Jack flicked his lighter and held it toward her. Kate cupped her hands around his, guiding them toward the cigarette tip. She smiled as she exhaled and offered the smokes to Jack.

He grinned. "My brand."

Then the lights dimmed except for a spotlit circle on the stage, and an amplified voice announced "Welcome—Christian Florin." A guy with curly red hair and the biggest nose she'd ever seen stepped into the light and began to strum his shiny electric guitar. His first song, heavy with blues, drew an occasional "oh yeah" from the audience. His smoky voice didn't belong with his pale appearance; it caressed and seduced.

Florin did a couple more songs, equally drenched in blues, bowed, and left the stage with applause echoing in the sudden emptiness.

Ryder came next, and Kate felt a surge of excitement when she saw him move into the spotlight with that six-string Gibson hanging from his neck. He ripped the audience out of their trance the instant he touched the guitar strings.

He seemed unaware of the people in the room, sitting at wobbly tables on a sticky floor, and when he started to sing, Kate shivered. The music penetrated her soul. Ryder's voice was every bit as rich and resonant as she remembered, but a cynical edge had taken over.

"One thing right, that's all I'm askin', just do me one thing right," he sang. The song had a beat that set Kate's feet tapping, even when she caught the lyrics. He was singing about a woman who'd broken his heart, sending an "I love you so much I hate you" message, strong enough to make Kate glad it wasn't directed at her. His voice soared; people swayed to the rhythm, and Kate realized she wasn't the only one transported by Ryder's music. The melody, if it could be called that, hypnotized.

She saw a line of sweat on Ryder's forehead, but he looked otherwise indifferent to his audience. He didn't acknowledge the applause at the end but went right into his next number, fast-paced and dissonant, with a chorus about "The dangerous season, people actin' without reason," and although once again Kate didn't understand all the lyrics, she got the protest behind them.

As taken as she was by Ryder's performance, Kate's awareness still centered on Jack Morrison, his arm draped around her shoulders, watching Ryder with a knowing half-smile, a proprietary expression. Kate thought Jack was the best-looking guy in the room and again felt a floaty sense of unreality at being there with him.

Applause crackled when Ryder finished. He didn't stop to enjoy it. His next song, which went from seductive to defiant, was about loss and redemption. *Pretty sophisticated stuff for a rock 'n' roll tune,* Kate thought as she heard Ryder sing, "The Devil is a personal friend of mine."

She turned to Jack. "I really like this one," she said, and at the same moment Jack told her, "I helped him with the lyrics on this one."

The disclosure left her breathless; she groped for a clever reply and came up empty. Jack had so many talents, but she didn't want to come across like some worshipful adolescent.

"It's the best," she said. Her words sounded lame.

When Ryder finished, to another deafening round of applause, he turned and stalked off the stage, his expression bordering on contempt.

"Is that an act?" Kate asked Jack as the lights went up. "He looks like he hates the audience."

"He doesn't want to let on how much he craves that applause."

A few minutes later, Ryder came out, pulled over an empty chair and slumped down at their table. Up close, he was even sweatier than he'd appeared on stage, and his eyes had a glassy sheen. He held a half-gone beer in one hand and a cigarette in the other.

"That was so cool," Kate told him.

Ryder accepted her praise with a shrug and took a hefty pull on his beer. "Long way from Bright Street, huh?"

Kate held back further compliments. She didn't want to gush, especially in front of Jack, and Ryder would probably mock her anyway.

A thin girl in a filmy yellow dress approached and touched Ryder's arm.

"When you sing," the girl said, "I forget everything else. You're so far out."

Ryder raised his beer to her in a toast, then turned away and ground out his cigarette. He didn't thank her or try to get her phone number; she might as well have been invisible.

What was it with him? Kate wondered. She thought of Jack's comment that Ryder didn't want to reveal how much the approval meant to him. But he took it over the line: as if the more people praised him, the more scorn he felt for them. Kate didn't know this adult Ryder.

He looked over at Jack and wiggled his eyebrows. "Come backstage in a minute. I've got something you might enjoy. In private."

Without another word, Ryder stood and sauntered off.

"We don't have to," Jack said, close by her ear. "He's inviting us to get stoned with him."

"That's cool," she said.

"You sure? We can stay out here if you want."

"Nah, we mostly came for Ryder, right? Besides, my eardrums hurt."

He laughed at that. "I get what you mean."

He took her hand as they went backstage. Several people looked up as they passed, maybe envying them.

The performers shared a makeshift dressing room, a partitioned-off cavern with a mirror, a table, some music stands, a little refrigerator and some rickety-looking wooden chairs. Ryder was leaning over the table, his nose almost touching its surface, and Kate realized that he was snorting cocaine. The girl standing beside him, her hand on his arm, looked vaguely familiar—and so did her dress. *I have a dress like that*, Kate thought, *only...*

The girl looked her way, and a shock wave hit Kate when she recognized her sister Debbie.

"What the hell?" Kate said before she could stop herself. *Tonight of all nights, why this?*

Debbie grinned. "Hey, Sis. I waved to you out there, but you looked right past me."

In four-inch heels and enough eye makeup for two women, Debbie was almost unrecognizable. She wore one of Kate's dresses—one of her favorites, in fact: a bright psychedelic mix of blues and greens, its soft jersey skirt cut to flatter her legs. Or rather, it used to. Debbie had sliced several inches off the skirt; it hit her mid-thigh and would ride even higher on Kate's taller frame.

"Damn you, Debbie," Kate muttered. She yanked her sister away from Ryder. "How stupid can you get!"

Fury bloomed in Debbie's kohl-lined eyes. "Fuck you, Kate. Mind your own business."

Kate's fingers dug into Debbie's shoulder. "Ruining that dress makes it my business."

Debbie's bright red lips curled. "You never wear it anymore—so what's the big deal?" She jerked free from Kate and strutted back to Ryder, chin tilted up. "He's *my* friend. He invited me."

Kate gestured to the line of white powder. "Are you nuts?" she said to Ryder. "She's *sixteen.*"

"Oh, and you're some big grown-up," Debbie said. "Leave us alone."

"Not on your life. Ryder could end up in jail. So could you."

Ryder watched the quarrel with a dazed look on his face.

Kate turned to Jack. "I apologize for my idiot sister. She's been practicing to be a brat all her life."

From the stage, slightly muffled, came a frantic drumbeat and the whine of a guitar, then a woman's voice, cigarette-hoarse. "Men don't know what we feelin'." The voice spiraled into a wail and then cried out, "Ain't it the truth, Baby? Yeah, ain't it the truth?"

Jack Morrison eased himself between the sisters and put his hand on Debbie's skinny arm like he'd known her all his life. He cocked his head toward the line of coke. "I love that stuff as much as anyone, Kid Sister. But Kate's right—you and our friend here could end up in a shitload of trouble. This isn't a very private place, and even I can tell you're underage. If somebody walked by and freaked out, we could all go down."

Debbie's anger faltered; her expression softened toward uncertainty.

"You've never done coke before, have you?" Jack asked. His voice was gentle and unjudging, but Debbie didn't reply.

"You have plenty of time," Jack continued. "Don't let this badass push you into something you're not ready for."

Confusion reigned on Debbie's face, and then she caved. With a huge sigh, she stepped away from Ryder. "Later," she said.

"Later," Jack affirmed. "Now—did you come here with anyone?"

Debbie shook her head.

"Do you have a car?"

Another head shake. "Took the *bus.*" She glared at her sister like this was Kate's fault.

In the horrible moment that followed, Kate anticipated what Jack was going to say.

"Then we're taking you home."

Debbie's face pinched up in protest. "No!"

"No arguments, Kid Sister. Now come on—*vamanos!*"

He jingled his car keys and gestured toward the exit. Radiating resentment, Debbie took a couple of slow steps forward, and Kate followed, fighting an urge to shove her sister out into the night and let her find her own way home. Her first date with Jack, and Debbie had wrecked it.

From behind them, Ryder asked, "One for the road?"

She turned and saw him holding up a small glass vial, half full of something white.

Jack waited a beat, then said, "No thanks, man. Not tonight."

Kate flashed him a grateful smile before she nudged Debbie out the door.

Jack drove a dark blue Volvo coupe with a stick shift, and from the backseat Debbie leaned forward and watched as he worked the clutch and the gears.

"So you're an artist?" she asked.

"A painter," Jack replied. "Not sure yet about the artist bit."

"What kind of painting?"

"You heard of Joan Miró?" He looked in the rear-view mirror. "No? Well, some people think my stuff is like that. Maybe sometime you can come to the studio with Kate and see for yourself."

"That would be so groovy," Debbie said. "But *she* probably doesn't want me to."

"That's between you and *her*," Jack replied, with a smile for Kate, who sat in mortified silence. Jack would never ask her out again after this fiasco. But then the meaning behind his words hit: he did mean for her to come to the studio again!

She turned and smiled at Debbie, whose eyes, fixed on Jack, glittered with admiration. Then Debbie gave her a look that said, "I can't believe he's wasting time with *you*" and stuck out her tongue.

Anger flooded back into Kate, only partly diluted by the pleasure of sitting beside Jack. She watched flashing neon signs flow past: liquor stores, bars, golden arches promising fast-food delights.

"So, ladies," Jack said as they cruised up Barham Pass, "did either of you expect the night to turn out like this?"

"No way," Kate replied. "And I am so sorry Dip-Shit here barged in."

"Hey!" Debbie protested.

"Be quiet, Deb. You were lucky to run into us."

Kate swallowed the rest of her tirade. More than ever, she wanted to turn around, grab Debbie and shake her to pieces for interfering with the scenario she'd concocted to end the evening: Jack taking her to the loft, where they'd stay up until dawn again, talking, maybe doing other things. Things she wanted to do even though she knew she shouldn't.

He put on his blinker and turned onto Bright Street, and Kate barely held back a sigh.

"Well, sister dear," said Debbie as the Volvo stopped in front of the Prescott house, "I guess this is the end of the road. For both of us. You should come in with me. You know how Mom gets if we're out too late."

Kate heard the satisfied smirk in her sister's voice. Her hand itched to slap Debbie. Hard.

Jack got out and pulled the seat back forward for Debbie to exit. "Run along, Kid Sister. I want to talk to Kate. Alone." He stressed the last word in a way that allowed no argument.

Debbie touched his arm lightly. "Thanks," she said. "You are far too nice to be hanging around with her, though."

She pranced up the walkway as if she didn't have a care in the world.

Kate stayed in the car until Jack opened the door for her. Then she got out slowly and started to apologize for the dreadful end to their date. He stopped her with a kiss, his tongue gently pressing against her lips until she opened them and let him explore.

When they broke apart, he touched her cheek gently. "There'll be other times," he whispered.

"Promise?" she asked, and then hated herself for practically begging.

"Promise," he affirmed. "I like it that you look out for the kid. She's going to get herself in more trouble than she can handle without a big sister to protect her. She's lucky you're there for her. I'm lucky you're here with me."

"We are all so damned lucky," Kate said, but when she smiled, she meant it.

He kissed her again, pulling her close to him, and she surrendered to the warm, protected feeling that washed over her. For the moment, she could relax and not worry about Debbie, or what people thought of her, or how her life would turn out. Jack would keep her safe. She knew that as surely as she knew her own name.

Chapter Seven
February 1969

"We've heard good things about you," said Paul Lange.

Kate sat across from Permian Oil's Employee Relations Director, trying to look poised and politely interested in the reason he'd called her into his office. She stifled a ripple of surprise, smoothed her skirt and wondered who "we" were.

When she replied, "Thank you," Kate hoped she sounded calm and matter-of-fact.

Lange shuffled some papers in front of him. His desk was *huge*, its glossy walnut surface covered with stacks of folders and a few thick books that looked like they'd actually been read.

"Marcie thinks you have a lot of potential, and I respect Marcie's instincts."

Kate smiled, trying to find a better response than "thanks" so he wouldn't wonder if she had any other words in her vocabulary.

* * *

Marcie Plesh, who ran the Personnel Department and reported to Lange, had been friendly from the start. Kate's job hunt had begun with a referral from one of her dad's golf buddies, a marketing manager at Permian. The guy must've had some clout because Kate landed a receptionist job on the spot.

"The oil business may not be glamorous," Marcie had explained when she conveyed the job offer, "but it's good pay and steady work."

Marcie didn't seem to resent Kate skating into the job. In fact, she seemed relieved to have filled it so quickly. She also mentioned that, although the receptionist job was merely entry-level, it was a high-visibility post that could lead to a move up.

Was she ever right: Kate met *everyone* in the company, from the janitor to the CEO, and discovered she had a knack for remembering names and faces. The executives noticed. Now, after less than a year, Paul Lange was interviewing her for a promotion to the steno pool—not a huge leap forward, but it carried a fifteen-percent pay boost.

Kate had studied shorthand and typing in high school, certain they'd come in handy at the university. Ironically, they turned out to be the most relevant job skills she possessed.

* * *

Now, in meeting with Lange, Kate told him, "Marcie's been very kind to me," and she meant it.

"And she doesn't give praise lightly." Lange peered at her over the top of his glasses. "I understand your college education was interrupted by family circumstances."

Kate felt a flush creep across her cheeks. "That's right."

"Any plans to go back?"

Behind Lange, through the plate glass window, the towers of downtown Los Angeles shimmered in morning sunlight. The sight reminded Kate of the view from Jack's loft.

"Eventually. Right now I'm focusing on…" She hesitated. "My career" sounded pretentious and wasn't quite true anyhow. "… on learning the ropes here and doing a good job."

Lange smiled. "Admirable. But don't give up on higher education. A bright young woman like you could really advance here."

"Thank you. I'll keep that in mind."

* * *

He didn't offer her the stenographer job on the spot, but Marcie Plesh came to the lobby later that day and leaned an ample hip against the reception desk. Half-moon glasses dangled from a chain around her neck, and her softly reddened hair framed a face full of kindness.

"Can you start Monday?" she asked.

Kate gripped the gleaming granite desk top. "I got the job?"

Across the lobby, elevators chimed, and people bustled in and out, on their way to one important meeting or another. The murmur of voices filled Kate's ears, words indistinct but tones all urgent and focused on company business. Or so she imagined. *This is my world now*, Kate thought. *I belong here.*

"You did," Marcie affirmed. Overhead lights bounced off her shiny curls.

And, just like that, Kate had a new job.

On Friday morning, Marcie phoned Kate at the reception desk.

"Did you bring your lunch today?" she asked.

"No," Kate replied. "I ran out of time."

She usually did bring a sandwich with her, both to economize and so that she could spend her lunch break in one of the vacant conference rooms, working her way through Janson's *History of Art*, one of the few textbooks she'd kept from her university classes.

She and Jack often spent Monday nights on La Cienega Blvd., where all the important galleries were clustered. They stayed open late on Mondays, and Jack was introducing Kate to a new world of painting and sculpture. Monday nights had become a special time for her, and Kate wanted to sound halfway informed when she discussed the paintings with Jack. The huge Janson book was a good start.

Much of the text was familiar, thanks to her dad's informal tutoring. Seeing pictures of some of her favorites—Van Gogh's irises, Hopper's cityscapes—was like meeting old friends and helped her relate to the art she saw on her gallery tours with Jack. Kate looked forward to escaping into the art world while she ate her lunch.

That morning, however, she'd been sidetracked searching for the sweater she planned to wear—which it turned out Debbie had "borrowed."

"Good," Marcie said. "I'm taking you to lunch at Dave's to celebrate your promotion."

Dave's was a popular local hangout with oversized sandwiches and the "Best Fries West of the Rockies," according to a sign in the front window. The atmosphere was noisy but comfortable.

"I should be the one taking you," Kate said as they scooted their chairs up to a table. "You were behind this—and I really appreciate it."

Marcie lit a cigarette and exhaled smoke from her nose. She looked incredibly sophisticated to Kate, who pulled out her Marlboros and tried to copy Marcie's easy grace.

"You deserve it, honey. Do you have any idea how many girls we went through on the reception desk before you came along?" Marcie held up her right hand, fingers splayed. "Five. In a year." She sighed. "And I'll bet you a hot fudge sundae the next one will fold too."

"Why?" Kate asked over the clatter of dishes and silverware. "It's not hard. It's even fun sometimes."

In fact, Kate had been surprised to find that she enjoyed her work. After the abstract world of textbooks and essays, she took pleasure in doing something measurable by more than a letter grade. And sitting behind the reception desk in that high-ceilinged lobby, she didn't feel scared. The crises that came up were small and manageable.

Marcie laughed. "To you, maybe. I knew from the minute I laid eyes on you that you were right for the job. You're smart, you pay attention, you remember things."

The description pleased Kate, although she hadn't realized she came across that way.

The gum-chewing waitress in her starched yellow uniform grinned at Marcie. "How ya doin', hon? Where ya been?"

Marcie took another puff on her cigarette. "Trying to count calories. But today I give up. I'll have the usual."

Kate hadn't even looked at the menu. "Same for me."

Marcie's "usual" was a massive beef dip sandwich with a pile of those acclaimed French Fries on the side. The food smelled heavenly, and Marcie dug into hers with obvious zeal.

"The raise comes at a great time," Kate confided before she took a nibble. "I'd really like to get my own place. Living at home is a drag."

Marcie licked off juice that had dripped onto her hand. "Play your cards right, and you'll be making even more money soon. Lange has his eye on you—and no, that's not my doing. He can see how smart you are, how hard you work."

Kate put down her sandwich and blotted her lips. "He thinks I should go back to college." She pulled out a thick slice of onion and pushed it aside.

"He's right," Marcie replied. "It'll open a lot of doors."

Kate wrinkled her nose. "Classes and homework *and* a job. Doesn't leave time for much else."

A police cruiser wailed past on Sixth Street, lights flashing. Kate winced at the noise. The city was never quiet. At night, sirens and truck engines and the clamor of winos' voices pushed their way into Jack's studio, no matter how late.

Marcie polished off the last of her beef dip and dunked one of her remaining fries in ketchup. "You mean time for the boyfriend? You don't think he'd understand?"

"He would."

Wouldn't he? Jack was graduating in June, and his mother was pushing him to go for his Master's. She'd promised to foot the bills so he could concentrate on his coursework.

"It's not as tough as you think," Marcie said. "I even had time to date while I was working on my B.A. at night."

"That's because you're super-smart."

"So are you, Kate. You have so much potential. I'd hate to see you waste it in clerical jobs the rest of your life." She tapped the back of Kate's hand. "I don't mean to be a nag, but I want you to succeed. Permian has so few women in management—you could be one of them."

Management. More money: enough to get her own apartment and still help her mom with the mortgage. To take trips with Jack. To buy new clothes when she felt like it. Marcie was right. Lange was right. If she ever hoped to make anything of herself, Kate acknowledged, she'd have to go back to college, bite the bullet and give up a big chunk of her free time. In the end, though, it'd be worth it. She didn't want to be some little twit following Jack Morrison around with nothing of her own to say. He'd get bored with that plenty fast. And so would she.

After lunch, Kate phoned the state college where Jack had applied to graduate school, and asked for her own admissions application.

Chapter Eight
June 1969

Ryder handed Kate a glass of champagne. "Relax. Jack's folks are cool; they won't check your ID."

Kate took a sip. "Are you sure? I think his mom hates me. She's always *glaring* at me."

Ryder drained his glass and burped. "Josie'd be that way if you were the Q of E. Nobody's ever gonna be good enough for her son. Get used to it."

"Get used to what?" Jack asked, sliding between Kate and Ryder. He put his arm around Kate's waist and kissed her.

God, he was handsome. In the months they'd been dating, his shiny brown hair had grown to his shoulders, and the beard he'd started last winter had filled in.

His white shirt and dark slacks were a concession to Josie Morrison, but as a shaft of afternoon sunlight fell across his face, Kate could see into his dark brown eyes, and when he winked at her, he was still Jack, even in a different costume.

He clinked his champagne flute against hers. "Is Ryder trying to get you drunk?"

"We can't do much else," Ryder muttered. "Weed is out."

Jack grinned. "Says who?" He tilted his head toward the staircase that led up to his old bedroom. "It's my graduation party. I say we can do whatever the hell we want."

Kate had been in Jack's room only once before, the night he brought her to meet his parents. Then, as now, it was a welcome sanctuary from Josie Morrison's penetrating eyes and Henry Morrison's clumsy attempts to joke about young love. Several of Jack's older paintings hung on the walls, along with a small pen and ink drawing of a desert landscape, rocks and succulents making exotic patterns beneath a rippling sky.

Kate had learned with surprise that Jack's mother had done the drawing years ago. Josie clearly had talent. Jack couldn't explain why his mother hadn't pursued drawing, but Kate guessed that marriage and raising a son had consumed all her energy.

Jack shut the bedroom door and opened a window. Ryder took a seat at the well-worn desk, which held a couple of chess club trophies and a photo of a grinning teenaged Jack, standing by a painting and displaying a blue ribbon.

Kate sat on the bed's edge, and Jack sank down next to her as the box springs creaked.

When Ryder pulled a baggie full of weed and some Zig Zags from his jacket, Kate reached for them.

"Here," she said, "let me do it. Jack's been teaching me."

Carefully, she licked and glued two papers together, tapped in a fat line of weed, thumbed the paper over it and rolled a respectably firm joint. She licked the paper's free edge and pressed it in place, then held it up. "Voilà."

"Not bad," Ryder acknowledged, flicking his lighter and holding the flame out for her.

Kate took the first hit and pulled it into her lungs. She no longer coughed when she smoked pot, thanks to months of practice. She didn't really *love* getting high; it tangled her thoughts, and she had trouble concentrating. But Jack liked it, and she wanted to share the experience with him. She kept hoping eventually she'd feel whatever it was he felt, but so far that hadn't happened.

"So, man," Jack said to Ryder, "did you come clean to your parents about leaving school? Or did they not know about graduation?"

Ryder shrugged. "They figured it out. Dad yelled at me, and then he went back to his poker game. Mom cried—that was hard. But I think I convinced her it'll be OK. When she hears me on the radio, she'll be glad."

He'd assembled a ragtag band over the winter: a bass guitarist, keyboard player and drummer. The group called themselves the Ryders and had been creating a little stir with "The Devil is a Personal Friend." They'd landed a few gigs at high school dances and held a couple of open-air concerts, but mostly the group got stoned and jammed at the loft. So far no record producers had come sniffing around.

"It's this close," Ryder insisted, holding up thumb and forefinger an inch apart.

And maybe it was, Kate reflected. Stranger things had happened. Besides, the band was actually pretty good—at least equal to most of the stuff being played on the radio.

Kate took another hit on the joint and tried to enjoy the balmy spring afternoon. Jack had his Bachelor of Fine Arts degree from Chouinard, and Kate shared his relief that the grueling senior year had ended. Summer stretched before them, shimmering with promise. She had two weeks of vacation saved up for long lazy days with Jack.

Fall seemed an eternity away, and that was fine with her. Jack had been accepted at L.A. State, and he'd be buried in class work again. Kate hadn't turned in her own admissions application, although she'd gone through the preliminaries, ordering transcripts from the university and confirming that she'd be able to transfer all of her class credits, thanks to her 3.4-grade point average.

Why hadn't she filed the application? She'd already missed the deadline for the fall semester, and she didn't have much time before applying for spring.

Kate frowned, thinking of summer's end. Why did she have to spoil the moment with worry about the future?

Jack caught her look and squeezed her hand. "You're worrying again. I can see it."

"No, I'm fine. It's all fine."

Jack winked at her. "I love you," he mouthed as Ryder took another hit and squinted from the smoke.

Kate felt a little thrill, and then doubt washed it away. Did he really love her? What would happen in the months ahead, when he went back to school and got involved in new art projects and made new friends?

Jack nuzzled her neck. He didn't usually give in to public displays of affection so Kate figured he was trying to reassure her, and she let him. He did love her, he wasn't afraid to say it, or show it. He was so perfect, so handsome and talented and sexy and kind. Could life send her any clearer signal that things would be okay? Kate surrendered to the moment and let well-being flow over her.

The doorknob rattled. From the other side came Josie's annoyed voice. "John Henry Morrison, are you hiding from our guests? Why is this door locked?"

"Sorry, Mom, I didn't know," Jack said. "Just a sec."

Kate and Ryder fanned smoke out the window while Jack took his time opening the door.

Josie peered over his shoulder at Ryder and Kate, her nostrils flaring. "You're being rude," she said to Jack.

"I'm sorry, Mom. I was showing Kate and Ryder some of my old stuff."

"Don't you try and fool me, young man. I'm quite aware of what you were doing, and it wasn't looking at your high school art project."

"Busted," Ryder said, hanging his head in mock remorse.

"Come along now," Josie commanded, stepping away from the door. When Jack hesitated, she repeated, "Now."

He looked back at Kate with a "what can I do?" expression and she smiled her understanding.

Josie was entitled to order him around that afternoon, Kate supposed, since she'd paid for—and would continue to subsidize—his education.

Kate and Ryder followed Jack and his mother, and at the foot of the stairs, Josie took Kate's wrist and gently drew her aside.

Oh, God, here it comes. The lecture.

Voices hummed from the living room, where friends and relatives mingled to celebrate Jack's graduation. Most of the guests were in the same age range as Jack's parents, Kate had noticed. She'd lost track of names and grew uncomfortable under the eager curiosity most displayed when they met her.

"This is an important step for Jack," Josie said.

"Yes," Kate replied. "I'm as proud of him as you are."

"He seems very... fond of you, Kate. You're the first girl he's gone out with in a long time." Josie patted Kate's hand before releasing it. "He's been so caught up in his studies that it seemed he didn't have time for fun." She flashed a benign smile. "I'm so glad he found you."

"Thanks," Kate said. What was Jack's mother getting at?

"Your opinion obviously matters to him," Josie continued.

"I hope so," Kate replied. "I can't control what he does, but please don't think I'm encouraging the... the smoking thing."

"Oh—that!" Josie laughed softly. "No—boys will be boys. I've known for a long time that Jack smoked marijuana. So many young people do these days. Especially artists." She narrowed her eyes. "He'll grow out of it, I'm sure. But I do want the best for him—the best education, the best chance for a useful life. A productive life."

"Of course," Kate replied. "I do, too. He has a brilliant future ahead of him. He'll be a famous painter."

"Perhaps. But the art world can be very cruel. That's why I insist he get his education. He needs a career to fall back on."

"But he's so talented. He can't give up on his dream."

"Dreams are easily broken," Josie replied.

Is that what happened to you? Kate wondered. *Is that why there aren't more of your drawings on the walls?*

"He needs to finish graduate school," Josie continued. "And I don't want him to be overly... distracted."

Kate studied the older woman's face for any sign of softness, and she didn't find it. Jack's mother, flawlessly elegant in a navy-blue shift, her hair going silver at the temples, had eyes the same color as Jack's, and they seemed to bore into Kate's soul.

Kate, in her well-worn pink jersey dress, which she saved for special occasions, felt common and helpless before Josie's intensity.

Someone—Josie or, more likely, a housekeeper—had strung glittery garlands along the staircase banister, and their sparkle reflected on Josie's face, an attractive face now set in a disapproving frown.

Kate wished she had something to hold in her hands, which hung at her sides; she fought an urge to curl them into fists.

"I don't intend to *distract* him," she finally managed to say without much acid in her voice. "I have plans for the future, too."

Josie studied her without speaking.

"I'm probably going back to school myself... next year," Kate continued.

"Are you?" Disbelief rang in Josie's voice.

"My boss has encouraged me to finish college," Kate told her, willing herself to sound dignified. "He thinks I have a lot of potential."

"I'm sure you do," Josie replied, although her expression said *I want you and your potential to leave my son alone.* "You're a smart young woman, and there are so many opportunities out there now for smart young women."

Kate had no idea how to respond.

"A good education is priceless," Josie continued. "When you're young, it's easy to lose sight of your goals, and I would hate for either of you to look back later and be sorry you didn't try harder to accomplish everything you're capable of. I want what's best for Jack, naturally. And for you too, Kate. Truly."

Damned if she didn't sound like she meant it. This Josie, the concerned, earnest parent, threw Kate off balance.

"I understand where you're coming from," Kate replied. "Truly." She tried not to mimic Josie's tone, to be genuine and gentle herself, but the words held more sarcasm than she wanted.

Kate waited a few heartbeats before she turned away and went looking for Jack. Josie's words had pried open the door to uncertainty.

Did she get in Jack's way? Was she distracting him from his destiny?

Deep within her thoughts, a tiny voice whispered, W*hat about my destiny? Where does that fit in?*

One thing for sure: she didn't want to end up like Josie Morrison, shoving her own dreams aside because she didn't have the guts to make them real. But what *were* her dreams, anyway? What *did* she want to do with her life?

Kate tried to put her questions aside. There was plenty of time to figure it all out. Wasn't there?

Chapter Nine

"Give me a lift home?" Jack whispered as the party wound down. His parents had insisted on chauffeuring him to the graduation ceremony and back to their house, and they hadn't offered Kate a ride so she'd driven by herself in her beloved Bel Air, a sixteenth birthday gift from her father.

The car hadn't been brand-new even then, but Kate had maintained it the way her dad taught her. It still looked good and ran well, and comforting memories arose every time she got behind the wheel. She imagined the smell of Dad's aftershave and the rumble of his voice, reminding her not to rely on the mirrors but to look over her shoulder before changing lanes.

Kate pretended to think about Jack's question. "Oh, so that's why you invited me? As a free taxi?"

He smoothed back her hair and kissed her forehead. "Can't fool you, huh?"

Her skin tingled. "How soon can we leave?"

"Was Mom that hard on you? I saw her give you The Talk."

"Nah, she was fine."

Jack squeezed Kate's arm. "You're a good sport, Babe."

* * *

She'd hoped for some private time with Jack back at the loft, but Ryder had gotten there first. He and his band were jamming, filling the air with a mixed noise of drums and guitars, as Ryder sang about salvation and intoxication.

Kate swallowed her disappointment. When the band stopped playing, the drummer called out, "Hey, Jack—congrats. I hear you're now officially an artist."

Jack pursed his lips. "Ask me tomorrow."

He put his arm around Kate. "Don't mind us," he said to the drummer. "Carry on."

Ryder cackled. "I think you two are the ones who'll be carryin' on. But before you disappear, I have a little graduation present."

He put his guitar aside and came up to them, holding a small black-topped vial.

Jack grinned, but he must have felt Kate tense up. He held her even more closely. "Want to try some, Babe? You'll like it, I promise."

The white powder in the vial looked harmless enough, and from the way Jack and Ryder talked about it, coke was a miracle cure for whatever ailed you. Tired? It gave you energy. Worried? It made you forget your troubles.

"Let's do it," she said.

Ryder set out a pocket mirror, laid down a line, and handed her a cut-off soda straw. "Go easy," he cautioned, "just sniff. Then hold your head up and breathe in through your nose."

Kate wrestled with self-consciousness as she leaned over the mirror, careful not to spill anything. Her nostrils reflected back at her, immense, as the powder disappeared. *Hey,* she thought, *this isn't so hard!*

Her nose prickled. The feeling intensified and moved outward, downward, surging through her whole body. Every nerve ending fired, and a feeling of intense power swept over her. Anything was possible. Best of all, the echoing insinuations of Josie Morrison finally shut up.

"Wow," Kate said after a minute.

Jack squeezed her hand. "Pretty cool, huh?"

She didn't know what to say. Words tumbled in her head but refused to form a coherent sequence. She was all feeling, no thought.

Jack had taken a turn at the pocket mirror too, and Kate noticed a spot of white powder on the rim of his left nostril. After she wiped it away, he put his mouth around her finger, rubbing it against his gum, all the while keeping his gaze fastened on her. The gesture made her shiver.

Kate was only partly aware of Ryder and his band, passing the coke and the mirror around, sniffing and muttering "oh yeah" and "far out." She and Jack were in their own universe—the way it had been that first time they met, among all those hippies in the park.

It might have been minutes later, or hours, when the band started playing: a song she'd not heard before, with a heavy, throbbing beat, seductive and slow. Jack pressed his body against hers and swayed with the music, and Kate, who always insisted she couldn't dance, let him lead her in a sinuous motion around the bare wood floor.

The music invaded her skin, and her heart beat in time with the drum, her blood surging through her veins. Ryder, his voice deep and suggestive, sang about drinking whiskey in smoky bars, fast women in shiny cars, and rockets to the stars. Jack's breath, warm on her cheek, smelled of cigarettes and champagne.

"Are you okay, Babe?" Jack asked, pulling her in tighter.

Kate could merely nod.

Gently he maneuvered away from the band, toward his part of the loft. The now-familiar smell of oil paint embraced her. A hot, moist yearning overtook her, a pulse that was both of and apart from the music.

Her body let Jack's know how much she wanted what came next: his lips on hers, their tongues touching, his hands sliding down, unfastening her clothes, pushing her onto the bed.

"You sure about this?" he asked, his voice low and breathy.

Kate smiled. "Never been more sure."

"Well then," he whispered, "this is the best damn graduation present anyone ever got."

From Jack's easy moves, Kate could tell he'd done this before. It was her second time. She'd reluctantly surrendered her virginity to

Ricky Tremaine the summer before she left for college, mainly because everyone else had had sex by then, and Kate wanted to join the club. She'd regretted it even before it was done, and so, apparently, had Ricky, who avoided her after that night.

With Jack, however, it *felt* like the first time. The coke fueled her desire and gave her a wild, crystal-clear energy. *I want this. I want* him. *And he wants me.*

At the same time—how could she have so many different feelings? —anxious thoughts tugged. *What if I get pregnant? What if I'm doing it wrong? What if he doesn't like it with me? What if I don't like it with him? I shouldn't be doing this.*

I DON'T CARE! roared another voice inside her head, one she'd never heard before. *This feels so right, so perfect.*

She was ready for him, more than ready, and she let the heavy beat of Ryder's drummer set the pace, and nothing had ever felt so good. It seemed to Kate as if she had been born for this moment, that making love with Jack Morrison was the sole reason she'd been put on earth.

When they finished and lay panting and sweaty, Kate basked in a glow of well-being and satisfaction, and Jack smiled at her—a slow, lazy smile.

"Too good to be true," he whispered, and pulled her to him, and they started up all over again.

Afterward, Jack rolled onto his side, kissed her again and traced a pattern across her naked breasts.

"Are you all right?" he asked.

His chest hair glowed golden in the slanting sunlight, and his eyes glistened. He touched Kate's cheek, and a quiver ran through her whole body, head to toe, an electric current set loose inside her. Her mouth tasted of Jack and something coppery-minty.

"More than all right," Kate replied. She kissed his lips.

The Ryders had taken a break. Only a curtain separated the bedroom from the open spaces beyond, and Kate hoped they hadn't heard her gasps of pleasure. Then again, she didn't really care. Nothing mattered except what had just happened between her and Jack. Then a guitar twanged and cymbals clanged as the band started up again.

Jack's hand beat out a tempo on the bed covers, and he winked at Kate. "How often do you get your own private serenade?"

Kate giggled. "Aren't we lucky?"

Ryder's voice rang out from the other end of the loft. "Jack and Katie, sitting up in a tree, k-i-s-s-i-n-g."

Another voice joined in. "More than kissing, you can bet."

Warmth flooded Kate's cheeks.

Jack sat up and stretched. "Ignore those clowns. All they're good for is making noise and getting high." He raised his voice. "Hey, you jokers—a little privacy, please!"

The guitar wailed louder in reply.

Jack tilted his head back, closed his eyes and howled, like a wolf calling to its pack.

The music quieted a little after that, but Jack let out one more yowl. Then he opened his eyes and smiled down at Kate. "*There* you are."

Kate returned the smile. "I've been here all along."

Chapter Ten

S unlight pierced the smudged window glass and pulled Kate from sleep. Her mouth tasted of stale tobacco, and her tongue felt thick and dry. For one panicked moment she didn't know where she was. Then she caught a whiff of linseed oil and turpentine.

Jack stirred next to her and opened his eyes. "Morning." He pulled her close. "So you weren't a dream."

When he kissed her, his flesh warm and welcoming, his touch brought back the night's lovemaking. They'd almost never left the bedroom, even after the Ryders took off to party elsewhere, leaving a vial of white powder behind with an invitation to use it. They had.

Much later, as physical and mental exhaustion claimed her, a nagging thought had tried to surface, something she needed to do. She'd fallen asleep before she remembered what it was.

The telephone's clamor shattered the early-morning quiet. Jack pushed himself up on one elbow. "What the hell?"

He threw off the covers and grabbed his pants, holding them against his nakedness as he thrust the curtain aside and hurried toward the phone, which hung on the kitchen wall partition.

"Hello? Yes, it's... yes, she's... calm down, Helen, I'll get her."

By then Kate remembered what she was supposed to have done the night before: call her mom and tell her not to wait up. It would've been an unpleasant conversation then, but nothing compared to what she faced now as she hurriedly slipped into her dress and ran barefoot to the phone, her only thought to keep Helen's toxic fury from scalding Jack.

Wide-eyed, Jack handed her the phone. Kate heard her mother's tinny rant even before the receiver reached her ear.

"Mom, calm down, I'm okay. I'm sorry I didn't call, I got ... distracted."

"And that makes it all right?"

Through Kate's distress, a realization came clear.

"How—how'd you find the number here?"

"How do you *think*? From your phone book!"

"You went through my desk?"

"What else could I do? I didn't know how else to track you down. For all I knew you were lying dead in a ditch somewhere."

"Mom, please, don't—"

Helen's tidal wave of indignation continued. "I expected better of you. Your father would be so—"

"You leave Dad out of this! And quit lecturing me like I'm a little kid."

"You think you're a grown-up now? Then act like one, not like some irresponsible—"

"Look, Mom, I said I'm sorry. I didn't do it on purpose. I forgot, okay?"

"No, it's not 'okay,' Kate. And your 'sorry' doesn't make up for the scare you've given me. Again."

Her words dissolved into a moist, noisy cough.

The futility of reasoning with her mother washed over Kate, and her arm felt too heavy to keep holding the phone.

"We'll talk later," she said. "Good-bye."

"You can bet we'll talk later. I only hope you haven't done something you'll be sorry for. You don't know how boys are. They get what they want, and then they're done with you. You young girls think you can—"

Kate hung up.

Jack had pulled on his pants while Kate absorbed her mother's wrath.

She turned to him. "I am so sorry you had to hear that."

He smiled. "I'll make us some coffee."

As the aroma of brewing coffee filled the air, Jack fired up a Marlboro and offered the pack to Kate. She sank into a chair as he lit her cigarette with intimate ease and moved the abalone shell ashtray closer to her.

Kate inhaled and tried to clear her head. Why had her mother gone and wrecked the morning's peace?

He knelt and rested his arms on her legs. "You okay?"

"Yeah," Kate replied, tapping ash into the abalone shell, working to recapture the lighthearted mood they'd shared before the phone rang.

Jack rubbed his hands along her bare thighs. "No regrets? About last night?"

"Of course not. It was the best night of my life."

Her mother's words, however, had planted their poison. Had she done something she'd be sorry for? She couldn't get pregnant from just one night—could she? But what about next time? She wanted a next time, and a time after that. She'd talk to Arlene at work; Arlene was far more experienced. She might know a doctor who'd prescribe birth control pills even if you were single and underage.

Jack rose and kissed her, ever so gently, and Kate's fears melted at the touch of his lips. He looked into her eyes, like he was trying to see behind them and to read her thoughts.

"No regrets at all?" he whispered. "I mean, I know girls worry about stuff."

Kate shook her head; she couldn't talk.

Jack smoothed back her hair. "You don't have to worry. I'll always take care of you. You're special to me, Babe."

His words eased her mind, but only a little. And she didn't want him to know how much she worried about things that other people shrugged off.

When she could speak again, Kate told him, "I'm still pissed off at Mom. Debbie stays out all night, and she's usually lying through her teeth about who she's with or what she's doing, but Mom never yells at *her*."

He brought her a mug of steaming coffee, strong and black. "Your mom expects it from her. But not from you. You're the good girl."

"Me?" Kate laughed at the notion.

"You. And you acted out of character. It's scary when people do what we don't expect."

"She gets scared, all right. Scared she'll lose her paycheck." Kate ground out her cigarette. "That's all I am to her, help with the bills. The rest of the time she treats me like a five-year-old."

"I noticed that."

"It's obvious, huh? I should move out, get my own place, let her worry about the mortgage instead of butting into my life."

Her own apartment. The idea had tantalized her for weeks, ever since her promotion, which brought a realization that she could afford it now. Somewhere she and Jack could have privacy.

The vision shimmered before her as she sipped her coffee.

"Don't jump into it, Babe," Jack said. "Give your mom a break."

Kate rubbed her temples. "She doesn't give *me* a break. The way I feel right now, I *never* want to go home."

Jack sat across from her. "Sorry." He looked like he meant it.

Half-joking, Kate said, "Maybe I'll hide out here today."

He didn't respond, and Kate wished she'd taken time to put on the rest of her clothes before dashing to the phone, instead of leaving them strewn around his bedroom. The morning air held a chill that brushed her bare arms and legs. The silence ticked on for several heartbeats.

"Uh, sure, you can do that," Jack said at last. "Stay as long as you want. The thing is, I have to go over to my folks' place in a while."

The words stung like cold water. "Oh. I didn't know."

"Yeah," Jack continued, and the word "sheepish" suddenly had a face. "Mom's having some lunch thing with my aunt and uncle from up north. They couldn't come to the party yesterday, so…"

The abrupt shift in his demeanor baffled her. Where had her tender lover gone?

"Oh," Kate said again, hardly recognizing the tight little voice that came out of her. *Your mom crooks her finger and you come running. And I'm not invited, of course.*

She tried to recover a breezy dignity. "You gotta keep the folks happy." *Especially when they pay the rent.*

"You know it." He seemed a little more relaxed. "But you don't have to rush off, honest."

"No," she replied. "I have to face Mom eventually. Maybe she'll have cooled off by the time I get home."

Kate's stomach clenched, however, when she thought of the scene she'd probably walk into: her mother's angry face, the nasty voice implying she was a tramp. Mom would find ways to skewer her with insinuations, and Jack wouldn't be with her to run interference; she'd have to confront it all on her own.

"I'm getting so damn tired of her temper tantrums," Kate continued. "She depends on *me* to pay her expenses—but I don't try to boss *her* around."

It came out harsher than she intended. Or did it? Everything she'd been trying not to worry about, all the possible disasters that could come from her night of careless fun, rose up and hummed furiously through her thoughts. Kate stiffened her back.

Silence hung in the air again, broken only by the flick of Jack's lighter, leaving a pungent chemical after-smell along with the scent of burning tobacco. He didn't offer the pack to Kate, and her cigarettes were in the bedroom. Her fingers twitched, but she didn't help herself.

Jack's face had closed up. Even bare-chested, he seemed to pull a cloak around himself, a separateness she could feel. Smoke curled upward from his cigarette as it consumed itself. She thought of how that bare chest had glowed in the sunlight yesterday afternoon, and a sharp longing pierced her, for something that had been snatched from her too soon.

When she spoke again, she was able to lighten her words. "Wouldn't it be nice if I had my own place? We could do whatever we want, whenever we want. You could take a *real* shower."

Jack had griped about bathing in the unheated loft, using a claw-foot tub that sat on a platform next to the toilet.

He smiled a little but still looked uptight.

"Just so we don't confuse things here," he said. "It's *your* mom caused the trouble, right? She's the one you're pissed at."

"Right," Kate agreed.

"Good, 'cause it sounded to me like you were taking a shot at me for letting my mom help out with the bills." When Kate didn't respond, he continued, "So what if I do? She doesn't run my life."

This was going so wrong, Kate thought. But she could no more stop it than she could fly.

"Oh really?" Damn it, why was he arguing with her, now of all times? "So I guess you *want* to spend your day entertaining your aunt and uncle?"

Jack exhaled a thick plume of smoke. His eyes narrowed. "What if I do?" he said again. It sounded more challenge than question.

Kate picked up her coffee; it had gone cold and stale. "Oh, excuse me for presuming you might want us to spend the day together."

He stared at her. So—the idea hadn't even occurred to him.

Her cheeks burned. She had been so wrong about him. He was just like those boys her mother had warned her about. *They get what they want, and then they're done with you.*

Shame made her reckless. "Okay, I get it. Sorry for being so dense. I didn't realize you like the way Josie has your life planned out for you: Master's Degree, teaching credential, then she'll set you up at some fancy college, teaching kids how to stretch canvas and mix colors. Too bad you won't have time for your own art."

"Is that what you think? Mom has plenty of faith in me. But she wants me to have some job skills to fall back on. She wants me to have a profession."

"A profession. Right. And she wants you with some girl who has a *profession* too, not some little typist in a dead-end job. Like this is all I'll ever be."

"I don't see you like that, Kate. But you're rushing into things I haven't even thought about."

Kate slammed her coffee mug down so hard a few drops splashed onto the tabletop. She ignored them.

"Well, maybe you should."

"Maybe I should. I tell you one thing I *have* thought about: I may not go to grad school, all right? I may take a year off, bum around Europe. They treat artists with respect over there."

"And when were you going to tell me about this?"

His eyes turned dark and flat in the harsh morning light. "I just did."

"I guess that settles it."

A stranger answered her, someone she didn't like. "I guess it does."

Kate turned away so he couldn't see the tears on her face as she went to gather up the rest of her clothes. He didn't try to call her back as she stomped down the stairs and got into her car. Kate held her breath and counted to ten before she started the engine, but he didn't come after her.

Chapter Eleven

Kate went through the motions. She showed up for work, did her job, lived her life like a bad dream. Most of the time she felt numb, and that was good. Better than the scalding emotions that ambushed her at all the wrong moments, leaving her tearful and trembling.

Helen must have sensed potential combustion in her daughter—and how could she not, given the way Kate had slammed the car door and stomped into the house that morning after leaving Jack's? Helen took a long look at her, then went into the backyard and began yanking up weeds.

Kate almost wished her mother *would* start another argument. Then she could let loose all the hurt and rage, spew it on the person she blamed for her blowup with Jack. Helen had pushed her into the need for her own apartment, the plan that had fizzled with Jack.

It had seemed such a perfect solution, but she'd handled it wrong. Or had she? Kate replayed the argument again and again and began to wonder if Jack didn't really want to be with her full-time, not permanently. Maybe she'd merely been a diversion, to amuse him while he finished art school.

No, she argued back with herself, they'd had a *real* relationship.

They'd been so right together, they'd had so much fun, they cared about each other and shared secrets no one else knew.

And making love with him—that had been spectacular. It had affirmed her belief that Jack was *the* one for her.

So why then, the minute she tried to get serious, had he turned on her? No matter what the reason, she told herself, it was better to find out early on that he didn't want to take things any further with her.

Early on? Who was she kidding? She'd fallen in love with him. She'd never again find anyone as special as Jack Morrison; he'd ruined her for anyone else. She'd always be making comparisons, and any man she met would come up lacking.

Kate sat through polite dinners with her mother and sister, and Jack's name didn't come up, although she caught Helen directing a warning glance at Debbie now and then. She usually volunteered to clear the table, wash the dishes, do whatever needed doing. Anything to keep herself busy, any distraction to keep from thinking. From feeling.

More than ever, Kate appreciated her job. It gave her a reason to get up in the morning; it filled her days with memory-blocking activity. Maybe the breakup was for the best, she told herself. Jack was like a wildfire that had consumed her, leaving nothing but ashes. She'd given up her own ambitions, stopped trying to figure out what she wanted from life.

Now she could get back on track. In the fall, she'd go back to college at night, and she'd fill those empty hours with classes and textbooks.

A guy at work asked her out, and she turned him down. Even the thought of dating made her tired. Trying to start a new relationship, suffering through the awkward moments, the disappointments. The boring conversations while she and her date sought common ground, groping for mutual attraction. It would never be as easy and spontaneous as it had been with Jack.

* * *

In early July a summer rainstorm blew through, dampening everyone's spirits as it filled the air with oppressive moisture. The cloud cover and drizzle darkened Kate's mood that evening as she buttoned her raincoat and trudged from Permian's offices to the parking lot across the street. She almost preferred gloomy weather to the taunting rays of sunlight that reminded her of Jack. Almost everything reminded her of Jack. She'd see a long-haired guy strolling down the street, hands in jeans pockets, walking Jack's walk, and not until he turned her way would she feel the stab of disappointment, and then a surge of relief, that came from realizing he was not Jack.

A man approached her in the rain mist, and again his silhouette, his gait, made her think of Jack. Kate wanted to yell at herself, "Give it up! He's gone! You drove him away, now stop thinking of him!"

This one looked even more like Jack as he got closer. *What in the world?*

Kate stopped walking. The drizzle coated her eyelashes, but she didn't want to blink and disperse the mirage. Dampness penetrated the soles of her pumps, but Kate scarcely registered it. Cars swished past on the shiny wet street, and the sound of their tires seemed to urge her, "Keep going. Keep going!"

Jack—it really *was* Jack! He held up a bouquet of roses. "They got a little wet."

He, too, was soaked; rain dripped from his brown curls, darkening his shirt and jeans.

Her mouth hung open; she must look like a dunce.

"I wasn't sure when you'd come out," he continued. "And I didn't want to miss you. I thought you got off at five...but I guess you worked late. Kate? Say something!"

Kate didn't have a reply. What could she do but accept the roses, lift them to her face and inhale their sweet fragrance, let it drive out the numbing sorrow?

"Thanks," she said when she finally trusted her voice. "They're beautiful."

"I was an asshole," he said. "But I didn't know how to fix things. I figured I'd start by meeting you head-on and apologizing."

That drove her back into silence.

"I'll get down on my knees if you want," Jack said, and when she didn't speak, he did just that. He knelt on the dirty, puddled sidewalk and reached out for her hand. "I am so, so sorry, Kate."

She finally found her voice. "Get up—you're drenched. Don't you have a raincoat?"

He stood, looking unsure of himself.

"I'm sorry too," Kate said.

That must have been the right response because he kissed her then, and the reality of his lips on hers swept everything else away.

"Come home with me?" he murmured.

She did.

* * *

Back in the loft, Kates watched him towel off and change into dry clothes. Her eyes couldn't drink in enough of him. *He came back to me.* The delicious realization sang in her mind.

A warning bell chimed faintly in the back of her thoughts, but Kate silenced it. He'd made a mistake, and he admitted it. So had she. *Put the past away.* Could she do that? Could he? *Don't go ruining things by worrying.*

She waited for him to make the next move, and she had no firm expectations, but the serious Jack who sat her down in the kitchen with a cup of hot coffee surprised her.

He lit cigarettes for both of them. "I freaked out, and I'm sorry. Guess I wasn't ready to think about tomorrow and the day after that."

"I know, and I—"

He stopped her with an upraised hand. "But I missed you. Felt like part of *me* was gone. I didn't like it. Besides, I *should* be thinking ahead. We both should. Here's what I came up with."

He took a drag on his Marlboro and squinted through the exhaled smoke. "You talked about moving out of your mom's. If you still want to, let's do it—get an apartment for the two of us. I'll put off grad school, get a job to make my share of the rent."

What had he said? Move in together? Kate was almost afraid to breathe for fear of breaking the spell.

"You were right about my mom," he continued. "The way she maps things out. I never minded before because—"

She had to interrupt. "Jack, I was mad and I said that to piss you off. I didn't mean it. Your mom is right. You need an education."

"I *don't* need it, not right away anyhow. You're more important. *We're* more important." He took her hand and kissed the palm. "I missed you, Babe. So much. And I'm sorry I fucked things up."

He ground out his cigarette.

"I missed you too," Kate said. "But you can't put off school. If you don't keep going, you'll always—"

"Kate, will you marry me?"

For a minute Kate thought she'd heard wrong. Marry him? That was like asking if she wanted to keep on breathing. She couldn't make her tongue work to answer him. *This is too much.* That damned alarm again. *Does he know what he's saying? Does he really want this? Do I? What if he changes his mind? Wait, give it time. Don't jump in again.*

She put out her smoke as she tried to make sense of it all.

"Want me to beg?" Jack's forehead wrinkled. "I love you, Kate. I want to spend the rest of my life with you. Please say yes."

That did it.

"Yes," she said. "Yes. Of course I'll marry you, Jack Morrison."

Kate's face was wet with tears. Jack stood and pulled her to her feet, then stroked her cheeks. "I didn't mean to make you cry. Was it that lousy a proposal?"

"No! It was beautiful."

"I don't even have a ring—didn't think this through very well, huh? We'll get one tomorrow. I promise."

"It doesn't matter," Kate murmured, although it actually did.

Jack wrapped his arms around her and squeezed, and Kate surrendered to the love and protection. Her life had a meaning at last, a story of its own. She looked up at him and could feel the idiot grin on her face. And she didn't care at all.

Josie Morrison was going to shit bricks when they told her, but that didn't matter either. They'd work around it. And Kate was sure she could persuade him to go on to grad school. That would appease Josie, and Kate decided right then she'd never let anyone blame her for making Jack cut short his education. Bitter seeds would take root from something like that.

As for her own college plans—she'd waited this long, she could put them off a while longer, until she and Jack settled in. Saying yes to Jack didn't mean saying good-bye to her education, or anything else she might want out of life.

She could do it all. The feeling intoxicated her. At that moment, everything felt possible.

Chapter Twelve

Josie hadn't been as hysterically opposed to the marriage as Kate feared. Publicly at least, she treated Kate cordially, murmuring about how happy she was that Jack found a girl who was both pretty and smart. But behind the shining brown eyes, Kate sensed an adversary, appearing at unexpected times.

For example, the wedding ring: "I have a lovely ring," Josie proclaimed. "My mother's. I've kept it all these years, especially for Jack's wife."

Because Kate had visualized a simple gold wedding band, she didn't care for Josie's mother's ring, a half-carat marquise diamond flanked on each side by six smaller stones. The setting looked dirty and old to her, even after the ring had been cleaned, polished and resized. It made Kate think of musty closets and dusty furniture. She tried to focus on the ring's sentimental value.

With both Kate and Josie insisting, Jack went ahead with his plans for grad school, and Josie pledged to finance it. She even thanked Kate for "talking some sense into him."

When Josie drew up a foot-long guest list for the wedding and proposed several upscale sites for the ceremony, however, Kate rebelled.

"This is turning into a circus," she'd grumbled to Jack one night at the loft. They were lying in bed, enjoying blissful solitude. The Ryders had a gig in Redondo Beach.

"Don't you like circuses?" he'd replied.

"Not when I'm in the center ring. Jack, my mom can't afford a huge wedding—and yeah, I know your folks would offer to foot the bill, but that's wrong. Do you even know half the people your mom is inviting?"

"Want to run away?"

Kate giggled. "Quit teasing."

"I'm serious, Babe. We can drive to Vegas over Labor Day weekend."

"Really?"

He smoothed her hair back from her forehead. "Really."

"You don't want the extravaganza?"

"I want you—the sooner the better."

Kate lit a Marlboro and considered the implications. "Your mother would never forgive me."

Jack took a drag from her cigarette and blew a perfect smoke ring. Kate watched it float away from them.

"Sure she will," he said. "She and my dad did the same thing."

"Now I know you're joking."

"True story, swear to God. So—let's do it."

"You are too full of surprises."

He shrugged. "I was wondering how much of Mom's planning it'd take before you freaked out."

Kate frowned. "So I'm a lightweight?"

"Not hardly. You lasted longer than I expected—and you still want to marry me, right? Right?"

She didn't answer, so he climbed on top of her and started tickling. Which led to kissing, which led to fondling, which led, inevitably, to sex. But then, even a long look from Jack usually led to sex when they were alone together. It was the most fun Kate had ever had in her life, and her newly-prescribed birth control pills made it even better.

* * *

Three weeks after her twentieth birthday, Kate stood beside Jack in a little chapel on the Las Vegas Strip, where a Methodist minister pronounced them husband and wife. They went to one floor show at the Sands, but neither of them even visited the gambling tables. They went back to their room, and to bed, but not to sleep. *I'm safe now*, Kate kept thinking. *I know what to do with my life.*

When they came back married, hell did break loose in the Morrison living room. All the disapproval Josie had harbored over Jack's choice of a wife bubbled out, drenching the newlyweds. Josie cried. She pouted. She stomped away, slamming doors behind her.

Henry, in contrast, seemed almost relieved. He poured his son a glass of whiskey and offered one to Kate, who let the bitter brown liquor numb the despair she'd felt when hatred flared in her new mother-in-law's eyes.

"Well, you kids, congratulations," Henry said, lifting his glass in a toast. "And now what?"

Relieved she had an answer, Kate told him their plans. "We found a nice apartment, and we can move in on the first. And Jack starts school next week."

Henry had smiled, all the way up to his kind, watery blue eyes; he looked wistful. "And you're still going back to college yourself?" he asked Kate.

That took her by surprise.

Jack replied for her. "She sure is."

"Probably," Kate amended. "But I'll wait until we get settled."

"Don't wait too long," Henry told her. Another smile softened his words, and despite his military buzz cut he looked gentle and benign. "Our dreams have a way of escaping if we put them on hold too long."

"I won't," Kate had assured him with fake confidence.

* * *

And although Kate sensed she'd somehow won over Jack's father, Josie Morrison never forgave her for eloping. She rarely even spoke Kate's name, referring to her as "she" or "her" in a voice as cold as an Alaskan winter. Josie conveyed an impression that the marriage was less legitimate because she hadn't witnessed it in person. She got even by staging a lavish post-wedding reception, and she gave Kate no say in the arrangements or the guest list.

Her own mother's reaction had been muted. She claimed to be happy because she liked Jack, but there was hesitancy behind her congratulations, even after Kate assured her she'd continue to help out financially. Helen dismissed the offer—she'd finally landed a job herself, at the local yardage store.

She did, however, contact Jack's parents about helping arrange the reception, and Josie cordially accepted the offer. Her bitterness was apparently focused on Kate.

"They seem very nice," Helen Prescott had said, voice tinged with awe, after her first in-person visit with Josie and Henry. "They want to have the reception at their house, which is very generous."

"They have a ton of room for it," Kate replied, wondering if Josie planned some public humiliation for her, among all their friends, to retaliate for the absence of a big fancy wedding.

* * *

But Josie couldn't have been sweeter—in a distant, overly polite way. The weather accommodated plans for an outdoor reception in the Morrison's large back yard, and Jack persuaded his parents to hire Ryder's band for the afternoon. Surprisingly restrained, the Ryders played music everyone could dance to—including Kate's kid sister Debbie, who danced with almost every man there, and twice with her new brother-in-law.

While Debbie monopolized Jack on the dance floor, Kate went looking for a glass of water. The champagne had made her dizzy and she didn't want to say or do anything that would embarrass Jack in front of his parents' friends. The empty kitchen gave her a moment of privacy to catch her breath.

She braced her hands on the spotless white tile countertop and inhaled the fragrance of jasmine, which spilled out of a green crystal vase on the window sill. Pale oak cabinets contrasted sharply with the worn maple ones in her mom's kitchen. The refrigerator's gentle hum soothed her, as did the sight of their wedding cake, a multi-tiered confection. Kate smiled at the tiny, formally dressed bride and groom atop the cake.

She filled a glass from the tap and sipped, savoring the shadowy quiet. Then she heard her mother's voice coming from the nearby dining room.

"She's the luckiest girl alive," Helen said to someone.

Josie Morrison's voice answered. "And my son is lucky to have found her."

Kate tiptoed into the hallway that led to the dining room, hating herself for eavesdropping but unable to stop.

"I hope she lives up to her father's plans for her," Helen continued. "He really wanted her to finish college. When she had to drop out, it nearly broke my heart."

"I'm sure it did."

"Well," Helen said, a sigh in her voice, "Maybe I worry too much. She's getting married, not resigning from life. And things are different now than when you and I were girls. Kate has all kinds of possibilities in front of her. She can do anything she wants."

"But *will* she?" Josie replied.

The hallway walls, covered with photos of smiling Morrisons, seemed to close in on Kate. Her party dress, selected mainly for its on-sale price tag, felt scratchy and confining, and her high heels made the balls of her feet ache.

For a second, she couldn't breathe. Then she backed into the kitchen and paused to splash cool water on her flaming cheeks. Kate studied her reflection in the kitchen window glass. Did she look happy? She *was* happy.

Then why did Josie's words echo? "But *will* she?"

Why did she have to do anything more? She was Jack Morrison's wife now. Wasn't that enough? A treacherous voice hissed in her head: *Is it enough? Really?*

Chapter Thirteen
October 1969

A week after their wedding reception, Mr. and Mrs. Jack Morrison moved into an apartment in East Hollywood, south of Melrose and West of Normandie: an area of elegant old homes that had mostly been divided up into rental units. Kate had found the place by accident, a happy coincidence resulting from a good deed on her part.

She'd been apartment-hunting ever since Jack's proposal, but the places she found were too expensive or too shabby. Three days before she and Jack eloped, one of the other women in the steno pool, stranded by car trouble, had asked Kate for a lift home.

She dropped her co-worker off and made a wrong turn on Kingsley, trying to find the freeway, and there, so small she'd almost missed it, was a "For Rent" sign in front of a beautiful two-story fourplex with a canopy of climbing roses arching over the front porch. Big bright windows invited her to come in. She did.

Jack didn't *love* the place as Kate did, but he did like the air and light those big windows provided, plus a nice view of Griffith Park and the Observatory.

Ryder offered reluctant help with the move-in, and although he claimed to be sad at losing his roommate, in truth he came out ahead. Jack kept the loft for a workspace—he bargained with Josie to continue paying the rent there as long as he stayed in school, which meant Ryder could also afford to stay in the loft. And now he had the place more to himself.

* * *

"Why'd you pick a pad with so many stairs?" Ryder grumbled, sweat dripping from his forehead as he carried a carton of clothes upstairs.

"It's good exercise," Kate replied. She loved the staircase: it had a movie-star vibe. The whole building, even the neighborhood, held that kind of energy. "No more stairs than the loft anyway."

Ryder grunted and shoved open the door. Kate followed, clutching a lighter box full of linens, grateful for the towels and sheets she and Jack had received as wedding gifts. The Morrisons needed *everything* except furniture; lucky for them, the apartment came furnished with old but well-preserved pieces.

An untidy pile of boxes covered half the living room carpet, and Kate sighed at the thought of unpacking. However, as she took in the high ceiling, framed with crown molding, her spirits lifted like the front curtains billowing in a brisk autumn breeze. She was going to be very happy here; how could she not?

She went to the window and savored the view, especially the Observatory on its sentinel perch above Los Feliz Blvd.; the smooth curves of the Planetarium dome glowed in the afternoon light. *Back to work*, Kate admonished herself.

Ryder clattered down the stairs for another load. As Kate started after him, the door across the landing opened, and a young woman's freckled face appeared. She didn't look all that friendly.

"Hi," Kate said. "Sorry about the noise. We're almost done."

Jack came up the stairs, panting under the weight of a box filled with dishes scavenged from Kate's mother's kitchen, with Helen's grudging blessing. "When am I going to have company for dinner, anyway?" she'd replied when Kate asked about the stoneware accumulated in supermarket giveaways. He set the box down inside the apartment with an exaggerated sigh.

Her new neighbor smiled. "You must be the newlyweds. Congrat-ulations—and welcome."

Kate relaxed and introduced herself and Jack, and then Ryder, who huffed his way to the top of the stairs with a carton of Kate's record albums, almost dumping Joan Baez from one frayed corner of the box.

The young woman held out her hand to Kate. "Stella," she said. "Stella Barberini." She was half a foot shorter than Kate and had dark curly hair, and something about her said she felt sure of her place in the world.

She peeked in the open doorway of the Morrison's apartment, looking curious.

"Come on in and check it out," Jack said.

"I never wanted to go inside when that old guy was here." Stella wrinkled her nose.

"Now's your chance," Ryder told her. "I need a rest anyway. And a smoke." He looked at Kate. "I suppose a beer is out of the question."

"I have a whole fridge full," said Stella Barberini.

Ryder grinned. "I like your new neighbor."

Stella brought over four frosty Michelobs and a bag of Fritos. Kate, parched from the day's exertions, overcame her usual dislike of beer; this one actually tasted good. She took Stella on a tour of the apart-ment while Jack and Ryder brought up the rest of the boxes, re-ener-gized by the prospect of beer and corn chips as soon as they finished.

"This is like my place, only in reverse—and Mrs. B had it painted after the last guy left," Stella told Kate. "Sound really echoes in the hall, so don't say anything you don't want me to hear. And be careful about the weird Russian who lives under me—he's always staring like he's trying to hypnotize me. Sometimes at night I hear him moaning."

Kate shuddered. "What about Mrs. Bloomfield?" Their landlady lived in the apartment beneath the Morrisons.

Stella waved away her concern. "Don't stomp around late at night, pay your rent on time, and she'll love you forever. Trust me, she's glad to have you guys move in. So am I—that last tenant was older than dirt, and cranky!"

Stella grinned. She had a beautiful smile, Kate thought: the kind that could light up a room. What a lucky break to have such a neighbor.

Kate learned that Stella was a freelance writer who supported herself as a script reader at Warner Brothers. She was two years older than Kate but looked closer to Debbie's age; it was those freckles. Divorced, Stella lived alone except for her cat Whiskers, and she liked it that way.

"I've been here two years, ever since I got free from He Who Won't Be Named, and it's a really cool neighborhood. You're gonna love it."

Jack and Ryder had finished unloading Ryder's pickup and were sprawled on the living room floor. Each held a cigarette in one hand and a Michelob bottle in the other. Kate and Stella joined them, and Jack lit a Marlboro for Kate, then offered the pack to Stella.

"No thanks," Stella said. "I have enough bad habits without taking on that one."

Ryder pulled a joint from his shirt pocket. "This kind of bad habit?"

Mortified, Kate started to apologize, but the delight on Stella's face stopped her. "I knew you guys were cool the minute I saw you."

Ryder lit the joint and gave it to Stella, who took a healthy toke and passed it to Kate.

"Why not?" Kate muttered, taking a deep hit before handing it over to Jack.

Stella exhaled a thin stream of smoke and looked at Kate. "What do you do? For a living?"

Kate wished she had something exciting to say. "I'm a steno at Permian Oil."

"Downtown? No shit! The building that puts up a Christmas tree in lights on the roof every year?"

"That's the one."

"Cool!"

Kate shrugged. "It's only temporary—'til Jack finishes school and starts showing his paintings."

Stella looked at Jack like she'd forgotten he was in the room. "Oh, right—you're the artist. Mrs. B told me. She is a relentless gossip, by the way. Don't believe half of what she tells you. So—you paint?"

Jack nodded.

"Any of your stuff here?"

Jack pointed to a small seascape leaning up against the wall. Although Kate didn't understand why, he hadn't wanted any of his paintings in the new place. Kate, however, finally coaxed him into bringing this one.

Stella scooted over and studied the seascape. "This is really good, Jack. You are going to be famous someday."

Jack laughed. "Glad to hear it."

Stella turned to Ryder. "Are you an artist too?"

He shook his head.

"What *do* you do?" Stella asked.

"Guess."

She studied him and rubbed her chin. "Roadie," she said at last.

Kate and Jack burst out laughing. "You're close," said Jack.

Ryder's face flushed pink. "Maybe all I'm good for."

An awkward tension arose. "He's a musician," Kate said.

Stella took another long look at Ryder. "I thought so. You play at O'Malley's sometimes, right?"

Ryder's huge grin was answer enough. He loaded the roach into a Marlboro and fired it up. Stella shook her head when he offered her a toke, so he did the honors himself.

"Now and then," Ryder said to Stella. "Trying to get a recording contract."

"Man, that's a brutal business. Good luck to you." Stella looked at Kate and smiled. "To all three of you."

Beers drained, Jack and Ryder started setting up the stereo Kate had brought from home after a fight with Debbie. Since Kate had paid for it, she got her way. She accepted Stella's offer to help unpack and was relieved to find a shared sense of organization. Before long, they made the kitchen functional.

With Bob Dylan blaring from the stereo speakers, the cardboard mountain in the living room didn't look so intimidating. Jack and Ryder lay on the floor, analyzing Dylan's lyrics. Kate inhaled the crisp promise of fall through the open window. Seeing Griffith Park again, she thought about all the hikes there with her dad. Maybe she'd find time to get back to the trails. She felt the touch of her past, her present, and her future, swirling around in her bright, happy new home.

Stella joined her at the window. "After you get settled, I can show you around. There's the coolest clothes store over on Melrose, we can walk there. Their prices are unbelievable."

Kate was grateful for the young woman's friendliness and help, but she couldn't quite figure Stella out. Maybe she was simply happy to have neighbors again, and ones her own age. Kate was too tired to give it much thought.

Ryder lifted his head. "Hey, new neighbor woman. Can I trade you a joint for another beer?"

Stella looked at Kate, eyebrows raised as if asking permission.

"Why don't you go get your own beer?" Kate said.

"Hey, is that any way to treat slave labor?" Ryder replied. "Miss Stella, would you explain the meaning of kindness to Katie Heartless?"

Stella smirked. "I have *plenty* of beer," she told Kate. "But I wasn't sure you wanted your moving crew to get blitzed."

Jack, who had been staring at the ceiling, sat up and studied the move-in-progress. "I think we're done for the day, don't you, Babe?"

He looked at Kate, but Ryder answered. "Damned straight we're finished."

"In that case," Stella said, "let me get another round."

"You know what we need now?" Ryder asked.

Jack and Kate answered at the same time. "Pizza!"

"I know the best place," Stella said. "And they deliver—fast."

Sure enough, the food arrived in under half an hour. Kate's purse was near the door, so she picked up the tab and no one protested.

Stella *did* know the best pizza joint in the neighborhood. Or maybe Kate was starving—and stoned. She polished off three slices without a qualm of guilt after all those trips up and down the stairs.

When they finished, Ryder burped and squinted at Stella. "You do know your food, woman. And your beer. Where've you been all my life?"

Stella ignored him as she rose and helped Kate clear away paper plates and napkins. In the kitchen, Kate thanked her again for her help.

"Glad I could do it. I remember my first place, when Lars and I—"

She stopped and clamped a hand over her mouth. "Shit! I swore to never speak his name again."

"Was he that awful?"

Stella shook her head. "Probably not. But at the time I hated him."

"Not now?"

"Now I pretty much feel nothing for him. Hey, listen to me, spilling my life story and I've only known you a couple of hours. And I shouldn't talk that way to a newlywed—listen, not every marriage ends up in the trash like mine. There were... extenuating circumstances. Don't worry, you'll get the sordid details later."

"I'm counting on it."

Ryder lumbered into the kitchen, empty beer bottle in hand.

Kate felt rather than saw Stella tense up. "Looking for more?" Kate asked.

Ryder swayed a little on his feet, but at least he wasn't slurring his words yet. "I thought maybe I'd quit mooching off Stella and go buy some. Where's the closest liquor store?"

Kate shook her head. "You're in no shape to drive."

"Whoa! I'm not—"

"Yeah, you are, Ryder," Kate said. "Don't be a jerk."

"Yeah, Ryder," Stella echoed. "Don't be a jerk. I'll give you one more beer. You can pay me back some other time—sing me a song, or something."

Ryder scowled and tossed the bottle in the trash. "Okay—let's drink at your place. I think these kids want to be alone. Know what I mean?"

Jack crept up behind him and clapped him on the shoulders. "You're not as dumb as you look."

"I bet you're whipped," Stella said and turned to Ryder. "Okay, big fella, but if you're thinking of sobering up at my place, you have exactly one hour before lights out. And my lumpy sofa leaves bruises."

Ryder snickered. "My kind of woman."

"Don't be so sure," Stella said over her shoulder as Ryder followed her out the door.

"She seems nice," Kate said softly when the door closed behind them. "But should we have dumped Ryder on her like that?"

Jack kissed the back of her neck. "He's not so bad."

"True, but he's really hot for her. I hope he doesn't—"

"You worry too much," Jack said. "And I think Stella can take care of herself. Ryder may be in over his head."

"I guess." She kissed Jack, and her world slid back into sync. "Now, will you help me make up the bed so we can give it a try? Unless you're too tired?"

"Never *that* tired," Jack replied with a grin.

Kate started down the hall and squealed as Jack tackled her around the waist. Then she remembered Stella's warning and put her index finger to her lips. "Shhh—the sound carries."

Jack narrowed his eyes. "Well," he growled, "she may as well get used to it."

* * *

An hour later, as Kate started drifting into sex-sated sleep, an appalling thought yanked her awake.

"What's wrong?" Jack asked, his voice muffled and drowsy, as Kate staggered out of bed.

"Forgot to take my pill," she mumbled, groping in alien darkness for her purse.

"Oh, Babe."

Kate heard panic in those two words.

"It's okay," she assured him. "Not too late. Close call, though. With the moving and all, I forgot."

"You always check."

Until he said it, Kate hadn't realized that Jack noticed how often she checked the markings on the plastic disk that held her birth control pills. She looked several times a day, every day—not so much out of fear of pregnancy itself, but of the consequences. If she couldn't work, they would end up at the mercy of Jack's parents, or Jack would have to quit school and get a job. Either outcome was unthinkable.

On her way to the bathroom for water, Kate tried to slow her panicked heartbeat with a few deep breaths. The doctor had cautioned that even one missed pill might mess up her cycle.

She knew the pills' risks and was willing to take them on for the pleasure of unencumbered sex with Jack. The pleasure, however, came with a price tag of constant vigilance, and she'd almost failed herself. And Jack.

"But I didn't," she whispered to her wild-eyed reflection in the mirror. "I remembered in time."

She tried so hard to be careful, to remember important things. *Did I take my pill? Did I put out that last cigarette? Did I unplug the coffeepot?* She looked both ways before crossing streets, never ran red lights, paid her bills on time. Still, she often fought a sense of disaster lurking out of sight, ready to clamp down and crush her. Again.

The world was a dangerous place. How naïve of her to believe falling in love made it safer. In truth, it added to the threat. Now she had more to lose.

Kate swallowed her pill—a pill so small that she had to pay close attention to be sure it went down her throat. She took one more breath and switched off the light. As she fumbled down the unfamiliar hallway toward the bedroom, Kate tried to recapture the pleasured drowsiness she'd fallen into before she remembered the pill. But it was no good; her tranquility had been shattered.

From the other side of the wall came voices: Stella and Ryder.

Clear as a bell, she heard Ryder say, "What are you so afraid of?"

And for a second, Kate thought he was talking to her, and she whispered, "Everything."

Jack had drifted off to sleep, his chest rising and falling in a steady rhythm. As Kate eased under the covers, he stirred and drew her close to him, and for the tiniest of instants, Kate let herself feel safe. She was in bed with Jack. She was married to Jack. And she wasn't going to let random glimpses into an imaginary abyss wreck her joy in those simple facts. Not tonight.

Chapter Fourteen
September 1972

G litter. Through Finelli Gallery's front window, Kate watched the crowd inside, overhead track lights illuminating the scene as if someone had flung handfuls of sparkling confetti all over the place.

And there in the center of the scene, glowing bright, was Jack. A cluster of well-dressed women surrounded him, heads cocked like attentive spaniels as he spoke.

"Are we gonna stand out here breathing exhaust all night?" asked Stella.

Kate pulled out a Marlboro and lit it, inhaled a bracing dose of nicotine, and then released it into the muggy darkness.

Stella's hands went to her hips. "You were in such an all-fired hurry to get here, so what's wrong?"

Kate's whole body throbbed with longing to join the shiny celebration inside the gallery. "I'm late, and I'm dressed all wrong."

"You look fine, and you're only gonna be later, the longer you hang around out here."

"I know, but..."

But what? Damn it, Jack's first important gallery show, and already she'd messed up her part in it. Why hadn't she left work on time? Instead, she'd let a last-minute request from her boss delay her, and then had rushed home to jump in Stella's Mustang and race toward the Valley.

She'd wanted to get to the gallery opening early, not almost an hour late, but traffic had delayed them even more. Now she was sweaty and out of breath, still in her bland brown jersey work dress instead of the midnight blue mini she'd planned to wear that night. Her sensible beige pumps, the traitors, had begun to pinch her toes.

Stella, on the other hand, looked supremely ready to join the people inside. Dressed in black from her open-necked silk shirt to her jeans and high-heeled boots, she radiated confidence. And impatience.

Hard to believe it had finally come together. Ever since Jack got his Master's Degree, he'd been knocking on gallery doors, but aside from a couple of low-key shows in makeshift galleries downtown, he'd been largely ignored. Then Gino Finelli had called and invited him to show with three other local artists. He'd seen Jack's work in one of those low-rent galleries and "fallen in love with the colors and forms."

The Finelli Gallery, sandwiched between a dance studio and a bookstore in the heart of Encino, was known for discovering and nurturing new L.A. artists. It was huge for Jack to be included in a show there.

"Okay, fool, stand out here all night if you want, but I'm going in," Stella said, taking a step toward the door.

Kate ground out her cigarette: the cigarette she didn't even want because she'd been trying to quit. "Wait. I'm coming too."

The hell with it. This is the best I can do. She squared her shoulders and followed Stella.

Cool air drew them in, the air scented with expensive perfume and cheap wine, cigarette smoke hovering overhead. Voices rose and fell, a clamor punctuated by bursts of laughter. Energy circulated, and Kate caught the buzz.

She smoothed back her hair. In the car, while Stella drove, she'd undone her French twist and tried to comb out the kinks and bends. Instead of trendy, she'd probably achieved messy, but it was too late to fix that.

Jack's brown eyes zeroed in on Kate. He winked, and time stopped. Her feet quit hurting, her nerves stopped twitching, her heartbeat slowed to a steady thump. Instead of stale nicotine, she tasted something cool and soothing.

Jack spoke to one of his admirers, who glanced toward Kate and nodded; he left the group and made his way to Kate for a kiss, his lips lingering on hers. "I was getting worried."

"I'm sorry," Kate said. "I had to type up some last-minute contracts for Paul."

He squeezed her hand. "You're here now, that's what matters."

Stella tugged his shirt sleeve. "Congratulations. Where's the bar?"

He pointed toward the back of the gallery, where wine jugs sat on a cloth-draped table. Stella glided away, moving through the crowd like a ribbon of black silk.

Kate looked around. "Your folks aren't here yet?"

Jack shook his head. "Dad has the flu. Mom's playing nurse."

"Oh." Josie's absence, even to care for Henry, disappointed Kate. Jack's mother had gotten all bent out of shape when he didn't go into teaching after getting his Master's Degree. This show was proof he'd made the right choice, and Kate had longed to see Josie's reaction to Jack's paintings, hanging in an important gallery.

Kate wondered if her sister Debbie would show up. Probably not. Deb no doubt had a more interesting offer. She was dating a Ryder clone who probably thought graffiti was high art. Kate had invited her mother, too, but Helen didn't like to drive after dark.

"Want a drink?" Jack asked.

Kate took his hand. "No, first I want to see your paintings."

"Right behind you."

Kate turned. Three of his paintings hung side by side, radiant and beautiful. She could barely suppress a schoolgirl squeal.

"Oh, my God! They look ...wonderful," she said.

And they did. So different from when they sat on an easel at the loft or competed for attention with other artwork in dimly lit storefronts downtown. Here, in the full light at Finelli, they showed up as the masterpieces they were.

Jack's face was flushed, and his dark eyes shimmered. "People really like them, Kate. I think we maybe sold one."

Before she could respond, a skinny man with a pencil mustache fluttered up to them, and Jack introduced Gino Finelli, the gallery owner. He kissed the back of Kate's hand, and she caught a strong dose of English Leather.

"At last I get to meet Kate," he purred. "You're even lovelier than I imagined."

And here came the blush she'd never learned to control. "Thank you," she replied.

Jack put his arm around her and drew her close. "I owe everything to her," he told Gino. "She's stuck by me, and sometimes I don't know why."

More blushing; her cheeks must be neon. However, it was fun being in the spotlight for a minute. *What was I so worried about? I am a part of all this.* The realization brought everything into super-sharp focus: Kate could feel every inch of her skin, the air in her lungs, the pressure of Jack's hand on her waist.

Gino's full lips curved upward. "Your faith is about to be rewarded, dear. This one's going to be famous. And with a woman like you behind him…" He spread his arms, palms up.

Possibilities danced in her mind: Jack, so famous everyone knew his name, famous as a movie star. Signing autographs, buying sports cars, trips to Europe. His paintings in every major museum in the world, collectors begging to see the work, begging to own it and display it.

"I hope so," said Kate.

"I know so." Gino tapped the side of his head. "Jack tells me you helped choose the paintings for the exhibition. Besides beauty, you have a fine eye for art."

Although she was basking in the glow of approval, Kate couldn't think of a clever reply.

Gino saved her by announcing, "And now, we must mingle, yes? Have you met Trudy Zelnik?"

Jack shook his head. "I keep trying, but she's been surrounded all night."

"Come along, then, I'll handle it."

Gino touched Kate's arm. "Trudy Zelnik—major collector, or soon to be. Her husband's a plastic surgeon, very successful. Trudy is dying to spend his money. On art. And she has exquisite taste." He rolled his eyes. "Although she's also a world-class bargain hunter."

"By all means go meet her," she told Jack. "I'll check on Stella."

In truth, she wanted a few moments to absorb her encounter with Gino Finelli.

As Gino led Jack away, he called out to a young man passing by, "Adam—say hello to Jack Morrison's wife." He gestured toward Kate and kept going.

The man Gino had addressed frowned at Kate. He was tall, with dark curly hair almost as long as Jack's, but not as glossy. The woman clinging to his elbow wore a gold blouse and black velvet pants—perfect for a gala like this. She glanced at Kate with cool indifference.

Kate tried a welcoming smile and held out her hand. "Kate Morrison," she said. "You must be Adam Fletcher. Your work is very striking."

She'd seen Fletcher's paintings in one of those low-rent galleries. A recently transplanted New York artist with a growing West Coast following, Fletcher painted large, colorful, hard-edged shapes, so different from Jack's careful gradations of forms and hues. Kate liked his work well enough, but there was something impersonal and cold about it.

Fletcher's handshake, lukewarm and damp, ended quickly as he refocused on the crowd around them. He didn't introduce the woman clinging to his arm, so Kate turned to her.

"I'm Kate," she said.

The woman brushed a lock of silver-blond hair off her face. Her immense, exquisitely made-up gray eyes blinked vacantly. "Morel," she said.

"Are you a painter too?" Kate asked.

She caught Fletcher's smirk. An uncomfortable silence followed until the woman spoke. "I work at Pierra."

Kate couldn't figure out how to respond until Morel lifted her chin and added, "The *boutique*."

"Oh—right." Pretending to know of it. "That must be interesting."

Morel didn't acknowledge the remark. She stroked Fletcher's arm. "Adam's work is very tactile, don't you think?" she said.

"Very," Kate agreed, without a clue as to what Morel meant.

Kate scanned the gallery and saw Jack and Finelli talking to a pudgy woman who wore oversized eyeglasses and a calf-length fringed buckskin shift. She'd taken the Native American look all the way, Kate thought, down to her purse: a soft leather pouch with feathers stitched to the bottom. The woman gnawed on her lower lip as she extended her hand to Jack.

"Is that Trudy Zelnik?" Kate asked, unable to mask the surprise in her voice.

That got Fletcher's attention. He followed her gaze and nodded. "An important woman to know." He spoke slowly, as if imparting essential information to a dimwitted child. "And Morrison's monopolizing her. Can't have that."

He turned to Morel. "Get me a drink."

Morel waved with elegant nonchalance as Fletcher hurried off to intrude on Jack's conversation with Trudy Zelnik.

So much for mingling, Kate thought as she followed Morel to the bar. Where had Stella gone? Morel got some wine, turned her back on Kate, and drifted toward Fletcher.

Kate fortified herself with glass of inexpensive but decent Chablis and went looking for her friend. She found her studying Jack's paintings.

"They look right at home here," Stella declared.

Kate murmured in agreement. The pieces were three of her favorites. The first one, if she used her imagination, was a landscape: moonrise on the desert, Kate thought of it. The shapes implied rather than depicted rocks and cactus and lizards, and the tawny background enhanced the effect. She'd suggested the title: "Homescape."

The middle painting, "Garden," was more specific: a conflagration of disarrayed flower petals, pinks and yellows and whites tumbling into one another without apparent order—until you took a few steps back. Then the shapes formed sunflowers, camellias, and chrysanthemums—although again it took a leap of imagination to see the patterns.

The last one, untitled, portrayed a sort of funeral service, with a tiny bird covered in white fabric except for beak and feet, resting on a twig-framed platform; ghost shapes congealed around the body, and a pale disc beamed wavering light on the scene like a benediction.

All three paintings had an inner glow that reminded her of Rembrandt's work. Three hundred years earlier, Rembrandt had captured light on canvas like no other painter she'd seen. Her father adored his work; the first time he took Kate to see a Rembrandt exhibit, his eyes had filled with tears when he tried to explain the technique to her. The memory made Kate smile.

Stella raised her wineglass. "Congratulations. You did it. And somebody turned on your lights, didn't they?"

Did it show that much? The memory of Gino Finelli's exuberant praise had faded with Adam Fletcher's chilly treatment, but excitement still buzzed in Kate's brain.

"Boo!"

Hands gripped her shoulders, and Kate almost spilled her wine. She pulled away and scowled at Ryder. Like Jack, he'd abandoned the tie-dyed, psychedelic look for solid colors and flannel plaids, and he seemed built for the bell-bottom jeans and thick-soled platform boots he had on that evening. But he hadn't lost that pouty, pissed-off demeanor, even with the minor fame he'd achieved.

"The Devil Is a Personal Friend" had been a significant hit—in fact, had gone gold—in 1971, and another couple of successes followed. The Ryders made an album that also did well, but now the group was falling apart. Kate didn't know why, but she had her suspicions. Drugs and money topped the list. Most of Ryder's income went right up his nose.

Judging by the size of his pupils, Ryder hadn't come sober to the opening. Not that Kate expected him to. She couldn't remember the last time she'd seen him when he wasn't high. Jack liked to get high, too—but he controlled the urge and took care of business first. Ryder, however, didn't have an "off" switch when it came to drugs, and Kate worried he'd end up singing for tips at nightclubs in North Hollywood, or working bar mitzvahs and weddings, muttering about his glory days with no clue that he'd trashed his own future.

"Where's Superstar?" Ryder asked.

"Schmoozing with the rich people," Kate replied.

"And hello to you, too," said Stella.

Ryder leered at her. "Vampire convention in town?"

Despite the sarcasm, Kate saw a flicker of longing in Ryder's blue eyes when he looked at Stella. He'd made several tries at dating her, and she'd rebuffed every one. "I don't date musicians," she'd said by way of explanation, and Ryder finally gave up, or pretended to.

Stella smirked back at him and didn't take the bait.

"Where'd you get the hooch?" he asked.

"Come on, Ryder, grow up. At least check out Jack's paintings first," Kate said.

Ryder planted his boots several inches apart and studied Jack's exhibit, stroking his chin. With Ryder, you never knew if he'd show up with a month's worth of beard or bare-cheeked. Tonight, he was clean-shaven.

"Far out," he muttered, his eyes moving from one canvas to another. "Far fucking out." He pointed at "Homescape."

"The lizards are really moving in there," he muttered. "I wonder if they hear us?"

Stella drained her wineglass. "You are so full of shit, Ryder."

"That's what they all say," Ryder replied. He laughed like a demon, and Kate wanted to sink into the floor.

Jack emerged from the crowd and slapped Ryder's back. "Heard you on the radio today, man. Sounded good."

Ryder didn't smile. He waved his hand toward Jack's paintings. "Stuff looks bitchin', man. Congrats."

"Thanks. Appreciate your coming."

Ryder was about to reply when his mouth fell open. "Sweet Jesus —what the fuck?"

He was looking at Trudy Zelnik. Kate suppressed a giggle while Jack explained Trudy's importance.

Ryder rolled his eyes in disbelief. "I need a smoke. Anybody want to join me outside?"

Kate started to point out he could smoke in the gallery and then realized he wasn't talking Marlboros.

Jack and Kate declined, but Stella seemed eager for a respite.

"Go ahead," Kate told her. Then she frowned at Ryder. "But if she's not back in twenty minutes, I'm coming after her."

Jack put his arm around Kate's waist. "You look nice, Babe." He kissed her forehead. "The prettiest woman here. And the smartest."

Pleasure eclipsed the fatigue, the sore feet. "You say that to all the girls."

"Only the sexy ones. I want to get you alone. Soon."

"I can hardly wait. Meanwhile: has Pocahontas made any offers?"

Jack glanced over his shoulder as if worried Trudy Zelnik would overhear. "She asked me, on the QT, if I had any 'less elaborate' work she could see."

Kate scowled. "What the hell does 'less elaborate' mean? Cheaper?"

"Probably. I told her to come by the studio next week and look around."

Kate shuddered, and Jack noticed.

"Trudy's a little odd," he said, "but she has great instincts. She's scored some good art—bought one of Fletcher's paintings and told him she has a sixth sense for who's going to be big."

Kate tugged at his shirt front. "Okay, Mr. Big Painter—let's hope her taste in art is better than her taste in clothes."

Jack grinned. "I better go make some more new friends. Come with?"

Kate shook her head. "No, you go mingle. I'll check out the rest of the paintings—not that any of 'em are half as good as yours."

He kissed her again and slid back into the crowd.

Kate started a circuit of the gallery to see the rest of the exhibit. Most of it came across as ordinary and lifeless to her. The evening's events, the proximity to fame, had made her dizzy.

She pondered a flat white canvas on which the artist had stenciled words like "fox" and "banana" and inside the stenciled letters had painted images of the words the letters formed. Tiny red foxes marched down the "f" and around the "o", then crossed one another in the "x." Vaguely amusing, she thought. But not very interesting.

"Pretty pretentious, don't you think?"

Had someone read her mind? Kate turned to see Trudy Zelnik beside her, squinting at the painting.

"Jasper Johns rip-off," Trudy muttered. She faced Kate. "We've not been introduced, but Gino tells me that you're Jack Morrison's wife. Kate, is it?"

"It is. And I already know who *you* are, Mrs. Zelnik."

"Trudy. Please."

"Trudy."

Trudy batted pale lashes behind her thick eyeglasses. "Your husband is very talented."

"Thank you," Kate said.

"I suppose you get tired of people telling you that."

Her voice grated like fingernails on a chalkboard.

"Not at all. It's not about me anyway. It's all Jack."

"Now we both know that's not true. Every artist needs a muse. And you clearly are *his*."

Good grief: more flattery. Kate felt her face grow warm again.

"We all have our purposes," Kate replied.

"Exactly! I have no artistic abilities myself, but I am awed by people who do, and I try to support talent. I envy you, Kate. Being so close to an artist like Jack. I imagine some of the magic has rubbed off on *you*. Or perhaps you brought the magic?" Her eyes had a moist, greedy sheen that made Kate queasy.

"With a woman like you to inspire him," continued Trudy, "he's definitely going places."

Still trying to figure out what this oddly dressed woman wanted from her, Kate tried to shift the conversation.

"You're very nice to say that—and it means a lot, coming from you."

Trudy scrunched up her face in a poor imitation of self-deprecation. "Oh, my dear, I'm strictly minor league. I really don't know much about art, but I know what I like. And I do like Jack Morrison's paintings."

Kate made herself smile. "That's something we have in common."

Trudy studied her. *Assessed* her. "And you: you work for a living, don't you? Pay the bills so Jack can paint without worrying where his next tube of Grumbacher is coming from?"

This was getting personal, but Kate didn't want to offend a potential patron, so she replied, "That's right. I do."

"Where? What do you do?" Trudy's hungry eyes widened even more.

Kate told her. The woman seemed genuinely interested, which surprised Kate as much as the questions.

"That is wonderful! I envy women who have a career. And you'll be a huge success. I have a sense of these things, Kate. It is, sadly, my only talent, but there you have it."

"I hope you're right."

Trudy Zelnik grasped Kate's forearm, and a weird, jittery current passed between them. Maybe the woman wasn't as kooky as she appeared. Maybe there was something behind the odd clothes and overstated mannerisms.

"I am seldom wrong, Kate," Trudy said. "And I hope that you and I can become friends. We have so much in common."

Yeah, right. So much in common.

"Not in terms of material things," Trudy continued, pointing to her chest. "But here—in the heart. We share the same instincts."

Kate overcame a powerful urge to pull away from Trudy's sticky, magnetic grip. "You're very kind to say that."

Trudy looked over Kate's shoulder as a cloud of English Leather enveloped them.

"See," crowed Gino Finelli. "I told you they'd hit it off. Two of the most important women in the art world, here in my humble gallery."

Trudy finally released Kate's arm.

Jack stood next to Gino, pleasure dancing in his eyes. Kate felt almost embarrassed that he'd witnessed the scene with Trudy, but if it made him happy, if it helped him succeed, she'd overcome her distaste for the strange woman who apparently held at least one key to his future. Maybe Trudy would buy an "elaborate" painting after all.

If only, Kate thought, she knew for sure how things would turn out. Jack's career could go either way. In one scenario, Trudy Zelnik helped make him a star of the art world. In another, he got tired of trying to interest collectors in his work and ended up in a drab little classroom in the Valley, teaching drawing to gum-snapping teenagers and hating every minute of it.

And in the worst case, he gave up trying to earn a living at all, succumbed to booze and drugs, and the two of them became dependent on Kate's meager paycheck, one step away from camping out on a bench in MacArthur Park, sleeping on last week's newspapers.

Trudy beamed at Jack. "I was telling Kate how much I admire your work. You have genius in you, Jack Morrison."

Jack clasped Trudy's hand and kissed the back of it in a flawless Gino Finelli imitation as Gino himself asked her opinion of the exhibit. The woman's persona shifted from fan to critic as she assessed the art on display, dismissing several paintings as "pedestrian" and "boring" while praising the "formidable talent" of Adam Fletcher and, of course, Jack Morrison. As she spoke, Gino and Jack moved in closer, until the three of them formed a circle—one that excluded Kate.

Suddenly invisible, Kate turned away. She needed fresh air, a moment to regroup. Surely this place had a back door. There: beyond the bar, in the corner. Fighting shaky, sweaty panic, Kate pushed through the crowd; hot wine-heavy breath and discordant voices washed over her. She stepped out into the humid night and inhaled, catching a faint odor of garbage.

At least the alley was quiet. Its dark silence soothed her pounding heart and eased the claustrophobic tightness of her skin.

What had just happened, and why had she freaked out? Kate pulled a Marlboro from her purse and lit it, exhaling into the night.

Was this how the game worked? Lavish attention one minute, total indifference the next? Because she wasn't an artist—was that it? She didn't count. Oh, but she'd been so close to the center, she'd started to believe she belonged there.

Wait. She *did* belong there. She'd helped Jack work his way past other struggling artists. She'd encouraged him, paid the bills, given advice that apparently had value, based on the responses he was getting that night.

"With a woman like you behind him ..."

Behind, hell. She deserved to be *beside* him, to share the recognition. He'd promised her that. *"Stick with me, and I'll help write* your *name on the sky."*

The art world held more pretense than she'd expected. So be it. This was Jack's world, but she could fit in. She *would* fit in, even if her feet ached and her face hurt from smiling. Even if her skin crawled from being touched by people like Trudy.

Her dad had taught her a few tricks about getting along with people, even when you didn't like them. Time to drag those old lessons out of her memory and put them to work. How hard could it be?

This was what Jack wanted, and she wanted it for him, almost as badly as he craved it himself. She wanted it for both of them.

Kate took one last drag on her cigarette and ground it out underfoot. Then she fluffed her hair, touched up her lipstick and returned to the clamor of the gallery, smiling broadly at strangers she squeezed past on her way to find Jack.

She spotted him standing a little apart from the horde, smoking and holding an animated conversation with Adam Fletcher, who looked utterly bored but nodded at whatever point Jack was making. Fletcher's companion Morel stood behind him, a silent hanger-on.

I'm not like that, Kate promised herself. *No standing around, hoping they notice me. I'm important. I belong. I have a part in all this.*

Jack saw her coming, and his face lit up like Christmas. He turned away from Fletcher mid-sentence and held his arms wide to envelop Kate.

"Where'd you disappear to?" he asked.

"I needed some fresh air."

"Yeah, it gets intense, doesn't it?"

"Sure does," Kate replied. "You having fun?"

"Kinda. It's exhausting, though."

"You'd better get used to it," she said. "You're a big hit tonight."

He grimaced. "I guess." He stroked her cheek. "You made it happen, Babe. I owe you."

"We made it happen, Jack. We're in this together."

He leaned close and whispered, "No one else I'd rather be with."

That's what Kate had yearned to hear. She mattered to Jack. To hell with everyone else.

Chapter Fifteen
December 1972

The transmission on Jack's Volvo gave out after 150,000 miles, so for over a week he hitched rides from anyone with wheels—mostly Adam Fletcher, who had inexplicably befriended Jack at the Finelli show. Fletcher's motives baffled Kate, but Jack was happy to pal around with him and talk about art. More important from Kate's perspective, Fletcher provided Jack with access to art dealers and collectors who had once been unavailable.

When the auto mechanic claimed he needed even more time, Jack asked Kate to pick him up at the loft after work on Friday. They always went out to dinner on Friday night, no matter what. Kate looked forward all day to this reward for another week's hard work. They'd probably go to Felipe's, their favorite hole-in-the-wall Mexican restaurant in Atwater, for killer margaritas and the best tacos in L.A. Then home for some tequila-fueled lovemaking.

The work week had been grueling. Kate's "job" was morphing into a career, working directly for Paul Lange as his Executive Assistant. Her last salary increase had enabled her to take over Jack's share of the loft rent, which gave her immense satisfaction; it made a dent in her mother-in-law's leverage. Despite Jack's growing reputation as an artist, Josie had never let go of her disappointment that he hadn't pursued teaching. She kept threatening to close the money pipeline, but now it didn't matter so much.

When she reached the loft that night, Kate had to park several car lengths away. She shivered and pulled up her coat collar. Did she smell a hint of evergreen? Another two weeks to the shortest day of the year, and she'd barely started Christmas shopping.

Inside the loft, Kate cranked the deadbolt behind her and started up the stairs. Rock music throbbed overhead: the Ryders, but not live. Recorded. Heavy drumbeats underscored Ryder's baritone wail.

She came to a dead stop at the top of the stairs. Under a cloud of smoke, four people sat at the kitchen table, faces shadowed by the overhead light. The smell of marijuana hung heavy in the air. Kate recognized Jack, and Ryder, and then Adam Fletcher. The other unexpected visitor was Morel, Fletcher's quiet shadow.

What the hell?

Jack rose in one fluid, graceful movement and came toward her. "Hey, Babe."

God, the music was loud, its beat vibrating through the floorboards. And the suffocating smoke smell! Irritation flashed through Kate. What happened to their Friday date night?

"Hey," Kate said. "What's happening? I thought we were—"

The look on Jack's face said it all.

"Uh, change of plans," he began, and as Kate got closer she saw his reddened, unfocused eyes. *Oh, shit, he's not going anywhere right now. Damn it, Jack, couldn't you at least have waited for me?*

"We're celebrating," Jack continued. "Trudy came through."

"Huh?"

"Durant," Jack said, his words fuzzed. "From the museum. She's bringing him here."

"*Stephen* Durant? The Curator? He's coming here tonight?"

He shook his head and laughed. "Next year."

"Oh. Great. I can see why you'd want to get blitzed then."

Jack put his arms around her, but the stale smoke smell repulsed her, and Kate pulled away.

"Don't be like that." He probably meant to whisper, but it came out in a loud hiss.

She hated this, being yanked from her work environment, where people cared what she thought. Kate sighed and tried to make the mental shift into a setting where she was simply an accessory.

She unclenched her jaw. "Like what?"

"Like all uptight. This is happy time. Don't spoil it."

"Yeah, Kate," Ryder echoed, exhaling a puff of smoke, "don't spoil it. Your man's big day."

Kate felt other eyes on her, and her cheeks grew hot. She wanted to turn and run. That was stupid, of course. The switch in plans was part of the deal—part of being Jack's wife. *You asked for it; don't whine when you get it.*

Kate took a deep breath and found a smile for Jack and his friends. She tried to forget how she must look to the others in their laid-back, colorful clothes. Her navy business suit and sensible shoes didn't have any authority here.

She forced animation into her voice. "Tell me the whole story. Sounds exciting."

Jack's face relaxed. He led her over to the table and pulled out a chair, offered her the half-smoked joint that had gone out in the ashtray. Kate took it and squinted against the lighter's flame, inhaled deeply and held the smoke. She never coughed anymore, and in fact, smoking pot had become second nature. She smoked a joint after work the way some people had a martini.

"There," Jack crooned as Kate leaned back and let the weed take effect. "All better now, huh?"

She nodded and handed the number to Ryder, who puckered his lips at her. Asshole. Adam Fletcher was drumming his fingers on the tabletop in time to the beat, ignoring her. Morel had her eyes fastened on Fletcher.

"Hi again," Kate said to the woman, who gave her a blank stare.

"We met at the Finelli show," Kate reminded her, but Morel's expression didn't change. She had the kind of peaches and cream skin that most women would kill for, and her sparkly red tunic and silky black pants looked too fancy for the dusty old loft. She herself looked too fancy for the loft, and even for Fletcher. What kind of hold did he have on her? Oh, right: he was an artist. For some women, that was all it took. *Hell, look at me,* Kate thought. *I'm no different.*

Jack rubbed the back of her hand. "Want anything to drink?"

Without waiting for an answer, he pulled a beer from the fridge. Kate wrinkled her nose; she'd never learned to like beer. Better than nothing, though, and what everyone else was drinking, so she let him pop it open for her.

"Now tell me that happened," she said.

"It was incredible!" Jack pointed at Fletcher. "He did it. Called her bluff, completely."

Kate looked at Fletcher, trying to follow the sketchy thread of conversation. "How? When? Start at the beginning!"

Jack swigged his beer, then lit a Marlboro. "Adam took me to this show out in Venice, some guy doing these hard-edge acrylic pieces that everyone says are the next new thing, and Trudy's there too. She goes on and on about how she loves my work and wishes more people could see it, because this new guy's stuff is just crap, honestly just crap."

"It was," Fletcher agreed.

"So Adam starts sweet-talking Trudy," Jack continued with a grin. "Tells her he knows she's got pull at the museum."

"Last week I read in the paper," Fletcher said, giving Kate a rare moment of attention, "that she just donated a shitload of money to LACMA."

LACMA: The Los Angeles County Museum of Art, the top of the heap. Finelli had been right: Trudy Zelnik did like to support the arts.

"That would give her some clout," Kate said.

"Damn straight," Fletched replied with a cackle.

"So," Jack continued, "she just grins at us and says, 'Well, I guess Stephen and I have become close friends.' And Adam gets in her face then and says, 'Hell, Trudy, then bring him to see some *real* art. Bring him to see *our* stuff.' And next thing we know, she's using the gallery's phone and talking to Durant."

Fletcher grinned. "Yeah, it was a heavy scene, man."

"Durant's gonna come see our work—both of us." He punched Fletcher's bicep lightly. "I owe you, man. Big time."

Fletcher smirked. "Remember me when you're some hot-shit famous artist."

Fletcher's remark sounded wrong to Kate, but the marijuana was blurring her thoughts, and she let it go as Jack's excitement flooded over her.

"That's great," she said. "He'll see your work, he'll fall in love with it and make you famous. Right?"

Ryder glared at her. "Don't be sarcastic."

"I'm not! I think it's fabulous! What's with you, anyway, Ryder? You're awfully pissy tonight."

"You mean this isn't his normal mood?" Morel asked—the first time she'd spoken.

"Kate brings out the best in me," Ryder told her.

Jack pointed a finger at Ryder. "Now who's being sarcastic?"

"So," Fletcher said, looking from Ryder to Jack. "Where's this blow you were talking about?"

Aha, there it was—the lure: Ryder's prime white powder. Jack had been using it more and more, and she understood the attraction. She liked coke better than pot, actually—the surge of energy, the feeling that nothing could hurt her. But damn, it was expensive, and she wasn't sure how Jack managed to get as much as he did. The money didn't come from their shared checking account, that was for sure. Maybe he traded favors with somebody. She wanted to ask and was afraid of the answer.

Kate caught the glance that passed between Jack and Ryder. They were up to something, and her patience frayed. "I'm not up for this tonight," she said to Jack. "You guys do what you want. I'm too hungry—and too tired."

Ryder's face glowed like a maniac's. "We can fix that, Katie Girl. We can fix it good."

Kate frowned at Jack. Why was he letting this go on? His cheeks were ruddy, and his eyes glittered. How much dope had he smoked?

"We'll make a food run," Jack said. "Pick up some moo shoo at Man Fook Lo, okay?"

Kate's mouth watered.

"Far fucking out," Ryder muttered. "Let's do it."

But first he broke out his coke vial and tapped two lines onto a playing card: the Jack of Diamonds, Kate noticed. Weirdly appropriate. He snorted the coke through a cut-off drinking straw and passed the works around. When her turn came, Kate hesitated and then decided what the hell. It would stave off the hunger pangs.

Fletcher sat back and wiped his nose. "Man, that is some heavy shit all right."

When Jack and Ryder stood, he followed their lead like an eager puppy.

Jack kissed the top of Kate's head. "We'll be back in a flash."

Morel started to rise, but Fletcher put his hand on her shoulder. "You stay." She sank back into her chair.

After the guys left, Kate tried to engage Morel in conversation. She hadn't partaken of the coke, and somehow that made Kate feel superior.

"So, how long have you and Adam been together?"

Morel didn't reply at first. She lit a Newport, exhaled and stared at the ceiling. "A few months, I guess," she said finally.

The music stopped. Morel tapped out her half-smoked cigarette, went to the turntable, and started the record over again.

"I really dig Ryder." She stood by the stereo, swaying in time to the beat.

Acts like she owns the place, Kate thought, and the irony almost made her laugh. She paid the rent, but around Jack's friends she became a visitor. She eased off her pumps, rubbed her aching feet and thought about going home to a hot bath and her comfortable bed. But Jack would get all pissed off if she did, and Kate really wanted to be with him. But she didn't want to share him, not on *their* Friday night. Her mouth was so dry; she swallowed some beer, but its sour taste didn't help.

Morel glided toward Jack's workshop, moving in slow, rhythmic steps. She paused in front of the paintings Jack had hung on the big white wall.

"You paint?" Morel asked, her voice barely audible above the music.

"Me? No. Those are Jack's." Kate had to raise her voice to be heard, but she didn't want to get up and move closer. "I work for a living." Her words came out more self-righteous than she intended, but Morel nodded like she understood.

Kate tried again. "You work at a boutique? Pierra?" The name rose out of nowhere. God, her tongue felt thick. She sipped more beer, which only made it worse.

Morel shrugged. "And I make clothes sometimes."

Ah. That explained the elegant outfit that looked like it had been made for her.

Morel sauntered around the loft, inspecting the paintings. She possessed a casual independence, so different from the quiet deference on display when Fletcher was around. She peered past the curtain to the space where Jack still kept a bed for those times when he worked through the night.

"You live here?" Morel asked without a trace of curiosity.

"Not anymore. We live over on Kingsley. By L.A. City College."

Morel shrugged again, an elegant rise and fall of her shoulders that conveyed utter lack of interest. She lifted her thick blond hair off her neck and twisted it into a knot, then let it fall again. Her hair shone like sunlight on water.

Ryder's recorded voice reverberated through the loft, filling up the silence between Kate and Morel.

The minutes ticked away, and with each one Kate felt more and more dispossessed and acutely aware of the jarring contrast between her workday world, where she was known and acknowledged, and Jack's world, where no one wanted to know her, not even this odd visitor, another non-artist.

* * *

When Kate heard the downstairs door scrape open, followed by a chorus of gleeful male voices, she got up and went in search of plates and forks.

They ate like hungry animals, and Kate tried to forget her discomfort and enjoy the feast of moo shoo pork, orange chicken and shrimp fried rice. It was probably better than the tacos at Felipe's, but resentment still burned in her gut; she couldn't let go of her irritation with Jack, for getting her into something she didn't want.

They smoked another joint and did more coke after eating, and Kate let the rush take her away. Jack flashed her a smile that eased the bad feelings. Screw Adam Fletcher and his pretentious arrogance. Screw Ice Queen Morel with her pretty hair and fancy clothes. Screw Ryder and his surly innuendos. She was as good, as important as any of them. And she was with Jack, right where she belonged.

Kate gave up on beer to quench her thirst and took a chance on L.A. tap water. It tasted of metal but did the job.

Fletcher helped himself to Jack's Marlboros and watched his exhaled smoke drift upward. "This place is cool, man. Maybe I should try and find a space around here."

Kate surprised herself by asking, "Where d'you live now?"

He chewed his thumbnail like he hadn't heard her, and Kate wished she'd kept quiet. When would she learn not to even try with people like Fletcher?

"Venice," he said, although he still didn't bother to look at her. "Venice is heavy. If this place was in Venice, you couldn't buy a ticket to get in."

Kate couldn't think of a comeback to that one so she let it go. Morel stretched, yawned, and rubbed her back. "But you have better furniture," she said. "My spine aches."

When Fletcher paid no attention to her, Ryder got behind her and started massaging her shoulders. Morel leaned into him like a cat. Fletcher didn't react.

He doesn't even care if guys come on to her, Kate thought. *What is with these people?*

"So," Jack said to Fletcher, "Trudy, dude—you think she can really deliver Durant?"

Fletcher snorted. "For sure, man. She's connected. It'll be heavy."

Jack looked past him to the paintings on the white wall. "I should do some new stuff. Gotta get to work."

Fletcher grinned. "There's time, man. Chill out a little. Enjoy the moment. Nobody says you gotta work all the time."

"Yeah, but we're supposed to—"

"We're *artists*, man. No dumb-assed rules control us, you dig? Rules make zombies out of us."

Jack's head bobbed up and down. "Right on, man. We're different." His eyes widened. "At the core, we're better."

Oh, for God's sake, thought Kate. She hated to see Jack buy into Fletcher's smug superiority.

"There you go," said Fletcher. "Remember it. We're fucking artists, man. That's a heavy thing to take on. Did we choose it? I don't know about you, but I sure as hell didn't wake up one morning when I was a baby and say, "Hot damn, I think I'll be an artist when I grow up.""

With bored nonchalance, Ryder picked up his smokes. "Later," he said as he ambled toward his space at the back of the loft. Morel watched him go.

Kate made another try at joining the conversation. She asked Jack, "When *did* you know you wanted to paint?"

"I always liked to draw stuff," Jack replied. "Ever since I was a kid. It kind of grew from there."

"Yeah," Fletcher said, "everybody does that, man. Everybody has some little talent that pokes out when they're kids."

"I didn't," said Kate.

Fletcher kept his face turned to Jack. "And when'd you figure out you had to take it to the limit? Make it more than scratches on paper? Make people want to look at it?"

Jack shook his head. "No clue."

"Exactly! We got swept up in it without wanting to. It *takes* us. And here we are, the two of us, sitting around the table on a winter night figuring out how to get our paintings seen."

The two of us? Kate tuned out the rest of Fletcher's babble. Morel didn't react to the slight, but a hot tide of anger rose up in Kate, from her aching feet to her tired brain. *Two of us my ass. Screw you!*

She stood in a quick, jerky move. "I'm going home," she said.

Jack grabbed her hand. "No, Babe, please. Stay. I have a surprise for you."

She tried to break free, but it was a feeble gesture. She wanted him to want her to stay.

"What kind of surprise?"

Jack tugged gently on her hand, so she sat and watched, curious, as he went to the cupboard and took a small glassine envelope from the top shelf.

He turned toward her and held out his hand, grinning. She saw some little translucent squares inside the envelope.

"What's that?"

"Windowpane."

Of all the things she expected, this came in dead last.

"Acid? Are you out of your mind?"

He laughed. "Not yet—but we're going to be. Come on, Babe. Time to give it a try."

She knew Jack had taken LSD once or twice. You couldn't hang around Ryder without sampling his cornucopia of recreational drugs, and Jack claimed the acid bumped up his creativity. But Kate had also heard terrifying stories of bad trips, people seeing monsters and leaping from rooftops to stop the visions. She'd read of acid flashbacks coming on days, even weeks later, flooding a person's mind with hallucinations while they were driving or trying to earn a living. Not for her, not worth the risk.

"No thanks. I still need my brain," she told Jack.

The music stopped again, and in the silence Kate's nervous laugh echoed through the dark recesses of the loft. Jack, however, looked utterly serious. He really wanted her to drop acid with him, she realized. Now.

Is this some kind of initiation? Perhaps it was. If he really did think of her as apart from his world, maybe this would prove how much she belonged. Maybe it would finally make Jack's friends *see* her and *hear* her.

"Let's do it," she said, firing up another Marlboro for courage.

Chapter Sixteen

K ate let the Windowpane dissolve on her tongue, then sat back and waited. Nothing happened. Jack, Fletcher and Morel each took a tab, and soon Ryder sauntered back in.

"About time, dude," he said when Jack handed him the glassine envelope.

Kate felt nothing except the residue of high-wire buzz from the last line of coke, blurred slightly by the pot she'd smoked.

Good God, if the people at work saw me now. Their resident druggie. What's next—heroin?

Jack raised his right arm in a slow, lazy arc and tugged the chain that turned off the overhead light, putting them all in darkness.

A voice came from the shadows: Fletcher's. "Far out, man. This is some heavy shit."

Jack took Kate's hand and kissed it. "You doing okay, Babe?"

Kate shrugged. "I don't feel anything."

Ryder chuckled nearby. "You will. First time, it takes longer."

Morel hummed and Kate smelled her perfume—a trace of paradise. She wanted to ask the brand but couldn't form words.

And then, Kate realized, she could *see* Morel, leaning against Fletcher, fanning her silver-gold hair like a waterfall. She could see

Ryder, even before he struck a match to the tip of the joint in his hand, the whites of his eyes glowing in the dimness. And she could see Jack; she could make out every hair in his beard; she wanted to run her fingers through it, so she did. Jack smiled and put his arm around her.

"Still don't feel anything?" he whispered.

Kate shook her head. "I can see you," she said.

"And I can see you. I can always see you, Babe. Even when you're not here. I can find you, anywhere in the universe. Always."

Warmth flooded her; she could see love radiating from Jack, golden wavy tendrils caressing her, drawing her closer to him, closer than she'd ever been. Like they were inside each other's skin.

From somewhere in the night a siren screamed so loud her ears hurt, but she didn't cover them to blot out the sound, because she heard an answering call: some stray Skid Row dog, howling an answer. Kate closed her eyes and could *see* the howl, soaring into the black shimmering sky, swirling red and gold and purple and orange.

Ryder stood and stretched. "I'm gonna go on the roof and check out the stars," he said. "Anybody wanna come?"

Morel rose without speaking and followed him. Fletcher didn't protest. Kate saw a soft, wavy mist trailing after them.

How long since they'd dropped the acid? Five minutes? Five hours? Kate couldn't tell. Time lurched forward, froze, and turned back on itself. As she looked at Jack, a sparkling rainbow unfurled around his head. She reached out, and her hands went through the color bands and disappeared. She yanked her hand back and wiggled her fingers.

"Hey," Jack said softly, "tell me what you see."

"Colors. The most incredible colors," Kate began.

From far away, Fletcher spoke. "Man, where did you get this shit? It's amazing."

Oh, he knows a word besides 'heavy' Kate thought. Fletcher's outline retracted and then expanded; his face morphed into a dog shape and then back to a man. *Werewolf? Merewolf? Mere man.* The words tumbled around and rearranged themselves.

Jack tapped her skull gently. "What's happening in there, Babe? Talk to me."

"Talking is ...talking is weird," Kate said. "My tongue feels furry. I feel furry."

That got them both laughing. Overhead they heard footsteps on the roof: who was stomping around up there? Oh, right: Ryder and Morel. Fletcher—where was he? Kate looked around: there. Silent for once.

"We need some sound," Jack said.

"Not the Ryders," Kate told him, as Jack rose slowly. His body seemed to flow upward, like liquid; he vanished into the shadows. A moment later, Janis Joplin's scratchy-sweet voice rang out, telling everyone to try a little bit harder.

Then came another noise, one that didn't belong. Through the front window, bands of light flashed. At first, Kate thought it was another displaced rainbow.

Then words, amplified almost beyond recognition, drowned out Janis' voice.

"You—on the roof!"

"What the hell?" Jack muttered. He turned off the stereo and opened the window.

Kate saw him stiffen as a voice proclaimed, "You at the window—hands where we can see them."

Jack leaned forward, arms extending through the opening.

"Cops!" Fletcher hissed.

Kate heard Ryder and Morel walking around on the roof again. Why had they attracted the attention of the police? Her thoughts unraveled in a crazy tangle.

"I work here," Jack yelled down. "What's the problem?"

"Don't move—keep your hands where we can see them. Who else is there? On the roof?"

"My friends," Jack replied, still bent forward at an awkward angle to keep his hands visible. "It's okay—really."

"We're coming in," the cops responded.

"Don't break down the door," Jack shouted. "I'll unlock it for you."

Reality sliced through Kate's confusion. When the cops came upstairs and found all the shit lying around, they'd haul her and Jack and the others off to jail for drug possession, faster than you could say "Timothy Leary."

"Stay where you are!" the policeman ordered. "Don't move."

"My wife's here," Jack called out. "She'll come down and let you in. Just a minute. Please!"

Fear wailed in her head, and for a minute Kate felt like she was going to puke. Then an unexpected calm took over. *Don't panic. Think!*

She glared at Fletcher. "Go open the door."

"Me? No way! Jack said you'd do it."

"Go! Make a lot of noise going down the stairs, and move slow."

Fletcher didn't budge.

"Now!" she hissed, finally breaking through his trance.

While Fletcher clumped down the stairs, Kate groped in the dark to sweep the table clear of weed, Ryder's coke vial and the glassine envelope. She gathered up a roach clip, the soda straw, and two half-smoked joints. Where to hide them? She scanned the kitchen area and without further thought opened the refrigerator and stuffed everything in the vegetable crisper as she heard voices invade the stairwell, growing louder by the second.

Kate shoved some wilted lettuce over the top of the stash, barely masking it, with no time to think or to find a better hiding place. She closed the fridge door quietly, took a deep breath and moved as far away from it as possible.

A flashlight beam pierced her vision, and she raised her hands instinctively, unable to see much of anything in the glare. Something metal glinted below the flashlight. A gun?

"You got a light in here?" asked a voice behind the flashlight. Kate pointed to the pull chain.

"Turn it on," the cop said, and she did, blinking in the sudden brightness.

The gun barrel looked huge in the cop's hand, a tunnel of death. Kate's tongue stuck to the roof of her mouth when she tried to speak.

The lead cop appeared younger than she was, and nervous. One of the other officers had herded Jack in from the window, and another stood guard over Fletcher, who was sweating despite the chill coming in the open window.

"Who else is here?" the lead cop demanded. He moved closer, and Kate saw his name on a metal rectangle pinned to his uniform: Stark. Somehow knowing his name helped calm her; he was a human being with a name, a life.

She found her voice and pointed to the ceiling. "Our two friends are still on the roof. They're probably afraid to come down."

"How do you get up there?"

"I'll show you," Jack said, moving slow and careful toward the ladder to the roof, with two of the cops close behind.

"What are you guys doing here?" Stark demanded.

"Celebrating," Kate told him. She had to keep him talking, keep him from looking around; she probably missed a few things in her quick sweep. *Distract him, relax him, get him to leave.*

She struggled to keep her voice steady; her legs were trembling. "My husband—that's him going up on the roof—is an artist. This is his studio. We just found out some important people are coming to see his paintings, so we were celebrating."

"Celebrating, huh? How were you *celebrating?*"

"A little beer," Kate replied, gesturing to the Michelob bottles on the table, glad she hadn't had time to clear them away. "But no one was going to drive anytime soon, honest."

"There's a bunch of paintings over here," another cop confirmed.

"Your husband works here?" Stark said, like he still didn't believe her.

Kate nodded. "He's had this place for years. It's not illegal—is it?"

Stark scowled. "We've had four burglaries around here this month —and two armed robberies. For all we know your pals on the roof are part of that."

"They're not, honest. The guy on the roof—he's a musician. Maybe you've heard him? He's the lead singer for the Ryders, and—"

"Nope," said Stark. "Don't listen to much music."

"Well, he's had some hit records. I can show you his albums. And you can see his band's equipment there." She pointed, moving her hand slowly, to the back of the loft. "He was showing one of our guests the view from the roof. We weren't planning any robberies." She gestured to her rumpled navy blue skirt. "Do we look like criminals?"

Stark snickered. "Ma'am, you'd be surprised at how respectable criminals can look."

He approached the table, checking out the beer bottles. Kate's heart thundered: there among the cigarette butts in Jack's abalone shell ashtray lay one roach.

Footsteps scraped on the creaking ladder, and Jack, Ryder and Morel came down, followed by two policemen. Morel's eyes were huge dark discs, and even Ryder seemed scared.

"Which one's the artist?" asked Stark.

"I am," said Jack. "Jack Morrison." He started to extend his hand, then let it drop.

"Okay," Stark said, lifting his gaze to the ceiling and then taking in the rest of the kitchen area, head moving continuously, eyes not stopping—thank God—on the overflowing ashtray. "Big place you got here."

"Yeah," Jack agreed. "We need the space."

Stark holstered his gun. "You people gave us a scare."

Jack smiled. "Not half as much as you scared us."

"Okay," Stark said again. "Looks like we didn't stumble on a nest of criminals here. But you all might want to stay off the roof. And for sure never duck out of sight if you see us see *you*."

Kate glared at Ryder. "We'll be more careful, Officer Stark. Thank you. Sorry to cause trouble."

"Have a good night, ma'am," Stark said with stoic indifference.

Jack followed them down the stairs, and Kate exhaled a vast sigh and found a chair.

Ryder's eyes were glazed, his movements slow and jerky as he sat across from her and rested his arms on the table. "What the fuck happened?" He peered at Kate. "Tell me you didn't flush all my good shit."

She started to laugh then, and she couldn't quit.

Jack had returned; he sat next to her and folded his arms around her. "Babe, how'd you do it so fast?"

She leaned into him, and the laughter finally stopped. She pointed at the refrigerator. "It's in there. Under the lettuce."

"My girl!" Jack said, a wide grin lighting up his face.

Kate scowled at Ryder. "I can't believe the only thing you were worried about is your goddam coke!"

"All's well that ends well," Ryder replied. "Whatever the hell that means."

Morel, Kate noticed, no longer looked quite so elegant and detached. Her eye makeup had smeared, raccoon-like, and fear still darkened her expression.

Fletcher took a seat next to Ryder. "What a heavy scene! I have never been so fucking scared in my life. Man, those cops—did you see their *guns?*" He didn't even glance at Morel.

A lot closer than you did, Kate thought.

Jack picked up an almost-empty Michelob bottle and lifted it in a toast. "To Kate—who saved all our asses tonight. Thanks, Babe. You're amazing—but I always knew that."

"Yeah, good goin', Kate," Ryder echoed. "Now bring me that blow, will you?"

"Get it yourself, Fucker," Jack said, tempering his words with a chuckle. "My girl and I need some time together."

He led Kate toward the bedroom. The smell of oil paint and turpentine welcomed her home. With the immediate threat of arrest and jail—not to mention death—out of the way, the acid reclaimed her brain, and she slid into the bright rainbow that flared out around Jack.

She'd surprised herself, not for the first time, and she felt she'd earned whatever pleasure came her way the rest of the night.

Chapter Seventeen
June 1973

W hen Stephen Durant arrived at the loft on a bright Friday morning, he looked exactly as Jack had described him: tall, thin, and pale. Streaks of gray along his temples matched the shade of his crisp business suit. Kate hadn't expected the suit; she imagined a Modern Art Curator would wear trendier clothes, maybe even jeans. When he shook Kate's hand, his grip was firm, his voice earnest, and his deep-set blue eyes fastened on her face with intense sincerity.

He brought his daughter along—a horse-faced young woman with lank blond hair and badly chewed fingernails.

"Amanda's working on her MA in art history," Durant told Jack and Kate, "and she needs to see the kind of art being done today."

Kate liked him for that; it reminded her of her own father and the way he'd introduced her to fine art.

"You picked good examples," said Trudy Zelnik, who hovered inches away from the curator.

Trudy was dressed more conservatively than she'd been at the Finelli show, in a complexion-flattering burgundy Chanel suit. *Dressing the part,* Kate thought. She'd learned from Jack that Trudy had joined the Docent Council at the Museum.

Trudy greeted Kate coolly and seemed almost surprised to see her.

The soul-sister familiarity she'd displayed at Finelli had disappeared along with the look-at-me costume.

"This one in particular, Stephen," Trudy said to Durant, gesturing toward "Garden," the centerpiece of the display. "The moment I saw it, I knew it had to be seen in our museum."

She placed a subtle but distinct emphasis on "our."

Durant's expression remained neutral as he studied Jack's work, and he didn't speak. His daughter followed him down the wall of paintings, twirling a lock of her limp hair and looking bored out of her mind.

Kate could barely keep from gnawing her knuckles. Had she given Jack the right advice about getting ready for this visit? Her nerves sang with longing to participate, but she forced herself to stay quiet while the others examined Jack's art.

* * *

Weeks ago, Kate had caught the fever from Jack and jumped into the preparations, doing her best to make the loft look good. She'd convinced him to put away his petrified wood collection, the geodes he'd hauled back from a trip to Oregon, a plaster tyrannosaurus statue someone had given him as a joke.

"They're distracting," she'd insisted. "Everything has to relate to the paintings. *Everything.*"

It had been her idea to hang spotlights on a crossbeam above the display wall, to better show off the paintings.

"And start something new. Put it up in your workroom. Show a work in progress so he can get a feel for your *process.*"

Jack had created four new paintings for Durant's visit. Meanwhile, Kate cleaned the studio; she dusted every horizontal surface, scrubbed the floor, and removed years of grime from the windows.

When Jack got ready to hang the work, he asked her advice.

"You have a better eye than anyone I know," he said, and pleasure coursed through her. Thanks to all those museums and galleries she'd visited with her father, she *had* developed a sense of balance and proportion, and it resurfaced without her even trying.

"Higher, no not that high," she'd instructed from ten feet away. "Get them farther apart. Put that one first. Now stagger the height."

* * *

It had all made sense at the time, and the display had looked superbly *right*. Now Kate wondered if she'd gone too far. Did the studio look too bare, the half-finished painting setup too contrived? Maybe he should have hung everything at the same level.

The work covered a spectrum of colors and shapes. "Garden" was flanked by three older paintings and the four new ones. These last moved from gentle realism into full-on abstract shapes that, like "Garden," seemed utterly random until you moved away from the canvas, at which time they arranged themselves into recognizable patterns: trees and waterfalls, ponds from which deer and dog-like creatures drank, an ocean.

Durant's silence made Kate want to scream. What was the man thinking? His face gave nothing away.

Kate caught Jack's eye; he winked at her, and she relaxed a bit. *Oh, please like them, Mr. Durant. Please recognize how wonderful they are; put them in your museum.*

Trudy Zelnik launched into a smug, proprietary recital of how Jack's interest in painting had evolved and how pleased she was to have "discovered" him. Had she given the same spiel at Fletcher's? They'd been at his studio the week before, but Jack didn't know how that visit had gone.

Durant ignored her as he questioned Jack: had he studied painting under Emerson Woelffer at Chouinard? Did he feel that Pollock's work had influenced his own?

As Jack discussed his training and early influences—yes to both questions, but he felt a stronger kinship with Miró and de Kooning than with Pollock—Amanda's bored demeanor dissolved. Her head swiveled from Jack to her father and back again, and she focused her attention on "Garden."

Kate's feet, stuffed into Stella's borrowed boots, began to hurt. Stella had helped Kate pick her outfit for the visit, declaring it had to be "elegant but casual." She'd gone through Kate's closet and finally approved a pair of flowing black knit pants and a top with bright blue and green color blocks.

"This looks artsy enough," Stella declared. "But not too obvious." She'd shaken her head at Kate's shoe collection and handed over the black boots with platform soles.

* * *

Kate had taken a personal day off to meet the curator, and hours before his arrival she'd baked chocolate chip cookies from her mom's old recipe. The cookies were a pain in the ass to make, with lots of measuring and mixing, but they came out chewy and moist and oozing semi-sweet chocolate. People always raved about those cookies; everybody loved them, especially Jack. Surely Stephen Durant wouldn't be immune.

At the loft, she'd brewed a pitcher of iced tea to go with the cookies, and she hoped her refreshments would put the visitors in a cordial frame of mind.

* * *

Durant stepped close to one of the new paintings, then backed away and gazed at it from the side. He nodded his head, almost imperceptibly, but Kate caught it. *He likes them!*

Trudy picked up on the shift as well. "You feel it too, don't you? *Now* you understand why I insisted you see them," she said in an urgent voice.

Durant turned his penetrating eyes on Jack. "Very interesting—the way the shapes change. Quite original."

Jack's face lit up.

"You work exclusively in oils then?" asked Amanda. It was the first time she'd spoken, and the loft almost swallowed her voice.

Jack turned to her. "Nothing else gives the depth I want."

Durant smiled, revealing perfect teeth. "Or the texture."

"Yes," Jack agreed.

He kept reaching for the Marlboros in his shirt pocket and then retracting his hand. Finally, he gave in and lit one, waved out the match and inhaled deeply. Kate yearned for a smoke herself but resisted the urge.

Amanda started questioning Jack, tossing out terms like "neo-surrealism" and "representational imagery." When she started toward the workshop, her father and Trudy followed. Kate moved to join them, but Trudy blocked her way.

"Might I have a glass of water, dear Kate?" Trudy asked.

"I have iced tea, too—and cookies."

Trudy's smile was like a shard of glass. "That's very sweet, but water will be fine. Thank you."

She turned her back on Kate to catch up with the others.

The plastic sheeting that separated Jack's painting studio from the rest of the loft had grown semi-opaque over the years. He pulled back a section and motioned the visitors inside while Kate fetched a glass of water for Trudy.

Moments later, Trudy and Amanda emerged and Trudy mouthed "business talk" to Kate as she accepted the water. Kate offered some to Amanda, but the girl shook her head without a thank-you.

Amanda studied the paintings again, then pointed at Kate's favorite: the semi-disguised seascape with flying fish arcing out of the water. Closer up, it was a tangle of yellows, blues and greens, with the shapes emerging only gradually.

Kate pressed her lips together. Amanda Durant had good taste.

"That one caught my attention too," Trudy declared. "It's *very* good."

"It's spectacular," Amanda said. "How long does it take him to finish a painting?"

Kate paused before answering, to prolong Jack's time with Stephen Durant. "Some go quicker than others," she finally replied and pointed toward the seascape. "This one, though, took *months*. He was going to paint over it at one point—he got frustrated with the way it was going —and I talked him into finishing it."

Did she sound too boastful? Apparently not, for Trudy clasped her shoulder, suddenly all pals again. "How lucky that you have foresight."

In the workshop, Jack and Durant conversed, voices muffled. They stood beside the unfinished canvas, and the curator kept glancing at it.

"Dad's enthralled," Amanda stage-whispered. "He hasn't spent this much time in private with an artist since Eisenberg."

"Really?" asked Kate. She knew Simon Eisenberg only by reputation, and photos of his work in *Artforum, Art in America,* and a well-publicized show at LACMA two years earlier. He was the artist equivalent of a rock star.

"Really," Trudy confirmed. "Stephen's going to open doors for Jack. Doors you didn't even know existed."

Jack and the curator came out of the workroom, still deep in discussion. Durant studied the finished paintings again. "They're quite good, Jack. Quite good."

He turned to Kate and clasped her hand, and Kate felt the full force of his personality wash over her. She wanted to have *more* for Stephen Durant, something as spectacular as Jack's paintings, something far more significant than cookies and tea.

"Kate." Durant's cool hand squeezed harder. "How lucky you are. To have a part in all this."

Dust motes hung in the air as sunlight slanted across the floor, blinding for seconds, opening up caverns in the surrounding shadows.

When Durant released Kate's hand, it seemed as if the sunlight dimmed. *Say something important!* Kate urged herself.

"I am," she agreed. "It's very gratifying. I've learned so much from watching Jack work, seeing what goes into making art."

"Yes," Durant mused. "I'm sure it's been an education for you." His tone was benign, but the sensation of specialness Kate had experienced vanished like smoke.

Durant's hand swept in an arc along the display wall. "You have an excellent eye for overall composition—even with the way these are arranged. You've shown them at their best."

"It took some trial and—" Kate began.

Jack interrupted. "I guess those years in art school weren't wasted then?"

Durant's laugh rang like crystal.

Kate bit her lip at the slight. *Part of the game, kid.*

Durant extended his hand to Jack. "I'm so glad we had this chance to see your work. I foresee great things for you, Jack Morrison."

Jack's brown eyes glistened.

Kate pointed to the plate of cookies on the kitchen table. "I have some refreshments if you'd like to—"

Durant shook his head. "That's dear of you, but I have another appointment in half an hour."

Kate's breath froze in her lungs, and she felt a hot tingle on her face. Her clothes, her preparations for the visit: it all seemed suddenly pathetic and pretentious. The loft itself seemed pathetic, its space so full of dust, its shabby walls, the filmy windows she hadn't been able to clean entirely.

She grabbed a smoke from Jack's pocket and lit it.

Amanda cast a yearning glance at Kate's cookies before hurrying after her father. "Nice to meet you, Jack," she called out over her shoulder. Jack followed to show them out.

The visitors' expensive shoes clattered down the stair treads, and Kate watched from the window as they got into a black Mercedes, Durant at the wheel. Jack waved and looked on wistfully as they drove off.

"He's even more amazing than I expected," Jack said when he came back upstairs. He sounded dazed, and a flare of resentment jolted Kate.

It wasn't fair: she paid the bills, didn't pester him about keeping normal hours like the husbands of her women colleagues—or even about giving *her* moral support by coming to work functions. When he protested that he was too tired or too busy, she let it go, every time.

Don't be such a baby. You asked for this life. You wanted this for him. Kate tried to remember this was simply a business deal, part of the get-Jack-famous routine. Of course Stephen Durant would care only about the artist; that was his thing. The artist's wife had no value to him.

"He sure liked the work," Kate said. "I predict you'll have a museum show out of this before long."

Jack came back into focus. He put his arms around Kate and kissed the top of her head. "I hope you're right, Babe. I sure do hope you're right."

Kate rubbed against him, nuzzled his neck, and caught the exhilaration seeping through his pores.

He'd gotten what he wanted. Now they could break out the weed, the coke. They could celebrate, in their own private way. She was glad he'd kept a bed here, although she was ready to try the table, the bathroom, even the floor.

She tilted her head back, eyes closed, inviting kisses, but none came. When she opened her eyes, Jack was staring at the wall of paintings.

She gave it one last try. "We have the place to ourselves—for once. Let's not waste it," she whispered, pressing closer to him.

He finally kissed her again, but it was the kind of kiss you give a demanding child. Then he let go of her and wandered past the paintings, glancing now and then at his workshop. Kate had the weird sense he was communing with any trace of Stephen Durant left behind. His expression had tightened, and for a second he bore an eerie resemblance to Adam Fletcher.

She blinked and cleared her throat. "Guess I'll leave you to your musings then."

He nodded, but she doubted that he heard her words.

Outside in the cheerful June sunlight, Kate realized she had almost an entire free day ahead of her. *All dressed up and no place to go.* She could, of course, go straight to work, and she almost did. The office was *her* place, where people saw her, and listened to her, and cared what she thought.

Going there, however, would be a defeat. How pitiful, to have a day off and not know how to use it. Kate drove home, wondering why she felt like crying.

Chapter Eighteen

S tella's door opened by the time Kate reached the landing.

"What happened? How come you're home already?" asked her neighbor.

Stella drew her inside and gently pushed her into an armchair. "What's wrong? And don't say 'nothing.' You look like your best friend died. Did the honcho hate what he saw?"

Kate shook her head. "No, he liked it. A lot."

"Then you guys should be celebrating."

"Jack's under some spell," she told Stella. "I didn't—"

Stella scowled. "Bullshit. What's going on?"

Kate pulled off Stella's loaned boots and rubbed her feet. "I don't know exactly. After they left, he ...it was like Jack wasn't there. Like he was somewhere I couldn't reach."

"That is fucked," Stella said. "You worked your ass off for him, and when things get interesting, he shuts you out?"

Kate had no response. She almost told Stella about Jack taking credit for arranging the paintings, but she stopped. That would be whining about trivia.

"You know what you need?" Stella asked. "You need to go to lunch with me. Come on, let's head for El Coyote. A couple of margaritas will fix everything."

"I doubt that."

"Come on, don't even think about it, just come with me. Now."

"Fine. But first let me put on some shoes that fit my big feet."

* * *

All in all, lunch with Stella turned out to be the best part of the day. Almost. The actual best part had been when they were waiting in the bar area for their table. The place had been jammed, but two men in business suits stood and gestured to the bar stools they'd vacated.

"Can't let two pretty women stand while they drink," the taller of the men had said. He had a nice tan and very white teeth.

Stella narrowed her eyes at the men, but she took the offered seat. The other guy, younger, with close-cropped blond hair, extended his hand to Kate. "Larry Totten," he said, and his hand lingered in hers, gently squeezing her fingers.

The outer door opened and illuminated the room, sending a shaft of sunlight onto Larry Totten's face. The roar of bar noises receded. His hand was warm, soft, and dry.

"Kate Morrison. Thanks—glad to know chivalry isn't dead."

The maître d' signaled the men that their table was ready, and Larry Totten cocked his head at Kate. "I'm sure there's room for four at our table, if you ladies would like to join us?"

Before Kate could reply, Stella spoke up. "No thanks, fellas. She's married, and I'm the nightmare ex-wife your mother warned you about. Enjoy your lunch."

The tall guy flinched, and the two left without looking back.

"That wasn't polite," Kate said.

Her friend shrugged. "They wouldn't be so polite either, later on." She patted Kate's hand. "You gotta toughen up, honey. You're so busy being nice you don't see when people are gaming you."

They ordered drinks while Kate considered Stella's proclamation

Kate sighed. "I'm hopeless."

"You're not. Naïve, maybe—but there's a cure for that."

"The Barberini Cure?"

Stella's laugh rang out. "Call it what you will. It saves a lot of pain on down the road."

The drinks came, they toasted, and to Kate's relief when they finally got a table for lunch, it was in a part of the restaurant far from the two men they'd met. Still, the memory of Larry Totten's handshake lingered. A stranger had been attracted to her, even if only in a cliché way.

* * *

By late afternoon, Jack still wasn't home. He called a little after five o'clock to say the Ryders had returned and they were celebrating.

"Trudy phoned me," he explained. "She's coming back next week to buy the one you call the seascape. And get this: she thinks Durant wants me to be in a show he's putting on in the spring. It worked, Babe."

"That's great! All the hard work we did was worth it."

She waited for him to acknowledge the 'we.' He didn't.

Instead, after a brief silence, he said. "Hey, those cookies were good. We demolished 'em. You save any more at home?"

"No," Kate told him. "I gave you all I had."

The irony of her response fell over her like a blast of cold air.

"Okay, then," Jack said. "Don't wait up, OK?"

After they broke the connection, Kate realized that neither she nor Jack had signed off with their customary "love you." It was the first time she could remember that they both forgot.

Feeling empty and abandoned, Kate stood looking out the window toward the Observatory, which shimmered like a promise. She thought about phoning Stella but remembered her friend had plans for the evening.

"A date?" Kate had asked.

Stella had flushed. "Not a date-date. Meeting a friend for drinks is all. No big deal."

Stella met a lot of "friends for drinks." Always going out on her own; no guys ever came calling. Stella had explained that she liked her own wheels and paying her own way. Still, Kate often wondered what kind of people Stella met up with on those evenings out. She'd almost asked several times, but something in Stella's voice made Kate think she should mind her own business.

She did a half-hearted job of cleaning the apartment and then reheated the chicken casserole she'd made the day before, poured herself a glass of Chablis and stared at the darkening sky, feeling lonely in her own home.

The silence seemed louder than usual, so Kate turned on the stereo and let Carole King's voice fill the empty spaces while she ate dinner and washed dishes. Then she switched on the TV and tried to watch Sonny & Cher, but their easy banter depressed her.

She paced some more, wondering what Jack was doing. He hadn't said when he'd be home, and she hated waiting and not knowing. She tried phoning him at the loft, and the phone rang twelve times before she hung up.

That left her struggling to pull her thoughts away from dark explanations for Jack's whereabouts. Was this how her mother felt, the night the drunk killed her father? Did Mom keep going to the window, gnawing on her thumbnail and trying to persuade herself nothing was wrong, he was merely stuck in traffic, he'd walk through the door any minute?

The latest copy of *Artforum* sat on the coffee table, and Kate picked it up and flipped through its glossy, ink-scented pages, imagining the day it would feature Jack's work. Before long she dozed off on the sofa.

* * *

The sound of the front door opening pulled Kate from sleep. She sat up and rubbed her eyes, checking her watch: one-twenty.

"Hey, Babe," Jack said, shoving the door closed. "I told you not to wait up."

"I know. I was worried."

He laughed, but it was a nervous laugh, she thought.

"Went partying with the Ryders," he said.

"I wish you'd called." Kate heard the accusing whine in her voice and bit her lower lip. *I sound like Mom.* Jack studied her for a moment, and she realized how bizarre she must look—rumpled hair, wrinkled clothes, her face probably sleep-puffy.

Jack came close. His eyes were mostly dark pupils, and a mixture of marijuana and perfume came off his jacket. "I did call—we talked, remember? I said we were celebrating. Then we went out, and I tried again, but somebody was using the damn pay phone."

He kissed the top of her head and stroked her hair. Kate picked up a Marlboro but was too tired to light it, so she let it drop onto the coffee table.

A pause followed and then he said, "Let's get you into bed. You need your sleep, Babe."

He led her down the hall. "Man, those dudes know how to have a good time," he continued.

"Mmmmm," she replied, still groggy. "Musicians are supposed to."

"I couldn't keep up with 'em," Jack said, admiration flowing through his words.

Kate yawned. "Sounds like fun."

"It was. First time I've cut loose in a while." He shook his head. "Man, that Ryder—he has women falling all over him."

Kate pulled off her jeans and sweater and reached for her nightie. "And he hates every minute of it, right?"

Jack laughed. "Yeah. You bet."

She slid under the covers. "Aren't you coming to bed?"

He shook his head. "Too wired. I'll be in soon."

He kissed her, and hesitated before he spoke. "Kate, honey? You don't have a little spare change left over, do you? I bought a round of drinks at the last place and I'm tapped out."

Sleep evaporated. Money? *Now*? She pushed the covers aside.

"I thought we decided that—"

He held up a hand to stop her objection, like he already knew what she was going to say. Maybe he did. The Josie Morrison Money Train had derailed long ago, and despite Kate's steady upward progress at work, she and Jack lived paycheck to paycheck, with a little help from the occasional sale of a painting. They agreed a share of her take-home pay would go to each of them for spending money, and neither had to account for what they did with it. But it was supposed to last the whole month, and here was Jack, halfway through June and out of dough already.

"Babe, I'm sorry I even brought it up. I thought maybe this one time you could—"

"This one time? You go through money like it's water—meanwhile I'm rationing cigarettes and juggling grocery money so we can pay the rent."

He didn't say anything.

Kate sighed, overcome with fatigue. It was too much trouble to argue with Jack. He'd win anyway.

"You know where my wallet is. Help yourself. But leave me ten bucks, okay?"

He started out the door, but then stopped and turned around. "Did I ever promise you we'd have money coming out our ears?" The veins in his neck stood out and his arms hung stiffly, fists clenched.

Kate sat up and lit a cigarette as a thousand retorts flashed through her mind. She held back, barely.

"And if I want to show my friends a good time, it's none of your business," he continued, riding high on his anger.

Kate returned the volley. "Oh, really?" She gestured at the walls. "It's only my business that we have a place to live, and food in the refrigerator, right?"

Oh God, this was going to a bad place, but she couldn't stop. The unending worry over money, the injustice of her sitting home alone while he partied with his pals—rage took control of her.

"See, I don't exactly *love* working for a living," she said, "and it pisses the hell out of me when you act like you're entitled to do as you please."

"I *am* entitled," Jack said, in a deadly voice. "And if you think otherwise, maybe you're with the wrong guy."

"How are you entitled? Tell me! What gives you the right?"

He lit a Marlboro and exhaled, sending a thick cloud toward the ceiling. "News flash, Kate—making art is hard work. Some days my arms ache, and my head hurts, and I'm half sick from the fumes, but I keep at it. And then—listening to all those fucking critics, the pompous bastards who pretend they know what it takes to make a painting work. Yeah, that's a ton of laughs. And making nice with collectors who can't tell their ass from a hole in the ground. So much fun."

He stopped his rant and pointed the cigarette at her, squinting through its smoke. "I don't always like it, Kate, but I do it because I'm an artist. At least some people think I am. Some people think I'm worth the sacrifice. I thought you believed that, too. Looks like I was wrong."

He headed toward the door again but stopped, his back to her. "Thanks a lot, Kate, for making me feel like shit. I coulda stayed out all night with Ryder and his little groupies, but instead I came home to you. And this is what I get for it."

He stomped down the hall. Kate heard his footsteps stop, the sound of her purse opening, then the front door's slam, and the rattle of the Volvo's engine.

"Shit," she muttered as she crushed out her cigarette and sank back onto the pillows, stunned by his tirade and too pissed off to cry. How had it gotten like this? What was wrong with her, to begrudge the man she loved a little pleasure? He had never complained much before about his life; where had all that anger come from? Where had their happiness gone?

I wonder where he went, Kate thought. The loft probably, but if not, then she had no clue where to find him. The realization left her breathless.

* * *

In the morning, she tried to ignore Jack's absence as she stumbled out of bed and brewed coffee. She felt *sore*—not in her muscles, but in her feelings. And a long, lonely day stretched ahead, a Saturday that should have been spent with Jack.

Maybe Stella would be up for a hike. Kate peeked out the front window but didn't see Stella's Mustang. So, the sort-of date must have gone okay. Oh well—not the first time she'd gone hiking alone, and it probably wouldn't be the last.

She picked a steep climb, up to Five Points and then Glendale Peak, one of her dad's favorite routes.

"The thing is never to give up," Dad would say as she panted up the grade. "One foot in front of the other. You'll get your second wind anytime now. Keep going."

When she reached the summit, heart pounding, lungs heaving, Kate could imagine her father beside her, smiling approval. She straightened and let the breeze dry the sweat as she took in the view: Los Angeles sprawled in glittering splendor to the south, the San Fernando Valley to the north. And her friend and guardian, the Observatory, its domes shining under the blue sky. The sight was worth the climb.

Thoughts of Jack resurfaced on the way down. How had he changed direction so swiftly? He was hanging out with Ryder too much, that was it. Ryder's lousy attitude had infected him.

* * *

Jack got home around seven o'clock that night, acting as if their fight hadn't happened. Kate was tearing lettuce for a salad and baking another casserole—tuna this time. He came up behind her and kissed her neck. She breathed in a comforting whiff of varnish mixed with sweat and cigarette smoke, a combination forever linked to Jack.

"How are you?" he asked.

Kate put down the lettuce. "Okay. You?"

And that's how they played it, making polite conversation. An empty space lurked between them, and Kate had an odd sense she was talking to a stranger who'd stolen Jack's face and voice.

The distance diminished as the evening passed. Kate curled up on the sofa after dinner, and he sat next to her. She held out her hand, and he drew her into his lap. His kiss reassured her; it was Jack, really Jack, in the room with her again. The temporary loss had terrified her, though. How had it happened? What could she do to keep it from happening again?

Chapter Nineteen
April 1974

K ate stepped into the warm, moist evening, and nothing seemed real—not her hand on the doorknob, not the bumpy concrete walkway underfoot, not the pale green dress that swished against her legs, its hem grazing her kneecaps. Jack looked real, but even he might be the product of wishful thinking.

They were on their way to LACMA for the opening of Jack's first museum exhibition. LACMA: the Los Angeles County Museum of Art. When Kate spoke the acronym aloud, she imagined a key turning in a lock, opening a doorway into an insider's world, where artists and collectors mingled, and those collectors clamored to buy Jack's paintings, outbidding one another for the privilege. A silly, overambitious dream, but it seemed closer to reality that night.

The museum exhibit, titled "New L.A. Visions," featured the work of twelve up-and-coming artists: painters and sculptors, along with three conceptual artists, whose work Kate had trouble appreciating. Jack's inclusion was a clear sign of his growing importance. And they had Trudy Zelnik to thank for getting him in.

Adam Fletcher was also part of the group, but the easy camaraderie between Jack and Fletcher had dissolved over the past months. They were outwardly cordial to one another, but Kate noticed tension between them on the rare occasions they were together.

* * *

The houses they passed grew larger and fancier as they neared their destination. Jack parked on 6th Street, behind the museum, and clasped the steering wheel for a few seconds.

He turned to her. "Gimme a kiss for good luck."

"You don't need luck, Mr. Hot-Shot Artist."

The kiss, long and deep, made her quiver. What fun they would have tonight, especially after the show.

Outside the car, Jack squeezed her hand; his skin was warm and damp. "Here we go."

"Here we go," she echoed as nervous energy transferred from his flesh to hers.

Kate heard voices and saw lights before they reached the courtyard, where knots of men in dark suits and women in long colorful dresses stood smoking cigarettes and drinking wine from plastic glasses. The Finelli opening redone on a grander scale: this, after all, was *the* Art Museum. Oh sure, Pasadena had one too, and Long Beach, and a bunch of lesser venues. But this was the Jackpot.

Trudy Zelnik rushed them immediately. "Jack! Come inside—come see!" She smiled at Kate as she pulled Jack into the gallery.

Jack, of course, had visited the exhibit pre-opening. Now, though, he put on a good act for Trudy, as if seeing it for the first time.

"Don't you just want to pinch yourself!" Trudy gushed, then lowered her voice. "And *your* work is the best part of the show."

Jack flushed, and Kate guessed he must be torn between discomfort and pleasure at Trudy's praise.

"What do you think, Babe?" he asked Kate. "They look okay in here?"

Kate hadn't gotten a preview of the exhibit, but everything about the placement of Jack's paintings looked *right*: the lighting, the spacing, the distance from everyone else's work. A quick scan of the gallery confirmed her conviction that Jack's paintings were the best in the room. Everything else looked dull in comparison.

She touched his arm. "More than okay. Spectacular. They were meant to be shown here."

Jack's paintings had deepened and broadened. The newest ones were more dramatic, their shapes more defined, their colors bolder. And he'd gotten in the habit of titling them, relying on Kate's help but sometimes bestowing names that baffled and amused her.

Her favorite of the new work, "Featherstorm," depicted a riot of brightly colored shapes that, from a distance, morphed into a cluster of feathers, plumage that might have been shed by a mythical bird, or maybe an angel. The shapes seemed to move around on the canvas.

The second one, "Glossary," had portions of words embedded in swatches of green and blue paint that swept across the canvas. The letters could have spelled many things and left much to the viewer's imagination. Kate found "rtist" and "lo" among the clusters but didn't try to decipher anything.

Then there was "Garden," with its vivid flower-petal shapes.

The last was Kate's beloved seascape, with a placard that read

Nostalgia
Oil on canvas 1973
Collection of Stanley and Trudy Zelnik

Trudy paused in front of her painting, cocked her head and sent Jack a satisfied smile. Then she nudged him into the crowd to meet and greet, and he glanced back at Kate with a question in his eyes: *want to come along?* She shook her head, mouthed "go schmooze," and went looking for the bar.

The wine was higher class than Finelli, and so were the appetizers. Kate sampled both and then started a circuit of the gallery.

As she was studying a sculpture that appeared to be made from vacuum cleaner lint, she heard a woman's voice behind her. "How do you think Zelnik managed to get one of *her* trophies in the show? Stephen didn't ask *me*!"

A second woman, with a deeper, clipped voice replied, "Nothing she does surprises me. And just think—its value has quadrupled now."

They both tittered knowingly and moved out of range.

Interesting, Kate thought. So Trudy had clout—enough to evoke catty comments.

A moment later, Trudy reappeared and hugged Kate, who had a hard time not wriggling out of the Youth-Dew scented embrace.

"Isn't this the most exciting evening," Trudy stage-whispered. "You must be so proud to know you had a hand in it."

"I am," Kate replied, still absorbing the conversation snippet she'd overheard.

"I can't believe how many important people are here," Trudy continued. "I left Jack talking to Lawrence Grant—you know him?"

"The art critic for the *Times.*"

Trudy nodded. "You do your homework. I like that." She looked around the buzzing gallery. "And Nancy Yates is here, too."

"That name I don't know," Kate said.

Trudy leaned closer. "Pasadena high society. A snob, but she has a decent collection."

Kate followed Trudy's gaze and realized Nancy Yates had to be one of the two women she'd overheard earlier. She managed to keep from smiling.

Amanda Durant glided past them, without a greeting but with the same vague expression Kate had seen when Amanda visited the loft.

Trudy sniffed. "I do wish Stephen didn't insist on schlepping *Amanda* to these events."

Kate nodded. "She doesn't seem to enjoy it much."

"Don't let her waif-act fool you, dear. The girl is a human predator. Notice how she comes to life around men. And be sure *Jack* keeps his distance."

"Don't worry about Jack," Kate replied. Her gaze found Jack, conferring with Adam Fletcher. The two appeared deceptively friendly. Fletcher's girlfriend Morel stood next to him, looking elegant and bored. She moved a few steps away, and without even turning his head, Fletcher took her arm and pulled her back alongside him. Why did Morel let him treat her like that? She could do better than to serve as an ornament in Fletcher's orbit. Thank God Jack didn't expect that kind of subservience.

The notion of Amanda Durant as a manhunter amused her more

than anything, so when Trudy moved away, Kate searched the crowd to see if she could catch the girl in action. She didn't spot Amanda, nor did she recognize much of anyone. Stella had planned to join them but canceled at the last minute—a freelance assignment had her chained to her typewriter.

Then out of the crowd came Ryder, swaggering toward her with reddened eyes and an aura of marijuana.

"Katie Girl—been lookin' for you. Explain some of this shit to me, will you?"

Kate tried not to flinch as Ryder's whiskey breath assaulted her. His voice carried above the generally dignified murmurs and drew a couple of curious glances. Would anyone in this crowd recognize him? Would they even care who he was?

She spoke in a low voice, hoping he'd follow her lead. "I can't explain it to myself, Ryder, let alone to you."

He took a cigarette from his pocket—a legal cigarette, she noted with relief.

"Hey," she said, "let's go outside and smoke. I need fresh air."

"Whatever you say, Artist's Wife."

He held the door open for her, and she pulled a pack of Marlboros from her purse as the warm evening air embraced her. Ryder flicked his lighter and lit her cigarette.

Kate exhaled into the darkness. "What needs explaining?"

Ryder shrugged. "The whole fuckin' thing. Except Jack's—Jack's work I dig. But what was up with that little plastic statue thing glued to the blank canvas?"

Kate giggled. "That's conceptual art. It's very current. And I don't understand it either."

Ryder's laugh came out rich and deep, like his singing. "That's my girl."

Kate surrendered to the camaraderie and the fragrance of night-blooming jasmine.

"How's the band doing?" she asked.

He waved smoke away from her face. "It's cool, we have a few gigs. Times are tough, everybody wants to be a rock star. I don't know if we have the juice for it. I just show up, sing my songs, hope somebody hears 'em and likes 'em and wants to pay money for 'em."

"It's a tough field. Like art."

"Yeah, man, it is. Jack's lucky to have you covering his ass. I wish I had me a woman like you."

His words embarrassed her, even though she knew he was high, running off at the mouth, saying stuff he didn't mean.

"I bet lots of women would apply for the job," she said.

He shook his head. "Chicks attracted to me, all they want is the ride. And they want it for free."

They smoked in silence for a moment, then Ryder spoke up again. "Know what I like about you, Kate?"

She tilted her head. "I'm such a great dancer?"

He rewarded her with another laugh. "You are the worst dancer I ever knew!" His expression turned suddenly serious. "You're not a taker, Kate. That's rare."

She didn't know what to say in return, so she ground out her Marlboro in the pedestal ashtray and brushed some imaginary lint from her dress. "Let's go back in, and I'll make up some bullshit about the so-called art to entertain you."

He started to say something else, paused, then muttered, "I need a little jolt of something before I go back into that scene," he said, putting his finger under his nose with a sniffing motion. "Want to join me?"

Kate shook her head. No coke for her, not that night. People and situations were rushing at her fast enough.

She went back inside and checked out Fletcher's paintings, which still looked sterile and pretentious to her. *Yeah, Mrs. Art Critic, like you know so much.* She saw Ryder, wiping his nose as he came through the door and headed for the wine.

Then she caught sight of Amanda Durant, moving in on Ryder. Damn! Trudy had been right! Animation suffused Amanda's features as she put a hand on Ryder's arm, the gesture implying far more intimacy than Kate would have thought possible. The girl glowed; even her mousy hair seemed to shine.

As Ryder handed Amanda a glass of wine, he looked over at Kate and sent a broad, knowing wink her way.

She wished Jack's parents had come to the opening. They'd retired to the desert but were driving in over the weekend to see the show. Josie's relationship with Kate had thawed over the years, once she realized Kate was not a gold-digging parasite. Her attitude had shifted into a grudging respect for Kate's dogged support of Jack's talent, and last Christmas, after a few too many eggnogs and with the LACMA show on the horizon, Josie had acknowledged that Kate had been right to encourage Jack toward painting instead of teaching. Josie's admission was the best Christmas present anyone could have given her.

* * *

Jack worked his way back to her and kissed her cheek; his arm went around her waist, pulling her close.

"Having a good time?" Kate asked.

Jack nodded. He was radiant. "I had a great talk with Stephen Durant—what a nice guy! He's probably forgotten more about art than most people ever knew."

"And he likes your work—so he has good taste, too."

Jack looked away. "They're having a little private party after the museum closes, and Durant asked me to come. It's a big deal to be invited, Babe."

Kate suppressed a sigh. Her feet had begun to throb, and the evening had drained her. "Great. If you want us to go, we'll go."

"Not us, Babe. Me."

Kate couldn't believe what she'd heard.

"I asked Ryder if he'd give you a lift home."

Kate stared at him, speechless, and he finally realized the effect his words had had on her. "They're trying to keep it small, just the artists."

The longing in his eyes scorched her soul.

"Uh-huh."

"If you don't want me to, I won't. Your call. But Fletcher's going, so if I don't show up then…"

"Of course you have to be there. Have fun. Where's Ryder?"

"Right behind you," Ryder said. Kate hadn't heard him approach. "Hey, it's cool. Maybe we'll bar-hop on the way home."

Kate couldn't even laugh at the notion. Every fiber of self-control focused on holding back tears.

"Have fun," she said again and kissed Jack quickly on the lips.

He smiled at her. "You're the best, Babe. We'll celebrate on our own tomorrow, okay?"

"Yeah, sure. Now go."

She watched him catch up with Trudy Zelnik and the thin, pale curator, to whom Trudy had attached herself like a barnacle. The trio started off toward the museum interior. Artists only? Were the docents considered artists? Then Amanda Durant joined the group. Kate's cheeks flamed with resentment and humiliation.

Fletcher—solo—slipped in behind Trudy, and said something. Trudy turned her head for an instant and then looked away, as if from an unwelcome intrusion. Any other time, Kate reflected, she would have found that interesting. At the moment she didn't care.

Ryder took her arm. "Ready?"

Kate noticed Morel walking toward the parking lot. "I wonder if she needs a lift."

Ryder glanced in Morel's direction. "The Star-Fucker? Nah!"

The cold dismissal gave Kate no comfort.

As stoned as he was, Ryder still drove pretty well, and Kate was thankful for that. On the way home, he asked, "You okay, kid? You're awful quiet."

Kate shrugged. "This sure didn't turn out the way I expected."

"We really can go bar-hopping, if you want. I know a bitchin' nightclub."

Kate shook her head. "I'm not in a party mood, Ryder."

"Suit yourself," he said, upshifting and speeding them toward her apartment.

At least Jack had made sure she had a ride home; Kate tried to hold onto that thought, but it wasn't much consolation.

Chapter Twenty
December 1975

Christmas decorations turned downtown Los Angeles festive, if you didn't look behind the tinsel and colored lights. There you'd see homeless men in shabby clothes, drinking from brown paper bags. Or leather-jacketed thugs who preyed on the homeless and the unsuspecting. Last week there'd been a carjacking not far from Jack's studio, so Kate was extra vigilant, even on a crisp Saturday morning, as she drove to the loft.

Jack's overnights at the studio had become chronic, and Kate struggled to adjust. Waking up alone, she fought off the ache of abandonment. Once she got going, work filled the gap. Her increasing job responsibilities called for more and more overtime, so she wasn't home all that much herself.

Kate had a thermos of coffee and a box of Winchell's donuts with her. She and Jack had carved time out to go Christmas shopping together and then spend the rest of the day doing "whatever." Kate hoped "whatever" would include some steamy afternoon sex (their favorite kind because it always felt more spontaneous), a movie and dinner and maybe another round of lovemaking before they drifted to sleep curled up together. A perfect day.

Gino Finelli had offered Jack a one-man show next February, and the manic preparations were well underway. Three new paintings so far, and two sketched out. *When does it stop getting so frantic?* Kate wondered as she parked the car, checked to be sure no winos were lurking, and scurried into the loft. The dismal realization struck her that things would never slow down, not for someone like Jack. But, after all, wasn't that part of what drew her to him in the first place?

"Hello?" she called out at the top of the stairs. Her voice echoed through dusty silence.

A cough came from Jack's sleeping quarters.

"Jack? I have coffee and Winchell's."

The chilly air smelled of weed and cigarettes, and the ever-present oil paint. Kate set their breakfast on the table as she heard another cough from the bedroom. She sighed: nine a.m. and he was sleeping off whatever drugs he'd inhaled, sniffed, or swallowed the night before in pursuit of the Creativity god.

His appearance confirmed her suspicions as he shuffled toward her, red-eyed and disheveled.

"Hey," she said, "did you forget?"

He lit a Marlboro and gulped some coffee. "Forget what?"

"We're going shopping today."

"Right. Give me a few minutes to wake up, okay?"

"Sure. You did remember, right?"

"Yeah, of course."

His expression said otherwise.

"You and Ryder party last night?"

"Is that against the law?" he asked.

"I just thought—"

"Thought what? You're my timekeeper now?"

A rush of anger flowed in a hot red wave from her brain to her toes. "You promised to go shopping with me. How was I to know you'd blow it off so you could party."

Jack ground out his Marlboro. "Give it a rest, Kate! I said I'd go, I'll go. Not everybody leaps out of bed at the fucking crack of dawn like you, okay? All I'm asking is a few minutes to wake up. Don't make it a crime."

Why was he being so nasty? And why was she letting him get

under her skin like this? All she had to do was sit down, shut up, smoke a cigarette or two and let him wake up. But something in her rebelled. It wasn't fair. She didn't love getting up early, but it had become a necessary habit. And she asked so little of him…

"If you don't want to come with me, don't. I thought maybe you'd want to help pick out your parents' Christmas presents, that's all."

"News flash, Kate: there's more important stuff than shopping, than having *things*."

"Fine! Give *that* speech to your mom and dad instead of a package."

"There you go—put on your martyr suit again."

"I will. It goes with your Mr. Superiority act."

Jack picked up his coffee mug, knuckles white around it, and stared into the dark liquid. Kate thought he might smash it on the floor; sometimes he did things like that when he got mad. He never threw anything at her, though, even if she provoked him by making snotty comebacks like the one she'd just tossed out.

His beard was shaggy, his hair sleep-tangled. A cigarette burn darkened the sleeve of his red t-shirt, his favorite one with the peace sign stenciled on the chest. He looked like one of the vagrants who camped in the empty lot next door.

The fluorescent tube overhead flickered, and Kate heard her own breath whistle in her chest. Otherwise, a fierce silence wrapped around them.

Jack set the coffee mug down with a thunk. "Okay," he said in that put-upon voice she hated. "One more cigarette and I'll be ready."

He was anything but ready, and he made no move to even light his cigarette.

"You know what, Jack? I think I'll go on ahead without you. This is obviously not your thing, and I don't want to drag you along. Take your time, wake up, or sober up, or whatever you want. I'll see you later."

She grabbed her purse and stomped down the stairs to the sound of his protests.

"I'll catch up with you," he called out, and she muttered, "yeah, right" as she slammed the door.

* * *

Traffic was thick and sluggish, which added to her sense of annoyance and persecution. She finally got into the Broadway Plaza parking, creeping up the barber pole ramp to the upper lot, where she lucked out and found a slot by the elevators.

In the central courtyard, Kate debated where to go first, wishing Jack was with her. He'd blend in with the crowd at 7th and Broadway: skinny Asian boys, stocky Latina women, Black men holding intense conversations. In downtown Los Angeles, few people stood out.

Except for a neatly dressed white girl who clearly didn't know where she was going.

Kate bumped into a tall, thin man. "Sorry," she said, peering up into strange green eyes. He wore a leopard skin cap and leather vest, and when he grinned she saw a flash of gold; his dark brown skin glistened in the sunlight.

"Be careful, Little Sister," he said, reaching for her.

Maybe he was only trying to steady her, but Kate backed away and hurried into Broadway. Perfumes swirled around her and mingled with the smell of expensive leather. Gold and diamonds glittered inside glass cases.

Kate took out her shopping list: Jack, Josie and Henry, her mother, Debbie, Stella. She had a little over $200 in her Christmas fund, which she'd started in January, after coming up short on the rent because of last year's Christmas gift expenses.

Kate checked a few price tags and, with a twinge of regret, left the scented sanctuary and started walking toward May Company, a few blocks north and slightly more affordable. Her anger at Jack dissolved in the morning sunlight as the pleasure of walking quickened her pulse.

She hit the jackpot at May Company: a soft flannel shirt in a rich blue plaid for Jack. It would keep him warm, and he'd like the color. Kate's spirits lifted as she found fits for her family in Women's Clothing. By the time she left Housewares, she'd crossed all the names off her list except Stella's. Her arms began to ache from the heavy shopping bags.

Kate checked her watch. Not bad: she'd accomplished a lot in less than two hours. Time to head back to the car, get rid of the bags, and return to Broadway to find something for Stella. She could afford a tiny splurge—and get her parking ticket validated.

The day had turned chilly while she was picking out presents; clouds hid the sky. The shopping bag handles bit into her fingers. Why had she gone so far from the car?

Kate trudged south, her mood taking a dark turn, her annoyance at Jack returning. He'd really let her down, leaving her to lug the Christmas gifts around by herself.

This is so wrong—Christmas used to be fun. Even when we were broke, we had magic.

Snatches of memories arose: their first Christmas, the scent of evergreen suffusing the apartment. The shimmering tree, the whispered promise of bright packages under its branches. They'd shopped together, except for each other's gifts. Christmas Eve, Jack had surprised her with a bottle of *Je Reviens*, a fragrance she'd admired during one of those shopping trips. They'd spent the evening alone, listening to carols and getting high, making love in the golden glow of candlelight. The next day, as they shuttled from Kate's family to Jack's, neither minded the frenzy because they were together, holding hands and feeling a shared joy.

Now, six years in, much of the shine had worn off. Jack's compliments had given way to criticisms, with words like "shallow" and claims that she wasted time worrying about her looks instead of caring about important things like peace and inner beauty.

In the year and a half since the LACMA show, Jack had slipped more and more into the Artist role. He went to every gallery opening in town. The art scene had become one more addiction, like the coke he and Ryder used. He hung out with other painters, mostly men, whose attitude of superiority had infected Jack to the point where he scoffed at anyone who didn't make art—or, at the very least, *support* art. And even that was no ticket to approval, as Kate had learned.

What would it be like, when Jack became *truly* famous? Would he write her off as useless? Would he fall into a swamp of drugs where she'd never be able to find him? He'd described his trips on acid, mescaline, psilocybin, peyote—all in the name of widening his vision. Would he flame out in a cocaine-fueled explosion?

Kate herself never tried acid again after the night of the police raid and hardly even did coke anymore. She knew she should probably quit marijuana as well. It no longer gave her much pleasure, and Permian Oil, like a lot of businesses, was doing more and more employee drug testing. Office workers were usually exempt, but some companies randomly tested *everyone*.

* * *

A sound behind her, a wet, smacking noise, yanked her back to the present. Kate turned, and in her distraction stumbled over an uneven piece of sidewalk. She recovered quickly and hurried along, trying not to react to what she'd seen.

Three men were following her; one of them had made the wet-kiss sound. Kate processed impressions from her brief glimpse: denim, leather, boots, metal, baseball caps. Young? It seemed so. She didn't want to risk another look. Maybe they were harmless. Maybe not.

One of them said something like, "Hey, chickie," and another laughed—a deep, nasty sound. So much for harmless.

Shoppers flowed around her, oblivious, and not as many as you'd expect on a Saturday. A sharp breeze cut through her sweater.

Despite the heavy shopping bags, Kate picked up her pace, hurrying toward Broadway Plaza. Did it have a security guard during the holidays? She thought she'd seen one. At least there'd be more people around.

"Hey, Baby, what's your hurry?" one of the men called out.

Why had she been so damn stubborn? Why hadn't she waited for Jack?

Because then it wouldn't have gotten done. He's probably still sitting around, smoking and working up the energy to get moving. Or maybe he went back to sleep.

Why hadn't she paid more attention in the self-defense class she and Stella had taken last summer? She did remember one lesson the teacher had drilled into them: never look like a victim, never act like a victim.

Kate raised her head and straightened as much as possible with shopping bags weighing her arms down. She took a deep breath, waiting for a couple of people walking toward her to get closer.

Then she turned sharply on her pursuers and met the eyes of the middle guy. Her move seemed to confuse the trio. They all stopped, but at different times, so they appeared uncertain and disorganized.

She didn't say anything, just glared at them. They glared back.

Great. A standoff. Now what?

"Hey, Mama," the middle guy said, leering at her. "You need help with them shopping bags? They look *heavy*."

She hadn't expected them to speak.

"No, thank you," she replied, and her voice came out clear and firm. "They're fine."

Now what? She didn't want to turn her back on them, and they showed no sign of dispersing.

"Kate honey?"

Had she hallucinated Jack's voice, needing him so desperately? No, she heard footsteps behind her, saw the middle guy's focus shift over her shoulder. Kate risked a glance away from them, and there, six feet behind her, was her own private miracle.

Despite the overhead cloud cover, Jack wore sunglasses, and his hair flowed around him like a shampoo commercial. His flannel shirt hung open, revealing the red t-shirt with its peace symbol. His sneakers and ragged-edged jeans were covered with the colors of the past week's work: swipes of azure and brown, splatters of yellow ochre and magenta. His right hand held a burning cigarette. Behind him, downtown monoliths rose toward the sheet metal sky.

There may have been other times when Kate had been happier to see Jack, but at that moment she couldn't remember them.

She noticed him tense up as he took in the scene. He came up beside her, facing the men.

"Hey," he said to the guys, "you need something here?"

The middle one shook his head. "No, man," he replied, "we was offerin' your lady some help, that's all. It's cool."

Jack removed his sunglasses and stared at Kate's pursuers while he took a last drag on his cigarette, then replaced the shades and ground out his smoke on the sidewalk with a casual finality. "Cool," he echoed. "I've got it now."

He didn't move until they turned and retreated, looking over their shoulders now and then. Jack let half a block's distance open up before he hoisted Kate's shopping bags.

"Holy shit, honey," he said. "What'd you buy—a rock collection?"

"How'd you know?" she asked, her words coming out a breathy sigh.

"You bought *rocks?*"

Kate had to laugh then. "No, silly. I mean, how'd you know I needed you?"

He grinned. "I just had a feeling."

"But how did you find me? I could've been anywhere."

Jack kissed her cheek, quick and light as a hummingbird's wings. "I always know where you are, Babe. I always know when you need me. I *feel* it."

Kate didn't question him further. She wanted to believe, and maybe it was true. At that moment, all she cared about was the realization that Jack had come after her. He'd rescued her again. And the man walking beside her, making up a funny, lavish story about her encounter with the would-be hoodlums, was the man she'd fallen in love with, and loved still.

Maybe things would work out fine, after all.

Chapter Twenty-One
April 1976

"This isn't as bad as it looks," said Paul Lange, handing Kate a file crammed with papers.

Kate took the heavy folder. "If you say so."

"You have at least two weeks, and I only want a rough draft—it doesn't have to be perfect."

He wasn't fooling either of them.

Despite her lack of a college degree, Kate's writing skills had impressed Lange, and he'd begun delegating bulletins and policy language to her. Right after New Year's, he'd rewarded her with a promotion to Benefits Specialist, in charge of communications and policy development—her first professional position. And now Lange was giving her a real chance to prove herself, writing a recruitment policy for the expanding West Texas operations. The company needed to attract top talent to a part of the country where not everyone wanted to live.

Kate poured a tall cup of coffee and went to work, scribbling an outline and clipping sections of data together as the project absorbed her attention. Was this what Jack experienced when he painted? Kate envied his powers of concentration, the way he went into his work and neither saw nor felt anything around him.

Marcie tapped on her open door. "Lunch?"

Kate came back to the outside world with a jolt and glanced at her watch; three hours had passed. "Uh—no thanks. I'm really into this." Her stomach rumbled a protest.

"Overachieving again, aren't you?" Marcie said, a smile in her voice.

Kate winced. "Guilty. Can't help it."

"Paul wouldn't give you anything he didn't know you could handle." Marcie paused, but she didn't deliver her frequent pep talk: "Think how far you could go if you had your degree! This company has a piss-poor image where women are concerned, and you're limiting yourself."

And, Kate admitted to herself, she probably did have time for night school now. The solo show at Finelli in February had generated a surge of interest in Jack's work, a nice review in the *Los Angeles Times*, and several sales. Jack Morrison was moving into the big leagues—and working harder than ever to go all the way. When he wasn't painting, he was going to galleries or making connections with collectors and other artists. Sometimes it seemed like they lived on different planets.

"You haven't seen the last of me," Marcie said. She winked at Kate and disappeared.

Kate went back to her project, savoring the lunchtime letup in buzzy energy that suffused her workplace. She liked the clatter of typewriter keys, hurried footsteps only partly muffled by carpet, a shared sense of purpose and accomplishment.

Kate lost track of time again, but after what seemed like only a few minutes, Marcie bustled in with a white paper bag that smelled a little like heaven: cold cuts, pickles and Italian dressing.

"I'm going to sit right here and force you to stop and eat," Marcie proclaimed as she handed Kate a sandwich, removed a second one from the bag, and claimed one of Kate's visitor chairs.

Kate knew better than to argue with her friend, and in truth, it did feel good to let her eyes focus on something besides words. "Thanks, Marcie. You're the best."

"Possibly," Marcie said as she unwrapped her sandwich and inhaled dramatically. "And I have ulterior motives, in case you hadn't guessed.

Put your project aside for a few minutes and let me vent about something."

Kate did as she was asked and then started in on her lunch. "Mmmm, this is so good! Exactly what I needed. Now—what's up?"

Marcie finished chewing and set down her food. "It's that damned Jeff Gallo. His *wife* called me this morning."

"Is something wrong?" Kate asked, all thoughts of eating momentarily pushed aside.

"You don't know? The little prick—the little womanizing prick— has been carrying on with Dee Dee Carr in Purchasing, and his wife got wind of it. She wants me to fire Dee Dee."

"Jeff Gallo and Dee Dee Carr? How did I not know?"

Marcie gestured at Kate's project. "Because you've had your nose buried in work, and you don't have time for water-cooler gossip."

Kate absorbed the information. She didn't have much to do with Gallo, a cocky, slick-talking labor negotiator whose office was down the hall from Kate's. And her sole dealings with Dee Dee Carr had been as Lange's assistant, ordering stationery and business cards. Dee Dee had struck her as a bit of a flirt, batting eyelashes at every passing man, but there was a big leap from flirting to homewrecking.

"When you say 'carrying on,' Marce—you mean as in sleeping with, or just making eyes at each other over coffee in the break room?"

"If I had to guess, I'd go for sleeping with. It's not the first time Jeff's pulled a stunt like this. He's notorious."

"He's never come on to me."

"You have an IQ higher than your body temperature—unlike Jeff or any of his conquests."

"What are you gonna do?"

Marcie shrugged. "Not much I can do. Oh, I could get Paul Lange involved, sure, and make life miserable for Jeff and me and anyone else caught in the crossfire, but I'm too old to be a tattletale. I'm going to sit Mr. Gallo down and tell him that I know what's going on, and so does the rest of the department, and if he wants to keep on being the butt of jokes that's his business, but maybe he has more pride than that."

"Good luck."

"Yeah, it may not make a difference. But I can't tell him about the wife's phone call—that might nudge them into divorce court. I told her—I can't believe I did this—that sometimes a guy gets infatuated with someone in the office because things aren't so rosy on the home front. He comes home all tired and the wife's grumpy and gives him the cold shoulder, no wonder he's charmed by somebody at work who's cheerful and pays him compliments."

"That's brilliant, Marce. You should've been a counselor."

Marcie waved the compliment away. "You spend enough years in this job, you pretty much see it all. I hope it works. Maybe he can slide back into married life with only a ripple."

"Think that'll be the end of it?"

"Probably not," Marcie replied. "Some men are pigs."

"*Your* husband would never do anything like that, would he?" Kate asked. She liked Harold Plesh and the very notion of him cheating on Marcie almost made her laugh.

"I doubt it." Marcie sighed. "But he's a *guy*. For women like Dee Dee, that's enough." She chewed and swallowed a hefty bite of her sandwich and wiped her mouth. "You ever worry about Jack? Artists are probably real attractive to the predatory type."

Kate wrapped up the rest of her lunch; she'd had enough. "I don't know when he'd have time! Between painting and trying to sell his stuff, he's too busy to fool around."

Marcie took a last bite of her lunch, then stood and dusted off her skirt, as if putting the whole issue to rest. "Busy hands *are* happy hands."

* * *

After Marcie left, Kate fell back into the comforting details of language, explaining as clearly and concisely as possible how the company would give extra-special help to employees relocating to West Texas for the new venture. Time flowed around her, and she scarcely noticed its passing, or the rise and fall of activity outside her office.

Her phone rang, and she picked it up without looking, immersed in her project.

"You're still there?" Jack's accusatory tone startled her.

She checked her watch: 6:15. Not an unusual time for her to be at work, so why was he pissed off? Did they even have dinner plans that night?

"Did you forget Nikki Frank's opening?" he continued.

Oh damn—she had. Nikki Frank, owner of the hottest new art gallery in town, was staging a Simon Eisenberg retrospective, with an invitation-only reception that evening.

"I'm sorry, Jack. I'll leave right now."

"It'll take you forever, this time of night," Jack said. "I can't believe you forgot."

She was going to apologize again, but the words stuck in her throat. Where did he get off coming at her like this? "I'll hurry as fast as I can."

He didn't answer.

"Do you want to go without me?"

"I don't want to," Jack replied, "but maybe I have to."

"I can meet you there. I'll leave right now."

He hesitated. "I suppose that'll have to do," he said finally. Another pause. "Are you wearing something dressy enough?"

Kate looked down at her black gabardine skirt and wished she kept a stash of nice jewelry in her desk the way the fashion magazines advised. "It's not festive but it's clean. No, wait, this is silly. I really don't need to be there. You go to plenty of shows without me. Right?"

"I guess." His reluctance sounded fake.

"Fine, then. Go enjoy. You can tell me what I missed."

"I will." His voice softened. "Don't work too hard, okay?"

Kate wrestled with her feelings: a sense of being abandoned, mingled with relief. She'd started to dread the parties and gallery openings. Although she yearned to be a participant in Jack's world, most people wouldn't let her. When they did acknowledge her, it was not by her name. She was Jack Morrison's wife. A footnote. Never mind that she knew more about art than most of them. She didn't *make* art. She didn't matter.

She went back to work—the best antidote—and was proofing a rough policy draft when Paul Lange stopped by.

"I told you not to kill yourself on this. You have lots of time, Kate."

"I know," Kate replied. "But Jack's busy tonight anyway, and I wanted to get a head start."

He shook his head in mock frustration, but his expression radiated approval. "Sic 'em, Tiger," he said, giving her a quick wave before he turned away.

There: at least she hadn't disappointed the other man in her life.

Chapter Twenty-Two
August 1976

Summer blazed along, and Kate scarcely noticed. Her new recruitment policy helped draw all the skilled workers needed to West Texas. Paul Lange gave Kate full credit for the policy, and a flood of even more challenging assignments followed.

Meanwhile, Stephen Durant had invited Jack to be part of another major exhibit, showcasing painters from across the country. While Kate spent her days—and many evenings—in air-conditioned offices, Jack toiled away in the loft's stifling heat.

His new paintings fascinated Kate: trees that weren't quite trees, shiny river-ribbons, and vague shapes that could have been rocks, or animals. He'd finished two since Durant's invitation: "Periphery" and "Levitation." When Kate asked how he came up with the titles, Jack had laughed and said he flipped through a dictionary and picked out words he liked.

He hadn't titled the third one yet, but even in its incomplete state, the painting enchanted her. It was the best he'd ever done, and each time Kate visited the studio, she checked on its progress. Against a pale background, tree shapes hovered beneath the hint of an early crescent moon, and the foreground held a small furry shape, indistinct but somehow watchful. The painting radiated mystery and magic. It felt *alive.*

"I wish you didn't have to sell these," Kate said of the new paintings. "I'll cry when they go away."

Jack joked that she'd probably get her wish since neo-realism was neither trendy nor marketable, but Kate thought otherwise. People couldn't help but fall in love with his art. He was that good, that special.

She tried to believe that her own work mattered as much as Jack's growing reputation. But her career didn't sparkle with artists and fancy parties. It didn't take place amidst glamour and intrigue.

That glamorous art world could be cruel, however. People fell away from its edges. Adam Fletcher's star flamed out as Jack's rose. His paintings stopped selling, and Kate hadn't seen him lately at any gallery openings. When she asked Jack what happened, he said Fletcher had quit concentrating on his work and settled for merely playing a role.

"That'll never happen to *you*," Kate assured Jack.

"Never's a big word," Jack muttered.

The museum show was months away, but Jack continued painting like his life depended on it, and in a way it might, Kate reflected. Maybe sheer effort could ward off the failure and obscurity that had claimed Adam Fletcher. And how could she begrudge Jack the time and energy he devoted to his art, when the payoff was so clear? Especially since she herself was immersed in an occupation she enjoyed beyond her expectations.

* * *

One Friday night in mid-August, however, her bold reassurances failed her. She seemed to be the last to leave the workplace, and its deserted parking lot fueled her loneliness. A hot evening breeze grazed her cheek, and the sun, still above the horizon, filled the western sky with an orange glare. This was not just *any* Friday night; it was her twenty-seventh birthday. Her co-workers had celebrated with a strawberry whipped cream cake and cards and good wishes, but Jack hadn't mentioned it. He'd asked her to meet him at the loft before they went to Felipe's for dinner, which meant he'd no doubt go back to his studio afterward and work through the night.

Kate hadn't reminded Jack about her birthday. If he couldn't remember on his own, then it really wasn't worth it, but the disappointment stung. She shouldn't *have* to remind him.

Get over it, she told herself on the drive to the loft, cycling through her usual arguments about having what she needed, if not what she wanted.

She parked behind Jack's shiny new black Ford pickup. He'd bought it with the proceeds from selling three paintings earlier that year. He loved his new wheels, which were more than transportation for him. They meant he was making enough money to pay his own way. Kate wasn't sure exactly how she felt about that.

She let herself into the loft and trudged up the stairs.

"Kate? That you?"

"Yeah, it's me."

"You sound tired, Babe."

"I am."

He met her at the top of the stairs. "Happy Birthday."

Fatigue and self-doubt fell away. "You remembered."

"Important day. How could I forget?"

He kissed her, his tongue flicking over her lips. "Hungry?"

"A little."

"Before we go eat, I want to show you something."

He led her to the front of the loft, past the plastic sheeting and into his workshop. There on an easel sat the painting she'd been watching evolve. The background now suggested a sky impossibly blended from purple and crimson. A twilight sky: the magic, witching hour. Stylized trees spread their branches across the foreground, framing two smaller, more fragile-looking trees behind them.

Kate's imagination conjured a watchful, mysterious interpretation of the scene. The furry foreground shape now resembled a wolf with its head thrown back. The painting sang to her; it triggered a gut reaction, a sensation that someone—or *something*—was watching over that lonely little creature in the foreground.

"It's finished," Jack said.

Kate stood transfixed, gazing at the canvas.

Jack put his arm around her. "You'll never have to worry about me selling this one. It's yours."

"Huh?"

"Look closer."

She did. In the corner of the painting, above his signature, Jack had painted, "Happy Birthday Kate. 8/13/76."

A hot flood of tears spilled down her cheeks.

"Hey," Jack said, "You can't cry! It's supposed to make you happy."

"It does," she blubbered, her thoughts still churning. "Oh, it does." She swiped the tears from her face. "I don't know what to say."

"You could try 'thank you.'"

Kate wrapped her arms around him and kissed him for a long time, their bodies pressed together.

When they finally came up for air, she whispered, "Thank you. Oh, thank you, thank you, thank you."

She reached out toward the painting, and Jack grasped her hand.

"Don't touch it yet. The paint's not dry. That's why I needed you to come here—can't move it yet. When it's set I'll bring it home for you."

Kate couldn't take her eyes off the canvas. She took a deep breath and inhaled the smell of fresh oil paint and turpentine, her old friends.

"It's so beautiful," she murmured.

"You have to name this one, you know."

Without hesitation, Kate said, "Sanctuary."

"Okay then," said Jack.

"I'll always remember this birthday," Kate whispered. "This is the best present ever."

Jack kissed her forehead. "Still hungry?"

"Sort of. But I don't want to leave. I want to stay and look at it for a while."

"Babe," said Jack, "you'll have the rest of your life to look at it. C'mon, let's go eat."

She took another long look at "Sanctuary." The overhead light fixture illuminated sections of the painting, so that the wolf-shape appeared three-dimensional, and she could imagine the tree branches stirring in an evening breeze.

Jack led her out of the workshop as the downstairs door banged open.

Ryder's voice rose from the stairwell. "Yo, motherfuckers! Who took my parking place?"

He had acted more and more bad-tempered each time Kate had seen him over the past few months. The band had been struggling, unable to get any kind of air time. Their last single had faded into obscurity in weeks. Amid lots of finger-pointing, she had a pretty clear idea that Ryder's heavy drug use was the main cause of the group's deterioration. A damned shame. Ryder had so much talent, and it was all going up in smoke, or up his nose.

"Didn't see your name painted on the curb," Jack called out.

Ryder reached the top step and swayed, squinting at Kate. His blond hair looked dirty and lank, his jeans torn at one knee.

"Well fuck," he muttered. "Didn't expect *you*, Miss Business Suit. Slummin'?"

Kate ignored his sneer. "Just visiting, Ryder."

"It's Kate's birthday," Jack said, in a serious voice.

"Am I crashing your party?"

"Nah," Jack replied. "We're on our way out."

"Don't let me chase you off, I'm harmless." He paused. "Want to smoke with me first?"

Kate felt a surge of sympathy for Ryder. Where was his entourage? Where had all the groupies gone?

Before she had a chance to speak, Jack answered Ryder, and she saw an unexpected hardness in his expression.

"Not tonight. We're on our way to dinner. But listen: you have to start putting away your stash, okay? Last week, that couple from Beverly Hills—I'm halfway to selling them a piece when she noticed a bag of weed on the table. Then she sat down and nearly got your hash pipe stuck in her butt. Freaked her out. That's not cool, Ryder."

"That's how it broke?" Ryder chortled. "I thought I did it."

Jack held up his hands, traffic-cop style. "Doesn't matter who broke it. The thing is, you gotta clean up after yourself. Not everybody

likes the sight of bongs and baggies lying around. Put your shit away—
I don't want to get busted over your carelessness."

Ryder's reddened eyes blazed; his hands curled into fists. "Tight-
ass."

"If I really *was*, I'd've kicked you out by now. You haven't paid your
way for months, so don't go acting like you own the place."

Kate intervened before their argument ruined the evening.

"Hey guys," she said, tugging on Jack's arm. "No fair fighting on
my birthday!"

Neither man reacted for a few seconds like they'd forgotten she was
there. Ryder came back into focus first.

"You're right, Katie Girl." He rubbed his chin. "I feel bad I didn't
get you a present."

"You should," Jack said.

"I didn't expect a present," Kate said to both of them.

Jack refused to let up on Ryder. "Right. Nobody expects anything
from you, do they? They know better."

Ryder ignored him. "Maybe I'll write a song for you, for your
birthday," he told Kate.

"You do that," she replied, keeping her tone light and easy. "Maybe
it'll put you back on the map."

"Back on the map," Ryder echoed softly, a punishing longing in his
voice.

"Just what you need," Jack put in. "More fame and fortune to
blow."

Ryder scowled. "Back off, man."

The antagonism surprised Kate. Ryder's carelessness had always
annoyed her, but until now Jack didn't seem to mind it. She fished a
pack of Marlboros from her purse and held up her cigarette. "Who's
gonna stop this pissing contest long enough to give me a light?"

Ryder moved first, flicking his lighter open and thumbing it to life.
He held his arm out straight, keeping his distance, and Kate leaned
into the flame.

She offered the pack to Ryder. He only hesitated a second before
taking it and propping a cigarette between his lips. When he started to

put the Marlboros in his pocket, Jack reached for them. Ryder glow-ered, but he handed them over.

Kate pulled in the smoke, and it calmed her a little. Permian was starting to discourage its employees from smoking, and Kate felt silent disapproval whenever she lit up. Away from the office, however, she smoked to her heart's content.

Jack returned the Marlboros to Kate's purse without taking one, his face still taut with hostility.

"Don't go acting all high and mighty on me," Ryder said. "Looks to me like you came down with a heavy case of amnesia."

Jack's frown deepened. "What the fuck are you talking about? And why the hell do you have to barge in and ruin everything?"

Ryder fixed Jack with a rigid stare. "Not me doin' the ruinin', man. Go look in the mirror."

What the hell *was* he talking about? And when did Jack stop believing that Ryder could do no wrong?

A harsh silence hovered in the dusty air.

"All right, then," Ryder muttered at last. "Didn't mean to bust up your little party. Didn't mean to get in your way."

He wobbled to Kate and kissed the top of her head. "Happy Birth-day, kid."

The smell of him washed over her: nicotine and dope and beer and sweat, and something else, something dark and lethal. With every fiber of her being, she fought the urge to wipe at the spot where his lips had brushed her hair.

Then he staggered toward the back of the loft.

"Good night, Ryder," she called out.

No answer came from the shadows where Ryder lived.

Jack took her arm and led her downstairs.

"He's in a bad way," Kate said. "Isn't there something we can do to straighten him out?"

Jack shook his head. "You can't save somebody who doesn't want to be saved."

"He was acting so weird," Kate said, and thought *and so were you.*

Jack's voice was filled with contempt. "How could you tell?"

On the way to Felipe's, Kate pondered the angry exchange between

Jack and Ryder. Something was up—something she didn't understand. And it wasn't about Ryder leaving his dope around or not paying rent. There was nothing she could do about it, though. They'd work it out, or they wouldn't. But Ryder was hurtling ninety miles an hour into a brick wall, and Kate wished she knew a way to stop the collision.

But Jack had just given her the best painting he'd ever done. That awareness muted her concern for Ryder. This was her birthday party, and she was with the person she loved best in all the world. Nothing else mattered at that moment.

Chapter Twenty-Three
December 1977

The little brunette kept touching Jack's arm. From across the room, Kate watched the girl's predictability. They all had the same moves, these artist groupies—better dressed than rock-star groupies but otherwise interchangeable. She'd probably asked Jack where he got his inspiration, before assuming a sensuous pose and moving in to share a confidence. Her hand came up and brushed his upper arm again, and then she grew bolder, touched him again, more emphatically. She let go only long enough to flip her glossy brown hair away from her face.

Kate waited for the next move: Jack's. He looked over the heads of the admirers clustered around him, met Kate's gaze, and winked. The amusement she got from watching the scene play out, as it had more times than she could count, helped ease her boredom.

She drained her wine—a fine Napa Valley Chardonnay. None of the cheap stuff at Stephen Durant's holiday party. Time for a refill. Kate licked the last residue of black cherry gloss from her lips and headed for the bar, plowing through a wall of bodies that smelled of patchouli and peppermint.

The handsome young bartender smiled at her and raised his light brown eyebrows. Something about him reminded her of Ryder—a young, clean Ryder.

Kate smiled back. "White wine?"

He held out the glass seconds later. Their skin touched as Kate reached for the wine, and a tiny jolt of static electricity sparked.

"Ouch," he said. "Sorry." His smile displayed two rows of incredibly straight teeth; he looked barely old enough to be serving up booze.

Kate fought a weird urge to touch his hand again. Instead, she tapped her index finger on the linen cloth covering the bar. "Somebody didn't use their fabric softener."

He laughed and offered her a napkin. This time his hand grazed hers deliberately, and although no sparks flew, she didn't pull away for a few heartbeats. The bartender's white shirt sleeves were rolled up past his wrists, his skin tanned to a perfect toasty gold.

"So," he asked, "are you an artist or a collector?"

"Neither," Kate replied, pointing her thumb toward Jack. "I'm with him. My husband."

The kid seemed surprised. Why? Did she not fit his image of an artist's wife? For a flash, she wished she'd worn something glittery and black like most of the women there, instead of the crimson knit dress that quit just north of her knees. Did she appear to be trying too hard?

The bartender started rearranging wineglasses. "Didn't know Morrison had a wife. A *pretty* wife."

When Kate pulled a Marlboro from her purse, the bartender flicked a shiny chrome lighter and held it to the tip of her cigarette. He opened his mouth to say something more, but a silver-haired man claimed his attention, waving an empty glass over the bar. Kate moved toward the nearest ashtray and stood sipping her wine as snatches of conversations slid past: "...and then I told him, if you think I'm going to sit through that movie just so your son will think you're some kind of intellectual…" "It really does make a difference, you have to experience it …" "I swear, this is the last one, I'm really going on the wagon this time."

Her thoughts drifted back to Ryder, whom she hadn't seen for over a year. He'd finally crashed and burned, according to Jack. Moved out of the studio. Vanished from their lives. What a waste.

"Kate, isn't it?" The high-pitched voice startled Kate out of her reverie. Amanda Durant approached, limp blond hair floating around her homely face, stick-thin figure not doing an iota of justice to the snug black minidress.

Kate nodded. "Hello, Amanda. Yes, it's me." She lifted her wineglass. "Cheers. Your dad puts on a nice party."

Kate had learned via Trudy Zelnik that there was no Mrs. Durant. She had abandoned her husband and daughter, moved to Colorado with her ski instructor. Pity. Amanda could use a mother's touch—but maybe not *that* mother.

Amanda tucked some skimpy blond strands behind her ear. "It's good, right? I helped plan it, and I'm so glad Jack came—and you, too."

A flush crept over the girl's cheeks, mottling her complexion.

What the hell am I supposed to talk about with this kid?

"Your father's been so supportive—Jack and I appreciate it."

"I'm a huge fan of Jack's. He's amazing." Amanda's expression unnerved Kate: an "I've got a secret" look, the high school kind.

So the girl had a crush on Jack. Why did that annoy her?

Kate gave Amanda her best, most confident smile.

"And he talks about you all the time," Amanda continued. "How you two met and everything. I'm jealous that you knew him back when."

Honey, you were probably in elementary school "back when" and didn't know Pollock from Picasso.

Kate tilted her head. "How's school going, Amanda? You must be close to graduating."

Amanda flushed again. "Not exactly. I'm changing my major to business." She sighed. "I couldn't get into art, you know? It's so ... complex."

"Uh huh," Kate agreed. "It is."

"Well," Amanda said, "it's been nice talking to you, Kate. Enjoy the party."

"I'm trying," Kate said, but the girl had already wandered away.

Now what the hell was that about? Kate ground out her cigarette. An urgent need rose up in her, to escape the buzzing swarm of partygoers. She swallowed the last of her wine and headed for the powder room, tucked under the staircase.

The bathroom's pink and lavender striped wallpaper and soft lighting were designed to flatter and soothe. Kate pulled the door shut and leaned against it, breathing in a mild rose scent, until her ears stopped ringing.

She splashed a little water on her cheeks and reapplied her lipstick. Not too bad. She came off a damned sight better than Amanda Durant, right? Kate had never been able to assess her own looks. Was she pretty? Her father always claimed she was, and Jack now and then said "You're beautiful." But Kate herself had never come to a clear sense of what she looked like.

She snapped her purse shut. By the time the party was over, her face would hurt from forced smiles. But she and Jack would go home together and warm each other in bed, and maybe do more than snuggle against the winter chill. All she had to do to earn that reward was pretend to have fun for another couple of hours.

Back in the hubbub, Kate took out her Marlboros and discovered the pack was empty. How did that happen? She went in search of Jack, who was never without plenty of smokes, and spied him by the fireplace, deep in conversation with Little Miss Couldn't-Get-Into-Art.

Kate was struck by the change in Amanda's demeanor: her features were animated, and even from a distance Kate caught the sparkle in the girl's eyes. Trudy Zelnik's observation flowed back to Kate: *"Don't let that waif-act fool you, dear. The girl is a human predator. Notice how she comes to life around men."*

Trudy, apparently, had chosen not to attend the soirée. As Jack explained it, amusement dancing in his eyes, Trudy had clashed with Nikki Frank, the rising-star art dealer. "Probably over Trudy's bargain-hunting tactics," Jack had said. And Durant had definitely invited Nikki—Kate had spotted her earlier, in earnest discussion with her host.

The art world's politics *were* entertaining, but at the moment Kate didn't feel like laughing. Amanda Durant's posture, her proprietary attitude as she whispered something to Jack, really got to Kate.

Jack glanced her way as Kate approached, but his expression stayed neutrally distant, without a shred of recognition.

The floor gripped Kate's feet, and reality unspooled. Swarming voices pressed on her ear drums. In the mirror over the fireplace mantle, Kate saw a woman in a knee-length red dress, blond hair braided at the temples, face winter-pale and vacant.

Oh. There I am. Kate crumpled the empty cigarette pack still clutched in her right hand and waved it at Jack. The mirror woman did the same.

Jack blinked. Like a dog shaking off water, he turned back to Amanda, speaking into her ear. She nodded, her gaze sliding toward Kate. Jack touched Amanda's elbow lightly before he moved away, and the intimacy of that quick gesture made Kate want to scream.

So the bartender didn't know you had a wife, Jack?

She stood her ground as her husband approached.

"Having fun?" he asked, his voice cool.

"Not really," Kate replied, and the rest of the words slipped out before she knew they were coming. "I'm tired. My feet hurt. Can we leave?"

Jack frowned. "Don't be silly. They're about to serve dinner. We can't bail out—we'd insult Stephen. And Amanda."

"I don't care."

"I do. There's no reason to leave."

"Yes, there is."

Kate caught a burning smell, like toast starting to scorch. No, someone behind her had lit a cigarette, that was all.

"I'm out of smokes," she continued, like that explained it.

Jack handed her his Marlboros. "Now can we stay?"

She shoved the cigarettes back into his hand. "No."

"What is wrong with you, Kate?" His voice turned harsh.

"This whole scene is wrong. I worked hard all week. I'm tired. My life matters too, in case you didn't notice."

Somewhere inside her a child was raging, "Not fair! Not fair!"

How had things shifted in this unexpected direction and turned into a contest?

Jack didn't budge. "You're acting crazy," he said. "Leave if you want, but I'm staying."

His mouth made a hard, thin line.

Kate's right hand twitched. If only she could wipe that hostile expression from his face.

"God damn it, Jack!" Her voice rose, and when she said his name, thin beads of spit sprayed his chin. His eyes widened, but he didn't flinch.

She tried again, more gently. "Take me home. Please."

A few people were staring. The hell with them.

Jack held out the key to his pickup. "No. You really want to go, then drive yourself home."

An ugly smirk distorted his lips, like he was daring her. She held out her hand, and he let go of the key.

It fell forever, as if the air had become liquid. The key spiraled down and down and down until it landed in her palm like a slab of ice, so cold and heavy that it stunned her.

No! Take it back!

Kate wanted to hurl the key at Jack, but instead she said, in the calmest of voices, "Okay then. See you later."

She turned and walked out, as steadily as she could. Halfway down the front steps, she realized she'd left her coat behind, but she didn't go back. Her breath plumed up in the frosty darkness. Stars punctured the night sky, and the air smelled of pine trees and wood smoke.

Kate wasn't afraid of driving herself home; it was all surface streets, and she'd driven Jack's pickup before and figured out how to judge distances. She'd only had those two glasses of wine—or was it three? The cold and the fight had knocked their pleasant buzz out of her, and she had never felt more sober in her life.

She cranked the key, and the pickup roared awake. Damn it, though, she should have kept Jack's Marlboros. She checked the glove compartment; no cigarettes there. She took a deep breath, let out the clutch and gripped the steering wheel as she hit the gas.

Lights of oncoming cars separated into thin slices that pointed in so many directions Kate felt dizzy. She squinted at the white center line and used it to guide her, repeating over and over, "It's not that far. You can do it. You're almost home."

By the time she parked the pickup, she halfway believed herself.

The apartment was dark and cold, and her footsteps echoed through the emptiness. She fired up the wall heater and grabbed the nearest pack of cigarettes. As the nicotine did its work, she sank onto the sofa, gulping in smoke and exhaling in swift, angry bursts. The Marlboro was gone in less than five minutes, and she lit a second from the smoldering tip of the first.

Her eyes watered from the smoke, or so she thought until Kate realized she was crying—quietly, so as not to disturb anyone. When she remembered there was no one to disturb, the tears strengthened, and she had to grind out her cigarette because her whole body shook with deep, painful sobs.

The whole evening had gone so wrong. It should have been a happy time, a lighthearted holiday celebration. Jack's work was selling, his reputation growing, and their marriage, despite a few bumps in the road, was solid and strong. Jack loved her; she loved him, as fiercely as she'd ever loved anyone. He was good to her, he appreciated her, he wanted her. But this stranger he'd turned into tonight: where had he come from?

She had seen flashes of the stranger before and ignored them. Nobody's perfect, after all. Jack had a lot on his mind; it wasn't easy making a living as an artist, putting up with so much bullshit from the wealthy collectors he had to court in order to sell his work, get his paintings shown in galleries and museums. If he was a little irritable sometimes, no wonder. He was entitled to a burst of temper now and then.

Always before, he'd come back to himself, and back to her. Surely this time was no different.

She kept seeing that key falling into her palm, tumbling slowly from Jack's hand to hers while he watched with that cold, cruel expression.

Kate smoked five cigarettes before she calmed down, and by then her throat was raw and she hated the bitter nicotine taste that filled her mouth. The apartment had warmed up enough for her to undress, so she changed into her nightgown, brushed her teeth, and stumbled into bed.

The sheets were cold. Funny, she'd gone to bed alone more times than she could count while Jack worked at the studio, but that night more than ever she was conscious of his absence. Kate started to cry again, but after a couple of minutes, she made herself stop. Her tears might come alive if she let them.

Before she turned off the bedside lamp, she studied "Sanctuary" on the wall opposite the bed, and tried to latch onto the warm, happy feelings that surrounded it, the magical night Jack gave it to her. The painting had given her courage and strength. It was a tangible reminder that, no matter what went wrong in her life, she had the love of a good and talented man. She had earned it. But that night even "Sanctuary" didn't comfort Kate.

Who was the real Jack? The man who'd given her one of his most precious paintings, or the angry-faced Jack who'd let her leave the party alone? She had no answer as she finally fell into the mercy of sleep.

* * *

About four a.m., a noise woke her: the front door opening and closing, then slow footsteps down the hall. *Good,* she thought, *at least he came home. Now maybe we can talk it out. Maybe he'll apologize.*

"Hi," she said softly before her breath caught up and froze her voice.

Would he lean over then, stroke her hair and kiss her hello, like usual? Kate bit her lip and waited to find out.

"Hi." Jack's voice was empty and flat.

"How'd you get home?" If she could get a conversation going, they still had a chance.

In the dark she heard the click of his lighter and the slow hiss of exhaled cigarette smoke and evaporating hope.

"You don't want to know," he said.

He sat on the bed; Kate felt the mattress sag away from her. His shoes hit the floor one at a time, with sad, resigned thumps. Then he slid under the covers, way over on his side of the bed, without getting undressed.

Kate couldn't tell if and when Jack drifted off to sleep. She lay in the dark, listening to him breathe and wondering if he'd been this way all along, and she'd only just seen it that night. It didn't seem possible, but she'd lived long enough to know that life was always capable of sending nasty surprises, usually when least expected.

A dark, heavy fatigue took over, and she closed her eyes, but sleep eluded her. She lay silently in their bed, staring at a ceiling she couldn't see, waiting for something to happen and afraid that it would.

Chapter Twenty-Four

Sullen morning light outlined the window curtains. Kate had dozed on and off but had finally surrendered any hope of real sleep. Jack breathed quietly on the other side of the bed.

She slipped from under the covers and into jeans and a sweater, and went to brew coffee before he woke. Maybe that would start the day off right and erase the bad feelings from last night.

Her black wool coat lay on the back of the sofa like a reproach, but she took courage from knowing he'd thought about her enough to bring it home.

While the coffee perked, Kate thought back to what had happened at the Durant party. How ridiculous it all seemed in daylight. How could one disagreement derail what she and Jack had built together? How could one argument destroy years of happiness?

Just then Jack shuffled in, sleep-rumpled, as the coffee finished brewing. He squinted at the countertop and frowned. "Got any smokes?" asked, like he was expecting the wrong answer.

She took a pack of Marlboros from the cupboard and handed them to him with a book of matches. He acknowledged her with a lift of his eyebrows.

Kate filled a mug with coffee and dumped in his usual three

spoonfuls of sugar. He took the cup without speaking and sat at the dining room table, smoking and slurping coffee, his back to her. She fired up her own cigarette and joined him.

Pale winter sunlight slanted through the windows and fell across Jack's face. He didn't look at her when she sat.

"How was the dinner?" she asked, careful to keep her voice neutral.

He studied his cigarette. "Fine. You missed a nice meal, storming off like that."

Kate's good intentions faltered. "I didn't storm off. I was tired, and there wasn't any point hanging around. I felt like I was in the way."

He blew smoke at the ceiling.

"Jack? What's happened with us? It's like I don't even know you anymore."

His eyes, threaded with red, glared at her. "I'm still me. Maybe you had someone else in mind."

She reached for his hand, and he moved it away.

"No," she replied. "I didn't have anyone else in mind. You're still the guy I fell in love with. But you're treating me like I'm your enemy."

Jack ground out his cigarette and immediately lit another. "It feels like you are. You used to understand that I need the art scene. And you used to respect my paintings."

What was he talking about? She'd always ... Oh

* * *

The newest one; he'd shown it to her last week—she'd gasped at the sight: a black and white figure with wings instead of arms, its face obscured by bright copper flames. A rainbow spilled from a slash in its belly onto a black rectangle at its clawed feet.

"What do you think?" Jack had asked, and Kate felt like he was challenging her to say something positive. "I call it 'Angel.'"

The best response she had to offer was, "It's ... interesting."

* * *

He must have caught the lie in her voice at the time, but she'd thought he let it go. She'd thought wrong.

His coffee cup was empty. She got up and took it to the kitchen for a refill. "That new one," she said, over her shoulder. "It surprised me. I'm sorry ... it's taking me a while to get used to it—it's so different."

His voice came, unexpectedly, from right behind her. "Well, hurry on up, because there's more where it came from."

Hot coffee splashed onto her hand.

Kate gave the mug to Jack and rubbed her reddened skin. "What does Gino say about it?"

Jack snorted. "Finelli? That old fud? He hates it!"

"So—"

"Finelli's finished, Kate. He's old news. I'm not going to let him take me down with him." He stared hard at Kate and continued. "Nikki Frank likes 'Angel.' She gets it."

Nikki Frank, Nikki Frank. Kate was tired of hearing that name. Kate had first met the woman at her trendy gallery on La Cienega —*the* prestige location for showcasing modern art in L.A. Knife-thin, with a halo of curly black hair, Nikki had looked right through Kate and had only spoken to her once, addressing her as "Karen" until Jack corrected her. She was enthusiastic about Jack's work but kept urging him into darker and edgier paintings. Of course she'd like "Angel." She'd practically designed it.

"Nikki wants to represent me," Jack continued. "I'm finished with Gino."

"But he gave you your first show..." Kate protested.

Jack yawned and stretched. "So? Loyalty is overrated—haven't you figured that out?"

"I'm sorry I don't *get* the new painting, Jack. It's so ... so angry."

"There's a lot to be angry about, Honey."

When had she gone from "Babe" to "Honey"?

"I know there is, but—"

He leaned against the counter, his eyes hard and narrowed. "But you're so buried in your little corporate dungeon you don't see it. Look around. Quit being so wrapped up in—"

That did it.

"My little corporate dungeon paid your way for a lot of years."

Jack's right hand swooped through the air. "Here we go! Trot out the 'after all I've done for you' bit now. Wish I'd known your support came with a price tag."

"Stop it! We're talking like we hate each other."

She ran her hands through her hair and tried to step away from the angry words they were flinging at each other.

"I'm sorry," she said. "For everything. I won't get in your way again. And I'll learn to love your new stuff, I promise."

"Well, see, there's the problem." Jack held up his index finger. "For one thing, it's not 'stuff.' It's art. Until you get that, there's not much else to say. And you shouldn't have to work at liking it."

He lit another cigarette without offering the pack to her.

Kate took one anyway and struck a match to it.

"I'm sorry. I said the wrong thing. I didn't mean it like that."

"Yeah, you did. You can't help it."

She waved away cigarette smoke that was burning her eyes. "What next, Jack? What do we do? How do we fix this?"

"I don't know that we can."

She started to protest that of course they could find their way out of this mess, but Jack kept talking.

"I need some time away from you," he said. "Some breathing room."

She couldn't believe what he was saying. *Breathing room? What the hell?*

"How much more space do you need? You're gone more than you're here."

"A lot more." He paused and mashed out his cigarette. "I'm going to move back into the studio. Live there."

This was wrong. He was bluffing, surely. He wanted something from her, and if she gave it up, then he'd stop acting like an asshole, and things would shift back into place.

But she couldn't find the magic trick to make it happen.

Her cigarette had burned down to the filter, and she threw it in the ash tray. "So—just like that—you're bailing on me? For what? *Why?*"

He turned and started down the hall. "I've tried to explain it, Kate. You don't want to understand."

She followed. "I do. But you have to help."

He took his duffle bag from the closet and started stuffing jeans and shirts into it. "I'm tired of trying."

The absurdity of it overwhelmed her; fury replaced disbelief. Past hurts and disappointments boiled over.

"That's great, Jack. You decide I'm too much trouble—now—and just snap your fingers and say it's over. How convenient." Kate was screaming. Shrieking like a banshee. And she didn't care. "The hell with you, and your fancy new friends, and your ugly new painting. If that's how you want it, go ahead. I thought you were a better person than that. Stupid me. You act like you can live by a different set of rules than anyone else."

He zipped up the duffle. "There you go—that's what's wrong with us, Kate. You don't get it. You never did. There *are* different rules for artists. We can't live some tidy little life like the one you want, the one your parents had."

Her hand whipped out before she knew what was happening, and she slapped him, hard.

A red mark appeared on his cheek, and he smiled at her, like he'd wanted her to do that, and the smile fed her anger.

"I don't have a *tidy little life*," she said, in a voice so harsh she didn't recognize it. "In case you hadn't noticed, my life isn't all that easy. I don't always feel like going to work, but I do, so we can pay the rent and buy groceries. I'm your biggest cheering section. Or at least I used to be, when you let me. But you—you've bought into the bullshit those girls are telling you, the ones like that Amanda. They treat you like some kind of movie star."

"To them, maybe I am. They appreciate what I do."

"And I don't?"

He scowled at her. "No, you don't. You don't know the first thing about being an artist."

"And she does? That Amanda?"

"Why do you keep saying her name like that?" He mimicked

Kate's tone. "'That Amanda.' Believe it or not, Amanda knows more about what it takes to be an artist than you ever could."

The way his voice softened around Amanda's name told Kate the truth.

"You're screwing her."

Jack's mouth opened, but he didn't say anything. Then he picked up his duffle and turned away.

"You are such a cliché, Jack Morrison. I thought you were better than that."

"Guess you were wrong."

He took a step toward the door, and she blocked his way. "You can't leave like this."

"Let me go, Kate."

She had to stop him; if he left, she might never be able to get him back. This had all come on so suddenly, so breathtakingly fast. She fumbled for something to make him reconsider.

"You better not take my painting!" It was a stupid demand, but the only thing she could come up with that might strike home.

He smiled, but there was no happiness in it. "I won't." He looked over his shoulder at "Sanctuary" and hesitated, and Kate thought she'd found the key, the thing that would keep him at home. Then his expression shifted. "I gave it to you. I don't take back things I give away."

Kate hadn't budged. "You better not," she repeated, sounding like a scared little kid.

"Get out of the way, Kate."

"No!"

He pushed her, just enough to move her aside, but Kate hadn't expected it, and she stumbled backward, onto the bed. Her ankle struck the metal frame, and pain knifed up her leg.

She lay on the lumpy, jumbled bedcovers, too stunned to speak. Jack started to reach for her, and behind him she could see the silhouette of "Sanctuary." Suddenly, she hated it, and she hated Jack, and she hated herself.

"Get out!" Her words twisted with rage. "I can't stand the sight of you. I can't stand being married to you."

Jack nodded and turned away. "Fine with me," he called out on his way down the hall.

He didn't slam the door, but the sound of its closing struck Kate like thunder. She picked up an ash tray and hurled it at the space where he'd been. It hit the wall and thudded to the floor.

Unlike the rest of her life, it didn't shatter.

Chapter Twenty-Five

K ate had never liked Sundays. The world seemed to pause for
breath, and the ensuing quiet brought memories of starched
dresses and Sunday School. Loneliness thrived on Sundays.

But never had the empty silence ached as much as it did the
morning after Jack left.

She busied herself with mundane tasks, but when every piece of
furniture was dusted, every floor swept, every countertop scrubbed,
there was nothing left to do but sit and listen to her heartbeat.

She rubbed her burning eyes and studied the wedding ring Josie
had forced on her as an heirloom. Kate had never found the nerve to
replace it with something more to her taste. Now, as sunlight fell
across her hand, Kate realized she had neglected the ring; soap residue
clung to the setting, and the diamonds didn't shine the way they
used to.

Kate found a soft old toothbrush and went to work on the ring,
scrubbing away soap scum and polishing the stones. Maybe this would
help restore the strength in her marriage. Maybe this act of contrition
would bring Jack back.

He had to come back eventually. Didn't he? Sure, they'd had some
rocky times lately, Jack all caught up in his newfound celebrity, women

fawning over him, pawing at him like hungry cats. And Amanda—even Trudy Zelnik had picked up on Amanda's true nature. Trudy had warned Kate. Why hadn't she listened? Preoccupied with her own needs, her own career, she'd practically shoved Jack into Amanda's grasping arms.

Wait a minute. This was wrong. So what if she put her own needs first once in a while? Did that justify Jack's betrayal? She'd supported him in every possible way for eight years. *Eight years.* And he acted like it was nothing.

"What else are you gonna do for me?" That was his attitude.

And when he didn't get enough, he'd tossed her aside, like he had Gino Finelli, and moved on to someone new.

"Screw you, Jack Morrison," Kate muttered. "I don't deserve this."

The next minute she was bawling again, blubbering "Please come back. We can work this through. We have to."

When the doorbell rang, her thoughts ran wild, throwing logic aside. *Jack! He changed his mind!*

She scraped tears from her cheeks and ran for the door. Her throat ached from crying.

Stella Barberini stood in the doorway, biting her lower lip.

"Jesus, hon," Stella said, "you look awful. What happened?"

"Jack and I had a bad fight." More tears flowed. "He left."

"I figured. All that yelling yesterday ... these thin old walls ... I heard you crying."

Kate slumped into the doorjamb.

"Hey, you don't have to go spilling your guts to me if you don't want to, but sometimes it helps to have company. Why don't I come sit with you for a while?"

Kate didn't know what she wanted. Grief and disbelief numbed her. Stella slipped past her into the living room, looking around like she maybe expected to see smashed dishes or toppled furniture.

When Kate offered coffee, Stella nudged her toward the sofa.

"I'll get it," she said, and came back carrying mugs for each of them. The coffee was murky and stale, but Kate welcomed its bitter taste. She lit a cigarette and poured out the story, chain-smoking and choking on still more tears. Just when she thought she'd cried herself dry, another flood erupted.

"That bastard," Stella said when Kate finished.

"Something's happened to him," Kate said. Her tongue was thick and fuzzy from the cigarettes. "He's changed. And I never saw it coming."

"The wife is usually the last to know," Stella said. "She's too close."

"Did *you* know? With Lars?"

Stella took a sip of coffee and grimaced. "Sort of."

Kate's stomach twisted, and she clamped her hand over her mouth; for a horrible second she feared she was going to throw up.

Stella stood. "We need to get some food into you. Pronto. And coffee that doesn't taste like battery acid."

"I'm not hungry."

"Of course you aren't. But I'm gonna make you eat anyway."

In the kitchen, Stella opened the fridge. "Ah! Eggs! And spinach. I'm gonna make you a spinach omelet."

Kate leaned against the counter and watched Stella break eggs into a bowl. The shells fractured so easily, as if they'd been waiting for the blow; all it took was a sharp tap in the right place. She pushed the thought away and put bread in the toaster, took out butter to soften.

Stella whisked the eggs and poured them into a skillet, keeping up a steady stream of neutral chatter. Had Kate heard the new Bette Midler album? Did she think Jimmy Carter was doing OK as president? Was it possible Elvis had faked his own death? Kate murmured responses but couldn't remember what she'd said seconds after the words left her mouth.

The routine tasks and the comfort of Stella's company smoothed the edges of Kate's misery. She dumped out the last dregs of coffee and stared at the dark liquid flowing down the drain. Then she started a fresh pot—fresh coffee, fresh start. If only she could do that with Jack.

The toast popped up, and the heat of it, the slightly burnt smell, reassured her that her senses still worked. She spread butter on the toast and watched it melt.

Stella slid the omelet onto a plate and sliced it neatly in half. "Voilà. Bon appétit."

They carried their breakfast to the dining room and sat across from each other. Stella smiled, dusted her hands on her jeans, and lifted her coffee cup in a toast.

"Here's to survival."

Kate wasn't sure what that meant, but she clinked her cup against Stella's.

"This tastes really good," she said around a mouthful of omelet.

Stella smirked. "Told ya."

Kate laughed, then stopped herself.

"It's okay, hon," Stella told her. "It's okay to laugh."

Kate put down her fork and wiped her mouth. "What if he doesn't come back, Stel?"

Stella swallowed her food. "Wouldn't be the end of the world."

"Yeah. It would." She shuddered. "He has to come back."

"And then what?"

"We'll figure it out," Kate replied. We always have."

Stella looked down at her plate. "You need to start thinking ahead, kiddo. Focus on your future."

"Jack is my future."

"Really? And you're *his* future? You sure?"

Kate's appetite vanished. She shoved her food around for a minute or two and then lit a cigarette. Stella frowned but didn't protest.

Stella waved away the drifting smoke. "Man, this is such an old story. I really hoped it'd be different with you guys."

Kate sighed. "I never expected to become a cliché."

Stella patted the back of Kate's hand. "You're not." She smiled. "I predict a very bright future for you. You're young, smart, pretty. You have a good job, and—thank you, Gloria Steinem—women finally have a shot at some *real* careers."

"I guess." She thought about what Stella had said. Yeah, things had improved for women at work, even at old-school Permian. Ten years ago she'd never have advanced as far as she had.

Stella tapped her own head. "I *know*. Hell, when the ERA gets ratified—and it *will*, it has to—nobody's gonna be able to look down on us ever again. Women have been brainwashed into thinking we have no power. Wrong!"

Her dark curls swayed with every word.

"So," Kate said, "you're telling me that at least I have a career, even if my marriage is a disaster."

"The marriage disaster is not your fault, hon."

"It is. I got too caught up in my own career. I quit paying attention to him."

"Like that would have made a difference," Stella said. She snorted. "Jack and his big-shot artist act. I hate the way he gets when *art people* are around—like they're all that's important. Like he's better than the rest of us, because he's an *artist*."

"Maybe he is."

Stella glared at her. "Don't you believe that for one second, Kate. He used it as an excuse to behave like a shit."

Kate met her friend's eyes. "You knew something was up with Jack."

"Yeah, hon—and you did, too, but you didn't want to admit it. Hell, even your druggie friend Ryder noticed."

"You and Ryder talked? About us? Wait—I thought you guys hated each other."

Stella looked like a kid caught with one hand in the cookie jar. "Call it love-hate. I get pissed off when people squander their talent. He was trashing his life and ruining his voice. But at least Ryder had principles."

She paused and studied Kate for a minute. "That's why he moved out."

"He didn't move out," Kate protested. "Jack kicked him out."

The dark curls trembled. "Nope. He might have told you that, but the truth was Ryder couldn't put up with ... with Jack's Mr. Great Artist act."

Something in her expression bothered Kate.

"Stella? What are you not telling me?"

Stella pressed her lips together for a second before she answered. "Ryder told me he was sick of Jack bringing his groupies to the studio. For...you know for what."

The meaning of Stella's words sank in, and Kate set her coffee cup down hard. "That can't be true. Sure, Amanda seduced him, but..."

Stella put her hand on Kate's wrist. "She wasn't the first."

"Why didn't you tell me? We're friends!"

"I didn't think it was my place. And to be honest, I thought maybe you knew but didn't want to let on, or you were okay with it. Some women are."

Kate shook her head, still stunned. "No," she whispered. "I had no idea. And I'm still not sure it's true."

But reality crystallized. The times Jack came home late, smelling of stale smoke and wine and someone else's perfume. Women were always hugging him and transferring their scent, so it hadn't set off any alarm bells for Kate. Oh, how stupid she'd been! How blind.

Stella picked up their plates and headed for the kitchen. Numbly, Kate rose and followed. She needed to do something with her hands, something to take her mind off what Stella had told her.

She scraped the crumbs of their breakfast into the trash while Stella washed the skillet. Neither of them spoke. Kate's thoughts whirled in a tangled mess. Jack? With other women? How many? Who? When?

She started to cry again. Hell, would she ever be able to stop?

Stella turned from the sink and put her arms around Kate, patting her back. "I'm so sorry, hon. Maybe I should've kept my big mouth shut. But I couldn't stand to see you beating yourself up for his leaving. It wasn't your fault."

Kate tried to seize the reassurance, but it evaporated like smoke.

"Jack does love me," she said. "He always…"

Her brain balked. *He always what?* She broke away from Stella and lit a cigarette.

Finally, she picked up the thread of what she'd been saying. "Sometimes we're so tuned into each other it's scary. Like on my birthday when he gave me the painting."

The pity on Stella's face said it all. That had been over a year ago.

More caustic tears leaked out. "What am I gonna do, Stel?"

Stella took Kate by the shoulders. "You don't believe this, but you are going to be fine. Jack was draining you dry. Now you can have your life back."

"What if I don't want it back?" Kate whispered. Through the maze of feelings, one certainty reigned. If Jack walked through the door at that minute, she'd be down on her knees, apologizing, begging him to stay. She loved him so much, he was her whole life.

"What am I going to do on my own? I can't handle it. I'm all alone."

"In the first place, you are *not* alone," Stella replied. She released Kate and held up one finger, then a second. "In the second place, you've been on your own all along—you didn't know it, but you were. We all are."

"I am so pathetic."

Stella shook her head. "You're not pathetic. Just delusional."

Kate took a drag off her Marlboro and watched the exhaled smoke dissipate. "I can't think what to do next."

"You'll figure it out. You'll survive. I did, and I'm not half as tough as you."

"No way."

"Yeah, I've really had it easy. Oh, the marriage, Lars, that was fucked, yeah. But otherwise, things have pretty much gone the way I wanted. And you—I mean, the thing with your dad, having to quit school. That's big-time trouble. But look at you now—and you did it all on your own, hon. All on your own."

Kate gave herself a minute to think on what her friend had said. She *had* advanced her career through hard work and skill, along with some luck. She'd supported Jack for eight years. And her dad's death: the world had ended for her then, the world she'd known all her life. But she had taken the blow and kept going, worked through the chaos and the grief. She'd learned about survival when Dad died; she could use that knowledge again. Maybe she wasn't such a loser after all. Kate ached to believe Stella.

"This is a good time to be a woman," Stella continued. "I keep harping on this, but it's true. You'll see. You'll end up running your company someday, and you'll remember how Jack held you back and made you feel second-rate, and you'll laugh your ass off."

Kate managed a smile. "Maybe."

"Here's something else," Stella said. "I thought *my* life was over when Lars and I split up. But it turned out, the day our divorce became final was the happiest day of my life. I finally got out from under his shadow."

Kate nodded, dimly suspecting that Stella was exaggerating, and loving her for it. "I hope you're right."

"I'm always right."

Kate soaped and rinsed their breakfast plates and put them in the tray to drain. "Thanks, Stel. I feel better. Honest."

"You know what you need now? A nice hot shower, and then we'll go to the movies, see something funny and forget all about Jack Morrison, the creep." Stella gently pushed her aside and finished washing their dishes. "You'll be fine. You don't believe me yet, but you will. You don't have any other choice. Go on now. Clean yourself up."

Kate squared her shoulders and sashayed toward the bathroom. "I'll go clean myself up. Then I'll see about cleaning up my life."

Behind her, above the clatter of silverware, she heard Stella proclaim, "Now you're talking."

Chapter Twenty-Six
April – October 1978

"Kate, honey? It's me—Jack—but you probably figured that out...Babe, sure wish you'd call me back—I've left a ton of messages."

* * *

Jack had done more than that. As his voice spilled out of her answering machine, Kate reflected on the letters he'd sent: letters full of apologies and pleas for forgiveness and another chance. She'd crumpled the first one and thrown it in the trash. The next two she folded and put in a kitchen drawer.

He'd phoned her at the office, too, and each time she hung up on him and then sat with palms pressed so hard on the desktop that the veins bulged on the backs of her hands.

At home she let the machine screen her calls, and she lost count of the times Jack had tried to get through. She never responded, except to mutter to the machine, "You left *me*, dammit."

But she couldn't deny that she missed him. The holidays had been harsh and lonely, and she'd started the new year full of worry and regret.

* * *

"I know I hurt you," Jack's recorded voice continued, "and I'm so sorry, Babe. I was an asshole. I went crazy there for a while. But I miss you so much. I think about you all the time, and I'd give anything —*anything*, Kate—if you'd let me back in. I promise to make it up to you. Call me. Please."

Kate started to erase the message, then changed her mind. She walked away from the machine, but she couldn't escape her tangled feelings.

This was stupid. He wanted her back. Why was she fighting it? Had she given up on him, and her marriage? Wasn't Jack entitled to one mistake?

"Not me doin' the ruinin', man. Go look in the mirror."

"Hell, Kate, even your druggie friend Ryder noticed...he was sick of Jack bringing his groupies to the studio."

"But that was then. This is now," Kate whispered to the silent apartment. She turned toward the phone. *Don't go there.* Her hand hovered.

She turned away.

* * *

Jack's phone calls and letters continued, and Kate stiffened her spine and ignored them, but the interior argument continued, over and over.

Maybe he'd changed.

No, people didn't change that much, that fast.

"Not me doin' the ruinin', man. Go look in the mirror."

She enrolled in Cal State L.A. for the summer quarter, looking forward to being buried in coursework that would fill empty hours where temptation could creep in. As Jack's phone calls became less frequent, Kate almost convinced herself that her new life was better. She could set her own schedule and make her own choices with no guilt or scorn for her corporate ambitions, no put-downs or broken promises. No lies.

Stella urged her to see a divorce lawyer, but Kate delayed. No sense rushing into it; the process would be time-consuming and expensive. These thoughts played out like a phonograph record stuck in a groove.

* * *

One spring evening after work, she stopped by the Broadway Plaza downtown. The days were lengthening and warming, and she needed, or at least wanted, a couple of new outfits to go with the weather.

And there in the courtyard of the shopping center, she saw Jack Morrison. He was talking to a woman facing away from Kate, and something about her shiny silver-blond hair seemed familiar. Then she turned her head. Morel. Or, in Ryder's terms, "the Star-Fucker."

Kate almost dropped her purse. She blinked, and Amanda Durant's image flickered.

The scents of perfume and chocolate assailed her as shoppers jostled past, voices reverberating from window glass and terrazzo. Dusty green philodendron leaves spilled from pots that lined the courtyard. Kate noticed a woman's black stiletto, missing its heel, on the floor near one of the pots. Across the courtyard and oblivious to everyone but Jack, Morel appeared untouched by time as she caressed Jack's arm, her hand moving over the blue plaid shirt Kate had given him on that long-ago Christmas.

Kate turned toward the elevator and jabbed the call button, all thoughts of shopping abandoned. Inside the elevator, she moved behind a chubby teenage girl who tugged at a messy ponytail and gave Kate a curious look before popping a huge pink gum bubble.

So what! Kate chided herself. *It's not like we're still married.*

Early in the marriage, Kate had loved being described as "Jack Morrison's wife." It symbolized safety and gave her a sense of belonging. By the end, the label had become a burden.

She was no longer "Jack Morrison's wife." But who *was* she?

Time to find out.

* * *

Monday morning, she phoned Stella's divorce lawyer and started the process for a no-fault divorce. Jack barely protested. Why would he? There was little to contest: no children, no real property. Nothing to fight over, except the memories.

She and Jack eventually fashioned a truce, and after a while, when emotions had cooled, Kate could acknowledge Jack's good qualities, the ones that had attracted her to him in the first place. She wasn't *in love* with him anymore; that was too dangerous. But she didn't hate him either, not the way Stella hated her ex. And, even if he hadn't meant to, Jack had set her free, started her moving toward independence. It didn't feel half bad.

By October, Kate had completed two college courses with respectable grades and was in the third week of the fall quarter. She settled into her new routine: work and school, school and work. Sleep deprivation became a way of life.

* * *

One night she found herself overwhelmed with drowsiness as she sat through Management Principles in a stuffy Cal State L.A. classroom. The school's air conditioning fought a losing battle with an Indian Summer heat wave, and despite the uncomfortable chair and harsh lighting, Kate's eyes kept closing.

The instructor, Eric Ames, a forty-ish, fit-looking man, had a resonant voice that usually got through to her, and the discussion focused on conflict resolution, a skill she yearned to develop. Professor Ames had emphasized the importance of staying objective during workplace confrontations, and Kate wondered how a person managed that miracle.

* * *

She'd had a run-in that afternoon with Jeff Gallo, who had recently been moved from Labor Relations into Benefits as part of a cross-training initiative. Things were moving and shaking in Kate's work world, and Gallo's transfer was part of it. Paul Lange's newly-titled

Human Resources Department had taken on companywide responsibility for personnel issues, and Lange had charged Kate with developing consistent procedures across the board. She needed a helper, and Gallo was available.

Their reporting relationship was deliberately vague, and Gallo made it clear to anyone who would listen that he worked *with* Kate, not *for* her. Lange didn't like the arrangement, but Gallo had a college degree, and Kate did not. Yet.

At first, Kate welcomed Gallo and shared her knowledge and experience—until she discovered he was more hindrance than help. The guy was lazy. He interrupted her constantly, ignored her instructions, and if an assignment was done incorrectly he claimed it was because she hadn't explained it well enough. Sometimes she could barely disguise her dislike for him—a dislike fueled by the memory of his involvement with Dee Dee Carr years ago. Gallo had broken off the affair and apparently had managed to stay married, but Kate doubted that he'd stayed faithful. He had an attitude of entitlement that reminded her of Jack Morrison at his worst, although she struggled not to judge Gallo by her own sad experience.

That afternoon Gallo had shown a typical, patronizing response when Kate asked if he'd finished his part of a policy draft for the boss.

"What's the rush?" he'd asked with a lazy smile.

"It's already Thursday, Jeff, and Paul wants to review it over the weekend. I told you that when I gave you the paperwork."

Gallo shook his head. "No, you didn't." He put down his pen and leaned forward, hands splayed on his desktop. "You've had a lot on your mind lately, haven't you? Things slip through the cracks when you're stressed out. You need to quit trying so hard to please Lange. Hold back a little so he doesn't dump more work on you. Learn how to chill out."

"That seems to be working for you," Kate had muttered. She wanted to snatch the unfinished draft and do it herself, but that would let him win. No way.

* * *

Kate's attention was yanked back into the classroom when Eric Ames asked, "Anyone have an answer?" He scanned the classroom. "Ms. Morrison?"

Kate jerked upright as her brain scrambled to pick up the threads of the discussion.

"I'm sorry," she mumbled. "I lost track of the question."

This kind of disgrace was new to her. She'd been a good student, back when her only priority had been to learn. Now, juggling many roles, she wondered if too much time had passed since she left the university.

Professor Ames was standing a few feet away, and she saw no scorn in his expression. Clear hazel eyes sparkled behind his eyeglasses. "It *was* rather convoluted." He addressed the guy sitting behind Kate. "Mr. Graves, could you be more specific?"

Jerry Graves, whose perpetual smirk reminded Kate of Jeff Gallo, asked a lot of questions, usually designed to show off.

"I said," Graves replied, and Kate could *feel* his sneer even if she couldn't see it, "your *quid pro quo* theory isn't so easy to apply in the real world. Sometimes both sides can't get what they want. What happens then?"

Eric Ames looked at Kate, and she saw a kind of *acknowledgment* in his eyes, as if he was sharing a joke with her. "Ms. Morrison?"

Embarrassment clouded her thoughts. Then she heard herself say, "It's not so much both getting exactly what they want, as long as they get *something*."

Ames rocked back on his heels and smiled. "Can you elucidate?"

Damned if he didn't wink at her.

"What I mean is, suppose both people want..." she held up her pen. "This pen. They can't both have it, so one gets the pen, and the other gets ... a pencil. Or a sheet of paper."

A small wave of laughter rippled through the classroom.

"The principle of substitution," said Ames. "Exactly right."

"But they have to believe they're getting something just as good," she added. "Otherwise it doesn't work."

* * *

At the break, Kate hustled outside to the coffee cart. The brew they sold was thick and stale by nine p.m., but she didn't care. Anything to help her stay alert.

Freed from the claustrophobic classroom, Kate savored the night air before lighting a cigarette, once more promising herself to quit smoking. It was bad for her health and reminded her of Jack. But damn, that first puff tasted so good.

Some of her fellow students clustered a few yards away, talking and laughing. Not a smoker in the bunch, so Kate stayed away and took another drag on her Marlboro. Behind her she heard the click of a lighter and smelled burning tobacco. She glanced around—her fellow smoker was Eric Ames.

She smiled at him and pointed to the others. "That's where we should be. With the nonsmokers."

He waved his cigarette, trails of smoke fanning out into the darkness. "It's a nasty habit."

Kate took a hit off her Marlboro. "Addiction is vicious. It has us by the throat."

Ames nodded. "Quite literally." A vapor stream punctuated his words. After a pause, and without looking at Kate, he added, "I didn't put you on the spot in there, did I? I knew you'd have a good answer."

"No problem. And I didn't mean to drift off—it wasn't from boredom."

"You wouldn't be the first if you had."

His tone was humble, and Kate felt a surge of sympathy. "It has to be a challenge, keeping us all engaged. Everybody's worn out from work."

"Don't I know it."

He probably had a day job, too. Until that moment, Kate hadn't given much thought to her teacher's reality, but maybe he was just as tired as she was. As they all were.

The night closed in around them, bringing the sweet scent of clematis, underlaid with wood smoke. Steam drifted from their coffee cups, and the nearby benches and tables blurred into darkness.

After a brief silence, Professor Ames asked, "And what brings you here? To college, I mean."

"My job," Kate replied, and then added, "I'm a Benefits Specialist at Permian Oil." Did that sound pretentious?

His eyebrows went up. "Big company."

"Yes."

He took another drag on his cigarette and studied its glowing tip. "The oil business: I imagine the old-boy network still reigns?"

"It does, but I'm trying to break through it."

He raised his cup to her. "Good for you!" He paused. "Men have made some royal messes of the business world. I say, let's get women into management and let them clean it up."

She laughed in surprise, and the teacher cocked his head. "What? You didn't expect a man would think that way?"

"You sound a lot like my best friend Stella—and she's a radical feminist."

"There are worse things to be, Ms. Morrison."

He finished his cigarette—a power smoker, like Jack—and doused it in the ashtray but didn't walk away, as if waiting for Kate to finish her Marlboro, which she quickly did.

Checking her watch, she said, "Guess we should go back. Don't want to keep the class waiting."

Ames turned toward the classroom, walking slowly, like a person deep in thought. Kate matched her pace to his.

"You're going for your degree in Business?" he asked.

It sounded so straightforward when he said it, this trim, sandy-haired man, success radiating around him in his unrumpled gray suit. Up close, he was taller and better looking than she had realized.

"Yes," she replied, then gave him a brief version of her academic history, without explaining why she left UCSB. "But it was ten years ago, and I lost most of my credits. I have to make up so many of them."

They reached the classroom, and he held the door open. In the lighted doorway, Kate noticed Ames's eyes again: pale and almost transparent gray-green. Kind eyes.

"Don't let the difficulties stop you. You'll never regret finishing your education, Ms. Morrison. I promise you."

She held out her hand. "Kate. And thanks for the pep talk, Professor Ames. I needed it tonight."

He shook her hand with a warm, dry grip. "Eric. And you're most welcome."

With that, he returned to the front of the classroom, all business. Kate watched him transform into the professor role, straightening his jacket and tossing his coffee cup in the wastebasket with negligent ease. His kind eyes masked by reflections bouncing from his glasses, Eric lifted his chin and looked around the classroom.

"As I was saying before the break, conflict in the workplace is inevitable. But you can choose how it affects you. You can choose your battles."

Maybe it was the coffee, and maybe it was the conversation with her teacher, or both, but Kate had no trouble staying awake for the second half of class.

Chapter Twenty-Seven
November 1978

"Friday night in the big city," Kate muttered as she fought her way home in rush hour traffic. She should have stayed at work until everyone else got where they were going; her heavy briefcase would have been much lighter.

But the empty workplace had spooked her—so many darkened offices and silent telephones. She'd held out for half an hour, then packed up her files, turned off the light, and gotten sucked into commuter quicksand.

For what? An empty apartment, a frozen-food dinner, and an hour or two with her class homework. Why did life have to be so hard? With nothing to do but wait for the next green light, Kate let the dark thoughts in.

Thanksgiving lurked two weeks away. Without any special plans of her own, she'd accepted her mother's invitation to the family gathering, which would include the newlyweds: Kate's sister Debbie and her husband Roy Schlosser. Kate had been amazed when her serial-boyfriend sister had settled on *one* guy: a quiet, steady fellow at that. Thanksgiving, then, might be long and boring, but she was grateful not to be spending it alone.

"Enough!" Kate said aloud. She loosened her grip on the steering wheel and flexed her fingers, and finally traffic thinned out enough that she could use her accelerator more than her brakes. She turned onto her street and found a parking place right in front of the apartment.

As she looked up at her dark windows, Kate made a mental promise to buy a timer so the living room light would be on when she came home. When she passed Stella's silent apartment, envy flared. Her neighbor had gone to a writers' retreat in Palm Springs for the weekend.

"That's what I need," Kate mumbled. "A retreat."

She dumped her paperwork on the dining table, kicked off her high heels, and padded to the kitchen for a glass of wine and a survey of the fridge's contents.

Then she noticed that the back door was ajar. The door connected the kitchen to a narrow flight of outside stairs that led to the trash cans.

When was the last time she'd taken out trash, and could she possibly have forgotten to close the door?

"I don't think so," Kate whispered. She glanced around the kitchen for a weapon, breath freezing, mind churning.

The phone rang, shattering the silence.

Kate expelled a lungful of air and seized the wall phone. "Hello."

The word came out hoarse with fright.

"Bad time to call?" asked Jack Morrison.

Jack? Confusion at the unexpected sound of his voice mingled with grateful relief.

"Sort of," Kate replied.

"I had a feeling," he said.

Jack and his "feelings." *I always know where you are, Babe. I always know when you need me. I feel it.*

"What's going on?" he asked.

She told him about the open door.

"Is Stella home?" Jack's voice was filled with urgency.

"No. Gone for the weekend."

"Go outside. Right now. Wait in the car. I'm on my way."

Kate grabbed her purse and car keys, crammed on her shoes, and raced to her car. Then she started to regret alarming Jack, probably for nothing. But he had called her, he'd sensed something wrong. On that dark, lonely night, Kate didn't care if she looked like an idiot.

And what if there was an intruder in the apartment? Shouldn't she call the police? No, Jack would decide. He always knew what to do. And somehow their magical connection had withstood the divorce. Kate let that realization tumble through her thoughts, drowning out fear and embarrassment.

Ten minutes later his pickup roared up the street. Kate got out to greet him, and Jack hurried toward her, shoulder-length hair billowing out. A cigarette dangled from his lips, and he spit it into the street in a fiery arc.

"Hey," he said, and Kate fell into his open arms.

She'd left her coat upstairs and didn't comprehend how cold she was until Jack hugged her. He smelled so safe, so familiar—cigarettes and oil paint, and she'd probably see splatters of red and blue and brown on his jeans when they got into the light.

"Mmm, you smell good," Jack whispered, rubbing her back.

"Eau de fear," Kate said and forced out a giggle.

"Get back in the car," Jack told her. "I'll go check out the apartment."

"No way in hell are you going in there alone. I'm backing you up."

He pulled a crowbar from the pickup's bed and handed it to her. "Okay then. Hit first and ask questions later."

They went from room to room, yanking curtains aside and poking into dark closet corners. Kate's heart sped up every time they came to another possible hiding place. Her hands hurt from clutching the crowbar. They finished the search without finding anything out of place.

Kate rolled her eyes. "I feel so stupid, panicking like that. The dumb door sticks—I probably just didn't close it tight."

Jack patted her back. "We'll never know for sure. Maybe somebody was here, and you scared them off."

"Oh right, I'm so intimidating. More likely they hightailed it when they heard the cavalry was coming." She squeezed his arm. "I can't thank you enough, racing over here like this."

"I wasn't doing anything important anyway. It was a good excuse to see you." Jack chuckled. "I miss you."

The air softened and warmed.

"I miss you too," Kate said.

The words hung there like smoke.

Jack cocked his head. "All that adrenaline made me hungry. Want to grab a taco at Felipe's?"

How could she turn down an offer like that?

Chapter Twenty-Eight

F elipe's hadn't changed: same tacky mural of a Mexican village, same red-taloned hostess with her layers of pancake makeup and inch-long eyelashes. And the same frosty, lethal margaritas. Kate and Jack clinked glasses, took that exquisite first sip, and let the icy potion jolt their brains.

She took another swallow and felt her muscles unclench as she inhaled the aromas of cilantro and salsa.

"Mmmmm, this is just what the doctor ordered," she said.

Jack smiled and lifted his glass again. "Here's to vanishing prowlers."

He looked so appealing in the warm candlelight. And he'd come through for her that night, without asking questions or laying blame. Why *hadn't* they been able to make the marriage work?

A waitress sashayed past, a curvy young woman with dark hair cascading down her back; her very short skirt clung to her hips. Jack followed the girl's moves, his gaze lingering a few extra heartbeats.

Oh yeah, Kate thought. *That's why.*

"So," Jack said, "how are you? How's work? How's the family? Debbie finally married that goon, right?"

"Roy? Yeah. Last April. How'd you know?"

"She sent me an invitation," Jack replied. "But I didn't think it'd be cool to go. I sent a present."

"She didn't tell me. That was nice of you."

"Hey, I'm a nice guy."

"You don't have to tell me. Nobody else would come to my rescue tonight."

"Nobody? Really? You don't have some fellow on the hook, dying to play hero?"

Kate traced a circle in the margarita frost. "No time."

"Come on! Is work that brutal?"

"Work, and school. Yeah. The best I can do is squeeze in a movie with Stella a couple of times a month."

"She still hate my guts?" asked Jack.

"Let's change the subject."

He took another sip, then set his glass down. "Okay, enough small talk. Seriously—how are you doing, Babe?"

How could one little word pierce her soul?

She counted to ten before replying. "Seriously? I'm good. Most of the time. And you?"

He shrugged. "The show at Nikki's did pretty well."

"Yeah, that was a nice review in the *Times*. She called you the new de Kooning."

Jack flushed. "I'm not so sure that's a compliment."

His discomfort made Kate wonder if the reviewer had seen more of Jack than the paintings at Nikki Frank's gallery.

"Finelli must've been really sad to lose you."

Another shrug. "He still has a few of my paintings. He'll keep making money off me. And Nikki—man, that woman can *promote*."

"That's great, Jack."

"You got my invitation to the opening, right? I wish you'd've come."

"Couldn't get there," Kate replied. "But I did go see the show later. The work is beautiful, Jack. You keep getting better and better." She paused. "I'm glad you left that angry phase behind."

She said it lightly and was relieved he took it well. He chuckled, in fact. "You were right about that. Like always."

"Not always. So what are you working on now? More like the ones at Nikki's?"

He drained his glass and signaled their waitress for another round. *Go with the flow,* Kate told herself.

"I'm taking a new direction—again. I think you'll like these; they're...cleaner. Experimenting with abstract shapes, blending colors."

"Sounds intriguing."

He brushed a lock of hair from his forehead. "We'll see. Nikki's not so sure—she worries I'm losing my edge, but they feel *right.* I wish you could see them—I miss getting your take on my work. You have a better eye for it than anyone I know." He paused and sipped from his empty glass while Kate absorbed his remark.

"Anyway," Jack went on, "enough art stuff—how's the job?"

"It's good. Tough sometimes—but when I get it right..." She wiggled her fingers at him. "Like you don't know that feeling."

"And school? Getting straight A's?"

The margaritas arrived, and Kate took a drink before answering. "Not quite. Grades aren't as good as ten years ago, but I'm not flunking out."

"You're smart. You're gonna do fine."

"Glad one of us is sure."

The banter felt so comfortable, like old times, talking to Jack as if he was simply a friend.

"So," Jack said, "want to hear a funny Adam Fletcher story?"

Kate nodded. "I hadn't thought of him in ages. He really fell off the face of the earth."

Jack grinned. "Almost. He went to live in Alaska—Zelnik told me; she still keeps in touch with him. Anyway, he bought a cabin, did the whole mountain man thing, gave up painting."

"Doesn't sound so funny to me."

"Hang on, here's the good part. He grew a beard to keep his face warm, and one morning, it must've been 40 below, he goes out to chop some wood, and when he bent over the woodpile, his beard had frozen and he knocked a big chunk of it off."

Kate nearly choked on a tortilla chip, and she laughed so hard at the image that her eyes watered.

Jack was chortling, too. "And I guess he knelt down to look for it, and his knees stuck to the ground, and the woman he was living with had to come pour warm water on him to get him loose."

Kate held up her hand. "Stop before I die laughing." She wiped her eyes and took a breath. "And did he find the beard?"

That set off another round of giggles with both of them, and it took five minutes before Jack could speak long enough to give the waitress their dinner order.

While they waited for the food, Kate asked, "Have you heard from Ryder?"

Jack shook his head. "Another disappearing act."

"He's probably still looking for the path to enlightenment."

"Man, I hope he finds it," Jack said. "I could use some enlightenment too."

"Couldn't we all?"

Maybe it was the liquor at work, but all of a sudden she missed Ryder. He'd introduced her to Jack and had shared so many milestones in their lives. Should she have tried harder to help him? Jack's words came back to her: *"You can't save somebody who doesn't want to be saved."*

The tacos arrived and distracted her gloomy thoughts.

Midway through dinner, Kate said, "Thanks again for tonight. I don't know what I'd have done if you hadn't called."

"You'd've handled it. You're so damn competent."

"Yeah, right," Kate protested.

"That's the thing—you never give yourself enough credit. You're a strong woman, Babe, always were. Too damn strong for me."

"Not hardly."

He reached across the table and squeezed her hand. "I'm sorry, Kate."

She pretended not to understand. "For what?"

"For everything. For trashing the marriage. I was an idiot. I beat myself up every day for what I did."

"Don't. Water under the bridge. I survived, and so did you."

He put down his fork. "I broke it off with Amanda, you know."

"No, I didn't."

"Wish I'd done it months ago. You were the best thing that ever happened to me, and I went and ruined it. If I could take back anything, change anything in my life, it'd be the way I treated you."

How could she respond to a declaration like that?

"Listen, Jack, I had a part in it too. I think we just ... changed. Went in different directions. I'm sorry it happened, too. But I'm glad we can still be ... whatever this is ... friends?"

Jack picked up his fork and speared a chili pepper. "Damn straight. We'll always be connected in some weird kind of way I think. I hope."

"Me too."

The margaritas had done a number on her, and Kate was seeing double. She took a drink of water, but it didn't help.

"I'm getting kinda woozy, Jack. Can't drink like I used to."

He looked worried. "You okay?"

She blinked to clear her vision. "I think so. But I do need to pee."

He reached in his pocket for his smokes and then took her hand again and pressed something into her palm; when she glanced down, she realized it was a vial of white powder.

"That will help," Jack said.

Kate made her way to the bathroom carefully. Inside the stall, she froze. *What the hell are you doing?* Then she scooped up a tiny bit of coke with her pinkie fingernail and sniffed. The buzz hit her right away, and she let the feeling take her. How long since she'd felt that good? *This is so wrong,* she thought. *But I don't care. It's like old times. It feels good.*

Her head hit the clouds as she leaned against the stall's graffiti-etched wall and gave herself up to the surge of energy and power, nerve endings flaring. God, how she'd missed the thrill.

By the time she got back to the table, Jack had put out his cigarette and was polishing off his last taco. Amazing how much food he could pack away, without ever gaining an ounce.

Kate sat down and slipped the vial back into his palm. "Thanks. I needed that."

She slid her plate over in front of him. "I'm done—want the rest?"

He did.

"Feeling better?" he asked between bites.

Kate nodded. "Yeah. Amazing stuff—thanks. I haven't had any since ... since I can't remember when."

Everything looked so clear and bright. Her movements felt smooth and sure as she took out her Marlboros and fired one up, blew smoke upward and watched it dissolve into the nicotine-soaked ceiling.

"Yeah," Jack said. "I've tried to taper off, but—damn, I love the stuff. There's nothing like that rush."

"You feel immortal," Kate added.

"Exactly. And I feel like everything's right, everything's good. I can do anything. I can believe my paintings are the biggest deal since Van Gogh, and people should feel lucky just to look at 'em."

"Your paintings *are* the biggest deal since Van Gogh."

He sent her a smile that could melt icebergs.

When the check came, he grabbed it.

"Let me pay," Kate protested. "It's the least I can do."

"Absolutely not. It was worth it to see you again."

He held her hand as they left the restaurant, and they took their time walking back to his pickup.

Jack opened the passenger door for her. "So—want to run by the studio and see the new paintings?"

She hesitated a few seconds. Good sense told her to politely decline, but she was tired of good sense and hard work. The coke was singing in her blood, and words rushed out before she could stop them. "I'd love to," she said.

Chapter Twenty-Nine

"Are you out of your fucking *mind*?"

Stella slammed her wineglass down so hard the stem almost snapped.

Kate hunched her shoulders and drew her knees together. "It was just this one time."

Stella shook her head, disgust radiating from her like heat off a car hood. "I don't *believe* you."

* * *

In truth, Kate could hardly believe herself, couldn't believe she'd spent Friday night and most of Saturday in Jack Morrison's bed. The memory seared her—leaning against the wall just inside the studio like a pair of overeager teenagers while he pulled off her clothes. Sex with Jack had felt so good, so *familiar* and yet foreign, so exciting there in the stairwell, in a cocaine-fueled vortex. They finally got upstairs and made love again in bed, and again and again. Since their breakup, she'd only had one—lukewarm, as it turned out—sexual encounter and had begun to worry something was wrong with her. Jack erased those doubts.

They'd left the bedroom only for breakfast the next morning, and for Kate to see his new paintings, which were stunning: geometric shapes, filled with radiant color, merging and vibrating with energy that seemed three-dimensional.

"Just when I thought you couldn't get any better," Kate had told him, and Jack glowed at her praise.

"Glad you approve," he'd whispered in her ear. "Now I know I'm on the right track."

"Are you ever," Kate had murmured just before he tackled her and tugged her back to the bedroom.

* * *

She should have known better than to tell Stella about the encounter though, and she hadn't intended to when her friend invited her over for drinks Sunday afternoon. But Stella picked up on something; she had a knack for that.

"You're looking kinda ... glow-y," Stella had said as she handed Kate a glass of Chablis. "What kind of mischief were you up to this weekend?"

Kate had felt herself blush at the memory and tried to switch subjects, but Stella was like a dog with a bone.

"What gives?" she'd demanded. "Come on, don't hold back on me. You can tell me *anything*."

* * *

Not quite, Kate realized as the story spilled out. And she should have predicted the eruption. Stella had never forgiven Jack; it was like he'd betrayed Stella as much as Kate with Amanda Durant.

Now she tried to focus on damage control. Stella was her best friend in the world. Somehow Kate had to make her understand what had happened, and why.

It was hard to talk, though, with Stella glowering at her like that.

"I was high," she began, "and I'd been scared to death about a prowler. And there he was. And ... he's *Jack*. I missed him. I missed making love with him."

"And now? How much do you miss your self-respect?" Stella snapped. God, she was being a bitch about this, way out of proportion to what had happened. And it wasn't really her business.

Stella crossed her arms and glared some more.

"It's not like we're getting back together or anything," Kate said.

Stella's face filled with outrage. "Do I look like I care?"

Yeah, she sort of did.

"It was just this one time," she repeated.

"So you say." Stella's words steamed with sarcasm.

"So I say." But when she looked straight into her heart, Kate saw a glimmer of hope that it *wasn't* just this once. Then she flashed on Jack, admiring the waitress at Felipe's. *Don't be stupid again.* But that was nothing to share with Stella.

Her friend began rearranging the pile of magazines on her coffee table: *Ms., New Yorker, The Writer.* So different from Kate's collection, where *Glamour* poked out from beneath *Personnel Journal* and *Business Week.*

Stella had recently had her hair cut very short; the feathery style flattered her small face. It was an extreme look Kate knew she could never pull off herself. She'd always envied Stella's confidence, and never more than at that moment. Stella had no trouble saying no and letting go.

"I wish I were more like you," Kate said.

"What the hell does that mean?"

"It means what it means. I wish I was so sure of right and wrong."

Stella scowled at Kate, who rose and stood awkwardly in the middle of the room, waiting for some small peace sign.

"It's not so damn hard to figure out, kiddo."

"For me it is," Kate replied. She turned away and shut the door quietly but firmly behind her.

Back in her own apartment, Kate went to the bedroom and studied "Sanctuary." More than anything, the painting was proof that Jack *had* loved her, and they'd been so damned happy the night he gave it to her.

* * *

When Jack didn't phone the next week, Kate told herself she should have known it would go that way. They'd parted on friendly terms—very friendly—but when Jack dropped her off that Saturday afternoon, neither of them had said anything about getting together again.

The holidays spooled out, and Jack didn't get in touch. Disappointed at first, and then relieved, Kate admitted, if only to herself, that she really wanted to believe her declaration to Stella: "It was just this one time."

She needed it to be that way. Anything else was madness.

She and Jack had once been crazy in love, but those people were gone. Every now and then a transient longing would invade her, but she managed to brush it aside. This way was better. Safer. She'd come too far to backslide into the life she'd known as Jack Morrison's wife.

Kate and Stella picked up the threads of their friendship, but with a new caution on Kate's part. The memory of her friend's fierce disapproval still stung, and Kate censored what she told Stella.

Maybe I should move—get a fresh start in a new place—get away from the memories, find new friends. But where would she find the time to hunt for a new apartment, to pack and move? She barely had time enough to breathe.

* * *

When everyone returned to work after New Year's, Paul Lange dropped a surprise in her lap. Permian was bringing all its field personnel representatives to Los Angeles for a training workshop.

"I want you to lead it," he told Kate. "You wrote the manual. You know more about our policies than anybody."

"But I'm not a teacher," Kate protested, through the warm glow of pleasure at his words.

"Don't have to be. You'll have help—put Jeff to work. Marcie will pitch in, and we can pull in some people from Comp and Benefits. But I want you to oversee it."

Kate went back to her office and closed the door, trying not to freak out. This was a huge step forward, and Paul was acknowledging her potential.

But running the training? Talking to all those strangers, telling them how to do things, with Jeff Gallo smirking at her from the sidelines?

Her hands clenched into sweaty fists; the belt on her shirtwaist dress felt too tight. What a dumb dress, boring and safe. She'd need new clothes—maybe Stella would help. They could have a fun shopping trip, like old times.

Braced against the door, Kate studied her office: a small interior room without windows, but at least her own private space. The bookshelf behind her desk held several reference volumes, a well-thumbed dictionary—and the blue vinyl binder with notes from her Management class.

Her heartbeat steadied; here was a resource she could use. Eric Ames had devoted an entire class to business presentations, showing them the best way to use notes and how to make the most of gestures and eye contact. Kate had soaked it all up.

"Thank you, Professor Ames," she murmured as she pulled out her notes. Excitement flowed into her. "This isn't going to be so bad."

* * *

The morning of the workshop, Kate watched the personnel reps—20-plus of them—enter the room and take their seats around a long walnut conference table. Her nerve endings hummed.

I wonder if Jack ever felt this way, showing his paintings? The question popped out of nowhere, along with an awareness that she hadn't given more than a passing thought to Jack Morrison in the weeks of planning the workshop.

Kate stood at the head of the table. "Good morning."

Her voice rang clear and confident—as it should, after hours of practice in front of her bathroom mirror. Her dark blue knit suit and crimson silk blouse felt powerful, the pearl necklace—a good-luck gift from Marcie Plesh—just the right extra touch.

Everyone looked toward her; she'd met most of them at a reception the night before, and they'd seemed generally friendly and ready to learn. Ready to like her.

Marcie sat next to Jeff Gallo against the back wall, and Kate focused for a few heartbeats on her friend's smiling face, tuning out Gallo's already-bored expression.

Kate took a deep breath. "Welcome to our Employee Relations Workshop. I'm Kate Morrison, and…"

Her words flowed out, explaining the benefits of the whole company conforming its personnel practices. As she cited an example of things that could go wrong—and shared a vision of how they could go right—the faces around the table looked expectant and interested. The dark wood of the conference table gleamed, and as people picked up their pens and started taking notes, Kate relaxed into her talk. It all felt right; she was exactly where she belonged.

Chapter Thirty
April 1979

"So you haven't given up on school—or on smoking."

Kate turned around. "Eric! Hi! I'm glad to see you."

Last quarter their schedules hadn't coincided, and with all the other activity in her life, she hadn't given much thought to the professor until that very moment. The sound of his voice brought back pleasant memories of his Management class.

He lit up a Benson & Hedges and exhaled out the side of his mouth. "Likewise."

The damp spring evening wrapped around them. This part of the campus, where smokers gathered during coffee breaks, was mostly deserted, except for the two of them and another couple who stood near a metal trash can in the center of the cigarette-butt-littered courtyard.

"I never had a chance to thank you for the 'A'," said Kate.

"You earned it," he replied.

"True." She quickly added, "I worked hard in your class because I liked it—and I learned so much that I use all the time at work."

God! I sound like a teenager!

Kate cringed, but her words earned a smile from the teacher.

"I almost never hear that, Kate. I'm happy you got something from the class."

"I did." She sighed. "Unlike *Statistics*."

"Ah, Statistics. Not my favorite subject. Something in particular giving you trouble?"

"Everything. I've never been a numbers person."

"Me neither. But I figured out a way to get through it."

Kate cocked her head. "Share your secret—I could use a miracle or two."

He ground out his cigarette on the trash can and then tossed the butt inside. "Are you a gambler?" he asked.

"Excuse me?" Kate laughed at the unexpected question. "You mean like poker?"

Was he trying to learn more about her, or challenging her in some way?

Before he could respond, Kate shook her head. "Nope—never saw the point. Are *you*? A gambler, I mean."

His answering laugh came from deep in his chest. "You could say that. And I was going to dazzle you with ways you can use probability theory to predict a winning hand."

"You can do that?"

"Sometimes. But it's not very interesting, really, unless you have money in the game."

"Oh, I bet you can make it interesting."

He seemed to tense up at her remark. Did he think she was flirting? Was she?

"Maybe so. But not tonight." He tapped the crystal on his wristwatch. "Time to get back to the serious matter of education."

Kate thought his tone held a trace of sarcasm.

"Rats!" she replied, not entirely faking disappointment as she extinguished her own cigarette and dropped it in the barrel. "Until next time, then."

She suppressed an urge to extend her hand for him to shake.

"Count on it," he said. And in the dim lighting Kate thought she saw him wink at her as he straightened his elegant blue tie and motioned her toward the classrooms.

* * *

Back in Statistics, she checked the clock often, but the minute hand hardly seemed to budge as the colorless teacher droned on. Kate kept seeing Eric's wink and replaying his rumbling laugh. Why didn't *he* teach more of the classes she needed?

* * *

Eric was at the coffee kiosk ahead of her the following week, holding two cups, one of which he handed to her.

"I warned you I was a gambler," Eric said. "I gambled you'd be headed over here about now. And I didn't add anything to the coffee—you strike me as a black-coffee woman."

"Good guess. Thanks!" Kate didn't quite understand the rush of pleasure she got from seeing him and realizing he wanted to see *her* as well. For God's sake, he was a college professor. He lived an entirely different lifestyle than she did, and on an entirely different social level. They had nothing in common but this campus.

After that, they met up almost every week at the break, and their conversations were businesslike but enjoyable for Kate. In between giving her tips on mastering Statistics, Eric asked about her job. She told him, trying not to sound boastful, about her recent promotion to Benefits Supervisor.

"Or Stupidvisor, as they call it," she finished. "I actually have three people reporting to me. Feel sorry for them?"

"Not at all. But do you like it—the extra responsibility?"

Kate shrugged. "Most of the time. No two days are alike—that keeps it interesting."

"Variety is underrated," he said with a grin.

Eric spoke very little about his personal life, and Kate grew curious. What else did he do besides teach night classes? She made several tries at pulling information from him, but he deflected her questions and switched subjects.

As April melted into May and the days lengthened, Kate finally began to understand some of the material she labored over in Statistics —thanks to Eric Ames's break-time tutoring.

Then in mid-May, on a jasmine-scented evening, he surprised her by asking, "Do you like chamber music?"

The question stopped her. "To be honest, I don't know a lot about it... it's a smaller group of musicians than a full orchestra, right?"

Eric nodded. "Historically, it was meant to be performed in a palace chamber, but today, lacking palaces, they perform in other places. The reason I ask is that my neighbor's son is a violinist with the L.A. Chamber Orchestra, and they've given me two tickets for a concert next Sunday afternoon..." His voice faded.

He looked like he wanted to say more, but something held him back.

Was he offering her the tickets? Or asking her to go with him? If he *was* asking her out, how would that go? He was smart, sure, and a really good teacher. But intelligence might not guarantee good date material—not that she was any expert. She rarely dated; there wasn't time. Besides, she hadn't met that many eligible men—the ones at work were mostly married or "confirmed bachelors." None of the guys in class appealed to her; they all seemed too young, too preoccupied. Kate did realize, however, that she compared them all to Jack Morrison, and none measured up. Eric might be different, but what was his story? Did she want to find out?

"I'm being presumptuous," Eric continued, and even in the twilight she caught the flush on his face. "I never thought to ask if you're in a relationship, and I—"

"I'm not," Kate said quickly. "In a relationship. I'm divorced."

She wondered if he'd frown at that, but he didn't.

"Some of the nicest people are," he replied.

She let the silence between them play out for a moment while she came up with a reply. "I would very much enjoy going to the concert," she told him then. "With you."

* * *

By Sunday afternoon, Kate was feeling some first-date jitters but looking forward to seeing Eric outside of an academic setting. The weather cooperated in creating a cheerful tone—golden sunlight, air heavy with spring, roses bursting open.

Eric drove a shiny white Audi with creamy leather seats, and he wove expertly through traffic, never losing his focus on the road while telling funny stories about classroom projects that had gone horribly wrong. Kate listened and laughed and chipped in a few of her own experiences. It was fun talking with him: unlike so many men, Eric didn't monopolize the conversation.

Their route to the Mark Taper Forum, in the Music Center complex north of downtown, took them past Permian's headquarters. Kate pointed to it, and Eric glanced out the window.

"I've always admired that building," he remarked. "Interesting architecture."

It *was* an unusual shape, more trapezoid than rectangle, the north and south wings standing at slight angles to the main tower.

"What's it like inside?" he asked. "Lots of glass and marble, I'd imagine."

Was he hinting for an invitation to visit her at the office? Kate decided to play dumb and see how today's adventure turned out.

"More glass and marble than you'd ever want to see," she replied.

He steered the Audi into the Music Center's underground parking with a casual familiarity and then guided her to the escalators.

"Do you come here often?" Kate asked on the way up. "You seem to know your way around."

Eric buttoned his gray suit jacket. "Not often enough."

The jacket fit perfectly, shoulder seams falling exactly where they should, no straining across the front. Kate was glad she'd chosen an equally well-tailored pink sheath, even if she had to wear uncomfortably high heels to go with it.

Their seats were in the center of the third row, but as Kate glanced around she realized there were no truly bad seats in this semi-circular amphitheater with its outthrust stage.

"This is a treat," Kate told him. "I've never been here before."

"I hope you enjoy the concert," Eric replied. "I confess I've never heard them play, but they have a great reputation."

It wouldn't have mattered to Kate if they banged washtubs and strummed ukuleles. She savored the new experience, and Eric seem concerned that she have a good time. How long had it been since a guy took her someplace special and cared if she liked it? *Not since Jack.*

The lights dimmed, and five musicians filed onstage without introduction. The audience applauded lightly as the performers bowed and took their seats in a semicircle that mirrored the auditorium's shape. Two violinists sat in the outer chairs, with a viola player and a cellist between them, and slightly to the rear was a keyboard player.

"They look so serious," Kate whispered.

Eric chuckled. "It's an act."

After briefly tuning the stringed instruments, the orchestra began without preamble. Kate knew from the program that this was a Beethoven symphony, and as the music swept over her, she closed her eyes and felt her skin tingle with pleasure. She'd listened to classical music before, but never in this type of environment, and it seized her emotions as if the notes had taken physical form. The symphony conjured images of green grass rippling and gauzy curtains billowing in a pine-scented breeze, as if a long-buried memory stirred and caressed her.

When the sweet music stopped and Kate opened her eyes, Eric was watching her. "Are you all right?" he asked.

Kate nodded and touched his arm. "It's so beautiful," she murmured. "I didn't expect it to be this intense."

Accustomed to the disco beat of Donna Summer and the clamor of the Eagles on the radio during her daily commute, Kate felt as if she were sinking into a pool of clear water, cleansing and mild, as the orchestra began a Bach concerto that featured the violins.

Since they sat so close to the orchestra, Kate could hear each individual musical note. She watched the woman violinist in her sleeveless black gown, fascinated by the musician's constantly flexing arm muscles. *You have to be strong to do this!*

She thought back to that long-ago night at the Quartermoon, when Jack had taken her to hear Ryder sing. Ryder: worlds away from a place like this. She could imagine his dismissive snort if he saw her sitting in this cushy seat next to a man in a business suit, dressed in her Sunday best and listening to classical music. *Oh, Ryder, what happened to you? Are you still alive?*

Thoughts of Ryder led, invariably, to Jack. *I wonder if he ever comes here with his art-collector friends.* She made a mental note to check the names of donors engraved on the outside wall to see if "Zelnik" appeared. Then again, who cared about ancient history? Not here, not today.

* * *

When the concert ended, Kate felt a pang of regret; she wanted the music to keep going forever. They left the auditorium and stepped into a sun-washed concrete reality that jarred Kate out of her dream world. Eric pulled a pack of Benson & Hedges from his jacket pocket and offered a cigarette to Kate, then lit it with his slim lighter, cupping his hands with practiced ease around the flame.

He lit his own smoke and then waved to a middle-aged, well-dressed couple who approached. Between them was a handsome young man with shiny black hair, and Kate recognized him as one of the violinists.

"Kate," Eric said, "I'd like to introduce Gwen and Paul Farris—my neighbors—and their son Kevin."

Gwen Farris' eyes narrowed, and she studied Kate in silence until her ruddy-faced husband thrust his hand out and said, "So nice to meet you."

Kate shook his hand and thanked them for the tickets, praised Kevin for his playing and asked some polite questions about the orchestra. All the while Gwen Farris glared at her, and Kate grew nervous under the woman's scrutiny.

With a final thank-you, Eric led her away from the Farrises.

"That woman seemed angry with me," Kate remarked. "Did I say something wrong?"

He shook his head and looked embarrassed. In fact, the normally calm professor was actually perspiring. "I have to confess something.

Gwen has been trying to set me up with her widowed sister for months now, and I've been dodging her, making excuses." Eric stopped beside an ashtray.

He put out his cigarette and turned to Kate, frowning. "I should have simply told her outright that I wasn't interested in her sister, but personal confrontations are hard for me."

Kate took a final drag on her smoke and stubbed it out. "You used me as a decoy?" She didn't know whether to be amused or insulted.

He held up both hands and looked straight into her eyes. "No, no, no! I asked you to come with me for the pleasure of your company. Honestly."

His distress was so apparent that Kate felt a tug of sympathy as he wiped the moisture from his forehead.

The late afternoon sunlight warmed her skin, and she caught the scent of citrus blossoms as she bent and flicked ashes from her dress.

"Well, at least you're honest," Kate said, smiling to lighten her words. She couldn't bear to make him feel any worse than he obviously did; he'd been so kind.

"And socially inept, clearly."

"Don't worry about it. I'm only a little offended."

"Don't be!"

She linked arms with him. "Okay, I'll give you a pass on this one."

He clasped her forearm. "Thank you." He sounded so relieved that she almost laughed.

When they got to the Audi, he opened the passenger door for her and then glanced at his watch. "It's too early for dinner, but I really don't want this to end yet. Would you like to go for a drink or something?"

Without thinking, Kate asked, "How about ice cream?"

He looked surprised for a moment and then grinned. "Great! And I know just the place!"

Eric turned onto Temple, and as they left downtown behind, Kate remarked, "It looks so quiet and clean on the weekend. So *empty*."

Eric nodded. "A different world. There are lots of layers to the city —layers most people don't see."

"I know. I lived in one of those layers. Sort of." Now why had she blurted that out? Too soon, too soon, to be sharing her past. Eric seemed curious, however, so she hastily sketched out the details of her marriage.

"An artist! That must have been fascinating."

"It had its moments. But it wasn't all fun."

"I imagine. America doesn't treat its artists very well, except for the few very famous ones."

"Jack's moving into that category, but he's not there yet."

"From the way you speak of him, I gather the divorce wasn't too bitter?"

Kate fiddled with the clasp on her purse. "Sometimes it was, but overall we've stayed ... sort of friends, I guess. Jack's a better friend than he was a husband."

Eric followed Temple to Virgil and turned north without saying much more, so Kate dove in. Might as well get it all out there.

"How about you?" she asked. "Any ex-wives lurking around in your past?"

He hesitated for a minute, then answered without taking his eyes off the road. "Very long ago, and very briefly. We met in grad school. She was beautiful and shallow and we knew it was a mistake from the honeymoon but we held out for eight months. Mercifully, there were no children." He sighed. "I haven't thought of Dawn—that was her name—for years. She remarried—found the athlete she mistook me for—and last I heard had moved to Atlanta."

Kate didn't know how to respond. She hadn't expected that candid an answer.

"Well," she finally managed to say, "I guess that makes us even." *What a dumb remark!*

She let him shift the conversation to current events, and as he speculated about the chances of success for Margaret Thatcher as Britain's first female Prime Minister, Kate absorbed the information Eric had shared.

* * *

At Sunset Blvd., Virgil morphed into Hillhurst, and a few blocks south of Los Feliz, Eric pulled the Audi to the curb. On the sidewalk, Kate spotted a gigantic fake ice cream cone, topped with a white dome dripping brown paint that glistened like real chocolate syrup.

Eric walked around and opened the passenger door.

"How have I not seen this before?" Kate wondered aloud as she got out of the car. "I come this way all the time to get to the park."

Eric put his arm around her waist. "It's not exactly subtle, is it?"

Inside, the ice cream parlor was an old-fashioned wonder. White wrought iron tables and chairs, and a glass case displaying a dizzying array of ice cream: pinks and greens and blues next to giant tubs of chocolate chip, caramel swirl, and a mysterious mixture of fudge ribbon, nuts, and a few ingredients she couldn't identify.

"Cone or cup?" Eric asked, raising his eyebrows. "One scoop or two? Or three?"

Kate's mouth watered. "One scoop. In a cup. Otherwise I'll end up wearing it."

He laughed. "And which flavor?"

"Surprise me."

He did. One bite of the creamy concoction, and Kate was hooked. The tastes collided on her tongue: fudge and peanut butter, mingled with something fruity—grape perhaps?

She let the ice cream melt in her mouth, unable to speak for a moment.

"This is terrific," she finally got out when her tongue thawed enough to form words.

Eric had chosen the same kind for himself, and he winked at her. "I thought you might like it. He calls it 'Magical Mystery.'"

"I'm in love."

"Don't fall so easily. There are probably even better ones to try."

Kate took another spoonful of frozen heaven. *This is so nice,* she thought. *Quiet. Safe.*

When the ice cream was gone, Eric ushered her out to the shade-dappled sidewalk and motioned up the street.

"There's a nice bookstore on the next block, if you're in a browsing mood."

She was. The bookstore smelled like a library to her, paper and binding paste and ink swirling around. A display table by the entrance held some "gently used" hardcover books: *The Thorn Birds* sat next to *Chesapeake*—both of which Kate wanted to read if she ever again had free time. Eric picked up a book from the nonfiction table: *How to Achieve Financial Independence by Investing in Real Estate.*

"I should read this," he muttered. "If only for amusement."

Kate pretended to get the joke.

They ended up not buying anything in the bookstore, but afterward he took her hand and ambled up the street, away from where he'd parked the Audi. Kate's shoes began to pinch, but she turned her attention away from them because she was enjoying herself more than she expected to. Something about Eric made her feel peaceful and content as he swung her hand lightly. The sun's angle sharpened the afternoon shadows, and a cool breeze ruffled her hair.

"I don't live far from here," Eric said, pointing north.

"On Los Feliz?"

"Just above."

"Nice neighborhood." Nice *pricey* neighborhood.

He shrugged. "Lucky break. I dabble in real estate, and ... well, there's nothing like a motivated seller."

Now his interest in the real estate book made sense.

"You 'dabble?' When do you find the time?"

Kate had checked out his profile in the college catalogue and saw that he taught other Management classes three days a week and had published several papers on management theory and practice. The articles' titles were all long and scholarly.

Eric's grip on her hand tightened slightly. "Call it relief from academia. Comic relief."

She took the cue and laughed.

"A fellow teacher got me involved," he continued, keeping his focus on the sidewalk. "We bought a rental house together, made some money and got some tax breaks. Then we bought another one, did some cosmetic fixing up and sold it for a profit, plowed the proceeds into a nicer home, did it again. And somewhere in there I bought my own place." His voice rang with pride as he told her this.

"I envy you," Kate said. "I'm still renting—don't have the nerve to take the plunge."

He turned to her and smiled. "If you ever get the itch to buy, I'd be happy to give you some tips. You could learn from my mistakes."

"I can't imagine you making that many mistakes, Eric."

That got a laugh out of him. "Oh, you'd be surprised, Ms. Morrison. I make more than my share." He shook his head ruefully. "More than my share."

He seemed inclined to keep walking, and Kate didn't protest, despite the twinges her shoes caused.

"But enough of me and my sordid hobbies," he said. "What about you? How's the career going?"

Kate shrugged. "Well enough. I try to be patient and remind myself not to expect miracles. I'm lucky to have come this far without a degree."

"And what happened to interrupt your education before—if I may ask?"

"Ask away. It's not a happy story, though."

He stopped walking and faced her with concern in his gentle gray-green eyes. "I'm listening."

So Kate told him about her father and the drunk driver and finished, as offhandedly as she could manage, "... so that's why I dropped out of the university—had to go to work and help my mom out."

The sadness of Eric's expression touched her.

"Life is damned unfair sometimes," he muttered.

"It is. But I'm doing all right, and I appreciate my education more now. It feels more relevant."

He turned and started back downhill, toward the Audi, and for a moment Kate worried she'd depressed him so much that he wanted to get rid of her.

"We've talked entirely too much about me, Eric. And I know next to nothing about you—except for the ex-wife, of course. That and your great taste in music, and ice cream."

He looked up at the sky, as if thinking over his reply.

"There's little to tell," he began. "I'm quite ordinary, really. Born and raised in Chicago. My dad painted houses for a living. Went to U of Illinois, was going to major in business but switched to education. Got tired of freezing in the winter and came out here to grad school, got a job, and ... that's it."

He stopped and took out his cigarettes—they'd gone quite a while without smoking, she realized. When he offered one to her, Kate took it and savored the tiny ritual of having him light it for her. He touched the flame to his own and squinted against the smoke.

"I sense a lot of hard work in there that you've skipped over," Kate said.

Eric laughed. "Oh, there's been plenty of that all right. Plenty of that. But it comes with my territory—and yours."

* * *

He took her home after that. Kate was a little disappointed when he declined her invitation to come in for a drink.

"Tomorrow's a work day, and I have at least three-inches worth of papers to grade. You'll find me a terrible procrastinator, Kate, and I often kick myself, like right now, for letting the work pile up to the last minute."

But he didn't add anything encouraging, like "Rain check?" so Kate smiled and thanked him for a lovely afternoon. At the last minute, he leaned forward and kissed her lightly on the lips. It was a mild kiss, quick and soft as butterfly wings, and then he headed down the stairs without looking back.

* * *

Inside, Kate checked her answering machine: no messages. Not that she expected any.

She removed her pumps and sat on the sofa, massaging her aching feet. The afternoon had been worth the pain. Eric was an enjoyable companion, although she wouldn't describe him as "fun" or "exciting."

She replayed the afternoon in her mind as she changed into comfortable clothes and washed the makeup off her face.

"You're no prize either, you know," Kate told her reflection. "All you do is work and go to school."

But she hadn't been all that enthralling when she met Jack—and yet he'd made her feel special and desirable. She didn't get those vibes from Eric. And Jack would have taken her up on that drink offer, in a heartbeat.

Yeah, Eric Ames was no Jack Morrison, none of the drama and color. But maybe drama and color were overrated. Just look where it had led.

Time to move on, even if she didn't feel up to it.

What if Eric asked her out again? Kate doubted he would; he'd passed up a perfect chance to do that tonight. Maybe he really had invited her to the concert simply to get his neighbor off his back.

But *what if?* Kate put the question aside and opened the file of work she'd brought home from the office.

Chapter Thirty-One
May 1979

"But it's Mom's *birthday*," Debbie whined. "Can't you duck out of your job for an hour?"

Kate bit back an angry reply. "Tell me again why we can't do dinner instead of lunch."

"Because Roy and I *always* play bridge with Phil and Olive on Fridays. They count on us."

"Oh, *that* would be a hardship to miss."

Kate heard a sigh.

"What about Saturday?" she asked.

"Come on, Kate! It won't be the same if we do it another day. Please." Debbie drew the last word into an exaggerated bleat.

* * *

As a concession, Debbie chauffeured Helen, and they met Kate at Les Frères Taix, a ten-minute drive from her office. Kate turned her car over to the valet and let buttery spring sunshine warm her skin as Debbie's fire-engine red coupe pulled up.

Kate hugged her mother. "Happy Birthday, Mom."

"Such a treat—my girls making time for me." Helen's voice had thickened noticeably: too many cigarettes for too many years, but she hadn't been able to stop. *I should quit smoking,* Kate thought for about the millionth time. *Set a good example for Mom.*

As soon as they were seated, Helen lit up. Debbie waved the smoke away, face puckered, so Kate left her Marlboros in her purse. It was going to be a long lunch.

She glanced at the menu but already knew she'd go with soup and salad. The other two took time pondering their choices, and Kate stifled her impatience.

Debbie had grown into a pretty woman, although still with a me-first attitude that her husband encouraged. She did, however, give Helen more time and attention than Kate felt able to provide.

Helen had quit coloring her hair before Christmas, and the sight of those springy gray curls still jolted Kate. Her mother had been a good-looking woman in her prime, but time had faded her beauty.

When the waiter came for their drink order, Debbie passed on her customary glass of white wine and ordered iced tea. Helen looked puzzled but asked for a vodka tonic anyway. Kate hesitated, and Helen tapped the back of her hand.

"Don't make me drink alone, Honey."

Kate didn't. "Just one, though. I have to meet with my boss later. I can't come in reeking of booze."

Helen beamed. "My daughter the executive."

"Not quite yet, Mom."

Debbie pulled a small foil-wrapped box from her purse. "Happy Birthday, Mom."

"Oh, Honey, you didn't have to," Helen murmured as she slit the wrapping paper and opened Debbie's gift: a pair of dangly earrings with glittery stones at their tips.

Their mother had had her ears pierced the summer before, at Debbie's insistence. "You need a change, Mom," Debbie had proclaimed, whisking her off to a shop at the mall. Helen had seemed pleased with the new look, and Kate wished it had been her idea instead of Deb's.

"Oh, Debbie," Helen said, "you went way overboard."

"Cubic zirconia," Debbie admitted. "But you can't tell—can you, Kate?"

"No, they look like diamonds," Kate lied. "They're beautiful, Mom."

She held out her own birthday gift, and Helen tore it open, holding up the bright paisley scarf that had beckoned elegantly from the display case.

"Oooh," Debbie cooed. "Nice. Real silk?"

Kate frowned at her sister. "Yes." She restrained herself from adding, "Of course."

Helen stroked the delicate, glossy fabric. "It's so pretty. You'll have to show me how to tie it, though. I'm no good with those things."

"I'll help you, Mom," Debbie said, draping the scarf around Helen's neck and knotting it to one side. She patted it smooth. "There —perfect."

Helen smiled and clasped Kate's hand. "Thank you, Kate. You both are too good to me."

Debbie flicked a long fingernail against her water glass. "So, you two—don't you want to know why I'm not drinking?"

Kate sipped her wine. "Watching your weight?"

It was a cheap shot, and Kate regretted it immediately. Debbie could always bring out Kate's inner bitch.

"I'm pregnant," Debbie announced, ignoring Kate's remark.

Kate took a deep breath and her ears popped, as if she'd descended a mountain road too quickly.

"Oh, Honey, that's the best birthday present you could give me!" Helen cried out. "A grandbaby! You little stinker, keeping it to yourself. When are you due? Oh, I can hardly wait to be a grandmother. I can babysit for you, and…"

Kate let her babble on, glad that the news had invigorated their mother. She'd have a purpose now. And Debbie—Kate had to admit her sister was glowing.

"Congratulations, Deb," Kate said, lifting her wineglass for a toast.

"I'm due in November," Debbie said. She grinned at Kate. "*You'll* have to handle Thanksgiving this year."

"No problem," Kate replied. "I'll make reservations at McDonald's right away."

"Kathryn Ann!"

"It's okay, Mom," Debbie said. "I'm used to her."

"Sorry," Kate said, although she wasn't. "I'm really happy for you, Sis. How's Roy feel about being a dad?"

Debbie's smile widened. "He's over the moon. Well, both of us are a little scared, of course, but—"

"Don't you worry, Honey," Helen told her younger daughter. "You'll do fine. And I can help. I did okay with you girls."

Their food arrived amid a clink of silverware and the rattle of serving trays. Kate tore off a slab of bread and let her mother and sister prattle on about baby showers, baby names, baby food.

When the waiter cleared away their plates, Helen started to light another cigarette, and Deb objected.

"Mom, that smell makes me want to puke."

Irritation flicked across Helen's face, and she put her pack away.

Debbie turned her focus to Kate. "Ryder's folks got a postcard from him last week—from New Mexico. Ever hear from him yourself?"

"Not for years," Kate replied. "What's he doing in New Mexico?"

Debbie shrugged.

"I always liked Leonard," said Helen. "He was a sweet boy, before he got into all that...that *music* and such. His parents must worry." She shuddered. "I'm so lucky you girls didn't fall into all that."

Debbie pursed her lips innocently.

As far as Kate knew, her sister had limited her drug experiments to pot and had probably given that up when she married straight-laced Roy. And there was no way Deb could know the extent of Kate's own drug use when she was with Jack. Water under the bridge anyway.

"And," Debbie continued, "I saw Jack's name in the paper last week."

Kate took out her wallet; she figured she'd pay the bill and settle up with Debbie later. "Oh yeah? What's he up to?" Good—she sounded only mildly interested.

Debbie hesitated, like she was choosing her words. "Are you okay with him dating that socialite?"

Kate almost dropped her wallet. The air around her suddenly seemed too sharp to breathe.

"Sure," she said, hoping no one heard the tremor in her voice. "Why not? We're divorced. He can do—"

"You didn't know," Debbie said.

Kate pulled out her credit card and pretended to study the bill.

Happy now, you smug little brat?

She got control of her voice and her thoughts. "How would I? We hardly ever talk. Give me the scoop. A socialite? Really?"

Debbie's smirk faded. "Sounds like it. Divorced, lives in Brentwood, has a big art collection."

"This was in the paper?" asked Helen.

"Yeah." Debbie sounded almost sorry.

"Good for him," Kate said. "He finally found his patron."

When the talk drifted back to Debbie's pregnancy, Kate welcomed it. She signed for the lunch, told Debbie to consider it an early baby present, and fled to the certainty of her office.

* * *

Right before quitting time, Eric Ames phoned. "Are you avoiding me?"

"Excuse me?" asked Kate.

"You skipped our usual rendezvous last night. I thought maybe you'd had such an awful time on Sunday that you couldn't face me."

"Oh, no—nothing like that. I had to work. People from the Houston branch were visiting, and I took them to dinner."

Had he really fretted over her absence?

"What a relief! I thought ... well, it's not my business of course, but I worried."

Kate let the silence spin out for a few seconds, unsure what was on his mind. Then she gave in. "Did I miss anything interesting in the quad? Has the coffee improved?"

His laugh rewarded her. "No—the same wretched stuff." Another long pause followed before he continued. "This is unforgivably last-minute, but would you like to have dinner with me tomorrow? Perhaps catch a movie, if we can find one you haven't seen?"

Kate needed no time to consider his offer. *Time to get on with your life,* she reminded herself.

"I'd love to. I haven't been to the movies lately, so we'll have plenty of choices."

After they hung up, Kate's hand lingered on the telephone receiver. Eric Ames seemed to need some encouragement, and she might not be the right one to provide it. But nobody else was asking her out.

It wasn't a lifelong commitment, merely dinner and a movie. From what she knew of Eric, she'd have a pleasant enough time. And maybe that was the best she could hope for. It sure beat an evening alone.

Chapter Thirty-Two
April 1980

"Hey, stranger."

Kate recognized Jack's voice on the phone—she'd know it anywhere, any time.

"Hey there," she replied, trying for nonchalance. "Long time no see." *Brilliant.*

She stood and stretched out the phone cord so she could close her office door.

"How are you?" Jack asked, and Kate sensed he'd called for a reason.

"Good," she replied, keeping her tone light as she sank back into her chair. "Working too hard, but it beats unemployment. Oh—and I'm an aunt. Debbie had a baby girl last year."

When he laughed, her whole body trembled. God, he had the best laugh.

"Congratulations. How's she like being a mom?"

How strange, this ordinary conversation, like they'd spoken only weeks instead of months ago.

"Loves it. She was born for this."

In the intervening silence, the phone line crackled, and Kate filled the void. "So—the Whitney Biennial—the big time! Congratulations yourself. I read it was a smash."

"I don't remember seeing it described that way, but yeah, it went pretty well. Nice people. It was fun."

Another pause, and then they both spoke at once.

Kate said, "How are your mom and d—"

Jack said, "I need to tell you something." He sounded serious.

Kate's voice froze. She swallowed. "Okay. Lay it on me."

"I'm getting married. I thought you should hear it from me."

The clock on her desk continued ticking, but the rest of the world stopped. The telephone receiver felt too heavy to hold, and she propped her elbow on the desk. The taste of stale coffee filled her mouth and she almost gagged.

Say something, idiot!

"That's great, Jack. Good for you." The words seemed to go on and on, like a record on a dying turntable.

She imagined Jack on the other end, twisting the telephone cord, nervous, maybe embarrassed.

"Thanks," he replied. "We've been seeing each other for, I guess, over a year now. Neither of us wanted to rush into anything."

"Tell me about her: who is she, what's she like?"

Masochist!

"Her name's Eden Burroughs, and she's ... you'd like her, Kate. She kinda reminds me of you."

"Uh oh."

"No, really, it's all good. She collects art. That's how we met, through Nikki. She bought one of my paintings, and we got to talking, and…"

"She has good taste."

He chuckled. "Maybe."

"When is the wedding?"

"In a couple of weeks. We're keeping it small. Both of us have been married before, so we're not making it a big deal."

"I'm happy for you. Really."

"Thanks." She heard him sigh. "Anyway, we're gonna do the

honeymoon thing, and when we get back, we'll have a little party, to celebrate with our friends. It'd be great if *you* could come."

"Won't that be weird?"

"Not unless we make it that way. Honest. Her ex moved to Australia, but if he lived local, he'd come. They stayed friends, like you and I did."

Friends? Kate had wondered how to characterize their post-divorce relationship. "Friends" seemed as appropriate as anything. She was thankful they didn't hate each other, the way so many couples did. She thought of Stella, who could hardly say her ex-husband's name without spitting, who took back her maiden name before the ink was dry on the divorce decree. Kate, on the other hand, had kept Jack's name, since she'd used it professionally long enough to make switching a big hassle.

He let a few seconds go by and then said, "It's none of my business, but how 'bout you? Dating anyone special?"

"Actually, yeah. A guy I met in school."

"I hope he's being good to you."

"He is. Very good."

"Cool. Bring him with you to the party then."

"Nah, I don't think so. He wouldn't know anyone."

"Okay—but the offer's out there."

"I probably wouldn't know that many people myself. I've been out of the art scene for so long...I heard about Stephen Durant, though. Sad thing."

"Yeah, it was."

Durant, at a relatively young fifty-eight, had suffered a fatal stroke a year earlier, while vacationing in Italy.

After a pause, Jack added, "And Amanda. You knew about that too, right?"

"No," Kate replied, frowning at that unwelcome name.

"Stephen's death hit her hard. After the funeral, Amanda got blind drunk and wrapped her car around a light pole. Smashed her skull all to pieces. She's in some kind of special hospital—pretty much a vegetable."

"God! How awful." Despite her dislike of Amanda, Kate felt a surge of pity for the girl.

"Yeah," Jack replied. "Life's a bitch sometimes. But, hey, I didn't mean to bum you out."

"No, I brought it up. Jeez, makes you feel lucky to be you, doesn't it?"

"That it does, Babe. That it does."

How long since he'd called her "Babe?" The nickname made her want to cry, and she stifled the urge.

She took a breath to steady her voice. "Well, I'd better get back to work. I appreciate your calling ... about the wedding."

"Yeah, nothing worse than hearing third-hand that your ex got remarried, right?"

"Exactly. And I'm glad for you, Jack. You deserve to be happy."

"So do you, Kate. I hope you are."

After he hung up, she realized she hadn't asked any of those polite, intrusive questions people always threw at you when you announced a big deal like a marriage. How long had Eden been divorced? Did she have kids? Where were they going on their honeymoon?

Kate had practiced answering questions like that about Eric—not that they were even *thinking* about getting married; at least she wasn't, and he didn't act like a man anywhere near proposing. They saw each other almost every week, they spoke on the phone two or three times in between, and they still met at break time if he was teaching on a night when she had class. But their relationship felt more like a friend-ship than a romance, in spite of the roses on Valentine's Day and the trips they'd taken together.

They'd made love for the first time about two months into dating, and while he seemed enthusiastic and attentive, fireworks seldom happened. And although Kate tried not to compare Eric to Jack, she couldn't help it. No one else had ever made her feel that way.

On her way up the stairs to her apartment that night, Kate rang Stella's doorbell, even though their friendship had chilled since the blow-up over Kate's last fling with Jack. Stella never understood why Kate didn't hate Jack. And when Kate began dating Eric, Stella grew critical and remote, referring to Eric as "that teacher guy" and hinting the relationship was headed for disaster.

"I'm not ready to give up on men," Kate had protested, adding "the way you seem to have done."

Stella had stormed off, slamming Kate's front door behind her, and the two hadn't spoken for weeks afterward. Even now, Kate sometimes felt she was navigating a minefield in every conversation with Stella.

But that bleak evening, she needed a friend.

Stella must have read Kate's mood just looking at her. "What's wrong?"

"Jack's getting married," said Kate, and to her total mortification, she started crying like a kid who'd lost her favorite toy.

Stella gave her a drink, let her bawl for a while, and then reminded her that men are pigs—her favorite saying. She insisted Kate would be fine and should pity the poor woman Jack was marrying. The sympathy consoled her only a little, the bubbling rage underneath it not at all.

Why had she thought Stella and her man-bashing would help? Couldn't Stella sing *any* other tune? Kate finished her drink and left, pleading a monster headache, which was true by then.

Alone in her apartment, Kate went up to "Sanctuary" and stroked the frame, peered deep within the brush strokes for an answer that probably didn't exist.

"Were we ever a family?" she whispered.

Like the wolf-shape in the painting, Kate wanted to throw her head back and howl, but it would be pointless. No one would answer. She'd known it for a long time, but Jack's phone call had really hammered the message home. She really, truly was all on her own.

Chapter Thirty-Three
April 1982

"You're sure you want me to tag along?" Eric asked, re-folding the invitation to Jack Morrison's show at Nikki Frank's gallery. He ran his fingers along the crease.

"Positive," Kate replied. "Get a look at my past. Now that I've got you hooked, you won't turn and run." She poked his chest playfully. "I *do* have you hooked, don't I?"

He answered her with a bear hug. "Absolutely."

"It'll be fun," Kate continued. "Nikki always attracts an interesting bunch of people."

In the three years they'd been dating, she'd never introduced Eric to the art scene. It simply hadn't felt *right*. His nature was such a stark contrast to the glittering world she'd left behind.

Every now and then a fleeting desire pierced her, a longing for something more than Eric's steady predictability, for one more roller-coaster ride in the dark like the ones she'd known as Jack Morrison's wife. She chased off the yearning by reminding herself roller-coaster rides hadn't worked out so well for her. Eric was trustworthy and kind. That should be enough. And most of the time, it was.

She appreciated Eric's steadiness even more as Permian Oil became engulfed in a struggle to "grow the company in new directions, in response to an increasingly complex and competitive business environment"—as the propaganda from upper management described it. Some days Kate loved the charged atmosphere, even though it drained her energy and challenged her survival skills. Eric's calm presence anchored her. After a hectic day when she felt like she was running a footrace with Jeff Gallo, Kate relished an evening cocktail with Eric, who would let her vent and remind her that Gallo's behavior was merely a symptom of his insecurity—and inadequacy.

* * *

Standing at the entrance to Nikki Frank's Galerie Framboise, however, Kate hesitated. Eric was *so* proper—would this scene be too much for him? A wild mixture of perfume and cigarette smoke swirled over them, and the blistering guitar of Carlos Santana spilled from several stereo speakers. The room was awash in color: jewel-toned dresses, satiny paisley shirts. Eric's suede jacket, his navy-blue slacks and turtleneck sweater looked conservatively elegant, and Kate herself felt passable in black jeans and a beaded vest over her red silk blouse. For a minute she wished the two of them were dressed more outrageously, then changed her mind. She was there to see, not be seen.

She took his hand. "Ready?"

"Ready as I'll ever be. I'll try not to embarrass you."

"You could never do that, Eric."

Kate thought of Jack's first-ever gallery show, at Finelli, ten years ago. A lifetime ago.

Some things hadn't changed: the bar offered fancier wine, but the background patter still sounded shrill and vague, and barking laughter grated on her eardrums.

Kate guided Eric toward Jack and Eden; the cluster of people around them parted as Jack took a step toward Kate. He planted a quick kiss on her cheek, shook hands with Eric, and introduced him to Eden.

* * *

After Jack's wedding, Kate had gone, solo, to the post-honeymoon reception. She didn't know what to make of Eden but found nothing about her to hate. The woman was charming and cordial, even confiding to Kate that she was thankful she'd met Jack later in life, after Kate had done the heavy lifting at the start of his career.

Kate thought she'd heard a false note in Eden's remarks. However, an ex-wife would naturally be inclined to suspect the woman who'd taken her place—right?

Otherwise, Eden had seemed genuine and warm, leading Kate among the guests and introducing her as "Jack's first wife," which evoked a lot of curious stares and some awkward pauses in conversation.

When Kate got ready to leave, Eden had hugged her and murmured, "Thank you so much for coming, Kate. Jack thinks the world of you, and it meant so much to have you here tonight."

Kate liked Eden well enough that it bothered her only a little to see Eric's admiring expression as he shook hands with her. Eden *was* beautiful: blue eyes and creamy skin to complement her thick blond hair, and a slender athlete's body. Kate let him enjoy the view while she spoke with Jack.

"Good turnout tonight—congratulations." She scanned the room, took in a fast overview of the paintings. "The work looks great, Jack. This is a fabulous space."

He'd cut his hair short and trimmed his beard, and although his appearance had startled her at first, she recovered quickly enough to appreciate the new Jack as he adjusted the cuffs on his white shirt and fingered the buttons on his black corduroy vest. *Eden's fashion influence*, Kate thought with a smile.

Furrows appeared on Jack's forehead. "It looks okay to you?"

"More than okay. Fantastic."

His face relaxed, and he leaned in close. "Your guy seems nice."

Kate grinned. "You can tell by a handshake?"

"I can."

She touched Jack's arm. "You need to mingle. And I want a closer look at your masterpieces. Have a good time—you earned it!"

Jack clasped her hand. "Thanks for coming."

She reached for Eric and led him away.

"I've never met a famous artist before," Eric murmured while studying the paintings.

Jack's art had evolved into something Kate found more appealing than ever. The radiant color blocks she'd last seen now intersected wide curving lines, in unexpected ways. Colors that should have clashed, instead merged and blended, and the canvases glowed with inner light. When she looked away, the after-image stayed on her retinas.

"How do you like them?" asked Kate.

"Very interesting," he replied. "Striking use of form and color."

Kate giggled, and Eric winced.

"I sound like I'm reading a textbook." He turned to her. "What do *you* see in them?"

Kate gathered her thoughts. "I agree about the color and the shapes. And I'm always struck by the light in them. It's hard to capture that kind of light in an oil painting, but he does it so well—it makes them seem alive. To me, anyway."

Eric smiled, and it was Kate's turn to look abashed.

"Now *I* sound like I'm reading from a textbook."

Eric squeezed her hand. "No. You sound like you *wrote* the textbook."

Kate laughed and pointed toward the bar. "Shall we?"

"So," Eric asked as he poured her some wine, "do you miss this life?"

Kate looked around the room. She *did* miss the glamour, the sense of being near the center of the art scene—the buzz in the room, an energy that made her nerve endings quiver.

"Not really," she told Eric. "It was fun while it lasted, but most of these people are your best friend one minute and look right through you the next. When Jack and I divorced, I found out none of them were really *my* friends, even if they'd claimed to be."

He put his arm around her waist and kissed her cheek. "Their loss."

The sweet gesture brought warmth to her face. "I love you, Eric Ames." He'd been the first to say the word "love," and it hadn't come easily for Kate to say it back, but right then she truly meant it. She sipped her wine and savored the pleasure of being with Eric, not standing alone, waiting for Stella or Ryder to arrive and keep her company.

Ryder...where had he gone? Was he still alive? At times like this she always thought of him, and missed his wicked grin.

A hand touched her shoulder, and Kate turned.

"Are you two doing okay?" asked Eden Morrison. "I feel like we're neglecting you." She faced Eric. "Enjoying the show? And I don't mean the artwork."

"It's not what I expected," Eric replied. "It's more ... lively."

Eden's answering laugh made it clear she belonged in this world. She appeared so perfect at this opening—her clothes, her hair, her shoes—like she'd stepped out of a magazine ad.

"Eden, dear, I need you," whined a familiar voice, and Trudy Zelnik tottered up to them.

Eden recoiled, almost unnoticeably. "What is it, Trudy?"

Trudy ignored Kate and Eric. "Nikki is being impossible, she refuses to even listen to me, and she's blaming you for—"

"Of course she is," Eden interrupted. "It's always the wife's fault." She smiled at Kate and Eric with an apologetic lift of her eyebrows and drew Trudy a few feet away.

Nikki Frank, black curls bouncing with every step, joined the two women. Eden was talking to Trudy, apparently trying to explain something. Hands on her hips, Nikki glared at Eden and then interrupted. Her hands swooped through the air as she spoke. Eden glared back, posture stiffening, and Trudy looked from one to the other, apparently baffled.

Kate tried not to be obvious, but she had to watch the drama play out.

Nikki's voice rose. "This isn't an auction. You've made a fortune on Jack's work. If you want that painting, you pay retail."

Trudy looked at Eden who shrugged and lifted her hands in a "what can I do?" gesture.

With a huge sigh, Trudy stalked off, right past Kate without acknowledging her.

"Who *is* that woman?" Eric asked.

Kate gave him a brief version of Trudy's role in the art world and the part she'd played in Jack's success.

Eric chuckled. "A bargain-hunting art collector. I had no idea such a—"

"Kate, darling?" The whine came back, and with it Trudy Zelnik.

Kate forced herself to smile. "Hello, Trudy."

She linked arms with Eric as Trudy held out her hand to him. "Have we met?" Trudy asked.

Kate answered for him. "This is my friend, Eric Ames."

Trudy pursed her lips and scrutinized Eric. "You lucky man." She turned back to Kate. "Dear Kate, how have you been? I miss you." She lowered her voice. "Jack hasn't been the same without you."

"He's fine," Kate protested. "And he seems very happy."

"Isn't it interesting that he married someone who looks so much like you, but is ever so different?" Trudy emphasized her last words with a loud sniff.

Her comment surprised Kate. Why was Trudy cozying up to her?

She let go of Eric and lit a cigarette. "And how are you, Trudy? Who's your favorite new artist?"

Trudy flushed with pleasure. "You know I do have an eye for talent, and there's a young girl I discovered—although Nikki will probably take credit. Tatiana Kaminsky. Wait until you see her work. Neo-abstract impressionist. If you get a chance, snap up one of her paintings now before she hits it big. You won't regret it. I believe she'll be another Jack Morrison."

Eric pulled a thin notepad and a pen from his jacket pocket. "Can you spell that for me?" he asked Trudy, doing an Oscar-worthy job of looking eager and interested.

Trudy spelled the name. "Are you a collector, Mr. Ames?"

Eric smiled. "Of sorts. And always looking for a bargain. Do you have any other tips?"

Trudy's smile flickered. "Not at the moment."

Eden reappeared and took Trudy's elbow. "Trudy, I think you and I should have another talk with Nikki. In her office."

Annoyance flared across Trudy's face, but she went along with

Eden, and Kate let go of a breath she didn't even realize she'd been holding.

She turned to Eric. "You rascal!"

Eric grinned. "What?"

"Don't pull that innocent act on me, Buster. She thought you were serious. Be careful or you'll have a new best friend."

"I hope I didn't *really* embarrass you."

"Of course not. But what—"

"Sometimes it's fun to pretend, don't you think? It's harmless. Although…" He stroked his chin. "Art *can* be a good investment, no? If you know what you're doing? And from what you told me, the woman does know her art."

"Oh no," Kate said, half-faking dismay. "Not you, too!"

"Never ignore a hot tip, Love," Eric said. "But let's put that thought away for now." He returned the notebook to his pocket and took her hand as they made another circuit of the gallery, studying the people as much as the paintings.

While Eric went to use the restroom before they hit the road, Kate scanned the crowd, looking for Jack and Eden so she could say her good-byes.

Her gaze rested on an oddly familiar face, but it took Kate a moment to place Adam Fletcher, beardless and without the haughty Morel at his side. Back from the Alaskan wilderness after all this time?

As if he sensed someone watching him, Fletcher looked at Kate, but without a flicker of recognition. He walked toward her. *Oh shit.*

"Have we met?" he asked, his attitude betraying no shame at using the classic pick-up line.

"No," Kate replied, lowering her gaze and trying to act mysterious. *Sometimes it's fun to pretend, don't you think?* "But I know you."

"Oh, really?"

"I'm psychic," Kate said. "I know things about people."

Fletcher cocked his head. "Oh, really?" he said again.

He truly didn't remember her. Had she changed that much, or had Fletcher always been so wrapped up in himself that he'd never taken a good look at her?

Kate narrowed her eyes and studied his face. "You're … an artist.

But you turned your back on your calling for a long time. I see ... snow. Ice."

Fletcher's posture stiffened, and a mischievous thrill slid over Kate. She lifted her hand toward his face.

"You had a beard. To keep your face warm. A nice, thick beard. But..."

She widened her eyes and gasped in fake horror. "Did it hurt? When your beard broke off?"

Fletcher's mouth fell open. He nearly dropped his wineglass. Kate savored the moment: arrogant Adam Fletcher, artfully disguised in his gray velvet shirt and carefully worn jeans. All alone, no fans, no allies. What had he hoped to accomplish here tonight beyond revealing his own loneliness? These shiny, chattering people had no use for him.

If she hadn't taken care of Jack, would he have ended up like Fletcher? No, Kate decided. Jack had more substance at his core. He wouldn't have turned tail and run when things didn't go his way. He'd have made it on his own; she and Eden had simply helped it happen.

Kate's hand fluttered dramatically to her chest. From the corner of her vision, she saw Eric approaching.

"Watch out, Adam. These people can chew you up and spit you out."

She turned abruptly and hurried toward Eric.

"Making new friends?" he asked as she took hold of his arm.

"Not exactly," she replied. "Let's get out of here. I want to be alone with you."

He pulled her to him for a long, deep kiss. "Sounds good to me," he said when they came up for air.

Chapter Thirty-Four
October 1982

"Holy shit. You still live here." Ryder's ragged voice matched his appearance.

"I do," Kate replied, one hand on the door frame, the other holding the knob. "But Jack doesn't."

Ryder reminded her of a stray dog scrounging for food. His blond hair was shaggy, his beard in need of a trim. He didn't look dirty, however—just worn out.

"Yeah," he said. "I got the word. Came to see how you're doing."

What could she do but invite him in? Kate let go of her Saturday-afternoon plans to plow through the pile of work she'd brought home.

Ryder started to hug her; she moved back, and then shame washed over her. The moment passed, and she tried to recover by offering him food and drink.

He shambled into the living room. "Place looks the same," he said in a bewildered voice. Then, like an afterthought, he added, "Sandwich would be good. Thanks."

Kate went toward the kitchen. "How are you? Where have you been?"

He followed. "I'm staying with my folks—good old Bright Street. Man, that hasn't changed either."

Kate spread mustard on bread and layered slices of roast beef over it. "It hasn't. And you haven't answered my questions."

"Questions? Oh. Right. I've been around, man. Oregon. Utah. New Mexico. Ever been to Taos? That's a cool scene. I liked it there. Until winter—colder than a witch's tit then."

Kate scowled at him, but he missed it. "So for six years you've been bumming around?"

Ryder's mouth fell open. "Six years?" He shook his head. "Man, I lost a lotta time."

She gave him the sandwich and popped open two Pepsis, handing one to him. "What were you doing all that time, Ryder? Besides getting high?"

He followed her to the dining table. "Yeah, I did plenty of that. But I quit."

Kate shoved a stack of manila folders to one end of the table and sat down across from him. "Really? Just like that?"

He took a bite, chewed, rubbed his stomach. "Man, this is great. Thanks. I was starved. Mom fed me breakfast, but that was hours ago. No, not just like that. Withdrawal's a bitch, man. Saw monsters in the sky, bugs inside my skin, all that shit. But I did it—met an awesome lady in Taos, she helped me through. Been there herself, you know?"

"That's great," Kate replied. An unexpected jealousy overtook her. Why? She'd never tried to stop Ryder from using; she had nothing for that in her bag of tricks. But she should have tried; she could have been the one to save him, instead of turning her back and letting him drift away. She'd been so caught up in her own misery, the breakup with Jack, that she hadn't thought about Ryder until it was too late and he'd been lost to her. *Some friend you turned out to be.*

"Your folks didn't know where you were most of the time. I asked."

He put down the sandwich. "They knew. They were too ashamed to tell you."

"Oh." That made sense: the quick, fluttery replies from Ryder's mom—looking anywhere but at Kate. *Poor woman,* Kate thought. Mrs. Ryder had always been kind to her; why hadn't she seen through the deception?

"You couldn't have done anything about it anyhow," Ryder said, and Kate cringed. "I was hell-bent on ruining myself. Until Taos."

Kate reached across and squeezed his hand. "I'm glad you got clean. That took guts." The words weren't anywhere near adequate. She believed Ryder. Something inside him had shifted, and he truly seemed sober. How much suffering had it taken to get him there?

Ryder half-smiled at her and took another bite of his sandwich.

"So what now?" she continued. "Are you still singing?"

He shook his head as he chewed.

"How come?" she asked.

Ryder swallowed. "You can't tell? Fucking voice is wrecked, man. I sound like I've been gargling with drain cleaner."

He was right, but Kate had assumed the rasp in his voice was temporary, like he was getting over a cold.

"What happened?"

"Life," Ryder said, after a minute.

"When you sing, I forget everything else," the girl at the Quarter-moon had told him all those years ago. And Ryder had probably thought his gift was invincible.

"But you can still play guitar, right?"

Ryder took a big swig of Pepsi and burped. "Can, but don't. What's the point?"

He drummed his fingers on the tabletop. "So—you gonna clue me in on what went down with you and Jack? Where'd it go off the road, kid?"

"You already know," Kate replied. "Stella said that's why you moved out of the loft—you didn't like him bringing...girls there."

Ryder's expression darkened. "Maybe I shoulda said something to you. I told *him* off, plenty. But I thought maybe you knew and didn't mind." He laughed, but it wasn't a happy sound. "I mean, you guys were pretty *out there.*"

Kate shook her head. "No. I did mind. But ... hell, there was a lot more to it, Ryder. When he started getting famous, he changed. *You* changed when you hit it big, and so did Jack. Both of you started acting like the rules didn't apply anymore, like you could do whatever you wanted without any consequences."

Ryder had finished his sandwich. He rummaged in his shirt pocket, pulled out a half-crushed pack of Camels and lit one. "You're right. I got no defense for that one. But I only hurt myself."

"And your mom, and your dad, and anybody who cared about you."

He held up his hands like she'd pointed a gun at him. "Ever see Jack these days?"

"I went to a show of his paintings last April. He's doing good. Got married."

Ryder nodded as if he already knew that. "Mr. and Mrs. Famous. You okay with that?"

"Of course. It's over between us. The new wife is nice, and Jack ...well, he's calmed down. He deserves the fame, Ryder. He works at it. He earned it."

Maybe that last remark made Ryder uncomfortable, because he looked away, and for a second she thought he winced. Then he blew a big puff of smoke at her.

"And you," he said. "Speaking of working at it—you're some big shot at the oil company now."

"Your mom tell you that?"

"No. Deb did. She's proud of you."

The disclosure stunned her. Debbie usually yawned and changed the subject when Kate talked about her job.

"Did you see her kid?" she asked.

"Yeah—cute little devil. Gonna be hell on wheels, though—takes after her mom. If the new baby's anything like—"

"What new baby?" Another shock wave rippled over Kate. "Debbie's pregnant?"

"Oh, man—sorry. She said she wanted to surprise you. Jesus, I'm such a fuck-up."

Was he covering for Debbie? Kate couldn't tell.

"No, you're not. That's typical Debbie, always keeping secrets."

Ryder ground out his cigarette, stood and stretched. "Good grub. Thanks."

He picked up the plate and carried it to the kitchen. Then he prowled the living room, and Kate's framed MBA certificate caught his attention.

"Wow, girl—pretty fancy."

Kate lit a Marlboro. "Debbie didn't mention that?"

Ryder rubbed his right forearm like he was trying to massage away an ache. "She told me. But seeing it for real blows my mind." He turned to her. "You always did go after what you wanted, never let anything get in your way." His eyes lost their focus, and then he continued. "Remember that dork Jimmy Foster? Man, he never saw you coming!"

* * *

Memory ambushed her: Jimmy Foster had been Ryder's nemesis in grade school. Tall and hefty, Jimmy tormented Ryder all through fourth and fifth grade, calling him "Fatty" and "Pizza Face," shoving up against him in the hall, making fart noises in class and then staring at Ryder like he'd done it.

One time Kate had caught Jimmy shoving Ryder around on the playground after school, punching him in the stomach. Without thinking it through, Kate launched herself at Jimmy, and the surprise of her attack caught him off balance. He fell to the ground.

Kate had stood over him, glaring, hands on hips. "Leave him alone, you lousy creep," she'd shouted. "If I catch you hurting my friend again, I'll tell everyone how a *girl* knocked you down."

* * *

Kate's face warmed. "That was very unladylike."

"But it did the job! Fucker never came after me again. Man, you were fierce!" Ryder shook his head. "I wish I had as much ... as much of whatever it is you've got."

"You do have it, Ryder. You maybe lost it for a while, but you can still do something with your life. It's nowhere near over. You could go back to school, learn a new trade."

He waved the suggestion away. "I probably killed off too many brain cells."

"What *are* you going to do?"

"Not sure. Keeping my options open."

"You could teach guitar."

He snorted. "Yeah, I can see the ads now. Learn to play guitar from a has-been who trashed his shot at being famous."

"You don't have to tell 'em *that*."

He peered down the hallway. "That dyke still live next door?"

"Stella? Yeah, she does. But don't go slandering her just because you couldn't score with her."

Ryder hugged her. "You never did see it, did ya?"

"Stella's not a lesbian," Kate insisted, although puzzle pieces clicked into place. "And even if she is, it doesn't matter. She's been a real friend."

"Then why'd you get all uptight when I called her a dyke?"

"Because it's an ugly name. She's a good person."

"Well, she sure doesn't like men."

"Ryder—even if someone is gay, that doesn't mean they hate the opposite sex. Maybe she has her own history, and maybe *she* generalizes too. Just as unfairly as you do." Kate looked directly into his eyes.

He let it go. "Okay, you made your point, and it's well taken. Sorry." He lit another Camel and flopped on the sofa. "And Deb had one more news flash—tell me about this professor you're dating."

She did.

"He's a decent guy," she concluded. "He treats me well. We have fun."

"And how come you're not married to him then? He *too* decent?"

"Is there such a thing?"

Ryder laughed. "He's not Jack—is that it? There's no danger in him?"

"That's ridiculous. You don't even know him."

"No, but I know *you*."

"Not anymore you don't. I've changed."

"People don't change. Not that much."

"You did. You got yourself off drugs, off the road to hell."

"True."

He put out his cigarette and stood. "And I've barged in on you long enough." He pointed at the files on the dining table. "I'll let you get back to work. Thanks for letting me in."

"Why wouldn't I? We're practically family."

Ryder pulled her close and kissed the top of her head. He smelled of cigarette smoke and dust, but it wasn't a bad smell. "The sister I never had."

She walked him down to the street and watched him get into a rusted Ford sedan. The car, badly in need of a new muffler, backfired and shot out sparks as it rumbled away, belching acrid white smoke.

Kate stood at the curb and waved until the noise and exhaust fumes faded. So Ryder was alive and well.

As she climbed the stairs, Kate reflected that if Ryder had cleaned up his act, then miracles really did happen. She started to knock on Stella's door and share the news, then changed her mind when she heard women's voices from the other side.

So what if she's gay? The only thing that bothered Kate was Stella's failure to confide this important fact, if it were true. *We're friends. Why didn't she tell me? And why didn't I see it?*

What is wrong with me? Why don't I see what's going on right under my nose? She thought about Jack and his groupies. There again, she'd been stupidly unaware.

"I need to pay more attention," Kate muttered as she returned to the files waiting for her on the table.

Her thoughts tumbled over and over as she tried to pick up where she'd left off with her work. Ryder had given her too much to consider. If he could transcend his mistakes, then anything was possible.

As darkness settled in, Kate rose and switched on a couple of table lamps. She could still smell Ryder's presence in the living room, and it cheered her, filled her with gratitude for his existence. She'd already lost too much of her past.

Chapter Thirty-Five
October 1983

E ric grunted as he set down the packing box. "And I thought *I* had a lot of books."

Kate laughed. "You do. When we put my pathetic library next to yours, you'll see."

She knelt on the floor and opened the carton.

"I may need to clear more shelves for you," Eric replied with a wink.

Kate stood and dusted her hands on her jeans. "No, they'll fit. I'll make them. I really did weed out a lot."

She stroked his face, and the ring on her left hand—her *wedding* ring—caught her attention and sent a ripple of pleasure along her nerve endings. She and Eric had chosen the ring together, and it was exactly what she'd wanted for herself, a plain brushed-gold band.

They'd been married in a simple ceremony at a glass-walled chapel in Palos Verdes, overlooking the Pacific Ocean. Since Eric had no family, the only guests had been Kate's mother, Debbie and her husband, and a few work friends—Marcie Plesh and her husband, along with two of Eric's fellow teachers.

Stella Barberini had declined the invitation.

* * *

Kate had confided in Stella before anyone else, the morning after Eric proposed.

"Good for you," Stella had said in an icy voice. "I hope this one turns out better."

"Gee, thanks for the pessimism. Just what I was hoping for."

Stella scowled. "You got away free and clear once. Didn't you learn? This one'll hurt you too, sooner or later. They all do."

Kate stiffened. "How the hell do you know? You let one bad experience color your whole life! And you can't tell me gay couples don't hurt one another too."

"What the fuck, Kate? You think that's why I'm not all joyful that you're marrying this clown? You think I'm biased because I'm gay?"

Kate shook her head. "I don't think that at all. But I wish you'd told me, years ago. It might have helped me understand—"

"What's to understand? It doesn't change anything. I happen to like women—they're more honest."

"You weren't honest with me."

"And you were so damned clueless. If you hadn't been all wrapped up in yourself, you'd have picked up on it. I didn't feel like I owed you some big announcement. Besides, I figured you might freak, like you're doing right now."

"I'm not freaking. It's you who's carrying on like I'm betraying you by marrying Eric."

"You think I have a thing for *you*? Don't flatter yourself, honey. You are not my type."

"I never thought that! Jesus, Stella, what is wrong with you? I come here to tell you this great news, and all you do is yell at me."

"You're the one yelling."

That much was true. Kate hadn't been aware of how loud her voice had gotten. She took a deep breath and relaxed her fists. "Sorry." Consciously, she lowered her voice. "But you hurt my feelings—never telling me something that important. And sure, maybe I should've sensed it—if even Ryder, of all people, figured it out, I guess I was really dense. But I never thought ... I mean, you were married and all."

Stella didn't respond.

"Anyway," Kate continued, "it doesn't make any difference to me, okay?"

"How generous."

"Jeez, will you cut it out! Damn it, Stella—I thought we were friends." She paused. "But maybe I misjudged you."

"Meaning?"

"Meaning if you are my friend, how come you're not happy for me?"

Stella's nostrils quivered. "You love him? Tell me the truth. Do you?"

"Of course I do. He's good to me. He's kind and caring. And he loves me."

"Okay then. Hurray for you. Have a good life. But don't lose everything you worked for, Kate. Don't go back to just being somebody's wife."

She gestured toward the door, and Kate didn't need to be told. She left, being careful to close the door quietly behind her.

Kate had tried to forget about the fight, to find a chance to reconcile with Stella, but it didn't happen. Then she got caught up in the wedding arrangements and the reservations for their Hawaii honeymoon. Stella made no overtures either.

Kate didn't know how to heal the rift. Maybe, she reflected with a piercing sense of loss, their friendship had outlived itself. Nevertheless, she slipped a wedding invitation under Stella's door.

Stella returned the card declining the invitation. Along with the reply card was a box from Tiffany, and a note from Stella.

Dear Kate,

Sorry for being such a bitch about you marrying Eric. I do hope you'll be happy, honestly. I want the best for you, and I worry about you getting hurt. You're so soft-hearted, and people take advantage of softies. But maybe Eric's different. For your sake, I hope so.

I'm going away for a while, and that's one of the reasons I can't come to your wedding. A friend of mine just got an acting gig in France, and she's asked me to come with her. I've never been, and it seems like a good time to go.

By the time I get back, you'll be an old married lady, and you'll prob-ably have moved in with Eric, so here's a sort-of wedding gift. Imagine all my love for you inside it, and be happy, my sweet Kate. Nobody deserves it more.

Love,

Stella

Stella's gift was a heart-shaped porcelain box with bright flowers painted on it. Kate stroked the cool, smooth china and cried until she ran out of tears.

Apparently Stella had left for France right after she dropped off the letter, for when Kate knocked on her door, there'd been a hollow, empty echo behind it, and Stella's mustang had disappeared as well.

* * *

Eric thought they should wait until after the honeymoon for Kate to move in with him. Kate didn't mind; she had plenty to do without hauling boxes from her apartment to his house, a graceful two-story Tudor just off Los Feliz Blvd. The quiet street, lined with trees, was a world away from Kate's old neighborhood. Although not the largest on the block, Eric's house was big enough to absorb her belongings—it could have held *two* families.

And today they made it official, moving the last of Kate's posses-sions from her old apartment.

"So, Mrs. Ames," Eric said, "aside from clearing space for your impressive library, I made one other change. Can you see it?"

Kate studied the living room. The furniture, dark wood and leather, had a distinctively masculine aura, as did the clean, simple lines of the pale linen draperies. Eric had lived alone there for five years; his style was entrenched.

Then she noticed the empty space over the fireplace and remem-bered the Van Gogh print that used to hang there.

"Where'd you put Vincent's sunflowers?" she asked.

Eric chuckled. "They're comfortably stashed away in the front bedroom upstairs. I think they're happy there. And I thought you might want to put Jack's painting in here. I know how much it means to you."

Tears gathered in her eyes. "Are you sure?"

"Of course! It's a beautiful painting. Should I mind that your ex-husband painted it?"

She shook her head vigorously.

Eric got out a ladder, and Kate supervised as he lifted "Sanctuary" into place.

A shaft of late-afternoon sunlight set the painting aglow and heightened the magic watchfulness emanating from the tree shapes that guarded the little wolf as it cried out to the purple-crimson sky.

"There," Eric murmured. "Does it feel like home to you now?"

Kate nodded. "It does. I love it here."

Seeing "Sanctuary" above the mantle reassured her that Eric had taken on the whole package, her past as well as her present. And he was a good man, so clearly happy to have her in his life. He'd never betray her the way Jack had. And if he didn't have the "danger," as Ryder had put it, so what? She'd made the right choice.

He put his arm around her. "And I love you here." He swatted her fanny gently. "Now let's get to work on your copious book collection."

"I'll do it—you have papers to grade."

He didn't argue, and Kate went to work shelving books in the space Eric had made for her. As she pulled a tattered copy of *The Sirens of Titan* from the carton, a paper fell out and fluttered to the floor. Kate picked it up and unfolded it: the sketch Jack had made of her the day they met, at the Love-In.

She smoothed the creases from the sketch and smiled. How young she'd been. Young and silly and unaware of the huge adventure awaiting her.

Kate closed her eyes and let the memories take her away for a moment: the sunlight, the tambourines, and marijuana-scented air. And young Jack Morrison, coming to her rescue for the first of many times.

Well. That chapter of her life was over and done with, Kate reflected as she folded the sketch again and tucked it back into the book. A good, safe place for mementos from her past.

* * *

Married life had fewer ups and downs this time around. The trickiest thing had been the name change. Reluctantly, she parted company with Jack's last name; all her colleagues knew her as Kate Morrison—as did the Department of Motor Vehicles and the Registrar of Voters. But she gradually began introducing herself as Kate Ames.

The single syllable sounded incomplete at first, but as time passed she grew used to it. Aside from an occasional slip of the tongue, or signing a check the old way, Kate eased into her new identity as if into a pool of warm water.

Now that she lived at the foot of Griffith Park, Kate went hiking more often. She persuaded Eric to join her a couple of times, but he didn't seem to enjoy it and claimed he preferred to spend his free time pursuing less strenuous interests. However, she made friends with a few other hikers, so sometimes she had company on her climbs. And when she went alone, she could imagine that her dad walked with her, urging her on.

* * *

Outside her marriage, things weren't quite as rosy, especially at work. Jeff Gallo had used her honeymoon absence for some blatant sabotage, Kate learned via Marcie Plesh, who described a staff meeting at which Paul Lange had asked Gallo for an update on the new medical plan implementation. Gallo had claimed he had nothing to report because Kate hadn't left him the documentation.

"She was pretty distracted with the wedding and all," he told the staff with an innocent smile. "It must've fallen through the cracks. But I'll work something up for you ASAP."

If he had "worked something up," Kate knew, he'd have taken credit for the groundwork she laid before leaving on her honeymoon. She had entrusted the files to Gallo with instructions to take it to the next step.

As badly as she wanted to, Kate didn't confront Gallo immediately.

She was too outraged to do anything but rant, and she knew it. Instead, she confided her dilemma to Eric.

He'd rubbed her shoulders, kissed the back of her neck, and whispered, "Want me to go down there and beat up the little creep?"

Kate laughed at the notion, although it was tempting.

"You could probably get him fired, you know," Eric continued. "If he's as incompetent as he sounds."

"Wildly incompetent. But he has a wife and kids to support."

"Is that *your* problem?"

"No, but I'm making it my problem."

Eric hugged her. "You're such a softie. And I love you for it." He paused and then added, "The guy has to know that *you* know about the stunt he pulled, right?"

"I think so. Even Jeff's not *that* dense."

"He'll be expecting retaliation. Which is what he wants—some sort of emotional display on your part to prove his point. You know the line: women are too volatile for responsibility, blah blah blah."

"You rattled that off pretty easily."

Eric shrugged. "I've heard it often enough. But I never believed it. And you, my darling, are living proof it's untrue."

"So what do I do?"

"Nothing, at this point. But document *everything*. And let him see you do it. He's not as smart as you are, and I think he knows it. And your man Lange seems pretty perceptive; I'd be willing to bet he's on to the guy's game. Give it some time. Your problem child will trip up over his own incompetence eventually."

"Eventually is taking a pretty long time."

"Patience, my love," Eric counseled.

* * *

Eric's predictions came true. Less than a year after the marriage, Paul Lange offered her a promotion to Manager of Benefits. Lange mentioned that Gallo had also been a candidate, but Kate clearly had a stronger track record, and Lange himself favored her for the job. Gallo would inherit Kate's Supervisor title and report to Kate. He'd also assume her former workload, and it would be sink or swim. Lange didn't seem concerned with the outcome.

Kate didn't have to think it over before accepting.

As soon as the promotion was announced, Gallo came to her office.

"Congratulations," he said with his usual lazy smirk. "Guess all that bra burning paid off."

"Thank you, Jeff," Kate said, shaking his hand and looking steadily into his eyes. "But I think hard work had more to do with it. You should try it sometime."

She and Eric celebrated with a bottle of Moet & Chandon. Kate clinked her champagne flute against his and thought that life couldn't possibly get any better.

Which meant, of course, that it could always get worse.

Chapter Thirty-Six
April 1985

O n a drizzly spring evening, Kate and Eric were at home, working in their shared office, when the doorbell rang.

Eric looked up from the papers he was grading. "Did you order take-out?"

"No," Kate replied. "We have leftovers from yesterday." She put down her department's salary plan and went to the front door with a sense of foreboding that she didn't understand.

Ryder stood on the porch, ragged and damp, swaying like a birch tree in the wind. From three feet away, Kate smelled booze on him, and something else, chemical and sharp.

"Hey," Ryder said, lifting his hand in a sort of wave. "Found ya."

"I wasn't lost," Kate replied. From out of nowhere, Jack Morrison's voice echoed in her memory. *"We're all lost, but some of us don't know it."* She tightened her grip on the door's edge.

"I's just passin' through," Ryder said, slurring his s's. He shook his head like he was trying to rearrange the thoughts inside. "Nah—that's not true. Got your address—man, that took some work—after I went to the other place. Scared some old lady half to death."

He let out a deranged cackle, and Kate suppressed an urge to shush him.

"Deb didn't wanna give you up," Ryder continued. He wagged his index finger at Kate. "But I finally convinced her. So you're married, huh? My Katie Girl got married again!"

"Yeah. I did. I'd've told you if you hadn't pulled another disappearing act."

Ryder spread his arms wide. "What can I say? I fell off the wagon. Again."

"I see that. Why?"

"Why not?" Ryder said, doing a little sideways shuffle on the porch.

"You were home free, Ryder. You worked so hard to get there. Why'd you—"

"Hey missy—the devil don't let you go that easy. He's a friend of mine, y'know. The devil is a personal friend of mine."

Ryder started singing that old song in a hideously off-key voice.

Kate clamped her hands over her ears. "Cool it, Ryder!"

He stopped singing. "What the fuck, Kate? You lose your sense of irony? You used to have a *fine* sense of irony."

"Yeah, I lost my irony the same time you lost your mind. So where does that leave us? What do you want?"

"Right now? I want you to let me in. I gotta piss something fierce. Lemme in, I'll take a leak and then I'll vamoose. You'll never see me again, if that's what you want."

Kate sighed and moved out of the doorway. "Come on in." If she refused, he might well pee in the front bushes.

"Kate?"

Shit! Eric stood in the hallway, holding a sheaf of papers.

"It's okay," she told him. "Go back to work."

"Hey! Is that your husband?" Ryder leaned to one side and waved like a kid at a parade. "Hey man—congratulations! You got the prize in the Cracker Jack box."

"It's okay, Eric," Kate said again.

"Eric!" Ryder called out. "Hey, Eric. It's cool. I'm just usin' your facilities—had a bladder emergency."

Kate kept herself between the two men. "Come on, Ryder, I'll show you where the bathroom is."

Eric moved toward them. "What's going on?"

"Nothing to worry about," Kate told him, although she didn't believe it. "This is my friend Leonard Ryder."

She hoped that using his whole name would confer a smidgen of respectability on Ryder, but it didn't work. Eric's scowl deepened, and he stared at Ryder like he was looking at a rabid animal.

"We were neighbors back when we were kids," she continued.

"Yeah, man, me and Kate, we go back a long way." Ryder narrowed his eyes at Kate. "I can't believe you didn't tell him about me."

Eric blocked Ryder's way until Kate put her hand on his arm and eased him aside.

"Second door on the left, Ryder. Make it quick."

Ryder lurched past Eric and shut the bathroom door behind him.

"You know this guy?" Eric asked in a harsh whisper. The sound of splashing in the bathroom almost drowned his voice.

Kate nodded. "Since we were kids. I know he looks awful, but he—"

"And smells worse!"

"I'm sorry! His parents are my mom's neighbors. I couldn't send him away. He'll be gone soon, I promise."

Eric shuddered. "Not soon enough."

The bathroom door swung open and Ryder came out, wiping his hands on his filthy jeans. "Hey, man, that's a pretty fancy head there. Thanks. I'm good as new."

"Great, Ryder. Now you need to go—we're both busy, and we weren't expecting company, okay?"

"Aah, it's all cool. I just wanted to pay my respects, offer congratulations. Woulda brought a wedding present but I'm a little short on dough right now, y'know?"

Tension crackled through the silence, and Kate tried to soften it.

"Thanks, Ryder," she said. "No need to explain."

Ryder nodded. "I got it. No big deal, I'm outta here." He started for the front door. Then, like an afterthought, he swiveled around. "You wouldn't happen to have any..." He held his finger to his nose. "I'm tapped out, and—"

"No," Kate said, louder than she intended. "I don't even smoke cigarettes anymore, Ryder."

He rubbed his chin like he was trying to process this information. "Then could you maybe spare a few bucks? So I could score?"

Kate wanted to cry. "Wait here."

She left him in the hallway, and Eric followed her into the office.

"Are you out of your mind?" he hissed. "You don't give money to an addict—you know what he'll do!"

Kate opened her purse. "I have to. If I don't, he'll get it some other way."

"Then give him a can of soup or something! Don't enable him."

Eric put his hand on her arm, but she pulled away. He didn't try to stop her again. Of course it was wrong to give money to Ryder. But a can of soup wouldn't satisfy his urges.

She took out $50 and walked back to Ryder. He extended a grubby hand.

"Wait," Kate said, holding the bills out of reach. "I'm only gonna do this once. And you have to promise me something first."

Ryder's gaze fastened on the money.

Kate raised her voice. "I mean this, Ryder."

He looked at her then. "Okay."

"You have to get clean again. I don't know how to help you, but there are people who do. Your friend in Taos maybe. Or a doctor or a clinic. But you have to stop using. I can't stand to see you this way. Don't you ever come back like this."

"Hey, Kate, man, I—"

"No excuses. Time to grow up, *man*. You've broken my heart. I can't watch you trash your life."

Ryder's mouth moved, but no words came out. He grabbed the money and walked out the door, humming an off-key version of "Mr. Tambourine Man," as he merged with the drizzly darkness.

"What the hell, Kate?" Eric demanded as soon as she'd shut the front door.

Kate had never seen that much anger on her husband's face, not even when they'd endured the mood swings of quitting smoking, before the wedding. Nicotine withdrawal had been agony, and Kate could understand, a little, how Ryder might backslide into drugs. There were times when she still craved a cigarette. In fact, she could have used one at that moment.

"I'm sorry," she said for what felt like the millionth time. "I didn't invite him here."

"Was he asking you for drugs? Why would he expect *you* to have any?"

Kate bit her lip and tried to frame a reasonable reply. "When I was with Jack, we didn't sit around sipping iced tea and discussing art history, Eric. I experimented. We all did. I stopped because it made me paranoid and stupid. But Ryder didn't—he couldn't. And now he's...he's what you saw tonight."

Mouth open, Eric stared at her.

"If you'd known Ryder *before*, you'd understand," Kate continued. "He had the most beautiful voice. Yes, he's ruined it, and he needs help. I wish I knew how to—"

"Don't go getting any ideas about saving some poor lost soul, Kate. He'll only drag you into the gutter with him. If he ever—*ever*—comes here again, I'm calling the police." He shuddered. "Where's the air spray? The stink of him makes me sick."

Her husband still wore his work clothes, neatly pressed gabardine slacks, a long-sleeved blue shirt that somehow looked crisp after hours of wear. Behind him, Kate caught a glimpse of "Sanctuary" in the living room, and she drew courage from it. She was not a misbehaving child; she was Eric's equal, with rights and privileges of her own.

Kate quit resisting her own anger. "Will you knock it off? Nobody's perfect, Eric. Not even you."

She stomped into the kitchen, where she banged pots and pans around and tried to calm down. Her pulse continued to race as she relived the scene in the hallway, Ryder's tattered appearance, Eric's uptight reaction. It played and replayed like a bad movie, and her misery magnified.

She dialed Debbie's number, and when her sister answered, Kate lit into her. "What the hell, Deb? Why'd you give Ryder my address?"

After a brief silence, Debbie replied, "He really wanted to see you. I couldn't very well pretend I didn't know where you lived."

"Thanks a lot. He showed up stoned out of his gourd. Scared Eric half to death. And now *we're* fighting, too."

She heard Debbie laugh. Unbelievable!

"Eric sure scares easy," Debbie said. "Sis, this is *Ryder*. He wouldn't hurt anybody."

"He's using again! How could that happen, after all he went through?"

"Listen, if you had to live with his parents you'd need to get high too. Give the guy a break. He can't get a job, he can't sing, his life is pretty messed up."

"And getting loaded will fix all that? That's half the problem—people making excuses for him, looking the other way and letting him do what he wants. And when he ends up dead or in jail, you'll act surprised and sad—when you helped him get there."

"I'm hanging up now. You're hysterical, and I don't want to hear any more. I'm sorry I gave him your sacred address. But it's done, I can't un-tell him. And you no doubt made it crystal clear he wasn't welcome, so he'll probably never come back."

Kate slammed the receiver down. She couldn't say for sure who'd made her the angriest: Ryder, Eric, or Debbie. Or herself.

* * *

Less than five minutes later the phone rang.

"Hi, there," a man said, and for a few seconds Kate didn't recognize her ex-husband's voice. "You okay? You sound a little out of breath."

"I guess I am," Kate replied. "Things got a little weird here tonight."

"I bet it had something to do with Ryder."

"How'd you know?"

She heard the click of a cigarette lighter and could almost smell the smoke. "He's been on the prowl lately. I was going to warn you—sorry I was too late."

"He got to you, too?"

"Sort of. He wandered into Nikki's gallery over the weekend and caused a huge scene. I gather he was trying to sell an old drawing of mine. Nik turned him down, and he got pissed, knocked one of my paintings off the wall, broke the frame. Unfortunately, Eden was there too, and she got into a screaming match with him. He flipped her off and called her a bunch of names, most of which had "bitch" in them, and when she picked up the phone to call the cops, he grabbed her arm. Didn't hurt her, but just him touching her, that was enough. Eden keeps her cool pretty well, but when she loses it— watch out!"

"Eric had a similar reaction."

Jack chuckled. "Ryder does have colossally bad judgment, and when he's high there's no reasoning with him."

"I can't believe he's using again. He got clean—how could he—"

"Coke is hard to kick. Lucky you didn't get snagged."

"I wish I could do something for him."

"You can't save somebody who doesn't want to be saved."

How many times had she heard that from him? Kate wondered if Jack still got high. She hadn't even smoked pot since before she quit cigarettes, but if Jack still smoked...She decided it was none of her business.

She sighed. "What do you think will happen to him now?"

Jack echoed her sigh. "I don't know. I suppose if he got clean once, he could do it again."

"If only I knew what to do, how to reach him. That woman in Taos helped him once. She got him to quit using."

"The devil don't let you go that easy."

"True," said Jack. "But you can't do that sort of thing to please somebody else. Ryder has to save his own life. We're all on our own at the end of the story, Babe. No cavalry. No magic bullet, just you and whatever you have going for you."

"I suppose you're right, but I hate to believe it."

"Why? It means you're in charge. Isn't that better than looking for somebody to rescue you?"

She let the irony slide past. It felt good, though, talking to Jack—

despite a twinge of disloyalty. She could never have had a conversation like this with Eric. Could she?

From the office came sounds of Eric moving around, closing drawers with more force than necessary.

"Kate? You there?"

"Sorry. I was thinking about what you said."

A laugh, then a thick cough. "Sorry. Damn cold won't let go. Hey, don't take me too seriously. I didn't mean to go existential. Really, I only called to give you a heads-up about Ryder. Sorry it came too late."

"Nah, it's cool. It's good to talk to you."

"Yeah, we don't talk as often as we should. But the last time I phoned, Eric didn't sound so friendly."

"Really? When was that?"

"Sometime right after New Year's. You weren't home, and he didn't say much."

The fluorescent light over the kitchen sink buzzed in the silence that followed Jack's statement. Kate looked at the wall calendar—where a fat striped cat grinned under a full moon—as if the little numbered squares would help her understand what Jack was saying.

"He never told me you called."

"I figured that. I meant to phone again—I wanted to tell you about the show in Paris, that's what I'd called about—then things got so crazy I let it slip. But you got the flyer, right?"

"I did. That was such a big step up for you. I was tickled."

"Yeah, who'd have thought it? Me in the Pompidou, right up there with Dali and Pollock."

"I'm so proud of you."

"Thanks." After a moment's silence, he added, "Anyway, I'm glad to hear your voice again. I'll try and do better at staying in touch. You take care of yourself now."

"You, too. Thanks again."

She hung up, took a deep breath, and, recharged with indignation, went to confront her husband.

"Why didn't you tell me Jack had called?"

Eric was slouched over a pile of papers on his desk. He looked up, eyebrows raised in surprise. Clearly this was not what he'd expected her to say.

"Excuse me?"

"Before his show at the Pompidou—he phoned to tell me. You took the call and never gave me the message."

"I'm sure I did. But what does it matter? Would you have flown to Paris for the exhibition?"

"Maybe I would have. That's beside the point. You should have given me the message."

"Kate, if you're trying to take my mind off the seedier aspects of your past, it's not—"

"How dare you judge me and my friends! Ryder isn't 'seedy'—and he's a human being!"

The room closed in on her, its dark wood trim swallowing too much light. On the wall behind Eric, his framed university degrees flanked her MBA certificate. He'd opened up this space to her, Kate reminded herself.

Eric's face had lost the uptight anger she'd seen earlier. Kate saw her image reflected in his eyeglasses. His expression, if she read it right, said "I am not the enemy here."

Eric put down his pen. "I never said he wasn't human. But he surprised me—not the sort of fellow I come into contact with." His voice softened. "I'm sorry your friend has fallen on hard times."

Kate's anger began to fade.

"It must make you sad to see that happen," Eric continued. "I made it worse for you. I apologize." He paused as if waiting for her to say something. When she didn't, he added, "And I apologize if I forgot to tell you Jack had called. I never claimed to be a good secretary."

His tentative smile soothed her, and Kate unclenched her hands. She was being unfair to Eric, just as he'd been unfair to Ryder. So he made a mistake; sometimes she forgot things, too.

"That's true," she replied. "Good thing you have other ways to earn a living, huh?"

He stood and held his arms open wide. "Good thing."

Kate went to him and leaned into his embrace, sighing with relief as he kissed the top of her head.

"Our first fight," she murmured against his shirt.

"Thank goodness we got *that* over with. Now—is this the part where we kiss and make up?"

"It is." Kate grinned up at him. "And you know what they say about make-up sex."

"Why don't you show me?"

She did.

Chapter Thirty-Seven
February 1990

K ate dropped the day's mail on the kitchen table, kicked off her high heels and poured a glass of wine. For the first time in weeks, she'd gotten home before Eric. Her career demanded more time and energy than ever, but it also paid more money than she'd ever expected to earn.

Her salary made her feel like an equal partner in the marriage. Kate carried her share of the financial load, although she gratefully left decisions about investments to Eric. He was the financial wizard, after all, and unlike him, she didn't enjoy studying the real estate market or comparing mutual fund performance/earnings ratios.

As she sifted through the pile of mail that evening, Kate savored the crisp chardonnay and let it blur the edges of her thoughts. She picked up a white business envelope addressed to Eric; it stood out from the cluster of junk mail and advertisements. The return address read "Richland Services" and an address in downtown Los Angeles. Kate didn't recognize the sender's name. What was Eric up to?

She forgot her curiosity as she skimmed the pages of *Time*, the news magazine she'd relied on since college to keep her informed about what was going on in the world.

A photograph caught her attention, and an odd, disorienting sense

of recognition sparked. *Oh my God—that's* Jack! He looked contempla-
tive, a little grayer at the temples than when she'd last seen him. She
smoothed the pages and began to read.

A Modern-Day Throwback?

*Jack Morrison graduated from Chouinard Art Institute when avant-
garde art still flourished. Since then, he's moved from sparse Hopperesque
reality into Rothko territory and has flirted with icon status for over a
decade. He's hit his stride but is still incredibly tricky to label...*

The article described his "richly textured" canvases and used words
like "scale" and "context" in describing "simple images transformed
into complexity by lavish colors." Photos of his work accompanied the
text; Kate recognized some of the paintings, like old friends showing
up unexpectedly.

"Oh, Jack," Kate whispered. "You did it. You really are famous
now."

His work hung in permanent collections at the Los Angeles
County Museum of Art, the Whitney in New York City, the
Pompidou in Paris, and some other European museums with which
Kate was unfamiliar. The profile reported that he'd recently gifted two
paintings to the Museum of Contemporary Art in downtown Los
Angeles.

"And I have one of his best paintings," Kate whispered.

*Morrison continues to subvert the rules of form and composition to
reveal a deeper truth. His work addresses the twin themes of meaning and
reality effortlessly and enticingly.*

She didn't hear the back door open, or Eric's arrival. When he
called out a hello, Kate flipped the magazine shut, like a kid caught
raiding the cookie jar.

Eric set his briefcase down on the table and gave her a kiss. "What
are you up to?"

She took another drink of wine, more than a mere sip. "Nothing, I
was going through—"

Eric looked down at the mail spread across the table and seized the
envelope she'd set aside for him.

"What the hell? Why are they sending mail *here?*" he muttered as
he tore it open.

"Something wrong?" Kate asked.

He didn't answer, but his face turned pale.

"I don't believe this," he groaned.

"Eric? What is it?"

He cleared his throat. "Nothing, Love. Merely a misunderstanding I'll have to address. Minor but time-consuming." He smiled. "Where's my hello kiss?"

Kate kissed him again, and when he went into the office, she started baking chicken breasts for dinner. Then she went back to her wine and the magazine article, devouring each word and savoring her own private knowledge about Jack Morrison and his art. Sooner or later she'd show the profile to Eric, but this was apparently not the time.

What was that letter all about?

Dinner passed uneventfully. The chicken tasted fine to Kate, but Eric didn't clean his plate like usual. He didn't mention the letter from Richland Services, and she didn't ask. He'd probably tell her when he was ready.

They shared a laugh about one of Eric's students who had turned in a report on the marketability of mobile phones, predicting an ever-increasing reliance on them for more than mere telecommunication.

"They're so big and clunky," Kate said, giggling. "I'd have to get a bigger purse!"

Eric smiled. "Yes, young Mr. Riley is quite the visionary. I wonder if he'll be proved right."

Kate picked up their plates and took them to the sink. "Speaking of visionaries, I got a surprise tonight."

He looked up. "Really?"

She handed him the new issue of *Time*. "Check out the 'Arts' section."

He thumbed through the magazine and came across Jack's profile. "Oh."

"Yes," Kate said, trying for a casual tone. "He's really made the big time."

Eric scanned the article. "He should have given you credit for your role. You helped him get started."

"Ancient history, my darling."

He sniffed and flipped the magazine shut. "Do you ever regret the way things turned out? Do you miss all that excitement?"

She clasped his hand. "Not for a minute."

He studied her face but didn't say anything, so she continued. "I never enjoyed all the pretense, and having to be polite to people I really didn't like."

"I hope I'm enough for you," Eric said.

Where had *that* come from?

"Of course you are! More than enough. I love our life together."

"Even if it's not glamorous?"

"Glamour is overrated."

But even as she spoke, visions of an alternate universe glittered behind her words. *If I'd stayed with Jack, what would we be doing tonight? Having drinks on the terrace of some fancy condo? Fielding phone calls from collectors? Joking about the article? If we went to a glitzy night-club to celebrate, people would check me out and whisper, "That's Jack Morrison's wife."*

Wait. *Jack Morrison's wife.* Right. Would anyone even know *her* name?

Kate drained her wineglass and loaded the dishwasher.

Chapter Thirty-Eight
May 1991

"Vice President, Human Resources." Kate studied her face in the mirror and felt a thrill when she whispered the words. It could happen.

For months she'd been steeling herself for Paul Lange's retirement. He'd mentioned the possibility of her succeeding him, but no one had offered the job. She wanted it and feared it and dreaded the day her boss and mentor walked away for good.

"Of course you want it," Eric had insisted. "It's what you've worked for your whole career."

"You think I'm ready?"

"Certainly." He'd paused and then asked, "How much of a bump in pay would this mean?"

Surprised by the question, Kate had waffled. "I have no idea."

"Whatever they offer, ask for twenty-five percent more."

"You're joking!"

"No, Kate. I never joke about money. You know that."

Rumors had swirled through the department about Lange's successor. One widely-held belief had been that senior management would reach outside the company; that was the new business trend. "If you've been here more than ten minutes, you're old hat" was the way the cynics described it. Kate had tried to ignore the speculation.

* * *

When Paul Lange called her into his office on a Friday morning and she found Stan Shaw, Senior VP of Operations—Paul's boss—sitting in one of the visitor chairs, Kate shivered. The waiting was over.

Shaw rose when she entered, something close to a smile on his deadpan face. "Kate. Thank you for joining us."

Kate shook his hand. Shaw's grip was firm, his flesh cold.

Her boss didn't smile as he gestured to the second visitor chair. Kate sat. Lange had called her out of a meeting about impending layoffs at the West Texas refinery, and she hadn't had time to freshen her makeup. She had a run in her stocking that she'd tried to patch with clear nail polish, and it rubbed her calf as she smoothed her skirt and tried to slow her pulse.

Shaw cleared his throat. "Since Paul decided to retire, I'm sure you know we've done an exhaustive search for his replacement. It will be difficult to fill his shoes."

Kate started to speak, but Shaw silenced her with an upheld hand. "Difficult but not impossible. We had to carefully consider who was most qualified, and equally important, who could take over the reins with the least disruption." Shaw paused and studied her for a moment.

Kate's nails dug into her palms.

"Which is why we've decided that Jeff Gallo is the right choice for the job," Shaw continued.

Kate's vocal cords froze. *Gallo?*

"I see," she finally managed to reply.

Mr. Dead Serious went on in his monotone to explain that he and Lange had already spoken with Jeff, who had accepted the job (of course he would!) But all three of the men were concerned about Kate's reaction.

"You must know that your name was also on the list," Shaw said.

"I did," Kate replied. "And I admit I'm disappointed." She drew in a breath and looked at Paul Lange. "But I know you didn't make this choice lightly, and of course you have every right to offer the job to the person you think is best qualified."

"It's not only a question of qualifications," Lange put in. "It's a question of working relationships—with the unions *and* with the Board. There is no doubt in my mind that you could do this job blind-folded. But we couldn't be confident that the parties involved would *let* you."

How could she smile at him? Somehow, she did. "I appreciate your telling me before the announcement."

"And I appreciate the way you're taking the news," Shaw said. "You're a pro all the way. Always have been."

When he left, a chilly draft fluttered behind him.

Kate got up stiffly and followed him out the door. She didn't want to let Lange, or anyone, see her cry, but Lange looked almost on the verge of tears himself. She knew this wasn't his choice, but the man wanted out, and who could blame him? He'd been good to her, he'd promoted her and let her try her wings and learn all kinds of skills. But there was only so much a good boss could do—a good boss who wanted to retire while he still had his health.

* * *

She closed the door to her office and phoned Eric at work, praying she'd catch him between classes. She did.

"Those bastards!" he sputtered. "Those cowardly, short-sighted bastards!"

His response gratified her but did nothing to ease the ache of disappointment.

"It's bad enough not getting the job," Kate moaned, "but I don't think I can stand to work for Gallo. The look on his face, the way he ... I have to resign, Eric. I can't stay here."

"No!" Eric said, his voice louder than usual. "No, Kate. You can't quit. Think of what you'd give up, what we'd lose if you walked away."

He paused, then continued. "I didn't want to worry you, but we need your income right now. My finances have been a little dicey lately, nothing serious, but ... Please don't do anything impulsive. Give it a few weeks. I'm sure once the dust settles you'll—"

"I will," Kate said. She didn't want to hear any more. The panic in his voice alarmed her. Eric was having money troubles and needed her to keep working—how had that happened?

Kate longed for Marcie Plesh. Marcie would've taken her out for a good stiff drink, and maybe she, too, would have urged Kate to stay calm and not do anything rash. But cancer had stolen Marcie away three years earlier, and there was no one else at Permian to whom Kate could turn at that moment. She was on her own.

"Might as well get it over with," she muttered as she smoothed her hair, put on some lipstick, and went looking for Jeff Gallo.

Through her wretched disappointment, Kate told herself that Gallo was not totally untalented or stupid, and if he halfway tried he could do decent work. Kate had encouraged him with praise for what he did well, and they'd managed to craft a halfway cordial work relationship. She could only hope that, once he got in the VP's chair, he'd remember the kindness she'd shown him and let go of the times they'd clashed.

He was in the break room, and apparently the news had gotten out —he'd probably helped it along—because a cluster of co-workers surrounded him. Kate took a deep breath, looked him in the eye and shook his hand.

"Congratulations, Jeff," she said and was pleased at the surprise on his face. "I'm sure you'll live up to their expectations, and of course I'll do anything I can to help."

"I'm counting on it," said Gallo, returning her fake smile with one of his own.

Kate walked away while she was still in control of herself, and in the hallway, an old saying popped into her thoughts: *Keep your friends close, and your enemies closer.*

"I can hardly wait to see how *that* works out," she muttered to herself.

Chapter Thirty-Nine
August 1995

"Happy Birthday."

Kate recognized her ex-husband's voice on the phone, despite the months since they'd last spoken.

"Jack! You remembered!"

The irony of his call almost amused her, because her current husband seemed to have overlooked her birthday.

"Always." He chuckled softly.

A few beats of silence followed, and then Jack continued. "Hope I didn't interrupt anything important."

"You didn't."

That was true. Gone were the days when Paul Lange delegated choice, challenging assignments. Jeff Gallo saved those for his favorite minion, a drab transfer from marketing who showed no trace of competition.

"Good." Another brief pause. "This is short notice, but I'm on my way to New York later today, and I'd like to stop by and see you. I wanted to take you to lunch or dinner, but this trip came up last minute."

"Of course, come on by," Kate replied. "New York, huh?"

"Yeah. Nik's got me a show at some swanky gallery in September and I need to go meet and greet. You know the drill."

"Do I ever. That's great, Jack. Congratulations."

"Yeah, we'll see. Sometimes these things are more trouble than they're worth. But your office is on my way to the airport, and I haven't seen you in so long I don't know if I'll even recognize you."

"You will, trust me."

* * *

He got there a little after two p.m., and he looked as good as ever—slim and fit, in crisp black denim jeans and a black leather jacket that flattered his hair, which had silvered even more since she'd last seen him.

He hugged her, then stood back and grinned. "Best-looking executive I ever saw."

"I needed that," Kate replied with a laugh.

Jack studied her for a minute. "Seriously, Babe—you look good. I think you're even prettier now than when I met you."

"Flattery will get you anything."

Gracie, Kate's assistant, gave Jack her most brilliant smile as she came to offer coffee. She'd heard of Kate's famous-artist ex-husband and Kate could tell she was eager to get a good look at him. On her way out, from behind Jack, Gracie mouthed "Wow!"

"You have your own secretary!" Jack stage-whispered.

Kate giggled. "*Assistant*, Jack. They're called assistants now. Have a seat."

Jack sank into one of the visitor chairs in front of Kate's desk. "Pretty cool." He picked up Kate's bronze nameplate and studied it for a moment, then murmured, "Ms. Kathryn Ames."

Kate sat in the other chair, turning it to face Jack. "I couldn't very well keep Morrison—Eric's pretty understanding, but even he might object to that."

"I get it. And how is Eric?"

"He's fine," Kate replied, although that wasn't true. Eric assured her he'd conquered his financial troubles, but whenever she grumbled about the toxic atmosphere at work and speculated about quitting, he protested, claiming he was only concerned for her welfare—the job market was shaky and she didn't want to be perceived as a quitter, and so on. Kate wasn't entirely convinced of his motives.

"And Eden?" Kate asked.

"She and Nikki fight like a couple of cats, but they're both right in their own way. Nik wants edgy, Eden wants pretty. Sound familiar?"

Kate couldn't meet his gaze. "Yep." She pulled out some photos of her niece and nephew to ease the sudden tension, and finally she asked about Ryder.

Jack shook his head. "No idea where that guy went. Too damn bad. Such a waste."

"Such a waste," she echoed. From a couple of things her sister Debbie had said, Kate had a hunch Ryder was back in town, but she didn't pursue it with Debbie.

Jack pulled a small package out of his jacket pocket. "I picked this up in Santa Fe a few weeks ago. Happy Birthday."

The present surprised her; they'd stopped exchanging gifts after the divorce. *What a sweet gesture*, she thought as she wondered what prompted it.

Kate eased the ribbon off the box and peeled away the wrapping. When she lifted the lid, a glint of silver flashed in the afternoon sunlight. Cushioned in blue tissue paper, hanging from a silver chain, lay a pendant in the shape of a starburst, with a disc of perfect turquoise at its center.

Jack leaned forward, gripping the chair arms. "This made me think of you. I can't explain why, but I had to get it for you. To me it looks like the universe, with you the glue that holds it together."

Kate held the necklace to her throat. "It's lovely, Jack. Thank you."

"Here," he said, "let me help." He stood and fastened the clasp for her. His hands brushed her shoulders, and Kate's nerve endings tingled.

"Think of it as your good-luck charm," he said as he sat back down.

She pressed her fingers against the pendant. "Thanks. I could use some good luck."

Jack frowned. "Anything wrong?"

"Figure of speech," Kate replied.

Her phone rang. Gracie intercepted the call, but an awkwardness settled in as the phone trilled again, and Gracie's muffled voice drifted past the closed outer door.

"You're mighty popular," Jack said.

Kate shrugged. "Everybody has problems they think I can solve."

Her words and tone sounded bitter, even to her. Kate touched the pendant again.

"Maybe this isn't so much fun for you these days?" Jack responded.

"Things have changed," Kate acknowledged. "But mostly I still enjoy it."

She held back an urge to unburden herself to Jack. He was no longer her confidant. And had he ever been, really? Eric was—or used to be—a better source of reassurance.

"Well, you sure look successful to me," Jack said. His hand swept toward Kate's desk. "It feels a little weird to see this side of you, Babe. Did I *ever* come visit you back in the day?"

Kate rubbed her chin, trying to remember. "I don't think so. It wasn't exactly your thing."

She tried to see her office through Jack's eyes: the stack of folders bristling with "Sign Here" stick-on flags, the pile of correspondence in her inbox, the glowing computer monitor. The window beside them faced away from downtown but afforded a decent view to the west, including Griffith Park and the Observatory. Her desk was a glossy chunk of burnished oak, and the shelves behind it were full of books about health and welfare plans, retirement programs, employee stock ownership plans. The office made her look like she knew what she was doing.

"You really made something of yourself, Kate. I'm proud of you."

Kate almost blushed. "But not like you, Mr. Famous Artist."

"I don't feel famous. Some days I don't feel like an artist. I'm just a guy who slaps paint on canvas and for some reason people respond to it."

"Now who's sounding disillusioned?"

"No, not really. But I've been lucky—and I know it. Lots of more talented painters didn't get this far. And lately—call it my mid-life crisis—I've been wanting to give something back."

"That's nice, Jack. I bet you will. And for what it's worth, I still get a kick out of going to LACMA and seeing your paintings hanging there. Sometimes I think, 'I remember when he did that.'"

He reached over and squeezed her hand. "Glad I can still give you a thrill, Babe."

She hurried past the affectionate gesture. "And 'Sanctuary!' It's in our living room, and everyone who sees it is blown away."

He smiled. *He's never seen our house,* Kate realized. *I've never seen his.*

"So," she asked, "what are you working on now?"

He reached toward his shirt pocket and Kate feared he'd pull out a cigarette. Permian had recently banned smoking in its building.

Jack must have figured this out by the absence of ashtrays, for his hand dropped to the chair arm. "Trying out some new work, new images, funny stuff."

"Funny peculiar or funny ha-ha?"

He grinned. "Funny ha-ha. I hope."

"Like clowns?"

"Not exactly. More like fish and cows and—"

"Cows?"

"Yeah. Cows are inherently funny."

"If you say so."

He sipped his coffee and then added, "Nikki and Eden both hate 'em, by the way—first time in years they've agreed. Eden thinks they're stupid, and Nik wants me to do serious work. But I don't dig serious. I want to have some fun."

"Nothing wrong with that."

He coughed: a heavy rattle that made Kate wince.

"Are you okay?" she asked. "You look tired."

Jack waved away her concern. "Damn cigarettes are catching up with me." The furrows on his forehead deepened, and he seemed about to say something more; his mouth started to open, and his eyes fixed on her face.

Kate's heart did a funny fluttery thing—was that what "skipping a beat" meant?

In the space of that heartbeat, she saw her life with Jack spool out in her mind, from their first meeting at the Love-In, to the loft rooftop, the Vegas wedding, the apartment on Kingsley, the museums and galleries. The lovemaking and the fights. She had shared so much with this man. They'd grown up together. They had been so close, like they'd shared the same skin, the same breath. They'd been so irrevocably in love.

"I always know where you are, Babe. I always know when you need me. I feel it."

Jack's brown eyes seemed to be x-raying her, and Kate had the dizzying sense that Jack was seeing her, really *seeing* her heart and mind, thinking the same thoughts she was thinking, sharing the same memories and regrets. If they tried, could they ever slip back through time and become that magic, golden couple again? Did they want to, really?

The spell broke when Jack glanced at his watch, an expensive-looking thing with a slim silver band.

"Damn," he said. "I gotta get going."

Kate stood. "It was great to see you, Jack. Thanks for coming by. Thanks for the beautiful necklace."

"Wear it in good health, Babe. I wish...I wish I had more to give you. The world—I'd give you the world if I could. You know that."

She opened her arms for a hug. "I do. Thank you."

He didn't smell quite the same, not exactly the way she remembered. She caught layers of cigarette smoke and leather, intermingled with a musky cologne. No trace of linseed oil or turpentine, though. But when she looked up at him, she could still find traces of the old Jack in the angles and planes of his face.

He kissed her lips, really quickly, then backed away like he was embarrassed. He recovered, though, and looked right into her eyes again for a minute. "We made a good team back then, didn't we?"

"That we did, Jack. That we did."

"I still miss you, Babe. I miss your guidance. You're the only one who ever really got me, you know."

And then he was gone, whistling down the corridor to the elevators.

"So that's him," Gracie said as she watched him go.

"Yep. That's Jack."

"Pretty fancy."

"Pretty fancy," Kate agreed.

"Ever wish you were still with him?"

Kate couldn't answer for a minute.

"No," she said finally, as she picked up her message slips. "I like things just the way they are."

Chapter Forty
June 1996

Climbing a steep fire road in Griffith Park on a humid Sunday morning, Kate did a rough estimate of the miles she'd hiked over the years and figured she had done the equivalent of at least one trip around the earth. She paused to catch her breath and watch daylight spread across the city.

The air felt heavy and thick as she labored uphill, perspiration trickling down her back and gluing her t-shirt to her skin. Weather reports hinted at a thunderstorm on its way south, and the advancing moisture added to the dense atmosphere. Kate swiped away the sweat stinging her eyes; she licked her lips and tasted salt. When she stopped for a breather, she noticed banks of dark clouds looming to the north. No more rest stops, then; no acting like the wimps who turned back when the going got rough.

Where were the birds that usually serenaded her on morning climbs? Had the impending storm already driven the finches and sparrows to cover? A rough breeze stirred chaparral branches, lifting their pungent scent into the air, and then even the shrubs fell silent. Her hiking boots ground into the sandy trail, which was gritty and summer-dry already, the rocks underfoot threatening punishment for lapsed attention.

Suddenly, pain ripped through her. Kate doubled over, hands on knees. *What the hell?* The trail had been steep enough to set her heart thudding against her ribs, but not like this, not enough to bring on this sharp, crushing jab in her chest. Kate leaned against a nearby oak, fighting dizziness, fumbling open her backpack and grasping the water bottle with shaky hands. The tree's rough trunk bit into her side, but it held her upright while she tried to recover.

Kate got the bottle open and took a sip of water as the pain and dizziness subsided, although her vision blurred. On the trail ahead of her, a shape loomed out of the shadows. She blinked. Was that a dog? No, a coyote. The biggest damn coyote she'd ever seen, at that. Shoulders hunched, it stood in the center of the trail, watching her.

Wait. It wasn't a coyote. Kate's heart lurched again—it was a wolf, a big wolf. No way. Kate shook her head; she dropped the water bottle and rubbed her eyes with the heels of her hands. This couldn't be happening; there were no wolves anywhere in Los Angeles, except in the zoo. Could this one have escaped its chain-link prison? Maybe she was hallucinating. *Do you get acid flashbacks decades later?*

Why the hell had she set off alone? Why the hell did Eric always refuse to come with her?

If Jack were here ... The thought surfaced without intention. Jack claimed he could *feel* it when she needed him. But that had been in another life. And no way in hell would Jack Morrison be anywhere near a hiking trail, especially at seven o'clock on a muggy Sunday morning.

Kate touched the silver starburst pendant hanging around her neck. She seldom removed Jack's birthday gift. Her fingers caressed the necklace for a moment while her vision cleared and her heart resumed its normal rhythm, as if the very thought of Jack had power to calm her.

The wolf-shape on the trail evaporated. She was finally able to take in some air, but as she leaned over to retrieve her backpack and water bottle, Kate noticed her hand still trembled. Time to head back anyway.

* * *

Eric had the Sunday *Times* spread over the kitchen table, coffee in one hand and buttered toast in the other. He raised his face for a kiss as she came in.

"Good walk?"

Kate kneaded his shoulders for a moment while she considered telling him about her experience on the trail. "Very nice. I wish you'd come with me sometime."

He grunted and turned back to the newspaper. Eric *did* need to take up some form of exercise. His metabolism no longer vaporized every morsel of food, and she'd noticed a thickening around his waist, a jiggle to his stomach.

She ruffled his hair, still thick but going gray, then poured herself a cup of coffee and toasted a bagel for breakfast.

Without looking up, Eric handed her the Calendar section of the paper; he continued studying the front section, turning pages with sharp, snapping movements.

"Bad news?" Kate asked.

Eric looked up, jaw clenched, and for a moment Kate thought she saw annoyance on his face.

"The usual," he replied before his eyes went back to the paper.

She took a sip of coffee. "Would you like to catch a movie this afternoon? I didn't bring any work home this weekend."

She had a sense of him physically and reluctantly pulling his focus from the newspaper. "That would be nice."

* * *

A hot shower helped quell the itchy restlessness that had started on her morning walk. As she shut off the water, Kate heard the phone ring and Eric's muffled answer.

A moment later he eased open the bathroom door; he was holding the cordless phone receiver.

"It's Eden," he said. "Eden Morrison."

As if Kate knew more than one Eden—as if anyone but her ex-husband's current wife could carry a name like that.

Dripping wet but blazing with curiosity, Kate wrapped a towel around herself and took the phone. "Hi, Eden. What's up?"

Although she and Eden had always been cordial to each other, a Sunday-morning phone chat was unexpected.

"Kate," Eden began, and Kate heard a wobble in her voice. "I wanted to get to you before you saw it on the news. It's bad, Kate. It's Jack... He..." Eden broke into a sob. After a sharp inhale, she went on. "He died early this morning. A heart attack."

Kate noticed water puddling on the blue tile floor and thought, *I should blot that up.* She almost dropped the phone. She did drop the towel. Eric remained in the doorway, wide-eyed. He started to speak, but Kate held up her hand for silence. The light through the bathroom window seemed to dim.

"Oh," Kate said into the receiver. She didn't know what else to say.

She reached for the starburst necklace and then realized she'd removed it before her shower.

"What—what happened?" Kate pulled herself together with immense effort. She wanted to sink onto the bathroom floor, despite the hard, cold tiles. "I didn't know he had heart trouble."

"He didn't," Eden replied. "He seemed *fine* last night. But this horrible noise woke me this morning—he was sucking in air like he couldn't catch his breath. He wouldn't wake up. I called nine-one-one, and they came right away, they tried to revive him, but... his heart, Kate—it just *gave out.*"

Eden's voice faded again.

"I'm so sorry, Eden."

Kate's mind churned. *Say something comforting!* she told herself. *No, that's ridiculous, there are no words for this.*

"I apologize for telling you so abruptly," Eden continued. "I should have led up to it more gently, but I had to let you know as soon as possible—I hope you understand. A reporter has already called here, and I'm trying to notify Jack's family and friends before the news gets out."

"Thank you," Kate said in an empty, mechanical voice that shamed her, as she took in how incredibly painful this had to be for Eden.

"Jack would have wanted me to call personally," Eden said. "You were very important to him. I think you know that."

"I do." Kate paused to breathe. "Are you all right? Can I do anything to help?"

"I don't think so," Eden replied, and Kate couldn't tell which question she'd answered.

"I have to go now, Kate. There are so many more calls. As soon as I make the ... the arrangements, I'll be in touch. And would you do me one favor—would you tell Ryder? I don't know how to reach him and I don't care to speak with him anyway."

"I understand. Good-bye, Eden, and if there's anything else I can—"

But Eden had hung up.

Kate handed the phone to Eric without speaking. In the hazy bathroom mirror, she saw a woman with crazed eyes and pale skin, water-darkened blond hair hanging in clumps. It took a moment to realize she was staring at her own reflection.

She felt the most bizarre sensation, as if the earth had been yanked out of orbit and was spinning through space, coming apart at its seams.

Oh, Jack. Whoever thought it would end like this?

Chapter Forty-One

If Jack's death hadn't been shocking enough, Kate got another jolt when Ryder picked her up the morning of the funeral. His hair, now trimmed short, had turned white, and his face was scored with wrinkles. He wore dark glasses, and when he removed them to greet her, Kate saw sober clarity in his blue eyes.

Although he looked like an old man, Ryder's gait was vigorous and lithe. He'd explained to her over the phone that he'd gotten into Tai Chi to help stay sober. "It centers me," he'd said. "Keeps me flexible. It's all about flexibility now."

During their phone conversation, his voice had held clues of his physical transformation, but Kate still needed a moment to adjust.

Ryder laughed. "Yeah, people do that a lot. It's cool. Here—pinch me. I'm real."

* * *

As soon as she'd halfway recovered from Eden's phone call, Kate had contacted her sister Debbie, since Deb stayed in touch with Ryder's parents. Kate and Debbie had smoothed over old disputes, but their relationship remained easily irritated; it probably always would. Some people simply weren't meant to get along.

Debbie had shrieked when Kate broke the news about Jack. Her grief rang false to Kate, since Debbie hadn't mentioned Jack in years, beyond a snide remark now and then about Kate's "famous-artist ex."

"It's horrible," Kate said over Debbie's sobs. "And I'm sorry to drop it on you like this. But right now I need to find Ryder if I can, and tell him, before the word gets out. Do you know where he is?"

Debbie did. She gave Kate the phone number and emphasized Ryder's sobriety, how this time it appeared to have taken root. "But be gentle when you tell him, okay? Don't just blurt it out like you did with me. Show some sensitivity."

Stung by her sister's criticism, Kate thanked Debbie and hung up, but she did take the comment to heart.

The gruff, hoarse voice that answered his phone sounded only a little like the Ryder she'd last seen, and Kate tensed.

"Hi," she began, groping her way into the reason she'd called. "Deb gave me your number."

He didn't say anything, so Kate continued, "She said you're doing good now. I'm so glad."

After a moment's silence, Ryder murmured something noncommittal, and his voice held a wary edge. No doubt he sensed that she hadn't called simply to shoot the breeze.

"I have some really bad news," Kate said. Then she told him everything she knew about Jack's death.

There was a big whoosh of breath on the phone line.

"Man, I didn't think he'd go first."

Kate couldn't think of a better response than "Neither did I."

"Glad he didn't suffer," Ryder continued, and then he added, "There'll be a funeral, right? You'll go?"

"I think I should—you too."

"Man, I don't know. Eden, all that. She's a rough one, and I was an asshole last time I saw her. And your husband—he'd probably take a swing at me. I was an asshole with him, too. And probably with you."

"I wasn't sure you remembered that."

"Hard to forget when you make that big a spectacle of yourself."

"It's okay, Ryder. We all make mistakes. As for Eden—she asked me to tell you about Jack, so I'm sure she understands that you'll come to his funeral. And Eric won't be there. He barely knew Jack, and—"

"Can I go with you? I'll even drive."

It had seemed right, and the way Jack would have wanted.

* * *

The muggy start to June gave way to bruising sunshine the day of Jack's funeral. Ryder's nondescript compact car, however, had surprisingly good air conditioning; the vinyl seats looked like he'd just wiped them clean, and the interior smelled vaguely of pine. The ash tray appeared unused.

He drove with casual but careful attention to the road, shifting gears smoothly and checking traffic before each lane change. Every time Kate looked at Ryder, surprise fluttered in her chest. It was like riding with a stranger—until he spoke, and then beneath the roughened voice, she heard her old friend.

I didn't do very well by you, Ryder. I should have paid more attention. I should have tried to help.

"Think Eden will kick me out of the chapel?" he asked.

Kate took her time replying. "She may not even recognize you if you keep your mouth shut."

She regretted her pitiful attempt at a joke, because Ryder flinched.

"So," Kate said, "Deb told me you're teaching guitar now?"

He nodded. "I am. Turns out I have a thing for it. Kids like me. Maybe they hear the music inside me, whatever. It pays the bills."

"Great."

"Lucky for me I don't need much these days," he continued. "I get by. And you—Miss Hot-Shot Manager. Rakin' in the dough?"

Kate dug her nails into her palms. "Not as much as you might think. It's damned hard work. But I like it—some of it."

Ryder's head bobbed up and down. "Look how we turned out. Who'd'a thought it, back on Bright Street."

She turned toward the side window and blinked away tears.

Fountain spray lifted in iridescent arcs as they passed through the mortuary gates. Tall trees swayed in an afternoon breeze, and the setting, so deceptively tranquil and benign, almost made Kate forget why they were cruising up this narrow roadway. Then she saw the stone plaques in the ground, the occasional upright gravestone, and she felt another wave of grief.

Ryder parked amid a cluster of shiny cars, Mercedes and Lexus emblems gleaming in the sunlight. He turned off the engine, puffed his cheeks and exhaled noisily.

Kate clasped his hand. "I'm so grateful you're here. I'm glad ... glad you got your life back together."

His smile held a world of regret. "Yeah, I think I am, too. Some days, man, I get scared I won't be able to hang on, but somehow I do it. One day at a time, like they say. Hell, sometimes it's like I'm sittin' on the edge of a fuckin' knife."

"Don't fall off." She paused, wishing she had stronger encouragement to offer. "I can't claim I know how you feel, but I did go through hell when I quit cigarettes. I remember wanting to give up about a million times. And you—you've done something a lot harder. You've got the guts to see it through."

He grunted. "Let's hope you're right, kid."

Outside, people were walking toward the chapel, but Ryder made no move, even though the temperature inside the car rose quickly.

After a few ticks of silence, he continued with a shake of his head, "Man, I did love my blow. I loved it the way ... the way Jack loved you. For a while I loved it more than music. Now that was a major fuck-up."

"I liked it, too, Ryder—all that energy and confidence. But so damn dangerous."

"I get that now. But when it had me by the throat, I didn't care. I felt immortal. First time I did it, I felt the vibe in my skin, my gut— same thing I felt when I was playing guitar, only stronger. I knew everything was gonna be okay."

"Only it wasn't."

"Only it wasn't," he agreed, and opened the door.

Kate looked past him, down the sloping green lawns to the freeway and beyond, to their home town fanned out in the distance. She could almost see Bright Street, transformed over the years by ambition and passing trends, unrecognizable now. She took a deep breath and got out of the car. A warm wind struck her face, and the heat of the pavement penetrated her shoe soles. She linked arms with Ryder.

"You ready for this?" he asked.

Kate shook her head violently.

"Yeah," Ryder said, "I guess we never are."

Kate noticed his clothes for the first time. His suede jacket, worn thin in places but clean, covered a white cotton shirt, and his dark twill slacks seemed brand-new.

*   *   *

Kate did all right until they entered the chapel.

She should have expected the open coffin, all gleaming walnut and polished brass, but it knocked the breath out of her to see Jack lying there, cushioned in dark blue velvet.

Her feet stuck to the floor. Her heartbeat thundered in her ears.

"You okay?" Ryder whispered.

Every nerve ending screamed out, *No, not okay, not at all okay.* She bit down on her lower lip and made herself walk toward the casket. From the sides of her vision she saw people she probably knew, but her focus on the coffin made it impossible to acknowledge them. She concentrated on moving forward, holding Ryder's arm in a death grip. He didn't seem to mind.

The man—the *body*—in the coffin definitely resembled Jack. His expression was so peaceful that he could have been asleep, except the Jack Morrison she knew had never slept peacefully a night in his life. Carefully, Kate touched the back of his hand, so cold and firm, and whispered, "Oh, Jack."

Her legs gave way, and as she started to sag, Ryder—stronger than he appeared—wrapped his arm around her waist and held her up until she recovered.

He put his free hand over his heart and murmured to Jack. "Safe journey, my brother. Peace."

They took their seats for a mercifully short service. Kate barely heard what the minister said. Everything felt unreal: a bad dream, but one she couldn't escape by waking up. She stroked the pendant Jack had given her.

Afterward, as the coffin went into the hearse, Kate caught sight of Eden, tall and regal and all in black, with an elderly man and woman —her parents?—close beside her. Eden saw Kate and nodded a greeting.

At the nearby gravesite, Kate recognized a few of the mourners: artists, collectors, museum people she'd met through the years with Jack. Much of the Los Angeles art community had turned out to honor Jack Morrison. Even the ones she didn't know gave off a kind of vibration that told her they were part of Jack's world. She spotted Nikki Frank, dark hair springing out around her face, somber in a pale gray suit.

Trudy Zelnik was absent. Kate doubted Eden had slighted the woman intentionally; if she could include Ryder, then Trudy would surely have been invited. Kate realized she knew nothing of Trudy's current situation, or if she was even alive.

"Kate?" croaked a voice Kate couldn't immediately place. She turned to find Josie Morrison, although for a horrid second she didn't recognize the stooped old woman who came toward her, a cane in the hand not clutching Henry Morrison's arm.

"Oh, Josie," Kate said, embracing her former mother-in-law. Grief radiated from Josie so strongly that Kate felt singed. "I'm so sorry."

"It's a loss for us all," Josie said in a quavery voice that held no trace of the imperious woman whose approval Kate had never attained. "You loved him, too."

Josie squinted at Ryder. "I know you. You were Jack's friend." She held out her hand. "Thank you for coming."

Ryder mumbled something Kate didn't catch as he clasped Josie's trembling hand.

Henry looked dazed and uncomfortable, and Kate wished she could console him, hug him and tell him it was all okay. But that would be a lie. She thought, however, that Jack would have been pleased to see his mother and his first wife on good terms at last.

* * *

As the crowd dispersed after the burial, Eden approached. She nodded stiffly to Ryder before embracing Kate.

"Thank you for coming," she murmured. "And for your card. And the flowers." She gestured toward a tall spray of roses and lilacs near the grave. "They're lovely."

Ryder took a few steps away from them.

"How are you holding up?" Kate asked.

Eden wiped tears from her face. "I manage, but it's so hard to believe he's gone."

"For me too. Somehow I assumed he'd always be here. He was an important part of my life."

"And you of his, Kate. He cared very much for you."

After an awkward pause, Eden continued, "We're having a small gathering at my parents' house now. If you'd like to come…"

She glanced toward Ryder, who had his back to them. Kate got it. She wanted to assure Eden that he'd changed, but she couldn't make that guarantee, and this kind of scene might shove him off that knife edge. Besides, she had no wish to mingle with Jack's old friends.

"Thanks, but I'd better not. I have to get back to work."

It was a lie, of course, but it gave her an out.

"I understand," Eden replied. Then she took a breath; Kate could almost see the armor rising around her.

"Thank you for coming, Ryder," Eden said, raising her voice to be heard above the hum of voices and hiss of freeway traffic. "Jack would have appreciated it, and so do I."

Ryder turned, and Kate saw Eden gasp as she got a good look at his weathered face.

"It's cool," he said, "Thanks for including me. I'm sorry for your loss."

She lifted her hand in acknowledgment and slid back into the stream of mourners.

Chapter Forty-Two

R yder opened the compact's passenger door, releasing a stifling blast. Heat rippled off the car.

"Let it cool for a sec," he said, and they stood without speaking while wind scoured their skin. Ryder's hand went toward his jacket and then dropped to his side, and Kate recognized the gesture: he'd been reaching for his smokes. She'd seen Jack make that move a thousand times. Ryder said he'd quit cigarettes along with his other addictions, but old habits die hard, as she well knew.

Sunlight soaked into her skin as Kate took in the sound of tree branches swishing in the wind, overlaid with the call of voices and the slam of car doors. A dark bird shrieked as it soared overhead. To her mortification, she started to cry: huge gulping sobs that got louder and more uncontrolled as she tried to stop them.

Ryder patted her back. "Go on, let it out."

"I never got to say good-bye," she gasped as the tears flowed down her cheeks.

Ryder kept patting. "Hey. Hey. It's not over—you know that, right?" He paused. "You'll see him again."

Her voice was choked and shaky. "I wish I believed that."

"You might as well," Ryder said. "You got no proof otherwise."

He fished a Kleenex out of his jacket pocket and offered it to her.

"Thanks," she croaked. Her hot salt tears almost dissolved the tissue. She took a deep breath. "Whew," she said, exhaling. "I never do that."

Ryder studied her. "Maybe you should."

Kate forced a laugh out. "Yeah, it's great for the skin." Her eyes felt raw and swollen.

She swiped at her cheeks and slid onto the car's heat-softened upholstery. Ryder hurried around to the driver's seat and fired up the engine, then cranked the air conditioning up full blast.

"Better?" he asked as they left the cemetery behind.

Kate sighed. "Much. Ryder, thank you for being here."

"No—thank *you*. For needing me. Hardly anyone does anymore."

The comment, spoken without a shred of self-pity, scorched her conscience. Here she was playing Tragedy Queen, and Ryder was the one who was lost. Or was he?

"I bet your students need you."

He shrugged. "That, or their parents do."

The freeway entrance came up, but Ryder slowed. "Okay with you if we take the long way back, through the park?"

"I'd like that," Kate said.

He turned right, into Griffith Park. The tree-shadowed road, almost empty of traffic, soothed her like a lullaby.

She pointed toward Mt. Hollywood, a high peak off to the right. "I was on my way up there the morning Jack died. Had chest pains, so I stopped and came home. Isn't *that* weird?"

Ryder nodded. "Life's a mystery. And what's even weirder is the idea of you hiking up there. By yourself."

"Come on—don't you remember? Dad and I used to do that every weekend. I know practically every inch of it."

"Good for you, Mountain Woman."

They cruised along slowly, and after another minute, Ryder asked, "Want to stop and chill for a few minutes?"

Kate realized she did want to stop and chill, more than anything on earth at that moment.

He made a right, up to the parking lot above the merry-go-round.

When Kate got out of the car and saw the green slope flanking the carousel, ancient memories stirred.

"My God," she whispered. "This is where it all started. The Love-In."

She could almost smell the pot-and-incense suffused air, hear the bongos and cymbals.

"Back at the scene of the crime," Ryder replied. He gestured toward the swath of green lawn below the parking lot. "Sometimes I practice Tai Chi here, just when the sun comes up. It brings me peace. Sorta like ... meditation. Ever try it—Tai Chi?"

"Me? I get my peace of mind climbing those hills," Kate said, pointing behind them.

Ryder cocked his head. "This is different, kid. Honest to God. I've never done anything that made me feel so good. Come on—kick off your shoes and give it a whirl."

"Here? All dressed up?"

Her dark dress wasn't all *that* special, and he laughed off her protest as he shed his jacket and walked onto the grass. "Come on, Nature Girl! It won't hurt."

She followed.

"Okay," he said as he pulled off his shoes and socks. Here goes. Copy what I do."

It felt right, somehow, to be there, in the place where she and Jack first met. Symmetrical. Learning about something that had helped Ryder transform his life.

Kate shook off her shoes and stood next to him, mimicking his posture: feet apart, knees soft, hands raised at waist level, palms down.

Ryder lifted and lowered his hands. "Breathe, Katie Girl. Breathe. This we call 'Heaven and Earth'—we'll do it a few times to get you into the zone."

She felt vaguely ridiculous, but the movements began to relax her.

"Good," Ryder said. "Now try this. Pretend you're holding a big ol' ball and then turn."

He cupped his right hand over his left and pivoted. Kate copied the pose, breathing purposefully as Ryder glided through the moves and identified each one by name: "White Crane Spreads Its Wings" and "Repulse the Monkey" and "Carry Tiger to the Mountain." A river of poetry, those words.

After a few minutes, Kate slipped into his rhythm. Through her stockings, she could feel every blade of grass, the uneven tilt of the land.

Ryder looked over at her as leaf shadows slid across his face. "Hey kid, you're pretty good at this."

Her hands and feet mirrored his, a split second behind. It was a little like dancing, but easier than any dance step, with Ryder leading the way. Their movements synched and flowed as tree shadows lengthened across the field.

Time lost its power, and Kate sensed only the breeze and the grass and the fragrance of pine and eucalyptus. Peace rose up and filled her with consolation. Life still offered moments of delight like this, coming unexpectedly on the heels of devastation.

"And that's it!" Ryder said when they finished. "Those are the Twenty-Four Movements—basic form. Cool, huh?"

"Very cool," Kate told him. "I actually do feel better."

He grinned. "Told ya so. You should come to class with me sometime. Learn from a real teacher."

This close, she could see Ryder's eyes behind the dark glasses, but not enough to read what was in them. The trees shielded them from the strongest rays of sunlight, and the wind, gentle now, soothed her tear-chafed skin.

"Maybe I will," Kate said.

"The philosophy behind it keeps me sane," Ryder told her. "It's like there are two opposing forces, and they harmonize to make a whole. Up and down, right and left. Yin and Yang." He cocked his head. "Want to do another round?"

She did. This time her muscles caught on quicker, and she let go of self-consciousness and simply *was*. Her feet seemed airborne, and she wanted to stay there with Ryder forever, dancing on the gentle green grass of Griffith Park.

When they got to the end, Kate said, "You're good at this. You've worked hard at it."

Ryder nodded. "Muscle memory. You do it enough times and you don't even have to think about it anymore."

"If you say so."

"You'll believe me pretty soon. Some people get it—and some never do. They don't pay attention or they want to do it their way or they just plain can't do the moves—they're klutzes. Kind of like life."

"Like me and dancing?" Kate asked.

Ryder laughed. "But you get *this*—I see it."

"I almost believe you, Ryder."

He looked at her without saying anything and then ran a hand over his white hair.

"It's hard making amends," he said, out of nowhere. "Cleaning up unfinished business. Atoning for your mistakes, facing the people you've hurt. I don't know why, but doing Tai Chi makes it easier. For me anyway."

In his white shirt that almost matched his hair, Ryder looked so vulnerable, like he could fly apart if she said the wrong thing.

"I don't think you have all that much to atone for, Ryder—at least not with me. You never hurt me—not on purpose anyhow. And most of us can't help bumping up against each other sometimes."

Without even thinking, she leaned over to kiss his cheek, just as he turned toward her, and her lips brushed his. She backed off like she'd touched a hot wire. "Sorry."

"For what?" he said, cackling like the Ryder of old. "It didn't hurt."

Kate jammed on her shoes. "Guess I better head on home now," she said. "I brought a bunch of work from the office."

"Whatever you say." Ryder tied his shoelaces and strolled to the car.

They didn't talk much as he headed out of the park. Kate flinched when she thought of accidentally kissing Ryder.

He patted her knee. "It's okay, Kate."

She wasn't sure exactly what he meant, but she replied, "I think you're right."

Contentment from the Tai Chi practice still flowed through her, so Kate leaned her head back and relaxed, trusting Ryder to get her home safe.

Chapter Forty-Three

"That's weird," Kate said as they reached her house. Her husband's Lexus was parked at a sloppy angle in the driveway.

"Eric has a Thursday afternoon class. He must've forgotten his notes or something." She paused, then asked, "Come in for coffee?"

He shook his head. "I have a kid coming for a guitar lesson at four."

She squeezed his arm. "Thanks for being with me today. And for the Tai Chi—that was the best part of my day."

He hissed through his teeth. "The bar's pretty low for that."

With a twinge of regret, Kate got out of the car and waved as he drove away. She liked this new Ryder, and she wanted him to like her, too.

The front door was unlocked, and Eric didn't respond to her "Hello?" She found him sitting at his desk, surrounded by a flurry of documents, papers spilling onto the floor.

For a horrid moment she thought they'd been burglarized, that he'd been called home to deal with the mess. But the computer was in its usual place, and she'd seen no signs of a break-in on her way past the living room.

Eric didn't acknowledge her at first. His sleeves were rolled up, his hair sticking out as if he'd been tugging at it.

"Eric? What's going on?"

His eyes were wild. "Things fell apart. Where's the rest of it?"

"The rest of what? What's fallen apart?"

He seemed only then to notice her. "It's too hot in here." He *was* sweating, although the room was cool. In the pause that followed, Eric blinked and shuddered. "How was the funeral?"

"It was..." She groped for words that would keep him coherent. "it was sad," she finally said, worry still jittering along her spine. "Why are you home so early?"

He sighed. "I've lost it, Kate."

"What? What have you lost? I'll help you find it."

She touched his forehead; his skin was cool, almost clammy. His lips moved, like a fish trying to breathe through its mouth, and a low moan came out. His hands shook.

Alarm surged through her. "Do you need a doctor? Shall I call nine-one-one?"

She reached for the telephone, and he batted her hand away.

"Doctors can't help. No one can. I've lost it all."

"What are you talking about, honey? What have you lost?"

He stopped shaking. "Our money, Kate. It's all gone."

The story came out in disjointed pieces, only some of which she understood.

Once he'd said those stupefying words, Eric became icily coherent as he explained. He'd invested heavily in the real estate market over the years—she knew that—and he'd made a lot of money, so he kept buying and selling, because it seemed like the ride would never end. But it had. And he'd gotten reckless, made some bad investments, then made even worse choices trying to recover his losses. The reckoning had been a long time coming, but his maneuvering had finally caught up with him.

Ultimately he'd refinanced their home—*their home*—taking out an oddball mortgage that came with a now-overdue balloon payment. He had no money to pay it off. Worse, the mortgage exceeded their home's market value.

Kate remembered signing the refinancing documents—signing without reading, because she trusted Eric and assumed he knew what he was doing. Eric had more financial experience than she did, after all.

"How could this happen?" she asked. "We always have plenty of money."

Eric gestured at the papers strewn around him. "It only appeared that we did. I let you think we did."

"But the bills," she protested, "—they're all paid up, aren't they? The phone, the electricity, all that?"

"Yes," he muttered. "Thanks to your paycheck, we've kept up the illusion. Until now."

"How could you do this?" Kate demanded, with an unspoken question rumbling beneath her words: *How could I have let you?* "Where did all the money go? What did you use it for?"

He started to cry. "Remember the Paris trip?"

Their seventh wedding anniversary. He'd surprised her with first-class airline tickets, a room at the George Cinq, romantic strolls along the Seine.

"You told me you'd sold some stock that had peaked."

"I sold some stock, all right, but barely over what I paid for it."

"What else did you pay for with money we didn't have?"

He didn't look at her. "Your diamond bracelet. The Lexus."

The enormity of his deception blew her away. "*Why?*"

"I wanted you to have nice things. I wanted to make you happy. I wanted you to think I was as successful as Morrison."

"Oh, Eric. You never had to compete with Jack."

She studied the scattered papers—bills with red "Past Due—Please Remit" stamped across them in block letters. A sheet headed "Notice of Default" in boldface.

"Are we going to lose the house?" she asked.

He shrugged. "Probably."

"What can we do? There has to be something."

He glared at the mess on his desk. "I don't know, Kate." He sighed. "But I'll think of something. I always do."

"Do we have *any* money left?"

He didn't reply, which was answer enough.

"This is my fault, too," she said. "I didn't pay attention, but I know we can find a way out of this."

He crumpled one of the bills and tossed it toward the ceiling; it bounced gently down onto his head. "I'm sure we can, darling."

Kate left him mumbling over the wreckage of their finances. She went to the bar in the living room and poured an inch of whiskey into a tumbler. She rarely drank whiskey, but she remembered her dad sipping a glass of it when he was working out a problem. Maybe it would help her, too.

Then she sat in the darkening house that might not even be hers anymore, and tried to think of solutions to the mess Eric had made.

Chapter Forty-Four
July 1996

"I understand your position, Mrs. Ames," Ralph Conroy said, "and I'd like nothing better than to avoid foreclosing."

Kate concentrated on not letting the banker see her nervousness. "Foreclosures are messy, Mr. Conroy. And expensive. But if you can be a little flexible with us, I think we can come up with a better resolution."

In the days after Eric's confession, Kate had undergone a crash course in finance, helped by a colleague in Accounting. She'd taken him to lunch three days in a row and scribbled notes on everything he taught her. Now she was putting that knowledge to work.

The banker's voice dripped condescension. "I certainly hope so. But your mortgage is significantly in arrears. If you'd responded to the original Notice of Default, I'm sure we could have—"

Kate held up a hand to stop the lecture. *Rule One: Take command.* "Yes, but there's nothing to be done about that now. Let's look ahead instead."

Rule Two: Offer a compromise. She outlined her proposal: she would take a withdrawal from her employee savings plan for a big chunk of the mortgage in default. This carried a heavy tax and penalty burden, but she was willing to make the sacrifice if, in return, Mr.

Conroy's bank would agree to lower the principal—significantly—and recalculate the mortgage.

"It's a win-win," Kate said, forcing her fingers to unclench. *Rule Three: Stress the mutual benefits.* "You have money coming in rather than going out. My husband and I get to keep our house."

Conroy was a little man, at least four inches shorter than Kate. Everything in his office, however, was oversized: big desk, big chairs, big Mont Blanc pen in his hand. He had greedy eyes, shiny black hair, and a mustache that Kate imagined him twirling as he kicked widows and orphans out of their homes.

"You make it sound appealing," he replied. "And you clearly have a good sense of the gravity of your situation. Perhaps we can help you find a way out of this."

* * *

Everything changed in the aftermath. Kate took charge of the checkbook, canceled their vacation plans at Lake Tahoe, and drew up a budget that allowed bare-bones living expenses while they repaid overdue credit card bills. Dinners out, theater tickets, and $800 suits ceased to exist.

Eric, humbled by the near-miss of bankruptcy, turned quiet and tense. He walked around like a ghost, keeping his distance. He thanked her repeatedly, like he was reading from a script, for standing by him. Kate tried to give him time, and space, to adjust.

"I'm as much to blame as you are," she assured him. "I should have paid more attention to what was going on. But it's done now. Let's move forward. We'll be okay, as long as we watch what we spend and stay honest with each other."

He hadn't kissed her, hadn't even touched her, since the nightmare began. At first Kate had been too stressed to notice, but eventually his coldness annoyed her; she wasn't the enemy. One night as they were clearing the table after dinner—their housekeeper another casualty of the new austerity—he dropped a plate, and it shattered on the tile floor.

Eric stared at the broken pieces. "I'm so sorry."

Kate shrugged. "No big loss. We've got plenty."

She went to get a broom and dustpan and came back to find Eric in tears.

"I can't do anything right," he moaned.

"That's not true. This was a silly little accident."

She swept up the broken china and then reached for his hand, but he yanked it away like she'd burned him.

"I wish I had the nerve to kill myself and be out of your way," he groaned.

His complaint ignited her anger, and she couldn't tamp it down in time.

"Damn it, quit whining! This is hard enough without your self-pity!"

Eric paled, and his mouth trembled.

Kate's rage dissolved. She put her arms around him, and when he tried to pull away she held on tighter.

"Oh, Eric, please don't do this to us. I need you."

She didn't let go until he stopped struggling against her.

"Now," she said, "go fix our after-dinner drinks, and I'll finish cleaning up."

He backed away. "I don't deserve you, Kate. I'm a useless fool, and I've dragged you down with me."

"You're not a fool, so stop acting like one. Come on—this thing will blow over, and we'll get our lives back. Please try and believe that."

He straightened, took a deep breath, and went to pour their drinks. Later, when the liquor was gone and they got into bed, he reached for her, and kissed her the way he'd done when they first met, and Kate let herself enjoy a flicker of hope that the worst was over.

* * *

Two weeks later he came home with exhilaration dancing in his eyes, and for a minute Kate thought, *He's back. At last he's enthused about something.*

"I've been doing some exploring," he said, "and I think I've figured out a way to way to get our money back."

Kate set aside the report she'd been studying. "Really? How?" She had scant hope he'd found a real solution, but she gave him the benefit of the doubt.

"The real estate market's reviving, Kate, the signs are everywhere. This time I'll be smart, I'll go with a real estate investment trust. The risks are spread around, and the returns are unbelievable."

He spoke rapidly, and his flushed cheeks and glittering eyes set alarm bells ringing in Kate's mind.

She ran her thumb over the edge of the desk. "And how will we pay for this?"

He looked sheepish and sly at the same time. "You could take another withdrawal from your savings plan—a little one this time. And in a year, we could recover everything we lost."

"Everything *you* lost."

Kate hated herself for undermining his excitement, but she had to. *Not again. Eric. Please, not again.*

He frowned. "So there it is. You do blame me for what happened."

"I blame both of us," Kate replied, speaking slowly so she could collect her thoughts. "And I've read about real estate investment trusts, too. They're not foolproof, and we can't afford to gamble."

He deflated, like a kid who'd been told Santa didn't exist.

"Listen—we're doing okay now," Kate continued. "We're managing, we're paying off our bills. But another get-rich-quick plan would derail everything. You don't want that, do you?"

He shook his head. "No," he said, quietly.

She got up and hugged him. "I know it's hard. It's a big change. But we'll get through it. And we still have each other, right?"

"Right," he said, and she so wanted to believe him.

* * *

Despite all the turmoil, Kate found time to connect with Ryder and began shadowing him in his Monday night Tai Chi class. It was her one indulgence, and the lessons gave her a different kind of peace than hiking. The slow, gentle moves and the focus on breathing helped center her. The people in class had welcomed her as Ryder's friend; they knew nothing of her outside life, and that was fine with her.

Although she'd never experienced Ryder's mysterious "muscle memory," Kate felt safe in Tai Chi class. She quickly discovered there was no single "right way" to do it, so nobody judged her. No Jeff Gallos looking over her shoulder, daring her to make a mistake. No guilt trips or conflict or regret.

The classroom had mirrors on opposite walls. Kate hardly ever watched herself, but now and then, when she was at the front of a column of people, she savored the mirror image, everyone moving rhythmically in unison, arms lifting, feet gliding, like a multifaceted organism, each part sharing the breath of the whole.

"Stay present, in the moment," the teacher would tell them. "Don't *think*; simply *be*." Easy to say, but it took concentration to do.

* * *

Kate left work one autumn evening feeling lighthearted and upbeat. She'd finished a mammoth project that afternoon, and even Jeff Gallo had praised her work. Her financial outlook was improving, and Eric seemed to have accepted their new frugality.

His Lexus was already in the garage when she got home, and Kate smiled. They'd have a nice evening together, maybe open one of those expensive bottles of wine she'd stashed away for special occasions.

Like a kid up to no good, Eric slammed the desk drawer shut when she came into the office, and Kate's tranquility blew apart at the seams.

"Eric? What's going on?"

"Nothing," he said, in a stiff little voice that told her *everything* was going on. Everything she didn't want to know about.

Kate reached past him and yanked the drawer open.

She didn't understand every word of the document he'd tried to hide, but enough to figure out that it was a purchase agreement for shares in a real estate investment trust.

Kate's hands shook as she read through the lines of small print. "How *could* you?"

His face closed up. "I was merely considering the possibility."

"Is that why you signed this? What did you plan to use for money?"

The realization hit her before he could reply: she'd been building up a small reserve in their savings account, to cover property taxes and insurance. And Eric still had access to it.

Kate fought a sudden weariness that made breathing difficult. "I can't do this anymore. I can't give you the kind of help you need...I've tried to make this work, and I've failed."

He removed his glasses and rubbed his hands over his face. "Kate, please don't say that. No one has failed. We had a run of bad luck, but it'll turn around. Give me one more chance."

His expression broke her heart. She found enough energy to rip the documents into pieces and throw them in the trash.

"If you don't call a counselor and get help, I'll do it for you."

He stood, the veins in his neck bulging. "Don't you dare. I don't need that kind of help! What I need is understanding and support, not someone who doubts me. If you can't do that, then get out of my way. I won't let you hold me back."

Kate's fatigue morphed into rage. She turned and walked away, fists clenched. She should contact the bank and try to protect whatever was left of the savings account. But first she *had* to do something with the anguish boiling inside her.

She changed into jeans and laced up her hiking boots. Mother Nature's surefire cure—for grief, anger, and frustration.

"This'll be a long hike," she muttered as she got in her car and drove to the park.

Chapter Forty-Five
January 1998

"Cooking relaxes me," Ryder said as he stirred the concoction simmering on his stove.

Kate helped herself to coffee. "Lucky you."

Ryder's laugh filled the small, steamy kitchen. "You made a pretty good meatloaf as I remember."

"My big culinary specialty." She eyed the bubbling pot. "Where did *you* learn to cook?"

"Homeless shelter."

He often did that: nonchalantly dropped little fact-bombs from the years he'd gone missing.

"I got into it," Ryder continued, "making a big something out of a bunch of little somethings."

He tasted the pot's contents and added pepper. "I used to think, maybe that's how Jack feels when he's painting, smooshing colors together, making something different out of them."

Kate swirled the dark liquid in her cup. "You did that with music—blended notes into a symphony."

Ryder cackled. "Symphony! Woman, you have a talent for overstatement."

Kate's cheeks grew warm. She hoped he wouldn't throw out any more of those little zingers in that matter-of-fact voice, like he was telling someone else's story—going on stage so stoned he couldn't find the floor, canceling a concert because he'd torn up the lining of his nose from snorting coke and had bled into his throat.

Kate had trouble reconciling the reckless ruffian he described with the sober, white-haired man standing across from her, stirring a pot of vegetarian chili. But there he was, and how grateful *she* was that they'd reconnected.

He moved away from the stove, carefully stepping over Bailey, the collie-shepherd mix he'd adopted from an animal shelter. The dog clung to Ryder so much that Kate had nicknamed her "Velcro."

She unwrapped a slab of cornbread she'd picked up on the way over and then dumped some lettuce in a bowl. The two of them worked in companionable silence, and Kate relished the ease of Ryder's company after a hectic work week. These weekly dinners had become a comforting ritual.

Kate sliced a juicy red tomato and added it to the lettuce. "The final divorce papers came yesterday." Her voice sounded loud in that quiet kitchen.

Ryder stopped setting the table; his hand hovered with the knives and forks. "You okay?"

Kate tossed the salad. "Actually I am." She sighed. "I hope he keeps up his therapy—gets his life back together."

* * *

Ryder had witnessed the sad story unfold as Kate fought to keep Eric off the road to financial ruin. She found him a counselor, got him into a support group, stood by him in every way she could. It hadn't worked. He came up with one scheme after another; it was an addiction as strong as drugs. Despite her precautions, he'd secretly siphoned money from their checking account for another bogus real estate proposition, and Kate had to accept that she'd never be back on solid ground as long as she stayed married to Eric.

The decision to divorce him hadn't come without a lot of soul-scorching doubt and sleepless nights. Ryder became her confidant, letting her vent the self-loathing and frustration—an ironic turnabout that made Kate dizzy.

* * *

"I wish I could've saved him," Kate added.

Ryder put down the silverware. "Some people don't want to be saved."

"Jack said something like that. About you."

He snorted. "He was probably right. And you damn sure wouldn't have saved Eric if you'd stayed with him and pretended it was all good. He would'a brought you down with him."

"I've told myself that a thousand times. Wish I could believe it." She dusted her hands on her jeans.

Ryder came around the table and hugged her. "You did the right thing, Kate. You gave him one last shot at looking truth in the face. If that doesn't shock him back on the wagon, nothing will."

She shrugged. "I guess we'll find out eventually, huh?"

He seemed about to say something else but then smiled. "Let's eat."

* * *

After dinner they took Bailey for a walk. Ryder lived on a steep, narrow street in Eagle Rock. His house was sturdy and simple and almost paid for, thanks to a small inheritance from his parents, who'd died within a month of each other not long after Jack Morrison's funeral.

As they trudged up the incline at the end of their walk, Ryder chuckled. "Man, this is rough going! Imagine if we still smoked."

Bailey trotted ahead at the end of her leash, pausing to sniff grass and tree trunks. When Ryder stopped and bent over, resting his hands on his knees, the dog came back to him, nuzzled his leg and whined softly.

"It's okay, girl," Ryder huffed. "Dad's just feeling the after-effects of his youth."

"You'd think all that Tai Chi would build up our stamina," Kate said.

"You'd think," Ryder agreed.

She raised her face to the sky, where clouds masked the stars and the crescent moon she'd seen earlier. "Amazing we survived those crazy times."

Ryder straightened and took a hoarse breath. "Yeah, man—remember when the cops raided us? And you hid all our shit in the fridge so they didn't find it."

"And you—so worried I'd flushed it. Never mind that we might all have been arrested."

Ryder winced. "My priorities were a little fucked up back then."

"You think?"

He put his hand on her shoulder. "You saved my ass. And that wasn't the only time."

"Are you still hung up on that Jimmy Foster thing? Ryder, that was a million years ago."

He looked serious. "Not that. I mean the night I came to see you, right after you got married. I was real wasted, and you kicked me out."

Kate frowned. "You were pretty messed up. But I don't think I actually kicked—"

"That look on your face—I can still see it." He shook his head. "Like I was some cockroach, crawled up out of the toilet. I never wanted anybody, especially you, to look at me like that again."

"I never—"

"I was stoned, but I remember everything you said. Told me I had to get clean, or you never wanted to see me again. Told me I broke your heart and you couldn't watch me trash my life."

"I did mean that."

"Don't I know," Ryder said. "Going back to rehab was mighty rough. For a while I thought I was gonna die. Sometimes I almost hoped I would. But you know how it goes: just when things are at their abso-fuckin'-lute worst, and you want to give up, it gets better. And all those times I was tempted to quit, I'd conjure up that look you gave me, and…"

Tears spilled down her cheeks. "I'm sorry, Ryder, I didn't mean to—"

He squeezed her shoulder. "It's cool. Really. That's what I'm trying to tell you, that you probably saved my life, making me see how fucked up I was. So don't go beatin' yourself up about Eric, because you did the same for him. Not your fault he didn't follow through."

Bailey whuffed at a bug that flew past, and Ryder linked arms with Kate as they finished their walk.

"Thank you," Kate said quietly as he unlocked his front door.

Inside the house, he asked, "Coffee?"

Kate nodded. "I'll regret it when I can't sleep, but yeah. Please."

"Put some sound on, will you?" he called out from the kitchen.

Kate examined the stack of CDs on his makeshift bookcase of wood planks resting on cinderblocks.

"Don't you miss singing?" she asked.

Ryder's voice boomed through the little house. "Like you'd miss breathing."

He brought in cups of steaming coffee and handed one to Kate. "But I got only myself to blame. Took the one gift God gave me and trashed it all to hell."

Kate put down the Warren Zevon disk she'd been about to insert in the player. "You don't even try anymore?"

"What do you think?"

"I think, maybe you sound different, but different isn't always bad."

He rubbed his hand over his chin. "Where you goin' with this, Katie Girl?"

What *was* she doing? The words spilled out.

"Play me something on your guitar. Don't sing if you don't want to. But I want to hear *your* music."

Slowly Ryder pulled the old Gibson six-string out of its carrying case and lightly strummed some warm-up chords. Then his fingers started moving for real on the guitar strings, and the sound that came out made her quiver. She dug her fingertips into the chair arms. Ryder studied her like he was making up his mind about something. Then he started to sing.

"If you ever cared about me, if your sweet love doesn't doubt me, tell me now, oh honey, tell me now."

The gentle ballad was heavy with yearning. Ryder's jagged voice held none of the qualities she remembered from long ago, but its harshness made it haunting, and real.

The song ended, and Ryder put down the guitar. "Enough punishment for one day."

When Kate exhaled, it came out a gasp. "That was beautiful. I mean it. Really beautiful."

He shrugged and reached toward his shirt pocket, stopped, and picked up his coffee cup. "Lot different than 'Devil.' Lot older, too."

He leaned down and rubbed Bailey behind her ears. The dog moaned with pleasure.

"I wrote it in high school," he continued without looking up. "For you."

"For me? No, you didn't!"

His blue eyes, pale and vulnerable in the lamplight, focused on her. "Yeah. You never knew I had a thing for you back then, did you?"

Kate shook her head.

"Doesn't matter now," he went on. "You asked for a song, and I gave you one. Now we can let it be."

"Ryder—"

He put the Gibson in its case and snapped the clasps shut. "Nah. Let it go. I'm too used up."

"You're not! You made some bad choices, we all did, but you have a lot left to give."

"Bad choices! Man, that's a good way to put it."

"Hell, Ryder—you're probably the best friend I ever had."

He snorted. "Then, honey, you've had some mighty bad friends."

"That song—it's amazing. And your voice! I thought I'd have to cover my ears, but honestly, it...it's changed, sure. But it sounds good to me."

Ryder ruffled Bailey's fur and smirked. "To you. Not to me."

"But—"

"When you have something special, and you lose it—or throw it away—whatever comes after will never be as good. I don't know much, but I do know that."

He stood and stretched.

Kate gathered up her purse and car keys. She usually gave him a goodnight kiss on the cheek, but now she felt awkward doing that. Ryder solved her dilemma by wrapping her in a bear hug that almost knocked the wind out of her.

"Thanks for dinner," she murmured when she could talk again. "See you in class Monday."

"Catch you then," Ryder agreed.

He stood in the porch light glow, watching as she walked to her car.

Kate waved to him and headed home, Ryder's disclosure rolling around in her thoughts.

When would life quit sending surprises?

Chapter Forty-Six
February 1999

"Jeff Gallo's looking for you," Gracie said when Kate returned from lunch.

She took the pink message slip. "Did he say why?"

Gracie's dark brown hair swayed when she shook her head. "Anything wrong?" She looked worried.

"You tell me," Kate replied. "You always hear the scoop first."

"Something funny *is* going on ...you see all the closed doors around here lately?"

Kate had. Even preoccupied with insurance carrier negotiations, she'd noticed the shift in mood around the workplace.

"Guess I'll go find out," Kate muttered as she smoothed the front of her jacket and headed for Jeff Gallo's office.

* * *

Jeff looked up from a pile of papers on his desk. He didn't smile. "Have a seat."

Kate sat.

Outside Gallo's window, wintry drizzle coated the glass.

In the years since their roles had reversed, Kate had crafted a careful relationship with Jeff Gallo. She didn't like him, and he didn't like her; but he needed her and she needed her salary, so they made it work. Not without an occasional flare-up, but for the most part they kept it civil.

Gallo tapped his pen on the desktop and fidgeted, then peered at a spreadsheet in front of him. "You've no doubt heard rumors flying around, about the company's financial troubles."

Kate tilted her head. "I've heard those since the first day I came to work here."

Gallo's mouth curved into a thin smile. "Right." He sighed. "The latest ones have more behind them. Times are tough, getting tougher. The regulations, the taxes, the public dislike of our industry—you've heard all this."

"I have. Jeff, what's up? Don't sugar-coat it. Tell me."

He did.

"Permian's being sold, Kate. Genoco has made an offer ... The Executive Committee—and the Board—decided it's better than dismantling the company. They're selling it off in one piece."

Kate knew Genoco; she had met most of its HR staff over the years at industry conferences. The company, headquartered in Houston, was five times Permian's size, with five times Permian's staff.

"When?"

Gallo jabbed the spreadsheet with his index finger. "Soon. This has been in the works for over two months. I knew a little—not every-thing. God forbid they tell me everything."

That was the closest Gallo had ever come to confiding in her.

"You don't have to explain to me what this means," she said, although she hoped he'd contradict her.

"I fought for us, Kate, whether you believe me or not. I told Jack Slater our HR group could run circles around Genoco's, but..."

He trailed off, and Kate figured out the rest. Jack Slater, Permian's CEO, was a get-the-deal-done-at-any-cost kind of guy, and he'd sell off his own family if that's what it took.

Gallo continued. "Once the dust has settled, there will be some staffing redundancies."

"And I'll be one of those 'redundancies'?"

Gallo flushed and looked away. Kate expected him to gloat, but he didn't. "Your entire department. And I won't be far behind."

"You're kidding! How will they—"

He didn't let her finish. "I'm supposed to offer you a transfer to Houston," he continued. "And of course if you'd be interested, I'll push for you. But it would be a lower-level job, and the relocation package will be bare-bones."

"And if I don't go?"

He handed her a two-page document outlining her severance proposal: nine months' salary plus a lump sum payment based on Permian's profit picture at the time of the sale, continuation of medical coverage for 18 months, and "outplacement assistance."

Kate couldn't think straight. Why hadn't she seen this coming? Then again, what good would it have done?

He gave her three days to evaluate the proposal and give him her decision, but Kate didn't want to move to Houston, and she sure as hell didn't want to work for Genoco. The company had generated more than their share of employee-relations complaints over the years, and she couldn't stand to be a part of that environment.

* * *

That night, in the small Glendale apartment she'd rented after the divorce, Kate poured a glass of wine and went over the severance proposal. It was less than she'd seen other companies offer, but Genoco probably had a hand in that.

Kate sipped her wine and wondered what would happen next. She looked over at "Sanctuary," which was the first thing she'd placed in the living room when she moved in. The painting usually boosted her confidence: she'd been important to a famous artist. Her hand went to the starburst pendant hanging around her neck. Jack: what would he think of all this? Probably he'd scowl and say, "Assholes. This is the dumbest move they've ever made."

And Eric: the Eric she first knew, the wise professor who had all the answers. What would *he* advise now? Probably "Go where the money is."

But none of her speculation took away the sting: closing in on 50, she was back on the job market.

"But it's a good thing," Kate murmured as the wine blunted her distress. "A fresh start. Maybe a change in direction."

* * *

She signed the severance papers two days later, and that night she phoned her sister Debbie. The Genoco acquisition had hit the papers by then, and Kate wanted to head off any questions Debbie or their mom might have.

"Those jerks," Debbie said. "They'll be sorry."

Debbie's sympathy threw Kate off balance. "I doubt they'll even notice."

"Are you kidding? You're the best they'll ever have. Roy says the main reason Permian did so well for so long is that it attracted good people, and that's because you made it a good place to work."

Debbie and her husband discussed Kate's career? Astounded, Kate could only respond with, "Thanks."

"Will you be okay?" Debbie asked.

"I think so. They're giving me a decent severance. It'll take a while to land another job as good as this one, but—"

"Look, if you need to cut expenses for a while...when Lindsay goes off to college this fall, her room'll be empty. If you need a place to stay."

Kate almost started to cry. "Little Lindsay in college: I can't wrap my mind around that."

"Tell me about it!"

The sisters chatted for a few more minutes before Kate said, "Well, I better brace myself and call Mom."

"I'll take care of Mom," Debbie said. "You know how she gets."

When had Debbie turned so nice?

"I can't let you do that," Kate protested.

"Sure you can. You have enough on your plate now. And don't worry. You'll land a better job before you know it."

Kate thanked Debbie and hung up, wishing she had her sister's confidence in a good outcome.

* * *

On Friday night she told Ryder the news.

He studied her face for a minute before he said, "Man, that's hard."

Kate crouched on the floor to play tug-of-war with Bailey. "Things change. Life changes."

Bailey backed away, pretend-growling, and Kate let her have the toy, but once she got it, the dog shoved it back into Kate's hand.

"You'll be okay, right? You won't have to sleep on a park bench or anything?"

Kate shook her head. "Not right away."

"Listen, you'll get another job—companies should be falling all over themselves trying to hire you. But if you do get jammed up, you could always move in here. I've been meaning to clear the junk out of that spare room anyway."

Kate stood and wiped her hands on her jeans. Bailey retreated to her bed with the prize clamped in her jaw.

"That's quite an offer, Ryder. I appreciate it. But I don't think—"

"Bailey will chaperone us, if that's what you're worried about."

That made her laugh. "No, of course not, silly boy. You're too much like a brother. But I think I'll be able to manage the rent—it's not much. Let's see what happens."

* * *

Maybe this wasn't such a disaster after all, Kate reflected on her way home from Ryder's. She had a bigger support network than she realized. How many people were that lucky?

The search for new employment, however, rested entirely on her shoulders, and the idea of interviewing for a job scared the hell out of her. She knew all the tricks of the trade, and now they'd be turned on her.

Chapter Forty-Seven
May-August 1999

K elly Devereaux, Career Consultant, was a big, blandly cheerful blonde who studied Kate's résumé and began scribbling on it with bold red strokes.

She tapped a bitten-down fingernail on the paper. "You worked for Permian a long time."

"I did. Started on the reception desk and worked my way up."

Devereaux frowned at the résumé, "Worked your way pretty far up." She looked at Kate. "You were probably at the top of the pay scale."

"Possibly. And I understand I won't be able to start with anything comparable, but—"

"It's not just the amount that will trip us up, Kate. You're overqualified for a lot of positions."

"So where does that leave me?"

"We're not out of luck, but part of my job is to help you do a reality check. You're going to face a lot of employer resistance. They'll figure you're only taking the job until something better comes along—which may be true, but you have to find a way to convince recruiters that their job is the one you've been looking for."

"I can do that."

"I'm sure you can. And we'll help you find something acceptable, trust me. But you may have to broaden your definition of 'acceptable.'"

* * *

In the weeks that followed, Kate began to wonder just how broad that definition would have to be. She went on ten interviews in June, including one in San Francisco, another in Oregon, and a third in Phoenix. Devereaux hadn't been joking about "employer resistance." Time after time, the hiring manager implied the same thing, in varying ways: Kate had been highly placed at her last job and was not likely to be satisfied with the position and salary they were prepared to offer.

"Give me a chance," she'd finally said to the benefits manager at a bank in downtown Los Angeles. "I have a solid work record, and I started at the bottom of Permian's career ladder. I understand it takes time to move up. I'm prepared to wait, and to work my hardest in the meantime."

The manager, Dominique Sanders, had dark circles under her deep-set eyes and a very loud voice.

"I'm sure you mean that, Ms. Ames, but I've seen too many applicants change their minds when reality sets in." She leaned forward, narrow lips compressed. "I can't stress enough that this position is nothing near what you had. You'd be analyzing benefit trends and preparing reports for my action." She made a sound that was a cross between a sniff and a laugh. "I imagine you were the one reviewing those reports and making decisions about what needed to be changed. You probably had *my* job, in fact."

"I did," Kate replied with a rueful smile. "But before that I performed those same analytical duties, and I enjoyed that work, too."

"You might be working for people younger than yourself."

"Not a problem. I've worked with people of all ages, and we got along fine."

Sanders' eyes were unreadable, her body language closed off. "I appreciate your enthusiasm." The manager glanced at her watch. "We have a few other candidates to interview, but we'll be in touch when we get closer to a final decision."

* * *

Out in the sticky summer morning, Kate sat on a bench in the front courtyard and caught her breath. The hardwood slats beneath her felt unfriendly and cold despite the strong shaft of sunlight that sliced across her knees. A few feet away, water gurgled from a fountain on a base of fake rocks. A catering truck chugged past, spewing diesel fumes and the aroma of charred meat. Kate opened her purse, not sure what she was looking for, and then she got it: cigarettes. Cigarettes she hadn't carried, or even thought about, for over a decade. She closed her purse and pushed away the unexpected craving.

She'd so hoped that this one would work. Why had they even bothered to interview her? They probably hadn't known how old she was until they met her. Devereaux had counseled her to leave her employment dates off the résumé.

"Maybe I should get a facelift," Kate muttered. "Except I can't afford one."

If she hadn't dropped Tai Chi class, she'd at least have had something to look forward to that evening. But the lessons cost money, and as discouragement set in, Kate had found it harder and harder to walk into class and summon tranquility and acceptance of life's flow. She'd forgotten all the moves.

I will not cry. Other people she knew, at other companies, had been "displaced" and had found new jobs.

"But not right away," she reminded herself in a gray whisper.

* * *

She dreamed about Jack that night. In the dream, she was getting dressed for another job interview, and Jack walked in on her.

"Does this look okay?" She asked, turning around for inspection.

He didn't answer; instead he made a circular motion with his arms that reminded her of "Carry Tiger to the Mountain" from Tai Chi class.

Kate was so glad to see him, but she didn't know why his appearance was unexpected.

Then she remembered: "How'd you find me? I moved."

"I always know where you are, Babe. I always know when you need me."

"Oh, Jack, I do need you."

"Are you sure?" the dream Jack asked. His voice sounded hollow now, an echo in an empty room.

Kate reached out to touch him, and her fingers passed through nothing but air. A sharp and immense loss gripped her, so strong it woke her up, lungs screaming for air.

* * *

When bills arrived, Kate studied them grimly; she still had enough in the bank to pay them, but for how much longer? Even though Eric's follies had depleted her financial reserves, she was grateful that the brush with bankruptcy had awakened the budgeting skills she'd developed in the early years as Jack Morrison's wife. Back then, on a secretary's salary, she'd pared every expense to the bone, rationed every can of soda. Of course, back then a soda only cost about a dime. *But I did it once with Jack, and again with Eric. I can keep doing it if I have to. I sure know the drill by now.*

Chapter Forty-Eight
March 2000

K ate got plenty of practice in budgeting over the next few
months. Kelly Devereaux's job leads, the few she continued to
send, fueled Kate's discouragement. Same old story every time: she was
overqualified and had been overpaid. No one wanted to take a chance
on her willingness to start lower down the career ladder.

A new century had begun, and winter was fading into spring, but
Kate felt no sense of renewal.

On a gloomy Monday afternoon, she sat at her scuffed kitchen
table, shuffling bills and deciding which ones *had* to be paid. She
glared at her checkbook, where the account balance was down to four
digits before the decimal point. Her stomach clenched.

The phone rang, and Kate almost let the machine take a message.
She didn't feel like talking to anyone. But what if it was a job lead or
an offer?

"Yeah, right," she muttered before she picked up the handset.

"Kate? It's Eden—Eden Morrison."

Memories seized her: that awful phone call, the morning Jack died.
Kate's mouth went dry, and when she spoke, her throat felt rusty.
"Eden—how are you?"

"I'm well. And you?"

Kate hadn't spoken to Eden in over two years; they had no reason to talk now that Jack was gone. It would be ridiculous to mention her money troubles, so she cleared her throat and said "Fine" in her best imitation of cheerful.

"I'm sorry I haven't kept in touch," Eden said. "I've been traveling a lot."

Kate's curiosity stirred like an animal awakening at the sound of footsteps. It wasn't as if she and Eden had ever really been buddies. Why the apology?

"Life gets hectic," Kate looked out the window, where drizzle coated the glass, and gray clouds muffled the sky.

"It does," Eden agreed. She paused, and then continued, "I'm actually calling for a reason, Kate." Another pause. "Do you still own 'Sanctuary?'"

That really got Kate wondering what was up. "Sure do. It's the last painting Jack gave me."

"Yes. He told me about it—a birthday gift, as I recall. I've seen photos—it's breathtaking."

"It is."

Kate heard Eden exhale.

"I've made friends with a collector in Amsterdam—Dirk de Bruyn Kops—who's quite a fan of Jack's work. He owns the companions to 'Sanctuary.'"

"Lucky him."

"Yes, he is. Dirk knows of 'Sanctuary' of course—that it's the last in the series. He's asked if I thought he might be able to buy it. I discouraged him at first because I assumed you wouldn't want to part with it. But he can be very persistent. And persuasive."

What the hell?

Eden's tone grew less tentative. "And after a while, I started to think, who am I to decide what you'd do? I told him I'd check and see if you have the least bit of interest in selling it."

Kate looked over at "Sanctuary," with its swathes of purple and crimson folding into each other, the wolf-shape sheltered by stylized trees. The sight of it evoked memories of carefree laughter echoing through the loft the night of her twenty-ninth birthday, and the radiant pleasure on Jack's face as he told her the painting was hers. She took a breath, and it seemed for a moment that she even smelled cigarette smoke and oil paint. Jack had never made her feel more special than on that night, and the painting had kept that magic alive. *We were pretty good for each other back then, weren't we, Jack?*

"Thanks, Eden, but no. It means too much to me. I can't part with it."

"I thought as much. But you should consider his offer before you say no for certain. Kate—he'll pay you a lot of money. A *lot* of money."

When Kate didn't respond, Eden added, "His collection is very well respected, both here and in Europe. Museum quality. When I visited last week he was installing a Frank Stella he'd just acquired, and he owns some Old Masters as well—along with a very nice Van Gogh. I'm dropping all these names so you'll get the full picture of him."

"I get it—he's a real art-lover. But 'Sanctuary' isn't for sale."

"Would three million dollars change your mind?"

At first Kate thought she'd heard wrong. "Three million dollars?" She took a minute to absorb what Eden had said. "He really does want it."

"He does. And Kate, I assure you we'd ... he'd treasure it, every bit as much as you do."

A wave of vertigo swept over Kate, and the chair seemed to swallow her into its worn twill covering. Her jeans and shirt felt too big, as if she were shrinking inside them. Heat from the table lamp warmed her face; the phone was a dead weight in her hand. Outside, afternoon drizzle had turned to rain, drumming on the window panes.

Kate scrunched her eyes shut and then opened them and blinked. *Hey, Jack, this is a hell of a note.*

"I don't know what to say. I probably don't sound very grateful for the call, but I am. It's just so ... surprising."

"Of course. Don't give me an answer right now. Take some time." Eden paused and then said, "It's not my place to tell you what to do, Kate, but I do know this: Jack cared for you very much. He wanted you to be happy, and safe, and comfortable. And I do understand the significance of 'Sanctuary.' It's a link to Jack. But please consider that it would become part of a well-known collection. It would complete the series."

"I understand. And I'll think about it. I promise."

* * *

When Kate put the phone down, her hands were sweating. Three million dollars—the number screamed at her. Enough to pay past-due bills. Buy a real home. Surely enough to live on for the rest of her life without having to take a job she might hate. She'd be able to provide a comfortable old age for her mom, maybe even pay some of her niece's and nephew's college costs. She stood and went up to the painting.

She had other paintings of Jack's, but nothing as meaningful as "Sanctuary." Jack had painted it just for her. She had named it. "But you're not alive," Kate whispered. "You're paint on canvas. You don't have feelings. Right?" She stroked the painting's frame, her fingertips taking in every inch of wood as she scanned the ridges and valleys Jack's brush had created on the canvas. She could almost see the tree branches sway and the little wolf-shape's mouth move as it called out to its pack.

Darkness claimed the world outside her rain-coated windows. The dreary transition from day to night made Kate feel empty and uneasy. Discomfort lingered like smoke in the room.

She poured a glass of wine and muttered, "What the hell am I going to do *now?*"

Chapter Forty-Nine

"Don't do it," Ryder said.

"Seriously?" she responded to Ryder. "You think I should walk away from three million dollars?"

"In this case, yeah. That painting is more than a piece of great art. Jack painted it for you—not some fat-cat collector."

Over a meatloaf-and-mashed-potatoes dinner, Kate had told him the story. She'd brought along a green salad and Ryder's favorite mint-chocolate-chip ice cream for later, after they walked Bailey. At the moment, however, her stomach tensed, and even ice cream didn't appeal. She hadn't expected his reaction.

She stood and started clearing the table. "But Jack's gone."

"Exactly. Ain't no more where 'Sanctuary' came from. That's why you need to keep it. It's part of your past."

"There won't be much of my *present* left in a few months, pal. My bank account is almost running on fumes."

Ryder pulled her back down into a chair. "I told you before—I can help. Move in here, rent-free."

She squeezed his hand. "I appreciate the offer. But it won't solve the long-term zero-income problem."

"You'll find a job, Kate. It takes time."

"It's taking too much time. Every day that passes, my skills get more obsolete."

Ryder pulled away. "You were so strong into art, I don't get it. Not only with Jack, but your dad—he was an artist too."

"You used to call him a cartoonist."

"I said a lot of stupid things back then. It's in your blood, Kate, but it's like you're trying to forget."

"The art scene wasn't exactly nice to me, Ryder."

"Not always, sure. But you're turning away from it all, not just the bad parts. Don't you remember where you came from?"

Kate shook her head vehemently. "You're talking crazy, Ryder. I don't see any way around it: I have to sell the painting. I need the money. It's my life. My decision."

Ryder's posture went rigid. "That's right, Kate. It's you against the world. You don't need anyone else to fight your battles, right? So fucking strong."

Bailey had been lying beneath the table, whining softly. When the dog slunk away, Kate realized she and Ryder were yelling.

He got up from the table and stomped into the kitchen. "Your life," he muttered as he started the coffeemaker.

Kate grabbed her purse and stalked toward the door. "Thanks for the guilt trip."

Her hand was on the doorknob when he called out.

"Kate, stop! This is nuts. I'm being a jerk. Don't know how *not* to be. Help me out here."

Kate took her hand off the doorknob and turned around. "How?"

Ryder rubbed his head, and his hair stood in spiky white tufts. "Let me explain, okay? It's like this: I always wanted to repay you for all you did for me."

"I didn't do all that much."

"Yeah, you did. More than you know. And I'm not talkin' about Jimmy Foster or the way you kicked my butt into getting clean again." He held out his hands, fingers splayed. "You always treated me like a *person*. Like I mattered. Like you cared what happened to me, even when I didn't. You care about people, Kate. That's your nature."

"Ryder, I always ... you always—"

"Let me finish while I still got the nerve. I'm real sorry you lost your job and all, but when it happened I thought, now's my chance. I can do something real for you, give you a place to stay until you get back on your feet."

Kate's anger softened. "I get it. And I appreciate it, but you don't have to—"

"I *wanted* to! But then Morrison butts in again. From the grave, even. And I'm being a selfish asshole, wantin' to be some kind of hero, but it's more than that. I know that painting's important to you, more than money. It's a little piece of your soul." He exhaled noisily. "That sounds hokey. I suck at this."

Kate couldn't help laughing. "No, you don't."

"You mean a lot to me, kid. Always have, even when I didn't act like it. Come on, sit down, have some coffee, let's talk about something else. You're right. It's your life. You get to pick what you do, and I promise not to judge. Hell, you never judged me." He cocked his head and smirked. "Hardly ever."

Kate put her purse on the table, and as she sat, a piece of paper caught her attention:

Galerie Framboise: The Old and the New (Prelude).
Opening reception Friday, March 31, eight o'clock p.m.

Kate picked up the flyer. "Where did you get this? Don't tell me you and Nikki Frank have become pen pals."

He brought in the coffee and sat next to her. "I went to see her a while back, after Jack died. You know—making amends and all that. For the time I busted up stuff in her gallery."

"Uh-huh."

"Part of the program, man. And she was cool, really. Didn't chew me a new asshole or anything. She seemed different. Quieter. Jack's dying shook her up, too. We had a long rap about him, and art, and what it all means."

Kate shuddered. "Nikki never liked me. Couldn't even get my name right."

"People can change." His laugh had a nervous edge to it. "Anyway, she put me on her mailing list, and I've gone to a few gigs there." He paused, and there went that hand to the shirt pocket, reaching for cigarettes that weren't there anymore. "She still has some of Jack's paintings."

"I imagine she does." Kate pointed to the side of the flyer, where Jack's name was at the top of a list of artists being shown.

"I'm gonna go to this shindig," Ryder said. "Want to come with?"

Kate looked at the flyer again. Another name stood out: Tatiana Kaminsky. Where had she heard that? Then, clear as yesterday, she heard Trudy Zelnik mentioning her newest discovery, claiming that Kaminsky would be "another Jack Morrison." *I wonder what her work looks like.*

"Yeah, Ryder, I think I will."

"Seriously?"

"Seriously."

Chapter Fifty

G alerie Framboise had undergone a facelift since Kate's last years-ago visit. The place seemed larger and airier; its harsh white walls were now a soft gray.

The crowd prowling the gallery hadn't changed much, however; same loud laughter and mingled smells of wine breath and expensive perfume. And the same buzz, the vibrating if invisible energy field that embraced her the moment she set foot inside. Artists and their work mingling with taste setters and collectors, art students taking notes, and people like her and Ryder, there simply to see the art.

I missed this, Kate thought as she linked arms with Ryder. *I didn't realize how much.*

Her throat tightened as she got close to Jack's paintings. She'd recognize them anywhere by the technique. These had to be the ones he'd told her about the last time she saw him.

"Trying out some new work, new images, funny stuff," he'd said. Something about fish and cows, and sure enough, Kate could discern both shapes on the canvas.

"Cows are inherently funny," Jack had told her.

She smiled at the memory and at the paintings themselves. *Oh, Jack, you were so good.*

And then a sobering thought: these canvases might be the last he ever painted. She closed her eyes, wishing with all her heart she could open them and see Jack, amid a crowd of admirers, looking up and smiling at her like old times.

Ryder nudged her gently. "You okay?"

Kate nodded, even though she was really not quite okay.

She pulled herself away from Jack's paintings to check out the rest of the exhibit. Not much grabbed her. A lot of high-concept work, hard-edged and sparse, with meanings you had to work at divining. Kate had always suspected there really wasn't much meaning.

She came to a painting that did claim her attention: a big canvas, like many of Jack's, only darker: a mélange of seemingly random colors clashing for attention. Kate found that if she didn't look directly at the splashes of color but rather into the adjoining space, as Jack had taught her to do, all sorts of things emerged; the brush strokes formed patterns and shapes: tombstones and dead tree limbs, body parts scattered on the highway. Kate shuddered and admitted to herself that she *liked* this macabre display, without understanding why. The piece was called "Untitled." And the painter was Tatiana Kaminsky.

Next to it was another Kaminsky, an even larger canvas with hard pastel rectangles of blue and yellow fighting for dominance. This one had a name: "Imposition."

Well, well, Trudy—you were right, as usual.

"Kate?"

Kate turned and found herself face to face with Nikki Frank— impossibly thin as always, with a few wrinkles around her eyes to show the passage of time. Her springy curls had been smoothed to a sleek bob, but her hair—still dark as ebony—shone with verve.

"Hello, Nikki," said Kate. "The gallery looks terrific."

Nikki smiled, although her expression seemed to ask, "What the hell are *you* doing here?"

Kate felt a need to explain. "Ryder asked me to tag along."

Comprehension dawned, and Nikki shook Ryder's hand and gave him a warmer smile. "Of course—you two are old friends. Forgive my memory. But how lucky for me. I've actually been trying to find you, Kate, and I never thought to ask Ryder."

"Find me?" Kate's curiosity went on alert. She looked at Ryder, who shrugged, all innocence.

"Yes, I wanted to ask you about one of Jack's paintings." She glanced around. "It's insane out here. Come to my office for a minute, will you?"

Before Kate could answer, a tall forty-ish blonde woman stomped up to Nikki. She stabbed her finger at "Untitled." "You have to do something about that dreadful Cantrell person! He had the gall to ask me if I could paint another like this to match his living room colors!"

"He was joking, Tatiana. Calm down—and say hello to Kate Morrison. As in the wife of Jack Morrison."

"Ex-wife," Kate said, turning to the angry woman. "Your paintings are fascinating, Ms. Kaminsky."

The artist's scowl dissolved into a smile as she thrust her hand toward Kate. "Your husband—your ex-husband—was a genius."

"He was," Kate replied. "And you're very talented yourself."

"Thank you." Tatiana tilted her head, blue eyes wide. "That means much, coming from you. Jack Morrison exerted such an influence on me. Can you see it?"

Kate nodded. "I do. They look nothing like his, but they have the same kind of energy. The same sort of depth, and substance."

Behind Tatiana, Ryder wiggled his eyebrows. Kate ignored him.

"I admire his work so much," said Tatiana. "He came to talk at one of my first painting classes at CalArts, and what he told us—about art—it made so much sense. He was so encouraging, so generous with advice."

"Jack lived and breathed art," Kate replied, for want of a more articulate response.

"He talked about you, that time at CalArts," Tatiana added. "I remember that so clearly. He said every artist needed someone to believe in them and that you helped him survive when he was struggling to get his work shown."

Kate knew she was blushing but couldn't help it. "That's kind of you to say. I did believe in him. The first time we met, I could tell he had talent. I knew he'd be famous someday."

"Yes! That's why it pleases me that you like my work. You have an eye for these things. I feel it. And perhaps—"

"Tania," Nikki interrupted, "I see the Taylors just came in. They were so taken by 'Imposition' when they saw it the other day. Why don't you go say hi to them?"

Tatiana scrunched up her face and then sighed. She clasped Kate's hand. "Such an honor to meet you."

"It was my pleasure. And don't let that so-called collector Cantrell get to you. Jack never took him seriously, and neither should you."

Tatiana's eyes glittered. "Then I won't."

"You're the first person she's been even halfway polite to all night," Nikki murmured as she watched Tatiana weave through the crowd.

Kate shrugged. "Artists!"

Nikki turned to Ryder. "I'm going to steal her for a bit."

"Go for it," Ryder said, and strolled off toward a cluster of people he seemed to know.

* * *

Nikki closed her office door and exhaled a deep sigh. She pointed to the two guest chairs in front of her desk. "Have a seat."

Kate sat.

"Sorry I have to make this quick," Nikki continued, sinking into the chair opposite Kate. "I wish we had more time, but—you know." She gestured toward the door and the activity beyond it.

"Okay," Kate said. "What about Jack's painting?"

"You still have it, right? The big one with the trees and all?"

"'Sanctuary?' I do." The hair on Kate's arms stood up. *A lot of interest in my painting all of a sudden.*

Nikki put her hands on her knees and leaned forward. "I want to borrow it for a show I'm doing."

"What kind of show?"

Nikki waved her hand and looked impatient. "Long story. But the important part is this—Trudy Zelnik and I are staging a retrospective —artists who got their start in the sixties here in L.A. Back when real art was being done. We'll follow their careers up to now, and we're trying to get as much work as we can that hasn't been seen a lot. Including the painting you have."

"You and Trudy Zelnik?"

"I said it was a long story, and if I had more time I'd go into it all. You knew her husband died, right?"

Kate shook her head. "I didn't."

"Same week Jack died, in fact. Really devastated her. But after a while, she started looking around for something to keep her busy, take her mind off it. She and I never got along before, but I think we've both changed. We actually have a lot in common—we love art, and L.A. artists, and whatever else you say about the woman, she has infallible taste."

"Can't argue with that," Kate said.

"And she heard I'd been having money troubles—which was true, you know this business—so she invested in Framboise, helped bring in new talent." Nikki sighed. "She's the one who steered Tania Kaminsky here—although sometimes I don't think she did me any favors. Look up 'difficult' in the dictionary and you'll see Tania's picture."

"She did seem a little intense."

"And you caught her in a good mood! In fact, you *put* her in a good mood, for which I thank you." Nikki glanced down at her silvery watch. "I have to wind this up, sorry. So, Trudy has this vision of a *huge* retrospective of artists we've known, and she's even leased a big space east of downtown for it. We're reaching out to collectors and artists, lining up the best of the best if we can. Tonight Trudy's in New York trying to sweet-talk Nick Ferrier into loaning us some of his Foulkes and Nielsens. And of course I have some of Jack's work. But that painting of yours—it would be a real draw because not many people have seen it. What do you think?"

"It sounds great. But I can't help you. My long story's not as interesting as yours, but a Dutch collector wants it buy it, and much as I hate to part with it, I need the money. I'm out of work."

Nikki stared at Kate like she couldn't believe what she'd just heard.

"Dirk de Bruyn Kops?"

"How'd you know?"

Nikki rubbed her temples like she had, or was getting, a headache.

"The art world is one big gossip machine, remember? He and Eden are a couple now. You knew?"

"No."

"And you're thinking of selling him the painting?"

"I need the money," Kate repeated.

"I thought you had some hot-shot job at an oil company."

"I guess the grapevine only works in the art scene. That hot-shot job is long gone."

Nikki's mouth formed an "O." "You're kidding!"

The woman seemed genuinely surprised. *Score one for me*, Kate thought.

"Well," Nikki said, "so much for my big idea."

Kate laughed. "Sorry."

Nikki started tapping the desktop. "I had no clue. I'm sorry, really. I assumed ... never mind what I assumed."

She sat up straight, and Kate had a sense of Nikki literally pulling herself together.

"You do know that if you sell the painting to Dirk," Nikki went on, "it'll hang in a dingy climate-controlled vault where maybe ten people a year will get to see it."

"Eden said—"

"I wouldn't put much weight on what Eden says. That's catty. I know. She and I fought a lot over the direction of Jack's work. But ask anyone. Eden changed, Kate. Art has become an *investment* for her. And the woman is ruthless. She could give Trudy lessons!"

Kate laughed despite her discomfort.

Nikki stood and brushed imaginary lint off her black satin skirt. "I am really sorry to hear that, Kate. If I could, I'd match his offer, but I don't think even Trudy has that kind of money to throw around."

"I'm sorry, too," Kate said. "If things were different, I'd be glad to loan you the painting. Sometimes I wish it could be out there for people to see. It's so beautiful, and it means a lot to me."

"I'm sure," Nikki said, already on her way to the door. "Gad! Sometimes I hate the art scene. *This* art scene. I can't believe I'm opening another gallery—in Houston."

"Houston?" Kate echoed.

"Tons of art lovers in Texas."

"How will you run two galleries?" asked Kate.

Nikki shrugged. "A lot of frequent flyer miles, I guess. Actually, if I could, I'd sell Framboise, but Trudy wants to keep it going. She claims she can manage it for me, but I have my doubts. She's a first-rate collector, but I don't think she has the business gene. Stanley took care of all that. And," she added with a chuckle, "Trudy has pissed off a lot of artists, and a few collectors too, with her bargaining tactics."

She pulled the door open and shook Kate's hand. "Thanks anyway, Kate, and good luck to you. I hope you find a new job soon."

"Thanks. I'm afraid it won't be soon enough to save 'Sanctuary.'"

"You never know. Miracles happen."

"That sounds strange, coming from you, Nikki. What happened to your edge?"

Nikki laughed. "Edge is overrated, Kate. I finally figured that out."

And with that she melted back into the crowd.

Ryder materialized next to Kate and whispered in her ear. "Glad you came?"

Kate nodded. "It's been interesting."

Ryder smirked. "You missed it huh?"

"Yes, oh Wise One. I did."

They made a circuit of the gallery, but nothing else in the show resonated with Kate the way Tatiana Kaminsky's paintings did. Kate returned to them for one last look.

Beside her, Ryder said, "You dig these, don't you?"

"Don't you?"

"Yeah, they kinda grab me. But that bit you were feeding her— man, you spin a pretty good line."

"I meant it. So much of this," she gestured around the gallery, "seems shallow to me. But these are like Jack's. I can't explain it—it's a feeling I got with Jack's work, and not just because we were...in love, or anything. His work was—is—*real*."

Ryder put his arm around her shoulders and squeezed. "You're something else, Katie Girl." He studied Tatiana's canvases one more time. "You ready to split now?"

She was.

As they headed for the door, Nikki intercepted them and handed Kate her business card.

"Keep in touch, Kate. And let me know if your ... situation changes, please?"

"I will," Kate promised.

"Do you have a card?"

Kate felt naked as she replied. "Not anymore."

Nikki glanced at Ryder. "I could reach you through our friend here, right?"

"You could."

* * *

"So," Ryder said in the car, "you and Nikki have a good chat? Catch up on old times?"

"Not exactly." Kate turned so she could see his face in profile. "Did you know she and Trudy Zelnik are partners now?"

"Trudy Zelnik!" Ryder snorted. "That name's a blast from the past. She and Nikki in cahoots together? That I gotta see! But Trudy did buy a lot of great art for low-ball prices. She any good at *sellin'*?"

"Probably not without starting a fight." She frowned at Ryder. "Nikki wanted to borrow 'Sanctuary' for a show they're doing. I suppose you didn't know that either."

Ryder took one hand off the steering wheel and held it palm out. "Swear to God I didn't. Too bad, though. That'd be a trip."

"Yes, it would." Kate settled back in her seat. "Nikki did seem different. Nicer."

Ryder cackled. "Yeah, the old Nikki was a shark. This one, more a pussycat."

"Interesting analogies, Ryder. But pussycats have teeth too. And claws."

"Don't I know it, Katie Girl. Don't I know."

"She told me she'd like to close the gallery, though. Said she's tired of the L.A. art scene. Imagine that."

Ryder exited the freeway with practiced ease that Kate always appreciated. He never seemed to get angry in traffic.

"I told you, kid," he said. "People can change."

"She's opening a new place in Texas, and Trudy wants to run Framboise. Or run it into the ground."

Ryder parked in front of Kate's apartment. "Nikki won't let that happen. The gallery's too important. It's practically historical. She'll figure something out."

"Good luck to her." Kate reached for the door handle. "Want to come in for coffee?"

"Nah, gotta go walk Bailey."

Kate kissed his cheek. "Thanks for tonight. It was fun."

"Anytime, Katie Girl. You're the world's best date. And the cheapest."

* * *

The apartment was quiet and dark. She turned on a couple of lights and sank onto the sofa, staring at "Sanctuary." The painting was an old friend. It was her indelible connection to the art world. Selling it would expel her from that world.

Then she remembered the sketch Jack had made of her, the day they met. Another special gift—the very first thing he'd ever given her. Where had she stashed it? Kate pushed herself off the sofa; its weary springs creaked in protest, and she patted the worn upholstery fondly, like stroking a tired old dog.

There—the bookcase. She pulled out *The Sirens of Titan* and inside the front cover was the sketch, creased but not faded. The *Sirens* had kept it safe for her all these years. She put the sketch on the kitchen table, smoothed its surface, and marveled as she always did at how Jack had captured her essence in those few pencil strokes. The drawing had been an invitation from Jack—an invitation into his world. And what a world.

* * *

As she was getting ready for bed, Kate replayed her conversation with Nikki Frank. Something the gallery owner said kept nagging at her, but she couldn't nail it down.

How *was* Nikki going to run two galleries so far apart? Trudy—the Trudy Kate knew—wasn't cut out for the role of art dealer.

"I don't think she has the business gene," Nikki had said.

Kate spat a mouthful of toothpaste. "That's it!"

She looked at her reflection in the mirror and grinned. Nikki and Trudy needed her help. They needed Jack Morrison's wife. The *first* one.

Chapter Fifty-One

The next morning, Kate waited until ten o'clock to phone Nikki Frank; the woman had had a late night. She used the time to map out her plan so she'd sound coherent when she reached Nikki.

The more Kate thought about her idea, the more sense it made. She was at least as qualified as Trudy to run a gallery—probably a whole lot more so.

Nikki sounded tired when she answered the phone, but she didn't seem surprised to hear from Kate.

After a couple of pleasantries, Kate dived in. "I have an idea that will solve both our problems. And it comes with a bonus."

"Tell me," Nikki said, a wary undercurrent in her voice.

"Hire me. To run Framboise."

"Seriously?"

"Absolutely! I need a job—a salary—and I have more business skills than Trudy. I wouldn't displace her, I'd complement her. After thirty years in Human Resources, I can get along with anyone. Almost."

"You did work some magic on Tatiana," Nikki said, the words coming out so slowly that Kate could tell she was thinking as she spoke.

"I know a lot about art," Kate continued. "My dad was an artist—he taught me to recognize the good stuff when I see it. And all that time with Jack taught me more about art, and about artists."

"You do know your stuff. Trudy always said you had the best eye for art—next to hers, of course." Nikki laughed. "Jack said that, too. When we were setting up that last show of his, he said he wished you were there to help with the installation, because he trusted your judgment." Another laugh, heavy with irony. "More than he trusted mine, evidently."

"He and I made a good team... for a while."

"It's not a bad idea, if you're honestly interested. But I don't know if I can pay you enough."

That old line again. Kate was ready for it.

"I'd be okay to start at an assistant's pay, while I learn the ropes. If you'll agree to pay me a commission for the things I sell, and a bonus for bringing in new talent, we can make it work."

Nikki didn't speak, so Kate added. "Nikki, this is the first thing I've felt excited about in a long time. I know it's the right move for both of us."

"We'll have to convince Trudy. I already know she won't want to give up control."

"She won't have to. I'll work *for* you two. And here's the bonus. I won't have to sell 'Sanctuary,' so I can loan it for your retrospective."

"I'll set up a meeting for you with Trudy," Nikki said. "You convinced me, now sell it to her. It shouldn't be too hard. She always liked you, Kate. We both did."

You could've fooled me, Kate thought as she hung up the phone.

The audacity of her proposal had set her nerves jangling. But it made so much sense. It had to come together.

She laced up her hiking boots and headed to Griffith Park to burn off some of the adrenaline.

"Oh, Dad," she whispered as she started up the trail, "I wish you could see me now."

* * *

The following Monday afternoon, feeling like she was moving through a surrealist's dream, Kate drove up a broad semi-circular driveway and parked in front of Trudy Zelnik's home in the hills east of Laurel Canyon Blvd. Memories collided with reality as she turned off the car's engine and sat for a minute, untangling her thoughts.

"No big deal—just my whole future at stake," Kate muttered as she got out of the car.

The weather had turned early-spring benign, and sunlight warmed her back as she walked to the door, trying to remember the last time she'd seen Trudy Zelnik. Their relationship had usually been cordial, but Kate wondered if she'd ever seen behind Trudy's façade.

Life-size white stone lions guarded both sides of the front door, alongside terra cotta pots holding braided-trunked ficus trees. Quiet elegance emanated from the place.

Trudy answered the bell herself, and for a moment Kate didn't recognize her. The woman had undergone a dramatic transformation: gone were the coke-bottle glasses, along with at least thirty pounds, and she looked years younger than Kate had expected. Trudy's simple beige pantsuit flattered without screaming for attention.

"Hello, dear Kate," Trudy said, enveloping Kate in a Chanel-scented embrace. Even the voice had dropped an octave. "How nice to see you again. You look lovely. As always."

Trudy's house had a comfortable, lived-in atmosphere, tastefully decorated: spare, clean-edged furnishings, pale peach-tinted walls designed to show her art collection to its best advantage. The collection included several famous painters: Ruscha, Johns, Bengston. And among them, in the center—Jack Morrison's stylized seascape that Trudy had purchased all those years ago. Kate paused in front of it.

"This has always been one of my favorites," Trudy said softly.

Kate nodded. "Mine too."

Trudy guided her to a shaded patio overlooking green lawns and a sparkling turquoise swimming pool. The air smelled of citrus blossoms, and a glass-topped white wicker table held a tray of pastries and glasses frosty with iced tea.

"We have some catching up to do before we get down to business,"

Trudy said, handing Kate a small white china plate with one of the pastries.

Kate clinked her glass against Trudy's and bit into the most heavenly cherry tart she'd ever tasted. If she hadn't been so nervous, she'd have felt like a privileged society matron enjoying afternoon tea.

"I missed seeing you at showings," Trudy began, "after you and Jack divorced."

Kate didn't have a ready reply. In the years since she'd ceased being Jack Morrison's wife, she'd seldom thought of Trudy.

"We did have some interesting talks," Kate said finally. "I remember you telling me about Tatiana Kaminsky, and I finally got to see her paintings. You were right, as usual. She's incredibly good."

Trudy beamed. "She is, but temperamental doesn't begin to describe her. Nikki tells me you charmed her socks off, though."

"She was impressed that I knew Jack—that I was married to him. That gave me some leverage."

"Jack..." Trudy stared out at the horizon for a moment and sighed. "I was so shocked when he died—as I'm sure you were."

"I was," Kate agreed. "The last thing I expected."

Trudy's blond hair lifted in a breeze that swept in the smell of jasmine. "Life is so damned ironic. You knew my husband Stanley died?"

Kate nodded. "Nikki told me. I am so sorry."

"Emphysema. He hung on and hung on—and then the very week Jack died, so did Stanley." Trudy's left eyelid twitched. "I thought I'd come to accept that Stanley wasn't going to live much longer... but to lose both of them in a matter of days... I couldn't stop crying."

Kate reached out and patted the back of Trudy's hand. "That was brutal."

Trudy sniffed. "It was. And I couldn't bring myself to attend Jack's funeral. Stanley was buried the day before, and I couldn't face *two* funerals in two days."

"Of course. Jack would have understood."

Trudy pulled a tissue from her pocket and dabbed at her nose. "I'm sure he would have. He was a dear friend. A good man."

"Yes."

Kate sipped her tea, but her appetite for the cherry tart abandoned her.

Then Trudy straightened her back and took a breath. "But my darling Stanley did right by me. He'd made some very good investments over the years, made more money than I realized."

Unlike my darling Eric.

"You're lucky, then."

"I am." Trudy's demeanor shifted. "Now let's get down to business. Nikki of course filled me in on your proposal, and the reasons behind it. But what happened to you, Kate? You were such a rising star at that company."

Kate was prepared for the question. "Times change. The price of oil was in freefall last year, and Permian was overextended. Genoco saw a good bargain and snapped them up for their resources. But not for their support staff. Genoco has plenty of that."

Trudy clicked her tongue. "I can't imagine any as good as you, though."

"You're kind to say that, but the bottom line is all they care about."

Trudy tapped the plate in front of Kate and motioned her to eat some more. "And you truly think working for Nikki and me is the solution?"

Kate took another bite and swallowed, washed it down with some tea while she framed her response. "I do. I lived and breathed art when I was married to Jack. I learned a lot from him, and from my father. He was an artist, too."

Trudy tilted her head. "So Nikki said. I didn't know that. No wonder you always seemed so at home in the art world. They both taught you well."

Kate laughed. "They did. I have no talent for painting at all, but I do know a good one when I see it."

"And that is a skill that can't be taught, my dear."

"More than that, Trudy—I have a strong business background. I know how to bargain. I spent years negotiating contracts with insurance carriers and suppliers, and I learned how to do it without alienating them. Permian had some of the best terms of any company its size, and I think my strategy had a lot to do with that. I'm not an accountant, but I know how to draw up a budget and stick to it. I've spent a lot of years managing complex personalities. And from Jack I learned about the care and feeding of artists. I'd enjoy soothing their delicate egos."

Trudy was staring at her, eyes wide. "You present a very strong case for yourself, Kate. You've clearly given this some thought."

"I have. It would be a terrific opportunity for me to put my skills back to work, in a setting I get pleasure from. I understand there are no guarantees, and I'm willing to take a pay cut to do it—because frankly, some income is better than no income, which is my present situation."

"I respect your honesty."

"The other part of my proposal, as I'm sure Nikki told you, is that I won't have to sell 'Sanctuary' to Dirk de Bruyn Kops. I can loan it to you and Nikki for your retrospective. Jack would have liked that, I know."

There. She'd played the last card and given it all she had.

Trudy paused to sip her tea. "Yes—the retrospective. It's very important to me. I want to do something to honor Stanley. He was never really *into* art as much as I. He used to claim that he knew nothing about art, but he adored Jack, and his paintings. They had long conversations about their work. Jack was actually interested in Stanley. Most people think, oh plastic surgeons, they go around making movie stars look even prettier. But Stanley did so much more —children with cleft palates, burn victims, skin cancer survivors. And he did a lot of it *gratis*, thanks to those rich, beautiful celebrities."

"He must've been a good man, Trudy. I wish I'd known him."

"Yes. You would have liked him." She sighed again. "And this show will honor Stanley's memory *and* Jack's, and other talented artists— especially the ones who aren't with us anymore. I can't bear to think of them being forgotten." She bit her lower lip. "I believe art needs to be seen and appreciated, and I want to help inspire new artists to try and achieve what painters like Jack did."

"So you'd be honoring Stanley and securing Jack's legacy. A big task."

"And I'm very enthused about it. It's the first thing I've cared about since Stanley died."

"I'd like to help in any way I can," Kate said. *Don't act too eager.* But oh how she wanted to be a part of this project, and not merely for the salary.

Trudy rose and extended her hand. "I need to think this over, and I want to be sure you fully understand the risks. I would hate for you to pass on another opportunity that might be better in the end. We don't know how Framboise will fare without Nikki guiding every little detail."

"One thing I've learned is that life is pretty damned uncertain," Kate replied.

"True. But I didn't want to paint you a rosy picture with no thorns." Trudy chuckled at her own metaphor, and so did Kate.

At the front door, Trudy clasped Kate's hands. "You're a woman of many talents, Kate. I always said that about you."

"Thanks, Trudy. I hope you'll agree to my proposal because it would benefit all of us—you, me and Nikki."

"I'll let you know by the end of the week."

"Fair enough."

Kate walked through the door, trying to come up with a clincher to toss at Trudy.

She stopped and turned. "To clarify one thing, Trudy. Please don't think I'd be moving in on your territory. You would still absolutely control Framboise. You know much more than I about staging exhibits, doing publicity, all that. And you have the right connections. But I can finesse those connections for you. And take care of the back-room drudgery that you probably don't have time for."

Trudy smiled. "I understand. You make a very compelling case— you would do well in sales, my dear. If you were trying to sell me a Rolls Royce, I'd buy it this minute."

"I feel strongly about this idea. You know how you said the retrospective is the first thing you've cared about since Stanley died? I feel that way about Framboise—I haven't been this excited about anything in a long, long time."

Trudy seemed about to say something else. *Say yes! Just say yes right now!*

"Nikki and I have to talk before I decide, but I can't imagine any answer but yes, Kate. You make it very easy."

"Good. I really do think it would work, Trudy. Thanks for your time today. I enjoyed talking with you again."

"I did, too. And Kate? Thank you for not staring at my new face or asking any prying questions."

"Your face?"

Trudy smirked. "While Stanley was alive, I resisted plastic surgery. He wouldn't perform it himself, and no one else could ever meet his standards. But once he was gone…"

Kate studied Trudy's remarkably smooth skin and smiled. "You got your money's worth, whatever the price. You look stunning."

Chapter Fifty-Two

The sun slid toward the western horizon and tinged the sky brilliant crimson in Kate's rear-view mirror as she drove toward Glendale, replaying her meeting with Trudy. Had she come on too strong? Not strong enough? No, she decided—Jack Morrison's wife had done her best, and that had been damned good.

Instead of taking the Glendale Freeway, Kate pointed the car toward downtown L.A., drawn by a need to revisit the place it all started. Jack's old studio had been razed by a developer, and shiny new "artists' lofts" were rising on its grave, with glittering windows and smooth concrete walls. She found a parking spot across the street and turned off the engine. The lofts had taken over the vacant lot next door, too, where winos used to congregate, passing bottles around and throwing the empties to shatter on the side of the building. Where had they gone? Open space was scarce now, but the homeless population continued to grow. Had they drifted north, to the camps that lined the freeway entrances and exits?

Traffic flowed past her, thickening as the buildings emptied and their occupants headed home. After a few minutes of gazing into the past, Kate decided to join the homebound tide. In the distance, she saw the outline of the Permian Oil building, now missing its neon "P." The building still sat empty; Permian was long-gone.

"But I'm still here," Kate whispered as she transitioned onto Glendale Blvd.

* * *

Kate wanted to talk to Ryder, but she wasn't ready yet. He'd be pleased for her and maybe a little disappointed that she wouldn't have to move in with him to save money. Actually, that hadn't been a horrible idea. This little rented space had never felt like home and would feel even less so when "Sanctuary" went out on loan.

And Ryder was such good company. He made her smile, made her laugh. He'd been a catalyst for her biggest adventure, and he cared about her. She'd taken his friendship for granted, but that night she became acutely aware of just how lucky she was to have him in her life.

Trudy had seemed ready to make a deal right then if not for the need to get Nikki's buy-in. That shouldn't be too hard, given Kate's last talk with the gallery owner.

And if it didn't happen? She'd survive. She always had. There were other galleries, of course, and even museums that might welcome someone with her background and knowledge. Now that this direction had seized her imagination, a world of possibilities beckoned.

Kate looked at her beloved painting and whispered, "Whatever happens, I promise not to let you go. I might loan you out, but you'll always come home to me. Always."

It wasn't all that late, but exhaustion weighed her down, and Kate gave in to it.

* * *

She awoke early, before dawn, and further sleep evaded her, so she brewed hot tea and stared out the window as the eastern sky gradually lightened: first a graying of the dark horizon, then a deeper blue, and finally the first pink rays of sunrise. The sight reminded her of a Jack Morrison painting.

The kitchen clock read five-fifty-five a.m. Ryder would be on his way to the park for his sunrise Tai Chi practice. Kate traded her night-gown for workout clothes, swallowed some yogurt to quell her hunger, and drove to Griffith Park.

He was there, right where she expected. Bailey, tethered to a tree trunk, watched him intently, her head cocked to one side as if trying to figure out what her human was up to. Kate recognized the moves Ryder was performing: "Heaven and Earth," "White Crane Spreads Its Wings," and her personal favorite, "Carry Tiger to the Mountain," which Ryder had explained was a metaphor for letting go of fear. Ryder moved gracefully, arms circling, pushing and pulling, legs lifting effortlessly for the kicks. His lean body seemed part of the landscape.

A rising sun outlined the eucalyptus trees in pink and gold. Kate inhaled the sweet morning air and let the light flow through her. A breeze ruffled winter's fallen leaves; new growth sprouted everywhere. A shaft of sunlight illuminated Ryder, like the once-upon-a-time spot-light at the Quartermoon.

"Hi," Kate called out softly.

Ryder finished the sequence. Then he grinned, as if he'd been expecting her.

"You won't believe what happened yesterday," she said.

"Try me. But first, let's do the form together."

"I don't think I remember it."

Ryder reached out his arm toward her. "You do. You will."

After the opening moves, her muscle memory took over, that elusive grace she hadn't believed in. She felt it in every fiber of her being. How odd, since she had never really mastered the form before she dropped out of class. What had that been about, anyway? What else had been so all-fired important?

Now, here with Ryder, her truest friend in all the world, it was as if she'd never let her practice lapse. The moves came without fore-thought. It was not so very hard after all: simply take a deep breath, and dance.

Acknowledgments

Few authors complete a novel without assistance, and I am no exception. The feedback and support of my writing tribe helped bring this book into existence.

A staggering amount of gratitude goes to past and present members of the Pacific Online Writers Group: Heather Ames, the late great Terry Carr, Vance Gloster, Miko Johnston, and Christopher Page.

Thanks, too, to those who provided technical information, including Brian McCarthy for explaining the temperature at which hair might freeze in Alaska, and Patrick Huston for instructing me on the finer points of guitars. Bouquets also go to the late Waynna Kato Schroeder, who helped me stay in touch with the art world all these years.

I've said it before, but it still holds true and comes from my heart: I couldn't have done it without you.

Book Group Questions
Discussing Write My Name on the Sky

1. The book's title is a metaphor for ambition, and many of the characters hold ambitions that, when realized, conflict with the goals of others close to them. Are there people in your own life for whom this is true? What was the outcome?

2. Another theme running through the book is that of one person rescuing another. Jack saves Kate several times in the story; even after he's gone, how does he pull off one last rescue? Kate saves Ryder at least twice, but how does Jack's observation that "You can't save somebody who doesn't want to be saved" figure into this? Does Ryder save anyone? How? Could Kate have saved Jack from his fate?

3. Kate often identifies herself as "Jack Morrison's wife." Who does she become when she is no longer in that role? Or does she ever completely transcend it? Should she?

4. Ryder is a recurring character throughout the book. How does he act as a catalyst for some of the events in the story?

5. Did you have a favorite character? Did any of them seem more real and/or sympathetic to you? Why do you think that was?

6. Jack seems to think that artists are a special class of people with rules and entitlements of their own. Do you agree with his perspective? Have you ever known anyone who thought they were better than everyone else? How did that make you feel? How did Jack's attitude make you feel about him?

7. How did you experience the book? Did it pull you into that world right away, or did it take some time? Did the world eventually seem real to you? Did it mirror any of your own experiences?

8. Is the ending satisfying? Would you have changed it? How?

Preview

Read on for an excerpt from Bonnie Schroeder's first novel, *Mending Dreams*

Mending Dreams

Chapter One

Did you ever have one of those days that was so bad you thought, *Well at least it can't get any worse?* And then you realized, *Oh, yes, it could. It most certainly could.*

That August Monday started out hot, humid, and as wretched as Los Angeles can be. Somehow it always surprises us, the people who live here. "Where's the ocean breeze? Why is it so *hot?*" Because we live in a desert, that's why. It's been greened over with stolen water, but it is what it is.

The muggy weather came courtesy of Hurricane Isabel, which had devastated a bunch of towns along the Gulf of Mexico, and then brought her havoc further inland, even as far as California. Thick clouds held the heat in, and we baked, simmered, and stewed. A malicious pink sky tinged everything the color of thin blood.

Mechanical devices misbehaved. Traffic lights suddenly went dark. Internet servers spontaneously disconnected. Air conditioners strained and threatened to die.

I was late to work, thanks to some moron's car in the no-park zone of Glendale Blvd. When I finally arrived, caffeine-starved and out of breath, disaster awaited.

Over the weekend, I'd logged on to my office network and picked up my emails, even as "workaholic" hissed around in my brain. Jacobs Laboratories had sure been getting its money's worth out of me. I'd flown home late Friday night after five fun-filled days at our Dallas plant, and on Saturday I barely had time to take in my dry cleaning, mail my mom's birthday present to New Mexico, and restock my refrigerator. My houseplants begged for water, and so did my elderly neighbor's front lawn, which I'd helped take care of since she fell and broke her hip. Unpaid bills lurked in the pile of unopened envelopes scattered across the floor beneath the mail slot.

And I was desperate to get to the gym. Those days of enforced inactivity and hotel food had taken their toll. Maybe I was overly paranoid about my weight, but I'd been on diets since I was ten years old, and I'd finally learned that exercise helped silence the nagging little voice—my own or my mom's, I was never sure which—that whispered "fat, fat, fat" whenever I saw my reflection.

Not until Sunday did I even get time to catch up with my friends. Noah, the man in my life, was camping with his son in Yosemite. He'd left a message on my answering machine to welcome me home (as usual, I'd forgotten to turn my cell back on after the flight) and in some ways that was better than having him there in person.

* * *

My first clue Monday wasn't going my way at work came as a voicemail from my assistant, the inaptly named Angel Fairweather.

"Susan, I hate to do this, but I caught one mother of a summer cold," her recorded voice said between sneezes and coughs. "I know you'll be buried with work, but maybe one of those lazybones down the hall can help out. I'll try and be back tomorrow. Sorry." Another sneeze for good measure before she hung up. Her message had been time stamped at five o'clock Monday morning, and she sure sounded miserable—but Angel was an aspiring actress, and a couple of times before, she'd phoned in sick to go to an audition.

"Damn," I muttered as I booted up my computer and connected to the Jacobs intranet.

My email inbox was relatively clean, thanks to my weekend check-in. But sitting in the middle of my desk was a note from Derek Bord, my boss, asking for a time-consuming report on my year-to-date expenses compared with my budget. Double-damn. I went to the break room for coffee, and by the time I got back, I'd received three new emails, all way more urgent than Bord's request.

A few minutes later, Bord himself stomped into my office. He was a small man with dyed-looking black hair and eyes that didn't quite line up.

"Ah, there you are, Susan. Good."

I put all my energy into a smile and pointed at the computer. "Derek. I'm researching the expense data right now."

This was a lie, but he wouldn't know the difference. Bord's computer skills were somewhere below a first-grader's.

He waved a manicured hand. "Forget that. We have bigger fish to fry."

I bit my lip. "Fine. What's up?"

"I need a list of everyone in Benefits, how much they make, how long they've been here. And I need it right away."

I peered into his beady little eyes and wondered if he'd somehow forgotten that my job description—Manager of Corporate Compliance—didn't include keeping personnel records on individual work groups. I had enough of a challenge making sure the company maintained a semblance of ethical corporate conduct.

"Val should have that at her fingertips," I said without thinking. Big mistake.

My friend and co-worker Val Desmond managed Personnel, which also reported up to Bord and included recordkeeping. I overcame the urge to point out that last detail.

Bord's face scrunched up like a squirrel passing an acorn. "I'm not asking Val. I'm asking *you*. I have my reasons—and please don't cause another scene about this."

Another scene?

"I don't understand," I said, trying to figure out what had Bord wound up so tightly.

Again the squirrel face, accompanied by a heavy sigh. "I don't have time to explain it to you. I need the information, I need it *now*, and I need it done discreetly. If it's beyond your capability, I'll get someone else to—"

I held up my hands in surrender. "I'm on it."

He still blocked the doorway, studying me. I shuffled some papers to show I meant business. "Anything else?"

He shook his head. "An hour, Susan. I need it in an hour."

I went to work. The data wasn't that hard to come by, but the research kept me from what I considered more important matters. Every time I glanced at my email inbox, the number of unopened messages had grown.

I sent my query to the database, and an obnoxious little box popped up in the middle of my computer screen, informing me that the system was "WORKING... PLEASE STAND BY." While I waited, Ginny Loring tapped on my door. Ginny was Val's assistant, a pale, freckled woman with curly red hair and a bizarre sense of style manifested in the yellow sundress and purple sandals she wore that morning.

"No one's answering your phone," Ginny said.

I frowned. "I know. Angel's out sick, and I'm on a rush project for Derek. Just let 'em go to voicemail."

"Okay, but NitroLitho's calling—they really need—"

"Not now. Take a message. Thanks."

Back to the computer, where rows of data appeared on the monitor. I scrolled down to see if the names looked right. Wait—there was one I didn't recognize. Was it a mistake, or someone who'd just been—

Tap, tap, tap. Ginny again.

"What?" I snapped.

She flinched, and I felt a twinge of remorse, but I could practically hear Bord snorting for his damned report.

"Do you want your mail, or should I leave it for Angel to open when she—"

"Leave it! Please."

Ginny actually whimpered as she turned away. Belatedly, I called out "Thanks" as her sandals slapped down the hallway. I sighed and made a note to apologize later, when things calmed down. Even if she had a poor sense of priorities, Ginny meant well.

I found my place in the rows of data, found the unfamiliar name. A new hire. Okay. I downloaded the list, still trying to figure out what that little prick Bord was up to.

Lilah Cantrell, Bord's own personal Dragon Lady, glared at me as I approached, report in hand.

"Mr. Bord is on the phone," she told me.

I cursed the day I'd opposed Bord bringing Lilah with him when he was hired. She had to know about it, judging by the way she treated me. None of the other managers on Bord's staff got the chilly reception I did. Sure, I was just doing my job when I recommended he take one of the existing assistants rather than bring in an outsider, but I don't think Bord had explained my reasoning to her. Not that Lilah would have cared anyway.

I ignored the ice in her voice. "He asked for this report ASAP," I told her, fluttering the papers.

She held out a red-taloned hand. "I'll see that he gets it."

Yeah, right—in another hour or so.

"I'd rather give it to him myself. In case he has any questions."

She pressed her thin red lips together and glanced toward the heavy wood door that closed off Bord's inner sanctum. With a belabored sigh, she got up and knocked softly, then went in and pulled the door shut behind her. A moment later she emerged. "You can go in."

Still on the phone, Bord motioned me to a seat in front of his heavy walnut throne. Me, I'd have gone for a smaller scale in furniture, but I guess he thought it made him look important.

After a leisurely end to his phone call, Bord peered at me over his reading glasses. "What've you got for me?"

I handed him the report and he paged through it, frowning. No "thank you," no "good work, Susan." Just the Bord scrutiny.

"I don't see any ages on here," he said finally.

I fought down a wave of annoyance—at him for the belated request and at myself for not anticipating it.

"You asked for names, salary, and length of service," I said.

He shook his head with a well-crafted look of disappointment. "I expected better of you, Susan."

"It would help if I knew what was going on, Derek. I'm working in the dark here."

Bord looked at me blankly. An awkward moment passed.

"How soon can you get me more complete information?"

I checked my watch. "Fifteen minutes."

He gave me back the report, like it was too contaminated for him to keep. "Do it."

I went back and rewrote the query to ask for age data—plus gender and minority codes for good measure. That should give the little creep more information than he knew what to do with. I sent the request and then retrieved the voicemail messages that had piled up while I worked on Bord's pointless project.

As the query results began coming in, my phone rang. I picked it up without looking at the ID display, sure it was Bord wanting to know how long he had to wait.

"Hi there."

It took a second to place the voice, coming at me out of context like that.

"Bad time to call?" he continued when I didn't answer right away.

Is there ever a good time for a call from your ex-husband? Frank Krajewski and I had somehow forged an edgy truce in the shattered aftermath of our marriage, and even if he did still tell me every time he saw me that I looked just like actress Angie Harmon, *only better*, it didn't mean I was happy to hear from him. Oh sure, I kept his name after the divorce, despite the inconvenience. It's pronounced Cry-YES-ky, but I lost count of the times a sales clerk cheerfully addressed me as Mrs. Kurh-JOO-sky. My maiden name was Stafford, but I'd used Frank's name professionally for six years, and it was just too much trouble to change back.

Besides, the Stafford name was about all my father gave me. I never knew him, but I was pretty sure I liked Frank better. That's not saying much, though. Months of therapy and gallons of tears had worn away the sharp corners of my feelings, but sometimes I felt like my anger toward Frank was all that kept me going.

"No, it's fine," I said in answer to Frank's question, proud of how easily the lie came. "How are you?"

A pause. "Okay. I was wondering if maybe you'd like to have dinner at Emilio's tonight? Haven't seen you for a while."

Something in Frank's voice made me uneasy. I twirled my stainless steel letter opener and then pressed its sharp tip into the report Bord had rejected. Behind me, the computer hissed softly. A black plastic tray full of incoming mail sat on the far corner of my desk, and it wasn't going to magically disappear on its own. One of the fluorescent lights in the ceiling started to flicker and buzz; I scribbled a mental note to call Building Maintenance.

"Susie?"

"I'm here. Just checking my schedule. Ummmm, yeah, I can do that."

"Great!" He sounded relieved.

"How's Clayton?"

"Fine – he's up at Davis for some kind of training."

Aha, that explained it. Frank was on his own and bored; he never handled solitude well. We agreed to meet at seven. I went back to Bord's little emergency and put Frank out of my thoughts. Almost.

* * *

This time the Dragon Lady didn't even bother to look up at me. "Go on in."

Bord studied the report, lips pursed. He set it down and shook his head. *Oh great, he's going to find something else wrong.*

"A lot of people," he said, looking at me across four feet of gleaming walnut.

I nodded. "Anything else?"

Bord leaned forward and lowered his voice, even though the connecting door was closed. "This is highly confidential, but you're going to have a role in it eventually, so we may as well get you started."

I dug my nails into the padded leather chair arms. *Terrific—more pointless work.*

If you're beginning to think I didn't have much respect for Derek Bord, you're right. I wouldn't have liked him in the best of situations, but it so happened he was hired to replace my favorite boss of all time,

Paul Dumas. Paul had been tough on his people, but when they delivered, he wasn't stingy with praise. Or bonuses. Paul and I worked well together—until he dropped dead of a heart attack at the age of fifty-three. That had been two years earlier. When Paul died, Jacobs was in the midst of acquiring a medium-sized processing plant in Washington State; we needed to merge their workforce into ours without delay. As Vice President of Human Resources, Paul had been working twenty-four seven on the merger, which is probably what killed him.

Pressed for an immediate successor, Jacobs had opted for an outside hire with supposed credentials in the area of blending workforces. Enter Derek Bord.

And at that moment Bord was giving me an imitation of a benevolent smile from behind his desk, sure of his place in the Jacobs hierarchy. "We have decided to outsource our benefits work," he said.

We who, Derek? You and the rat in your pocket?

"What for?" There I went, speaking without thinking. But the idea sounded stupid, even for Bord. Our Benefits group was small and, except for a marginally competent manager, pretty efficient—too efficient to warrant outsourcing. In my opinion anyway.

Bord scowled. "There are a lot of reasons, but I don't have time to explain it all right now. The thing you have to keep in mind is that people will be . . . released. And we'll need to avoid the appearance of discrimination when we decide who to keep and who to let go."

He paused and cocked his head as if waiting for some sign of agreement from me. When I didn't offer any, he added, "That's where you come in."

Still trying to absorb the news, I nodded.

"So you need to be thinking about who's expendable and who's not. And I want you to think outside the box here, Susan."

"Outside the box?" I repeated like a moron. Was he asking me for ways to circumvent our normal Equal Employment Opportunity practices?

"Yes. For example, Jeff Tate. Jeff's a fine manager, but I'm not sure we'll need *his position* when the outsourcing's done. However, Jeff's skills are transferable—we could, say, move him into Personnel and—"

"But that's Val's—"

I didn't have to finish my sentence. Val and Bord had clashed several times when he tried to cut corners in the hiring process. This outsourcing would give him a prime chance to weed out the people who'd stood in his way, the ones he didn't like or want. Maybe even the Compliance Manager, if she gave him an excuse.

"Of course we have to obey the rules," Bord continued. "I'm not suggesting any wholesale disregard. Just . . . be creative. Think of ways we can *flex* the rules."

I got up and pretended to study the view. Bord's office had a nice set of windows, and I could see the glass cylinders of the Bonaventure hotel to the north. On bright days the reflection might blind you, but those thick, murky clouds had smothered the sun. I looked back at Bord's desk and his shiny brass name plate, and I pushed away an image of me bashing him over the head with it, blood splashed all over his crisp white shirt and gray silk tie.

Finally I trusted my voice enough to speak. "I'll see what I can come up with."

He nodded. "This is top-secret, Susan. I know you and Desmond are friends, and I'm counting on you to be discreet."

"Don't worry, Derek. I'm good at keeping secrets. I know where a lot of bodies are buried—figuratively speaking."

I hoped that sounded mysterious enough to make him wonder if I had anything on *him*.

I sprinted back to my office, closed the door, and leaned against it. My desk was exactly the way I'd left it, but I felt like my whole world had changed. Val was my friend. Should I warn her of Bord's plan? What good would that do? Was I next? Bord didn't like me, and maybe he knew how much I disliked him. And what about the other people who would lose their jobs? People with kids in high school, a mortgage, doctor bills.

Somehow I found my chair and sat down, hard; then I made myself inhale and exhale until I could feel my skin again. My hands shook so much that I spilled coffee when I tried to take a sip, but I didn't care. I just watched the pale brown stain, almost the color of dried blood, spread over my copy of Bord's report.

Then I decided the best antidote to Bord's toxic news was the comforting familiarity of my regular work. Among my unopened emails was one from NitroLitho, our printer. The subject line read "URGENT!!!" The message forwarded a draft of Jacobs' new employee handbook. They wanted comments by close of business. No wonder they got Ginny to bug me. Thankful for any distraction, I started editing.

Val tapped on my door just before noon and poked her head in. "Welcome back. Lunch?"

Val didn't look a day over thirty, but I knew she'd just turned forty-three. Compact and energetic, she had the mischievous grin of a teenager—always ready to laugh, and when she did, she put her whole body into it. She had straight, shiny brown hair, and her green eyes smiled with the rest of her face. I knew Val looked forward to lunch. She enjoyed her food but never seemed to gain weight, lucky duck. All that laughing must have vaporized the calories.

I marked my place in the handbook draft and shook my head, trying to avoid those smiling eyes and grateful for an excuse to pass on lunch. "I'm buried here. Rain check?"

"You got it. Want me to bring you anything?"

"Thanks, but I'm not real hungry. I'll survive."

I sent NitroLitho my comments on the handbook, answered eight other routine messages and returned all the phone calls. Things were looking up, except for the big, gloomy cloud Derek Bord had dropped on my world. I found some stale rice cakes in my desk drawer and washed them down with another cup of coffee, then decided I needed a stretch and a pit stop.

As I passed a bank of vending machines, the Snickers and Milky Way bars on display started calling my name. Damn, I was hungrier than I thought. Snickers had peanuts in them—that meant protein, right? *You deserve it. No, you don't. You don't deserve shit. You can hardly fit into your clothes now. Yeah, but it'd taste soooo good.*

The dialogue was tiresome but familiar. I gritted my teeth and kept walking. Some women would have caved, but not me—not that time, anyway.

As I reached the door to the women's restroom, Ginny Loring's voice came through from the other side.

"She's such a bitch," I heard Ginny say as I swung the door open, "I don't know how Angel—"

Ginny and Alice DuValle, another assistant, were washing their hands; Ginny had raised her voice to be heard over the water flow. She stopped mid-sentence as I came in, and the freckles on her face almost disappeared in the red flush that rose on her cheeks.

"… how she can wear those pointy-toed shoes," Ginny finished, carefully not looking at me.

Alice cringed, but I ignored both of them and locked myself in a stall. Only when the door hissed shut behind them could I let out my breath.

The women's restroom walls were a dull, sickly yellow, and the overhead lights put shadows on your face in places they didn't belong. Even drop-dead gorgeous Angel looked slightly jaundiced in there. The mirrors had dulled with age and abuse, and I think the idea was to discourage loitering.

I knew all this, but when I emerged from the stall I still flinched at the sight of my worn-out, scared reflection. Two weeks overdue for a trim, my normally flattering chin-length hair had morphed into a muddy brown fright wig with curls poking out in all the wrong places. My face looked like every one of my thirty-five years had told a story on it. And where did I get the idea I could wear black? It did nothing to hide the unwanted pounds I'd picked up during the funfest in Dallas.

When he saw me, Frank would probably shudder with relief that he didn't have to look at me across the dinner table every night. Would he still compare me to Angie Harmon? Not tonight—I'd lay odds against it. I smeared on some lipstick and fluffed up my hair, but that didn't help.

"The hell with it," I muttered, and then I went back to work. Some days you can't do much except grit your teeth and try not to notice how bad things are.

The rest of the afternoon swept past in a blur of messages, responses, and interruptions, but by the time I left work just after six-thirty, tired and famished, I'd done a decent job of clearing my desk. I hoped Frank was on time and ready to eat.

* * *

Emilio's Ristorante was the consummate Southern California Italian restaurant—big windows, lots of warm wood offset with marble and terrazzo, cozy glass-topped tables flanked by grapevines on the shaded patio. Interesting choice on Frank's part—our first date had been at Emilio's. The restaurant hadn't changed much over time except that the old neon sign had been replaced with discreet lettering in the window, the final "e" curling into the shape of a lush red rose.

I spotted Frank's silver BMW in the parking lot—at least I assumed it was his from the rainbow license-plate frame. I eased into a space next to the Beamer, took a deep breath, and tugged my dress into place as I walked toward the entrance.

The clouds had finally lifted, leaving a heartless blue sky that bounced a shaft of sunlight against the chrome trim on Emilio's front door, temporarily blinding me as I pushed into the dim lobby. Time warp: the burnished walls mimicked the inside of a cave—cool and dark. I could almost hear water dripping over rock. Even though smoking had long been outlawed inside Emilio's, as it had almost everywhere in California, decades of nicotine had saturated the dark paneling with a lingering tobacco smell.

How long had it been? Six months, at least, since I'd seen Frank.

I took one last glance at myself in the gold-veined mirror behind the host's lectern. The view was a little more forgiving, but I still hated my hair. Oh, well. I licked my lips and headed for the bar, where I knew I'd find Frank.

He was talking to the bartender so he didn't see me come in, and I had a chance to study him. Slouched over, right hand cupping his highball glass, he was, for just a second, still My Frank: the first man I ever loved. Frank was handsome, in the classic sense—a good, straight nose, black curly hair that he always wore just a shade longer than most men so it spilled onto his forehead and the back of his neck. Blue eyes so pale they sometimes seemed transparent. And artist's hands: long, slender fingers, capable and strong.

Violin music played softly from the dining room, and candles flickered in stubby little glasses along the bar and on the round tables by the window.

The bartender looked my way, and so did Frank. His face broke into a smile like sunrise over the desert. He slid off the bar stool and turned to me, arms open wide.

"Hey, Susie," he said, "you look terrific. Great dress—I was hoping to see those killer legs."

Suddenly, the extra pounds, the lousy hairdo, the shitty workday dissolved in a fizz of pleasure.

"Thanks. You're looking good yourself."

"Liar." He said it with a little laugh to take the bite out.

I hugged him and was surprised at the feel of his body. Frank had always been slender—a cosmic practical joke on me because he could eat his weight in M&M's and not gain an ounce, while I put on a pound just thinking about candy. But that night I felt his bones through his soft white shirt, every knob and junction of his spine. Had he always been that lean, and I just hadn't noticed? Or was Clayton wearing him down to nothing?

He kissed me, quick and close-mouthed. Too bad.

Damn you, Susan, don't go there.

I held him at arm's length. He looked okay, but something didn't feel right. He seemed pale, especially for the end of summer, the skin around his eyes and cheeks more deeply furrowed than I remembered.

The bartender put a tall vodka-tonic next to Frank's bourbon without being told; I pried my eyes away from Frank's face, slid onto a bar stool, and picked up my drink. So did he, and we clinked glasses.

"Cheers. Good to see you, Suse."

I took a hefty pull on the vodka and smacked my lips indelicately. Frank laughed.

I should say right now that Frank Krajewski was not the worst ex-husband in the world. And one thing that had drawn me to him from the start was that he made me feel like a woman. He noticed stuff— my perfume or my clothes or my hair. Thinking back, that should have tipped me off, but oh, no. And isn't it just the mother of all irony that he left me for a man, not another woman? But before and even after our breakup, my coarser habits, my height, my laugh—which some have compared to a donkey's bray—never fazed Frank. He took the whole package, and he never criticized me with one of those "Oh please!" looks designed to wither a person's soul. That wasn't in his repertoire.

When Frank told me about Clayton, I threw up. Really. Oh, not at the very minute. At first, I'd thought he was joking. And when I'd realized he was serious...

What kind of woman was I, that my husband would walk out on me for a man? And how stupid was I, to never have had a clue? I mean, I'd been so happy that he was interested in me. It's not like I had a hundred guys trying to date me. Being almost six feet tall kind of narrowed the field. My mom had seen to it that I never got really fat, but I'd never truly been cover-girl material either. I couldn't believe that tall, handsome, funny Frank Krajewski wanted to be with me. Too good to be true. Oh, yeah.

I looked around the half-empty bar: not like the old days when you had to be there by five o'clock to get a seat. Crowds change. Tastes change. I took another sip of my vodka.

"Are you starving?" Frank asked.

I shook my head. "We can drink a while first."

He smiled and took hold of my hand, brought it to his lips for a quick kiss. This was not normal behavior.

"So—how are things?" I asked, expecting to hear about Frank's job, Clayton's veterinary practice, their yard, their house. And maybe he'd drop the other shoe, the one hovering in my mind ever since he called.

Frank took a deep breath, drained his bourbon, and signaled for a refill. I passed. The vodka had gone straight from my empty stomach to my brain in a giddy rush.

"Not so good—truth be told."

Uh oh. I was afraid of this. Something's going on. Maybe he and Clayton are breaking up. Maybe he finally realized I was The One after all. Ha ha.

"What is it?" I tried to sound low-keyed but concerned.

The bartender slid a glass of bourbon with very little ice in front of Frank, and he took a swig before answering.

"I've been feeling kinda lousy lately, so I went to the doctor. He did some tests."

Oh my God. Clayton has given him AIDS.

Frank looked down at his drink. "I'm sick, Susie. I've got lung cancer."

His voice gave out, and he covered his eyes with one hand and grabbed onto me with the other.

Tiny dark sparkles erupted behind my eyeballs and for a few seconds I couldn't see Frank, or much of anything. I shook my head, the way you do when you get water in your ears, like maybe I'd heard him wrong.

I put my arm around him and pulled him close to me. "Jesus! What—how—when did you find out?"

He sat back and swiped at his face. "Sorry. I swore I wasn't gonna bawl like that. Friday. I found out Friday. Doc sits me down across from him and tells me—bam! Just like that. You've got cancer, Mr. Krajewski. Late stage, not much they can do. Just like he was reading me the menu in a restaurant, just that cold."

"Maybe you should get a second opinion."

Frank shook his head. "He was the second opinion."

"God, Frank. I don't know what to say."

I still didn't believe it. Oh, I knew he wasn't kidding, but sometimes you hear something so horrible, so unthinkable that you just won't let it into your head. Maybe, I thought, if I don't really hear it, if I don't believe it, it won't be true.

"Susie? You're not gonna pass out on me, are you? I'm the one who's sick, but you look like hell."

Breathe, Susan. My body felt like it belonged to someone else, but somehow I managed to inhale a few sips of air. There. The buzzing in my ears subsided. I took a hasty gulp of vodka to loosen my vocal cords.

"Oh, Frank." That's all I could say. Big-time comfort.

Frank rubbed my back. "I should've quit when you did. But no, I had to be the stubborn asshole, didn't I?"

I quit smoking the year Frank and I got married. It was the hardest thing I've ever done. Only the mercy of Prozac kept me from dissolving into tears and/or rage, and each day I grimly applied a nicotine patch to my upper arm, fearing that if I smoked with the patch in place, I would overdose on nicotine and die.

"Can't they operate, or—"

He shook his head. "It's late stage. He kept saying that. Late, late, late. Too late to cut it out."

"Chemo?"

He scowled. "I'm not gonna spend the last few weeks of my life bald and puking. The oncologist—can you believe it? They have their own special name! Anyway, he says I'm too far gone for chemo to help much anyhow."

All I could do was stare at him. My mouth probably hung open like an idiot's, but it would have taken too much concentration to close it.

Frank went on, "I could try some experimental drug, but that's not very promising either. The tumor has already spread to my back. That's how I noticed something was wrong—back pain. All the time."

"So what happens?"

He drained his glass and slammed it on the bar. "Nothing—yet. When it gets worse I'll go into the hospice program."

I wasn't sure exactly what that meant and, honestly, I didn't want to find out. Frank told me anyway.

"They set you up at home, keep the pain under control—they say —and…"

He waved his hand in the air.

And they let you die on your own?

"Did you tell your mom?"

He shook his head. "Not yet—haven't had the guts to. I don't want her roaring out here and taking over, dragging me to every quack in the country to find a miracle cure. No, thanks."

I couldn't think of a single helpful thing to say, no matter how much I rummaged through my mental collection of comforting phrases. Maybe none existed for this.

"I'm sorry, kiddo," he said. "I just kinda dumped this on you, huh?"

I rubbed the back of his hand. "I'm in shock."

"Yeah, I know the feeling. But for me the shock is wearing off, and I'm getting majorly pissed off."

He took a deep breath and then seemed to pull himself together a little.

"Is there anything I can do?" I had to ask.

"Yeah—find me a new body."

Back when we were married, that had been his stock response to my offers of help when he had the flu or a hangover or any other minor ailment.

Frank's "ain't-life-a-bitch" smile was as lopsided as ever; his mouth curved up more on the right than the left. "Sorry to bring you down, Suse. But I wanted you to know, and I felt like I needed to tell you face to face."

He turned on his bar stool, and I felt a twitch in my chest, that magnetic pull he exerted. Even then. Even when he was dying.

He put down his bourbon and signaled the maitre d' that we were ready for our table. I had no appetite by then and considered pleading a sudden stomach upset and fleeing. But I couldn't abandon Frank that abruptly, so I let him put his arm around me and lead me into the dining room.

I took a deep breath. "So—how is Clayton handling this?"

"Not real well. He's pretty much freaking out." Another drink arrived, and he took a sip. "Clayton is *emotional*—you know?"

I nodded, although I didn't "know"—not really. Aside from the fact that he'd taken my husband away from me, I knew little about Clayton Selden except that he was a veterinarian, he liked to grow roses, and he was a terrible cook. These informational treasures came from a few forcedly cordial encounters in the four years since Frank and I broke up. I no longer bore Clayton ill will, any more than I did Frank. What happened, happened. I accepted it and moved forward with my life. For the most part.

Frank took another hefty swig of his bourbon and shook his head. "Yesterday I found him in the garage, bawling his eyes out. He says, 'What am I going to do without you?'—like he hadn't made it through the first thirty years on his own. But that's Clayton. He doesn't handle trouble well. Not like you."

"Yeah, I'm such a beacon of strength."

"You are."

Yeah? But not strong enough to make you change.

I kept my thoughts to myself. Frank had enough to cope with. We ordered another round and studied our menus.

"Well, you *look* good," I said. *Let's try and redirect this conversation.*

Frank shrugged. "I feel okay, actually—except for the back pain. Most of the time I can't believe I'm sick."

"Are you going to take some time while you still feel up to it and do stuff you've always wanted to do? Travel, or sky dive, or anything?"

Frank put his menu down and took my hand. "I've pretty much done what I wanted all my life, now haven't I?"

Yeah. Come to think of it, he had. Including walking out on me when he met Clayton Selden.

* * *

He told me on a Thursday, and I've hated Thursdays ever since. I thought things were okay between us. Sure, I'd been putting in some long hours at work; the Department of Labor had been crawling all over our employment statistics, like they did every couple of years. Jacobs was a federal contractor and had to document fair treatment of its workers. But as the audit wrapped up, I looked forward to some quiet time, alone with Frank; maybe we'd go down to Mexico for a long weekend.

Instead I got the verbal equivalent of a kick in the gut. He'd met someone, he told me. He was in love. He was moving out. Leaving me. Oh, P.S., the someone was another guy.

"How could you not *know* you're gay?" I'd shrieked at him during one of the soul-scorching yelling matches that followed his defection.

He'd come back for some of his books and CDs a few days afterward. It was mid-afternoon, the house full of sunlight and the sweet smell of roses, strong enough to break your heart. Frank had probably expected me to be at work, but I'd phoned in sick ever since he left, lying on the living room sofa watching television without seeing it, eating Milky Ways without tasting them, and crying until my eyes were practically swollen shut.

He started packing the boxes he'd brought, while I glared at him from the sofa. I wanted to rip open his skin, shred his flesh with my fingernails. I wanted him to stop filling the boxes and admit he'd been playing a bad joke. Frank couldn't make eye contact with me. He looked so damn good. The bastard had on a turquoise shirt I'd given him for his birthday, and he had the sleeves rolled up above his wrists, a cruelly sexy look. New gray slacks—no doubt Clayton had picked them out. I still wore my pajamas.

He'd flinched when I yelled at him and then finally he looked at me. His eyes were a little red, so maybe this wasn't all sunshine and happiness for him after all, I remember thinking.

"Susie, it's something I fought my whole life, something I tried to pretend wasn't there. But when I met Clayton, I just—I couldn't keep on pretending. I was too damn tired."

I'd thrown an ashtray at him. I missed, and it rolled all useless across the floor. He'd finished loading up his stuff and left without saying anything else.

* * *

"Susie? You in there?"

I blinked away the memories. "Sorry."

"You haven't asked the big question yet."

I had no clue what he meant, and it must have shown.

"How long?" He wiggled his eyebrows. "How long do I have?"

"Oh." Jesus, when did I turn into such a brilliant conversationalist? "I didn't want to—"

"It's okay. You can ask me anything, kiddo. Anyway, the doc says three to six months. Everybody's different, blah de blah."

Those goddamn sparkles came back, pushing in between Frank's face and my eyeballs, and I felt like my head was about to explode. Three months? Three *months*?

Frank kept talking, and finally I could hang on to his words again.

". . . but the tumor's gonna grow, and spread, and they'll put me on morphine. Right now Vicodin does the job. Vicodin and Zoloft. Yum."

When the waiter brought our drinks, I pointed to his bourbon.

"Should you be drinking?"

Frank laughed. "I'm probably doing irreparable damage to my liver."

To my horror, I laughed along with him.

We ordered dinner. Funny the things you remember: he got the salmon and I got the sea bass—accompanied by Emilio's famous pasta, of course. Alfredo for him, Marinara for me. Just like always.

He skipped on to other subjects, but I had a nervous feeling one more bomb was going to fall. I crunched on a thick slab of bread to drown the alarm bells, as my thoughts jumped all over the place. So Clayton was panicking, and Frank was looking at a slow and miserable death. Hospice or no hospice, he wouldn't be able to take care of himself, and he didn't want his mom's interference. Who was left? And wouldn't that just be the shittiest outcome in the world, if that's what he was leading up to? Now, after all that had happened, was he going to ask *me* to be his caretaker? Hey, like an idiot, I'd even offered my help.

Please don't ask for it, Frank. Please please please. I wouldn't be able to do it anyway, I have my job, my life, Noah ... I practiced excuses with half my brain while the other half talked with Frank about mutual friends, his garden, my work.

He brought me up to date on my former in-laws, who lived in Chicago, Frank's home town. His sister Zoë and her husband Henry had a daughter now to go with the son who'd been born while Frank and I were married; his mother Elise still ran most of the family business; and his grandfather was still going strong at eighty-plus—which pleased me because Grandpa Krajewski had always been kinder to me than the rest of Frank's family.

And, oh yeah, Frank and Clayton had a dog—a Max look-alike, he said. Not that any dog could ever replace the late, great Max, who had died the summer before at the ripe old age of fourteen.

* * *

Frank had always loved dogs. When we started dating, I was surprised the first time he took me home to meet Max, a Golden Retriever mix Frank had rescued from the animal shelter. Lucky for me, Max and I hit it off. Frank later confided, and I think he was only half-joking, that I'd passed an important test when I picked up a slobbery tennis ball and threw it for Max to fetch. Again and again. And again. I'd been a non-animal person until then, but I grew really fond of Max, with his dark unjudging eyes and sloppy pink tongue. I liked the way he'd lean into me as if this simple physical contact was enough to make him totally happy.

I never dreamed that Max would cause the greatest disaster in my life, though.

Here's what happened: the dog, a prodigious glutton, had a yen for people food. Late one afternoon, he gobbled up a whole dish of cellophane-wrapped chocolate mints that Frank, oh careless man, had left on the coffee table. An hour later, Max started convulsing. I was still at work, so Frank took him to the emergency veterinary clinic on his own.

Clayton Selden was the doctor on duty, and while he pumped the dog's stomach and reassured Frank that accidents happen, my sweet, proper husband fell in love with him. Right there in the treatment room. Max survived, but our marriage did not.

* * *

Normally, I'm a pretty hearty eater, but that night at Emilio's I scarcely tasted my food. Frank pushed his salmon around on the plate, but I didn't see him take many bites.

The voices around us blurred into one wide murmur, like a swarm of bees. Our forks clinked against our dishes. Otherwise, we ate in silence. I chewed and swallowed and tried to think of something clever to say, something positive and comforting. Words had always been my forte, my weapon of choice, but they let me down, badly, that evening.

Finally the wretched meal was over, and I practically leaped up the minute Frank remarked that it was getting late.

He walked me to my car. "Thanks for coming, Susie. I've been missing you."

I tensed. He wanted something else from me; I could *feel* it. What? *Out with it, Frank!*

He hugged me, and he smelled of bourbon and cigarettes, just like I remembered. Frank was still pretty strong, and he held onto me so tight that I feared he might crack a rib. When he let go, he was crying, and I stroked the tears away.

"Thanks for listening," he said. "It helps to talk about it."

Okay. He just wanted to tell me the news, he doesn't want anything else from me. Thank God. I'm safe now. I'm safe.

Then why did I feel the teeniest bit disappointed? I *wanted* to do something to help Frank, but I sure didn't have a cure for cancer up my sleeve.

"No problem."

"You're the best, Suse. You always were."

A quick kiss on the cheek, and he let me escape.

After I started the car, the sparkles came back and blocked out my view of the instrument panel. I sucked in a big lungful of air and let it out in a whoosh. The sparkles intensified for a second before they dissipated. Frank was standing by the Beamer, head cocked. I waved and backed out of the parking space.

Over and over on the way home, I swiped at the tears trickling down my cheeks. It didn't seem possible. How could he be dying? I cringed at the memory of all the times I'd wished calamity on Frank for abandoning and humiliating me the way he had. Before I moved past it all, I'd torn up most of the photos of us together or scribbled "Eat shit and die" on them. And now . .

I comforted myself by thinking of the fate I'd escaped. To watch someone you love die, piece by piece. That had to be the worst thing in the world. Thank God I wasn't married to Frank anymore. Thank God I wasn't in love with him anymore.

I was so deep into these thoughts when I turned into my driveway that I almost forgot to open the garage door. Zeus, my neighbor's cat, a big tom the color of night, liked to sprawl on the cement apron flanking the garage. Normally the opening door's rumble startled him into motion, but since I didn't push the remote until I was two-thirds of the way down the driveway, he was blinded by the oncoming head-lights. I saw his eyes flash green as he leapt up, not knowing which way to run.

I hit the brakes, hard. Zeus escaped by a whisker.

"One down, eight to go," I whispered as he scrambled over the fence.

About the Author

Bonnie Schroeder was bitten by the writing bug in the fifth grade and never recovered. Among her published short stories are "The Go-Between," "A Losing Game," "Vigilantes," and "Fault Lines." In the nonfiction arena, she wrote a weekly column in *Drama-Logue* on the subject of "survival skills" for actors and other theater professionals and has written e-newsletters for a chapter of the American Red Cross. She has also completed two feature-length screenplays, one of which, *Smoke and Mirrors*, was a semi-finalist in the Monterey County Film Commission's competition. Long-form fiction, however, remains her first love.

If you enjoyed *Write My Name on the Sky*, please post a review online. Visit BonnieSchroederBooks.com for more on Bonnie.

Made in the USA
Monee, IL
02 September 2024

64341994R00223